EDGE OF A LONG SHADOW

NIGEL MILLINER

Special thanks to Alan Ayres

Edge of a Long Shadow

© Nigel Milliner

Cover illustration © Alan Ayres 2009

First Edition published 2009

Published by:
Palores Publications,
11a Penryn Street, Redruth, Kernow, TR15 2SP, UK.

Designed & Printed by:
The St Ives Printing & Publishing Company,
High Street, St Ives, Cornwall TR26 1RS UK.

ISBN 978 1 906845 00 1

Part One

GENESIS

THERE must be an exact point in a person's life when the scales are precisely balanced between what has gone before and what is to come. The moment comes when that person stops and assesses mortality and then decides that the time has arrived for the remaining years to be filled with worthwhile and meaningful activity. This in turn is the instigation of a desperate surge to achieve the ambitions of youth before the final curtain falls. And the driver of course is the desire to expunge as many deathbed regrets as possible.

The only trouble with mortality is that few of us knows exactly how much longer we have to breath, to make decisions about the future, or to what extent we have any control over that future. In the end it whittles down to a simple formula: we are born and we die and everything in between is mere self-indulgence.

Although there are extreme and indisputable examples of self-gratification, such as the man who squanders all his resources on drink, gambling and sexual pleasures, there are less obvious instances of self-indulgence. Take, for example, the nun. She dedicates her life to God, but she is also exercising a kind of masochistic self-fulfilment. After all, God did not give her life simply to have it flung back in His face, but it suits a certain type of person to make such a sacrifice. In the case of the nun it may be worthy self-indulgence, but it is self-indulgence nevertheless.

So at that point of balance, where the joist of life is horizontal to the fulcrum of destiny, just before we begin to stare down the slope to oblivion, what turmoil goes through the human mind? Is there an acceptance of our own mortality, a resignation to the boredom of treading steadily and inexorably to our graves, or is there a sudden surge of frenetic activity; a desperation to fit in as much as we can before the lights go out?

Looking back in the autumn of his life Brendan was never quite sure precisely when these thoughts began to disturb the humdrum processes of his mind. Perhaps he had always questioned mortality from an early age, or maybe, recognising that he was a fatalist he had simply tried to make some sense of the life he had been given. Or then again, maybe he had just been born to feel forever unfulfilled.

But, if pushed on the subject of when he had first attempted to analyse the meaning of his life, he might well have plumped for that spring of 1967, at about the time he had had the urge to go westward in order to relieve the ennui of his daily existence at the parental home.

He was just eighteen, a couple of weeks into the Easter holiday and he was bored rigid. His father, a civil engineer, had recently completed a two-year contract on the island of St Lucia and he and Brendan's mother were busy re-establishing their home near Westerham in Kent. The house had been let for the past eighteen months to an Indian family and the entire place reeked of curry and spices. His mother had spent a week removing all the curtains and soft furnishings and ferrying them to and from the drycleaners, while his father, cursing from the garage, had been attempting to repair the mower, which he was convinced the tenants had been running on chip fat.

His sister, three years older, lived with a drummer in a rock band, in a flat just off the Cromwell Road in London. That was the fact of it, but her parents believed she lived with a nice girl who had been educated at Cheltenham Ladies' College. Brendan knew otherwise, having enjoyed some hallucinatory parties there, the memory of which were now a blur on his mental horizon. In any event, he knew there was little chance of seeing Alice down in Westerham this side of Christmas.

But there was a consolation. The car. Brendan had saved for it, his parents had reluctantly approved it and so he had bought it. The *it* was a lime green Volkswagen Beetle, with 75,000 miles on the clock and the slickest gearbox in the county. It was one of his boasts that he could slip from third to fourth without using the clutch, simply by changing on the engine's revs.

He had found the car through the medium of the local newspaper and without any hesitation had cycled round to inspect it. After a brief turn around the block he had made an offer, one hundred pounds below the asking price, and the owner had eventually agreed to drop fifty in exchange for the price in used notes.

That was on the second day of the spring holiday. He spent the third cleaning the car, already named Limey, inside and out. By the fourth day boredom and frustration had set in like a fog bank in November.

It was while he sat clutching Limey's steering wheel one morning, watching his mother practically tearing down bedroom curtains and while his father drained the mower's oil sump into an old vase, that he had the first vision of his life sliding down the plughole of eternity.

It was also at that point that he decided to do something about it before he was much older.

The family had not lived long in Westerham, so Brendan had no real friends in the area, his sister was in London, his head was stuffed full of pre 'A' level gunk and Bob had a boat down in Lymington. He slapped the steering wheel, set his eyes on the horizon and exclaimed, 'I'm bloody well going to Lymington.'

So, after making the necessary arrangements and reassuring his mother, he had set out on a south-westerly course for his friend's home. His parents were quite easy about the situation, but that was almost to be expected. Over the past year and a half they had grown accustomed to being apart and, now that they were involved in recovering their home from the aftermath of the Indian invasion, it almost suited them to have Brendan elsewhere. He had phoned Bob who had cleared it with his parents for Brendan to spend a couple of nights with them and then he had worked out the route.

It sometimes amused him over the ensuing years to wonder what those few days would have been like, had he ever reached Lymington.

His carefully planned route took him through Hampshire along the A303, very close to the village of Lower Deeping, where he had spent four carefree and untamed holidays while his parents had been abroad. Deeping Manor was a private house of rambling proportions in the centre of the village, but the owners, having suffered a family misfortune, now supplemented their income by offering a holiday home to boys and girls in Brendan's circumstances. Lady Mary Cargill's husband, Sir Ramsay Cargill QC, had suffered a debilitating stroke two years earlier and was now severely paralysed and largely confined to a bedroom on the ground floor. Brendan had met him only once, but the tortured sounds resulting from an astute brain trapped in a damaged body could sometimes be heard through the oak door and along the stone-flagged corridor.

Lady Mary, the mother of one daughter, an Oxford undergraduate with a booming voice, coped stoically with her various burdens, but she was reluctant also to take on the role of mother hen to her young paying guests. So, the four or five adolescents in her charge during any given holiday period had the run of the house and, within reason, the county. All she asked was that they told her where they were going and check in when they returned. And they all loved her for the freedom she gave them and almost invariably respected her few cardinal rules.

Brendan now felt drawn back to Deeping Manor, if only for a fleeting visit on his way to the coast.

The weather was unusually warm for late March, a sure sign that there would be snow in April, but he had packed optimistically. He wore his faded bell-bottomed jeans and a wide-collared blue and pink cotton shirt for the drive, but his best clothes were packed in a pigskin suitcase on the back seat. There were two pairs of coarse cotton flares and two psychedelic shirts in there, together with more sensible sailing wear and some boat shoes. His pointed ankle boots were in the passenger well beside him as his socked feet caressed Limey's pedals.

Two hours into his journey he switched on the radio and tuned into Caroline. News of the stricken oil tanker, Torrey Canyon, and of a suspected foot and mouth outbreak had prompted him to turn off earlier. But now Bobbie Gentry was halfway through singing her *Ode to Billy Joe* and he was wondering yet again what the devil they were throwing off the Tallahatchie Bridge, when the sign to Andover loomed ahead.

If Lady M could offer him a bed for the night, then that would be great. If not, then he would simply motor on down to Lymington that evening and arrive late at Bob's. He smiled at the thought of what his friend might have lined up for them. After a day's sailing and then a couple of drinks at the yacht club there was bound to be a party somewhere they could crash. Bob had lived there all his life and had loads of friends.

8

As an afterthought he patted the buttoned down breast pocket on his shirt, where he kept a slim cigarette case. A frisson of illicit pleasure made his scalp tingle at the thought of what was in the cigarettes. Yes, there were bound to be a few raves around.

He slowed to negotiate a tight bend and the strangely fractured wail of Leonard Cohen's voice began to squeeze out his gothic song, *Suzanne*. His father called it music to commit suicide by. Brendan laughed out loud and flicked back a stray lock of his dark hair. His father could be right. But then suicide was always an option: the antidote to an empty life.

Huxley's *Doors of Perception* was not new, but it had awakened ideas for him when he had read a battered copy at school the previous term. When you sat in a bare room and stared cold sober at the folds in the curtains, what did you see other than folds in patterned material? But enhance your vision with mescaline and the hallucinatory effect passes a fresh awareness to the brain and ordinary things take on a newly enriched form. A more substantial meaning. Those folds become rippling waves of wondrous visual poetry. Surely there can't be anything wrong with that? Many poets, artists and songwriters had produced their finest works thanks to the effects of mescaline, hash, or call it what you will.

And she feeds you tea and oranges that come all the way from China . . .

Lower Deeping next turning on the left. Brendan concentrated on the road again and within a few minutes he was in the village and at the entrance to Deeping Manor.

It was all so familiar. The short pitted drive with straggly rhododendrons up either side, the circular rose-dotted lawn encompassed by a gravel turning area, the looming copper beech soon to display its leaves of shiny rust, which would shade Sir Ramsay's study – his spiritual home – until autumn.

He parked Limey under the beech and reached into the back seat for a bunch of flowers he had bought at a garage along the route. Before he had time to knock at the front door it opened and Lady M – as he always called her – stood with a welcoming smile.

She wore one of her favourite cardigans over a paisley patterned dress and on her feet the maroon house shoes that Brendan also recognised. Her lustrous grey hair was brushed high above a broad forehead in a sculptured perm.

Brendan glanced admiringly at Limey before mounting the porch steps. He brushed her cheek with his lips and then rather coyly handed her the flowers.

'Oh, my dear, how lovely. You remembered that I love chrysanthemums.'

Brendan, who had not been quite sure what they were, remembered no such thing, but smiled broadly at his unwitting social bull's-eye.

'Well, it's not much, Lady M,' he shrugged. 'I'm just glad you let me come and see you, specially at short notice.' He stood awkwardly with one foot on the step below her and wondered when would be the best time to ask if he could stay the night. Her pale blue eyes, level with his, were welcoming but somehow not quite as bright as he remembered.

'Come in, Brendan.' She turned and he followed her into the dark hall that led towards the kitchen. 'Not many students with us at the moment, so we're rattling around a bit in the old manor.'

They entered the kitchen and the heels of his leather boots clicked pervasively on the slate floor.

'Tea?' Her hand rested lightly on the handle of a substantial range kettle.

'Please.' He flicked his hair back in a practiced gesture and then glanced around the room. It was one of his favourite in the house: large, warm, full of pine furniture, old cooking utensils and a massive fridge that had supplied hungry youths with so many late night snacks. He rested his behind on the kitchen table and watched her as she filled the kettle.

'So, who's here? Jack, Mary . . . ?'

'No, just three, and one of those is in London for a day or so. Do you remember Luis? He's gone up to a function at the Spanish Embassy. The other two are a pair of sisters. They're out for a walk at the moment.'

'And Sir Ramsay, how's he?'

She put the kettle onto the Aga ring and he saw her back stiffen before she replied. 'I'm sorry, dear, you obviously don't know.' She turned now to face him and suddenly he knew the reason for the dullness in her eyes. 'He died two weeks after Christmas, after another stroke.'

'Oh!' he exclaimed and then felt himself blushing. 'Oh, I'm sorry, I didn't know. I'm really sorry, Lady M.'

'Don't worry, dear. It was not unexpected.' She noticed her young guest's embarrassment and, acknowledging that youth usually finds the termination of life awkward to handle, added, 'He went quite quickly and painlessly and it was probably for the best. He hated being useless.'

Brendan remained uncomfortable as he wrestled mentally with his vocabulary to find an appropriate phrase for the occasion. Nothing came to mind, so he pulled a chair out from under the table and sat down.

'I was going to ask if you'd like to spend the night with us, but I expect you're in a hurry to go on down to Lymington.' She sat down at the end of the table and Brendan looked up and grinned.

'Well, I am expected, but . . .' He grasped the moment, '. . . yes, that would be fab . . . I mean, lovely. I'll have to ring my friend.'

'Good. I'll let you have the small room at the end of the corridor – the one that Jack had last summer. And there's plenty of food now that there are only four of us in residence.'

So, that was how it came about.

Brendan phoned Bob and, with the crassness of youth, said that he would not be coming that night, but expected to arrive some time the next day. There was no thought of his friend's mother being inconvenienced, or of any other plans being disrupted. One day very much looked after itself, as did the next and so on.

He went out to the car and brought in his case and transistor radio and then ran up the uncarpeted oak stairs two at a time. The room was very familiar. It was here that he had enjoyed many midnight feasts with his American friend, Jack. Large chunks of Edam cheese and condensed milk on malt bread had been favourites. He wondered vaguely where Jack was now.

He unpacked carelessly, changed into the paisley shirt and his blue flares and ran his fingers several times through his thick dark hair. Whilst studying the result in the mirror on the windowsill a movement in the yard below caught his eye. Two girls were walking slowly across the circular lawn towards the front door.

One looked about thirteen years old and wore jeans and a chunky sweater with arms that were too long, so that only her fingertips protruded. The other girl made him hold his breath. She had long auburn hair, straight, but flicking up where it met her shoulders. Her pale blouse was tucked into the waistband of a knee-length skirt, which swayed in rhythm with her hips as she walked. There was no time for a longer appraisal before they disappeared from sight under his window, but just from that brief teasing glimpse and the fact that he was breathing a little faster made him very glad that he had decided to accept Lady Mary's invitation.

He looked into the mirror again, drew his lips back to study his teeth and then set off downstairs.

The room where the young spent most of their time at the manor had been built as a ballroom and it still sported a polished parquet floor, albeit somewhat pitted now as a result of youthful antics and high heels. There were a few battered armchairs at one end, a table tennis table in the middle and a scratched Dansette record player in a corner near the fireplace. There were also some bookshelves in one of the alcoves, adorned with dusty, shabby and unread books. He looked around fondly and breathed in the seductive aroma of ancient soot and floor polish before sitting down. She would come into this room – he was sure of it.

Many minutes passed and he was growing tired of maintaining an air of cool indifference, when the door opened.

Lady Mary came in first, bearing a tray with fruit juice and three glasses and she was followed closely by the two girls. He stood up.

Lady Mary put the tray down and began to make introductions. She knew better than to linger at times like this: the young are better at making acquaintances without the presence of an adult. Brendan caught the names Lucy and Fizzy before she turned to leave.

'Supper at eight,' she called over her shoulder as she left the room.

Fizzy? Had he heard right? He grunted a greeting at the younger girl and then turned to her sister.

'Fizzy?' He inclined his head and a cocky smile played on his lips.

She laughed. A coy sound, yet full of merriment and her face shone with luminous animation. Blue-grey eyes, slightly almond-shaped under arched brown eyebrows, twinkled with natural good humour as she clasped her hands under her chin in a swift, shy gesture. She shrugged.

'Yes, everyone calls me that. Since I was about five, I think.' She shot a glance at her sister. 'And don't you tell him my real name! It's too hideous.'

Brendan stared. Her skin was pale, but with the suggestion that it would tan easily. Her teeth were very white and even and her lips were . . . well, simply luscious. And her boobs . . . but she was talking to him again.

'Lady Mary says you stayed here for a few holidays?' She tipped her head to one side as she waited for his answer.

'Um, yes.' He cleared his throat and tried to recover his nonchalant air. 'I spent four holidays here, while my parents were in the West Indies. Great place. Do you like it?'

'I've never actually been to the West Indies, so I don't . . .'

'Sorry,' he laughed. 'I meant *this* is a great place. I didn't think you'd . . .'

'Oh, yes, great.' She blushed and he saw the blouse tighten against her chest. *Yes, fab tits!*

Suddenly he remembered that Lucy was still standing awkwardly in front of him and he turned to her.

'Would you like some juice?' And then to Fizzy, 'Lady M would never have us drinking booze in here. She doesn't ask what goes on outside, but it's always squash in the house.'

Lucy went across to the table where the tray had been left.

'Would you like some, Fizz?' Lucy piped.

'OK, if there's no gin and tonic . . .'

Brendan looked at her doubtfully and then saw from the twinkle in her eyes that it was a joke. She held his stare and it was he who broke first with a quick gesture to the record player.

'What records do you play here?'

'We've got a lot of 45s,' Lucy volunteered. 'Some Cliff Richard, Elvis and The Beatles.'

'Have you heard their latest LP . . . The Beatles, I mean?' he asked Fizzy, ignoring the younger girl. 'It's called *Sergeant Pepper's Lonely Hearts Club*. Funny title, but it's really fab. Nothing like their earlier stuff.'

Fizzy took a glass from her sister and frowned thoughtfully.

'No, I don't think so.'

'Actually, it's not coming out until June, so I'm not surprised,' Brendan put in quickly and also took a glass from Lucy, nodding to her as he did so. 'I heard some tracks on Radio Caroline. Who else do you like?'

'The Doors – I'd just die for Jim Morrison. Procol Harum. *Whiter Shade of Pale* is really dreamy.' She took a sip and then moved across to the record player. 'It's here somewhere.'

He followed her over to the pile of carelessly stacked records and stood as close to her as he could without actually touching, while she sifted through the 45s. Her hair smelt of wild flowers and something else fresh that he could not put a name to. He closed his eyes for a couple of seconds.

'Here it is.' She pulled the record out and turned her head so quickly that her hair brushed his cheek.

'Sorry,' she said abruptly, but he wasn't sorry at all.

She smiled with a jerky little twitch of her lips and then bent over the player to put the record on the turntable. She turned the volume up, pushed the play lever and then went to sit on one of the chairs. He hesitated and then chose the chair next to her just as the first chords of Bach's Air – or Procol Harum's version of it – began to cut through the mesh of the bruised speaker. Lucy plonked herself noisily in the third chair and slurped loudly on her drink.

We skipped the light fandango; turned cartwheels in the air... Fizzy's eyes were closed. Brendan's were wide open and fixed on her face. Lucy slurped again.

They said nothing until the record ended. The arm lifted with a robotic lurch and returned to its rest. Fizzy let out a long sigh and opened her eyes.

'Dreamy,' she repeated as he gazed at her half open lips, which were moistly reflecting the glow from the wall lights. He had only just met her and already he wanted to kiss those lips.

Lucy coughed and he shot her a sudden glance, as if suspecting that she had read his thoughts. There would certainly be no kissing while young sister was around. He looked surreptitiously at his watch. It was after half past six.

'Lucy.' He smiled ingratiatingly at her. 'I don't suppose you'd go and ask Lady M if she needs any help with the supper?'

'Ask her yourself!' came the immediate and indignant reply.

'Lucy!' Fizzy looked sternly at her sister.

'No, it's alright,' Brendan said, grasping the arms of the chair as if to rise, 'I'll go.'

'No, I'll go,' Lucy got up with exaggerated effort and went huffily over to the table where the empty glasses stood on their tray. '*And* I'll take the glasses with me.'

'Thanks,' Brendan said indulgently and then, after the door closed behind the girl, he exchanged a conspiratorial smile with her older sister.

'What do you do with yourself here all day?' Brendan stretched his legs.

'Sometimes we go to the cinema, watch TV, read, listen to records, go riding.' She drew down the corners of her mouth. 'Or go walking.'

'Lady M doesn't mind you wandering off on your own?'

'I'm not on my own,' she said defensively. 'If Lucy isn't with me then Luis is. And anyway I *am* sixteen.'

Brendan, who up to that point had not given serious thought as to her age, now felt a sudden pang of jealousy at mention of the manor's other resident.

'Oh, I see. What d'you think of Luis.' He recalled a boy of his own age, overweight and with spots on his neck, but it was best to check her opinion.

'He's nice enough.' She wrinkled her neat slim nose. 'But he has sweaty hands and . . .' she shrugged and raised her eyebrows.

He felt relief.

'When's he coming back?' He didn't want to go into how Fizzy knew about the state of Luis's hands.

'Not for another two days I think. Why?'

'Oh, no particular reason. I know him, so I'd have said hello, that's all.'

There were a few moments' silence and he peered out of the window at the fading light.

'Had you planned to go out tonight?' he asked suddenly and then wished he had not. Mustn't sound too eager.

She put her head to one side and stared at a point above his head. 'No,' she said slowly, 'not tonight, I don't think. There's something good on telly.'

'Right.' He looked down at his hands and time seemed suspended for a long while until the spell was suddenly broken by a creak from the opening ballroom door. As usual, the resulting movement of air released a waft of tired soot and floor polish. Lucy was back.

15

The meal was an unbalanced affair. Lady Mary always ate with her young guests and tried to draw them into conversation on all manner of topics, but on that evening she experienced some difficulty in achieving her aim.

Brendan was happy to fill her in on what he was doing, his hopes for a university place and opinions on life in general, but he did not want to be centre stage for the whole meal. He also felt self-consciously that his outpourings might sound like bragging in front of the girls, although he did note that Fizzy was watching his face intently as he talked. She did not herself have much to say and Lucy devoured her food – shepherd's pie with peas and carrots – as if no one else was at the table.

At the end of the meal they carried the dishes to the kitchen sink, washed up and put it all away. Brendan then looked at Fizzy.

'So, what were you going to watch?'

'Oh, there's a programme about the Beatles.' She glanced at the kitchen clock. 'It's on in ten minutes.'

Lady Mary Cargill closed a cupboard door, picked up her cardigan and sighed.

'Well, I'm going upstairs to make a phone call and then I'll probably read until bed.' She turned to Brendan. 'Will you lock up, dear? You remember the procedure.'

He smiled back at her. Indeed he did: dog out in the yard for a pee, dog in with biscuit, lock front door and back and, in the winter, guard in front of the fire and finally, all lights out except for the one in the hall.

'I remember. Goodnight, Lady M.'

'Goodnight all. See you in the morning.' And with that she walked slowly up the stairs.

They settled strategically in front of the television, which was situated in the smaller sitting room next to the kitchen. Lucy plonked herself in the chair directly opposite the screen, but Fizzy hesitated, pondering the options between the large leather pouffe and the sofa. Brendan, waiting patiently for her to make up her mind, tried to influence her choice.

'I once saw the dog being sick on that,' he said, inclining his head towards the pouffe.

'Eeeough,' Lucy exclaimed vehemently and Fizzy wrinkled her nose and promptly sat down on the sofa.

Brendan turned on the television, made sure it was on the correct channel and then came back to sit at the other end of the sofa.

Later he could not say that he remembered much of the programme, which by happy co-incidence was about the making of the Sergeant Pepper album. The music was out of sight, but there were other things closer to hand that needed his attention during the hour-long programme.

In fact those things were not so close at hand to begin with, but became progressively more so as the hour wore on. Through a series of manoeuvres, such as shifting cushions, stretching one side more than the other and leaning over the back to see where the dog was, he managed to create far more space between his body and the left arm of the sofa than between himself and Fizzy. Occasional rhythmic body movements in time with the music also helped his gradual magnetic orientation to the right.

Fizzy meanwhile appeared to be entranced by the Beatles' activities on the screen, although, he noticed, her left hand occasionally tapped out a beat on the space between them. Was this an invitation? God, this would be so easy if he did not care one way or another, or if they were on their own.

His arm had just snaked around the back of the sofa behind her neck when the hour was up and the credits began to roll. She turned to him excitedly, seeming unsurprised at how close he was.

'Wasn't that the grooviest music!' she exclaimed. 'Lucy, we must get that LP. When are we going to town next?'

'Thursday, I think.' Lucy shrugged and turned back to the screen.

'I've already got it at home,' Brendan lied again, trying to win favour. 'I should have brought it with me . . . except I didn't know we were going to meet.'

'I thought you said it isn't out until June,' Lucy challenged and he glowered at her.

'That's right . . . the first of June . . . but I've got a friend in the music business and he sent me a tape.' He gave the younger girl a self-satisfied smirk.

Fizzy stared at him open-mouthed, as if seeing him for the first time as an enlightened demigod of the pop world. He smiled modestly and hoped he was not blushing.

For a moment he was tempted to embellish the lie with more such claims but then thought maybe this was pushing his advantage a bit too far.

Lucy gave a loud yawn and announced that she was going upstairs to read. Fizzy closed her mouth and stood up, brushing Brendan's arm as she did so and then straightening her skirt.

'I'm going into the ballroom to play some records. You coming?'

'I'm coming.' He stretched out his arm. 'Pull me up.'

She tossed her head coquettishly and lowered her eyelids. 'Pull yourself up, Mr Brendan.' And then turned and hurried out of the room.

He sat for a while and tried to analyse the situation. *How was he getting on?* He really fancied this bird, but he only had a few more hours to make his move. Did that make it easier or more difficult? If the time was short then he might have to act sooner than he normally would – rather like striking at a fish that had only just begun to play around the bait. He liked that simile and decided to store it for his friends when relating holiday conquests. Or, perhaps, because he would be on his way tomorrow and might never see her again, it didn't matter if she bit or not. He couldn't lose, could he?

Brendan heard the music drifting along from the ballroom. Scott McKenzie singing *San Francisco*. '. . . *be sure to wear some flowers in your hair* . . .' He ran his fingers through his own and pushed himself out of the chair.

She was swaying gently in time to the music, with her eyes closed and her arms raised beside her head. Her hair flopped lazily against her neck with each movement and her lips silently recited the words. Yes, he really fancied this bird.

He moved silently into the room and began sifting through the records on the table, selecting a few, including *Whiter Shade of Pale*.

'When are you leaving tomorrow?' With the ending of the record she had opened her eyes and now took the record from the turntable.

'I told my friend that I'd be there in the afternoon, so I'd better leave at about lunch time.'

'Will you be staying for lunch?' She put another record on the turntable.

'I haven't been invited.'

'Oh.' She glanced up at him and held out a disc. 'Do you like this one?'

'Not much.' It was a Monkees number, but he was thinking ahead to the next day. 'Would you like to go for a walk tomorrow morning?'

'What?'

He leant over and turned the volume down a notch. 'I asked if you'd like to go for a walk tomorrow morning. It should be a nice day and I know a lot of good walks around here.'

'OK,' she said nonchalantly and then added, 'but Lucy will have to come too.'

'Fair enough.' But he really wanted to say *Bugger!*

And so, the next day the three of them went for a walk after breakfast. Brendan told Lady Mary his plan to leave at about lunchtime, but there was no invitation to stay for a meal. His welcome then, it seemed, would expire just before that. He had packed hastily, put his possessions into the back of Limey, slipped on a leather jacket and met the girls at the back door.

Fizzy wore the same skirt as the day before, but she had changed her top to a pink roll neck pullover and her hair was drawn back with an Alice band. There were sensible walking shoes on her feet. He did not notice what Lucy was wearing.

He took them along the path behind the house, down the side of a wheat field and over a style by Deeping Wood. A small stream ran alongside the wood and ended up, he thought, in the River Test. The dog ran ahead of them.

They talked casually about inconsequential matters for half an hour before they reached a second style. The dog ran under the lower bar and Lucy, wearing jeans, hopped over it with ease. Brendan glanced at Fizzy and then seized his opportunity.

He darted ahead of her, climbed to the top bar of the style and held out his hand.

'Here, let me help you. You might snag your skirt.'

She reached up and took his hand. He jumped down on the far side of the style and then guided her up and over. As they went on their way he kept hold of her hand and she made no attempt to withdraw it. It was as easy as that.

They were still holding hands as they completed the circuit back to the manor and by then even Lucy seemed to accept the situation as normal. Only discretion forced him to let go as they entered the garden. Lady Mary did not encourage relationships between her young people: one never knew where it might lead.

But Brendan now knew definitely where he wanted this to lead and had already formulated a plan. As he changed his shoes he felt his heart accelerating. He had less than an hour before departure and he had to see her alone.

Then suddenly the situation resolved itself. Fizzy came round the corner of what was known as the boot room, looking agitated.

'Luis is coming back early,' she said with a heavy sigh.

'I thought you liked him.' Brendan gave a final tug on his ankle boot and it slipped over his heel.

'I don't dislike him, but I wouldn't have minded another day to myself.' She looked directly at him in the dim light of the boot room. '. . . or with you,' she added with a quiet note of defiance.

He stopped and looked up at her. 'Well,' he said slowly, 'that can be arranged.'

'How?'

'You said you ride?'

'Yes, Lucy and I go up to the stables sometimes twice a week. What about it?'

'Is it too late to arrange a ride for tomorrow morning – before Luis gets back?'

'I shouldn't think so.' She looked puzzled. 'How will that help?'

He pulled on the second boot, leaned back on the bench and swept his hair into place. Now for the sixty-four thousand dollar question.

'If you and Lucy go off riding, could you bunk off to meet me without Lucy sneaking to anyone?' His eyes narrowed and he held his breath.

She hesitated as she thought it through and then her eyes flashed with a spark of excitement. 'Of course I could. And I trust Lucy completely. We never sneak on each other.'

'Good.' He stood up, grinning and clutching his walking boots. 'How do you get there? To the riding stables, I mean.'

'We take the bus at the end of the lane. The stables are only two miles away.'

'And Lucy'll be able to make an excuse for you . . . one that they'll believe?'

'Yes, of course. Don't worry.' She was now fully hooked into the conspiracy. 'Where will you meet me?'

'Where you get off the bus. I'll be parked nearby and I'll look out for you.' He guided her out of the boot room. 'What time is it due to arrive?'

'Should be about ten, but it's usually late. Where will we go?'

His grin broadened. 'Wait and see. I know some fab places around here. Wear walking shoes. I'll bring something to eat and drink.'

They went into the hall and found Lady Mary wandering around looking mildly agitated.

'Ah, there you are Brendan. I've been looking for you to say goodbye.' She came forward to give him a kiss. 'It was so nice of you to think of me and visit.'

The gates of hospitality were closing.

'Thank you, Lady M.' He glanced over her head at Fizzy. 'I'm glad I came too. Give my regards to Luis.'

'I will. Safe onward journey.' She opened the front door. 'Are you sure you've got everything you brought?'

'Yes, it's all in the car.' He went quickly down the steps and only glanced back once he was in the driving seat.

They waved him off and a few minutes later he was on the road to a pub where he had spent many past evenings, drinking the local brew and playing darts with the regulars. After a ploughman's lunch, he booked in for the night and then went to the telephone to make another difficult call to Lymington. Something had come up, he had said, apologies to Bob's mother and all that. Tomorrow afternoon definitely, unless Bob just wanted to tell him to bugger off after causing all this trouble.

Yes, Bob had said, it was all very inconvenient and he did not understand what it was that had turned up. Never mind, Brendan had reassured, all would be revealed soon. And with that tantalising morsel he had hung up the phone. The intention had been genuine, but, as events rolled out, he never did reveal anything to Bob. Not then, or at any time in the future.

On reflection in later years, Brendan could not remember exactly how he had spent the hours between lunch and bed above a noisy public bar, but after a couple of pints and a discreet smoke from his silver case he had slept soundly.

The next morning he paid the landlady three shillings for the night and then drove off. On the way to the bus stop he pulled up outside the village shop and bought two pork pies and a large bottle of Tizer. As an afterthought he picked up two Mars Bars as well and fumbled in his flares for a pound note.

Brendan did not have long to wait for the bus. He had parked Limey by the road fifty yards short of the stop and as it overtook him he could see five heads above the bus's window line. Two of them belonged to Fizzy and Lucy.

'Oh, my God,' he exclaimed as the girls stepped down to the side of the road. 'Bloody jodhpurs!'

He sighed, the bus drove off and the girls stood looking back at him. Naturally she was wearing jodhpurs, she had to keep up the pretence of riding. He got out of the car and walked briskly over to greet them.

'Hello,' he said cheerily and then looked at Lucy. 'Where's the stables then?'

She smiled cheekily and pointed across the road. 'Along that lane, where the sign says *Deeping Riding School*. That's the clue.'

'Ok, Ok,' he grinned back at her. After all, she was doing them a favour. 'How long will you be there? How long is the ride?'

'We usually pay for three hours,' Fizzy replied and then looked at her sister. 'I'll be back here then, Luce. Ok?'

'Ok.' She grinned back at Brendan. 'Have a nice time.'

'Thanks, Lucy,' he said with feeling as the young girl turned and crossed the road to the riding school. She was indeed doing him a great favour.

'Come on.' Brendan seized Fizzy's hand eagerly and they walked briskly back to the car. 'We're going up to Canbury Rings.'

The Rings was an ancient burial site, which was located at the top of a prominent hill topped by a circle of beech and oak trees. The land below the trees was pasture, pitted with rabbit holes and dotted with grazing sheep. It was a place that he had visited from school on a geography project, a place of mystery and romance, where dappled light filtering through the branches played tricks on the imagination. It was not somewhere he would like to linger after dark, but it was somewhere to take a bird he fancied on a mild spring day.

They did not talk a great deal on the drive there, each having individual thoughts about where this clandestine tryst might lead. Five miles from the bus stop the Rings suddenly loomed over to their left and Brendan turned the car down a narrow lane. He drove on for a while and then pulled into a lay-by.

'Should be Ok here.' He turned off the engine and then leaned over to the back seat for a brown paper bag. 'I've got some food and drink here. We'll need it after we walk up there.'

'How long will it take?'

'About twenty minutes I think.'

'Twenty minutes?' she asked incredulously. 'To get up there?'

He got out of the car.

'Well, quarter of an hour, but it's further and tougher than it looks. It's worth it when you get there though.' He slammed the car door and patted the roof. 'Right, there's the pathway, just by the gate there. Let's go.'

Was God looking down on the young couple on that particular spring morning? Had He planned the simple natural event that would affect their lives, mould their notions of human relationships and to a considerable extent channel the course of their lives? Or was it simply that it was almost April in Hampshire, when the most natural of events is a sudden downpour of rain? For, whether it was God's little joke or not, that is precisely what happened when they were through the copse and halfway up the hill. It began to rain.

'Oh no!' Fizzy yelled, turning up the collar of her cotton jacket, 'we'll have to go back to the car.'

'No!' Brendan shouted. 'We're nearly there. We go on. There's shelter under the trees.'

He gripped her hand tightly and made to run on, but she held back and looked yearningly towards the car at the bottom of the hill. Brendan stopped and gazed pleadingly into her eyes.

'Come on, Fizzy, it's only a shower. We can't turn back now.' His dark eyes under a damp mop of hair searched into hers. 'There may never be another chance.'

'All right, you win.' She shrugged. 'But, we'll be soaked. This better be worthwhile.'

It will be, it will be, Brendan thought, as they turned and trotted on up the hill.

A hundred yards from the outer ring of trees the shower stopped abruptly and they slowed to a walk, breathing heavily.

'There's an old shack over there,' Brendan gasped, 'where the shepherd shelters sometimes for the night. We might be able to dry off in there.'

The shack was a bothy made of rough timbers, with corrugated iron sheeting for a roof. There was one small glassless window above eye level and a doorway no more than five feet high. The corrugated iron sloped steeply down to the entrance and the sheet directly above it had been bent upwards to allow the door to open fully.

The door was ajar when they arrived and Brendan cautiously pulled it open wider. The top of the door caught the corrugated iron and some trapped water splashed onto the ground by his feet. He peered inside.

'It's all right,' he called over his shoulder, 'no shepherds in residence.'

She followed him inside, brushing a spider's web from her face with a quick flick of her hand. The sun now shone weakly through the window via the lower branches of a beech tree and shadows darted playfully across the floor.

'Ugh! What a disgusting place you've brought me to.' She stood in the middle of the floor and glanced around at the contents of the small hovel.

'It's not the Ritz, I know, but it's not actually as dirty as it looks. And it's a good place to dry off.' He went over to look out of the door and peered up at the sky. 'There'll probably be another shower before long, so we'd better wait until that's over.'

She sighed and slipped her jacket off for inspection. It was very wet down the back. She found a nail by the door and, with a resigned shrug, hung it up. Brendan cleared a space on one of the ledges and spread out the contents of his soggy paper bag.

'Lunch,' he announced proudly.

'But, it's only just after eleven.'

'I know,' he said patiently. 'But it's there for when we're ready. Come and sit down.'

She frowned dubiously at the sacking that he was patting, so he grunted and took off his leather jacket, spreading it out for her. She looked at it for a moment and then giggled and sat down next to him. He glanced at the jodhpurs and groaned inwardly.

'I could do with a drink,' she announced, feeling the damp patches on her blouse.

Brendan hopped up, reached for the bottle of Tizer and then sat down again. He unscrewed the top and handed it to her.

'Sorry, no glasses.'

'No matter.' She put the bottle to her lips, drank and then handed it to him.

'How much longer have we got?' he asked as he screwed the cap back on.

'About two hours. Why?' Her wide-eyed stare was one of mock challenge.

'Then we'd better make the most of it, hadn't we?' Brendan smoothed his damp hair with the flat of his hands and then appeared to become distracted by the state of his trousers. She watched with mild interest as the fiddling around with his flares went on, until he stopped suddenly and slowly raised his eyes until they focused on a point somewhere above her head.

'What is it?' she demanded urgently, a look of alarm in her eyes.

'Don't move,' he whispered. 'Stay very still.'

'Brendan . . .'

'Sssh! Very large spider coming down.'

She screamed and tried to leap up, but he caught her arm and started laughing. She lost her balance and fell back towards him, sprawling across his chest, her face upturned.

'Oh, you . . .' she spluttered, but any further expletives were stifled as he covered her mouth with his.

It was a clumsily calculated ploy, but when he felt no more than a couple of seconds' resistance from her he relaxed, folding his arm comfortably under her back. She was a good kisser, he reflected, as she responded to his exploratory tongue and he wondered fleetingly where she had gained her experience. Not from Luis, he hoped.

'You taste of Tizer,' he said gently as their lips eventually parted with a small pop of shared saliva.

'Mmmm,' was all she said and prepared to give him some more, slipping her hand up his back and into his damp hair.

25

The sun faded and very soon another sharp downpour rattled onto the corrugated roof, making any conversation impossible to be heard. But, for several minutes Brendan and Fizzy were not conversing.

The rain stopped as suddenly as it had started and she pulled away from him slowly, tapping his breast pocket.

'What's that?'

'My cigarette case,' he murmured and contemplated tapping her chest and asking the same question. 'Want one?'

'I don't smoke.' She stroked his hair. 'Tried it once, but didn't like it. I couldn't stop coughing.'

'You'd like these.' He pulled himself up into a sitting position and reached into his shirt pocket. 'Could you get the lighter out of my jacket pocket?'

She knelt as she felt inside the pockets of the leather jacket that had been her mattress and he had a clear view down the front of her blouse. Involuntarily he licked his lips as he opened the silver case and removed a slim tapered joint. She handed him his Zippo and then nestled up against him again.

He flicked the lid open, spun the flint wheel with a practiced motion and the flame leapt two inches.

'Don't burn the place down.'

'Well, it would be one way to dry the clothes.' The cigarette bobbled between his lips as he spoke.

He applied the flame, the lid closed with a sharp metallic click and he drew the smoke slowly into his lungs. She watched intently as he put his head back, closed his eyes and exhaled lazily into the bothy's cobweb-strewn air.

Brendan could not afford to smoke his secret joints that often, so it was usually a time of private contemplative pleasure when he did. This was the first time he had smoked in front of a girl and he probably would not have done so now had it not been for her curiosity, plus a certain amount of personal bravado. But then, with the second draw, as he felt the uplifting calm of the weed coursing through his body, he wanted to share the experience with her. And, as the effect grew, so did his desire to share everything with her.

Everything.

'Try it.' He handed it to her delicately 'Don't inhale too fast, then hold it in for a few seconds before breathing out slowly.'

His own voice sounded as if it belonged to someone else and already his head felt light, as if all negative thought was being purged from the recesses of his skull. She took it from him suspiciously and pursed her lips to accept the tapering, smouldering white shaft. She drew on it tentatively and almost immediately spluttered and recoiled, her face screwed up in disgust.

'Oh, Brendan, how could you?' She held it out to him, but he didn't take it back.

'I said slowly,' he reproached her gently. 'Wait a few seconds and try again.'

'What's it meant to do anyway?'

'Make you feel wonderful, relaxed and happy. You'll see everything differently.'

'But I'm happy already.' She smiled broadly and tickled him under the chin. 'See?'

'Ok, give it back,' he sighed and held out his hand.

She hesitated, pursed her luscious lips and inclined her head. 'No, I'll try once more.'

He said nothing, but lowered his eyes to the top of her blouse and studied the delicate line of her cleavage as it descended to the point where a pearl button strained taught against its retaining hole. Propped on one elbow she assumed a serious face and then put the cigarette to her mouth again.

This time she did not splutter or cough. She held the smoke in and then, as he had done, tilted her head back, closed her eyes and exhaled towards the corrugated roof. Then, without a word, eyes still shut, she passed it back to him.

Brendan took another draw and looked at what remained, before turning to Fizzy again. She was now reclining against a hessian sack that lined the rough wall, leaning on both elbows, her facial expression halfway between bewildered and mellow. She opened her eyes slowly, turned her head and looked at him. He smiled encouragingly back at her.

'It's working,' she said hoarsely and stretched her arm out, thumb and forefinger extended.

'Don't overdo it.' He handed it back to her. 'Not on your first go.'

27

'Silly boy,' she said lazily and patted him on the cheek. The sunlight through the small window played tricks on her face and ignited her hair and he felt desire stirring down below.

Then just as suddenly the sun went out and in seconds there was another sharp fall of rain, tapping urgently on the tin roof. With the rain came a gust of wind and for a few seconds he thought he could hear the new spring's tender leaves rustling from the twisted branches above the bothy.

The world seemed to stand still for the two of them, completely still, except for the slow movement of his fingers as he undid the buttons of her blouse.

'Do you know what I'd like to do?' She turned to him suddenly, eyes bright with anticipation, seemingly oblivious of what he was doing.

'Have a pork pie?' He popped open the last button and slipped his hand around her naked waist.

'Don't be daft, Brendan.' She sat up and with one motion discarded the parted blouse. 'I want to dance. I want to dance to the arrival of spring, under the trees, in the rain.'

He sat up as well. 'Dance in the rain? But, that's crazy. Anyway the rain's stopping. And you'll probably fall over.'

'The rain brings everything to life, you know. Come and dance with me, Brendan. Join me in coming to life with spring.' Before he could stop her, she was on her feet and reaching for the bothy door.

'Fizzy!' he shouted after her. 'Wait. Don't push the door too . . . '

But it was too late. She had shoved the door wide open, knocking the overhanging corrugated sheet upwards. The trapped water sped up the sloping roof and then came down again as she half-closed the door with her bare foot. The cascade caught her from behind and she shrieked as her jodhpurs took the full load.

'Still feel like dancing?' he called through the door.

'Of course! What's a little water?' And through the gap in the doorway he saw her skipping around to a secret and silent melody. 'Oh, come on, Brendan, you booby,' she cried. 'It's lovely out here.'

He pinched the end off the cigarette, put what remained in its case and then got to his feet and pulled off his boots. It was ten past twelve.

Brendan waited just outside the door and when she did a pirouette close to him he grabbed her arm and pulled her back into the hut. Her legs tangled with his and they fell in a heap onto his jacket. She shrieked and then tried to sit up, but he had other ideas.

'What are you doing?' she said between breathless gasps.

'I'm taking off your jodhpurs of course. They're soaked.' He wrestled with the side buttons. 'You and your dance . . .'

'Then stop fumbling,' she said impatiently, deftly undoing the remaining buttons and then wriggling out of the seemingly impenetrable garment. 'Now, what about you? Your shirt's wet too.'

She was a good button undoer and not bad at slipping off a young man's shirt either. Work done, she studied his chest and then gently tickled the incipient growth of dark hair on his sternum. He rolled towards her and caught her lips in his, at the same time reaching behind her back for the brassiere hooks.

Fizzy pulled away indignantly. 'No you don't. First, *your* trousers.'

'Ok.' He needed no further prompting, pulling the zipper down and then easing the flares over his buttocks to reveal a pair of Union Jack underpants.

'Very patriotic,' she said admiringly.

'Carnaby Street. It would have been cheaper to have bought a flag and cut it up.'

She laughed and plucked at the pants, accidentally touching him on a hard but sensitive area as she did so.

'Sorry.' She began to blush.

'Any time.'

His whispered reply was almost inaudible, but she didn't need to hear the words. Very tentatively she reached out again and rested the palm of her hand on him, feeling the surge and sensing the power of her touch by an almost imperceptible shudder through his body. He needed no further invitation and slipped his hand down the back of her pants and between her thighs, his gently probing fingers urged on by her little grunts of delight.

In a series of swift movements the brassiere lay on the floor, her arms were around his neck and they were locked in a squirming embrace, oblivious of the rough straw that scratched an unheeded warning on tender skin.

Discarded clothing lay scattered about. Raindrops from the overhead branches tapped gently on the tin roof and disregarded time ticked on towards the top of the hour as the two young tyros of romance melded into spring's primeval awakening. No visiting shepherd, no unsuspecting rambler, no otherworldly interruption could have stopped what happened that spring afternoon in the shepherd's bothy by Canbury Rings.

To Brendan, looking back later that day and for the rest of his life, there was a destiny in the proceedings of each act of the play until its climax, the like of which for him would never quite be repeated. It was not merely the consummation that clenched his insides, gripped his heart and curdled his mind; it was all that lead up to it – as if he were merely a puppet, acting on the whim of an unseen string puller.

When eventually he and Fizzy descended the hill from Canbury Rings, hand in hand in their soggy clothes, clutching uneaten pork pies, it had become in that short period of time as if they were one. There had been no need to speak afterwards, because to have done so might have woken them from a dream or broken a beautifully spun web.

There had been one lingering kiss as they stood by Limey, before they got into the car and drove away from Canbury Rings, back to the humdrum world that they had so recently left behind. They were re-entering the world of other people.

'You're late,' Lucy accused. 'And we've missed the bus.'

'Don't worry, Lucy.' Brendan said patiently, 'I'll take you back to the Deeping stop.'

Lucy nodded and then studied her sister's face curiously, but said nothing until they were in the car.

'Brendan, your parents, they're trying to find you.'

He looked sharply over his shoulder at the younger girl in the back seat. 'What? How do you know?'

'A telephone call from Lady Mary soon after you left me. Your parents had a message for you and they didn't know where you were.'

'Lucy, you didn't tell her that I wasn't there, did you?' Fizzy asked urgently.

'No, of course not,' she huffed. 'Anyway, Brendan, it's about your grandfather. She said he's very ill.'

'Who said?'

'Lady Mary, of course. They think he might be dying and your parents want you back home.'

Brendan took in this sudden piece of news and then exchanged desperate glances with Fizzy, realising with a sickening jolt that this meant an abrupt end to their newfound union.

The spell was broken. There would be no tomorrow, no meeting at the same place, no more walking in the springtime air, no loving and no more magic. Someone had pulled the plug and the music had stopped on an ugly discordant note.

They reached the bus stop before he had decided what to do next, but it seemed that Fizzy was ahead of him. She turned to her sister.

'Lucy, go back to the house and say that I got caught in the rain and have gone to change, then . . .'

'Suppose she asks why I didn't get wet as well?'

'Think of something! Maybe you were back before me and grooming your horse in the stables. I don't know . . . anything.'

'Ok. What then?'

'I'll be in soon after you and I'll go up the back stairs to the bath. Whatever you do, don't say you've found Brendan. All we know is that he left to visit his friend in . . .'

She turned frantically to him. 'Where was it?'

'Lymington.'

'. . . his friend in Lymington.' She swallowed hard, as if something was stuck in her throat and Brendan saw the tears pricking her eyes.

He leaned across her and opened the passenger door. Fizzy shot him a despairing glance and then got out, pushing the seat forward for her sister. Lucy struggled out of the car, ducked down to say a quick goodbye to Brendan and then walked briskly up the lane.

The next few minutes proved to be the most painful in Brendan's short life and the scar left by the wound of that parting was to remain with him for many years to come. Sometimes it was pale and faint, sometimes more livid, but the final lingering kiss that sealed their afternoon's magical experience was always there achingly to haunt him. She had branded his lips indelibly with hers.

Brendan glanced in his mirror just once after he drove off and caught sight of her profile as she looked back over her shoulder. Then he was around the bend in the lane and heading for the A303 and home. They had barely had time to exchange addresses.

The suddenness of their parting left him numb. His heart was carrying a millstone and yet his head was filled with helium and his perspiring hands gripped the steering wheel as if he were trying to maintain a grasp on reality. He felt that what had happened had been uniquely wonderful and momentous, but at the same time ephemeral.

Brendan did not know it then, but the events of that day would soon become a tableau in his mind: a mystical laminated tableau, sealed, unalterable and yet strangely incomplete, like a symphony that is forever stuck on its final poignant note.

He joined the main road and automatically turned on the radio.

. . . *and so it was later, as the miller told his tale, that her face at first just ghostly, turned a whiter shade of pale.*

The lump in Brendan's throat turned into an uncontrollable sob.

32

Part Two

REVELATIONS

Chapter One

THE sea was smooth, with only the faintest ripples serrating the surface and tickling the rocks with its incoming tide. On one of those rocks, fifty feet below the lookout, a cormorant perched, drying its wings in the afternoon sun, while a little way further out its mate carried on a relentless search for fish.

The shadow of the flagpole reached across the uneven scrub in front of the bowed window and pink thrift nodded on their long stems before a light breeze.

Out on the horizon a tanker headed southwest for Falmouth and, closer to shore, three small sailing boats leaned lazily as if reluctant to catch the wind.

Robert Sinclair stared out at the scene he knew so well. He had been there on coastal watch in all weathers. He had seen all the tides, heard gales whipping the radio mast, felt the rain pelt his face as he struggled to lower the flag and watched a wave upturn a rowing boat. Today was different. It was calm and quiet, with very little to enter in the log.

Nothing of note that is, until the jet skier came round the point and began buzzing the bay. Never, he thought, has a water sport been invented that could cause so much disturbance to so many, for the pleasure of so few. In this case the few was a single, young white male in a wet suit and he was going around the bay in tight circles, disturbing the half dozen swimmers who were braving the May Cornish waters.

Robert sighed and reached up to the shelf where they kept the air horn. He put on his peaked cap for added authority, stepped out of the lookout and waited for the jet ski to complete a circle and face in his direction. He was about three hundred yards away, but he knew the horn's volume was more than enough to cut through that distance.

Robert raised it at arm's length and pressed hard down on the button and winced. Even behind the sound he rocked back at the volume that blasted out and across the bay. He saw faces suddenly turn in his direction and the sun-drying cormorant took off clumsily. The man on the jet ski waved at him cheekily.

'The bugger!' Robert exclaimed. 'He thinks I'm joking.'

He gave three more blasts and, when that did not seem to have any effect, he turned and darted back into the hut, his anger now rising. He opened the cupboard under the map drawer and pulled out the megaphone, turning the switch to full volume. The megaphone was a relatively new toy and few of the watchkeepers, if any, had had reason to use it before. Certainly Robert was one who had not and he took a moment to check the mechanism. Satisfied, he switched it on and put it to his mouth.

'ON THE JET SKI . . . CUT YOUR SPEED AND GET OUT OF THE BAY.' He paused to check that he was being heard and then continued, 'I GIVE YOU ONE MINUTE BEFORE I CALL OUT THE HARBOURMASTER.'

The jet skier had heard and raised his arm in acknowledgment. He slowed, turned his craft and headed back towards the point. Robert heard a distant ripple of applause from the people on the beach and bowed self-consciously from his cliff-top perch. He switched off the megaphone and went back into the lookout. At least there was something to enter in the log now.

Down on the rock below the cormorant had returned to its wing-drying routine and all was quiet once more.

He glanced at the wall clock. Twenty-two minutes past four. In just under ten minutes he would make the buddy call to Poltock, five miles up the coast, and then at five he would be closing the watch down for the day. He sat down on the high stool and leaned back to reach for his thermos flask.

Sipping a mug of tea, Robert let his eyes wander lazily around the small confine of his little kingdom. A shelf above the cupboard was stacked with important looking lever arched files, bearing legends such as *Shipping Identification*, *Watch keepers' Notices and Health and Safety Observation*. There were also Health and Safety instructions on a laminated card above his head and another on procedure to be followed in the event of a fire. The latter began with what Robert regarded as an extraordinary instruction in bold, DO NOT PANIC, and on a point of principle he had ignored the rest of the notice.

There were other notices: asking for sightings of basking sharks and dolphins to be reported to one of the marine authorities;

advising of the tide times during the current month; and another form interpreting weather conditions into an abbreviated format.

A pair of binoculars was mounted on a fixed brass pelorus and a chart was spread on the small table below it.

Robert picked up the telephone from the ledge beside his elbow and pressed the speed dial button that connected them with Poltock. In the top right hand corner of the observation window a spider crept insidiously from its lair and advanced on a fly that had become be-webbed. The call was answered just as the spider pounced on its prey.

'Hello, George, Pengarth NCI here. All well?'

'It's not George,' came the reply. 'He's gone out for a pee. Yes, everything's quiet over here.'

'Good.' Robert never quite knew how to proceed these buddy calls beyond the banalities of greeting, so ended lamely with, 'Ok then, have a good watch.'

'Same to you.'Bye now.'

He put the phone back and then drained the last drops from his mug.

The Pengarth lookout of the National Coastwatch Institution had ten active volunteer members, all trained to the standards required by that organisation. Because there were so few of them, seven men and three women in total, the small station on the promontory above Pengarth Bay was manned at weekends only, with each person on watch for a two and half hour spell. It was reckoned that ageing bladders might not stand the strain for much longer spells. Even the rocks gave scant cover in the holiday season and members of Pengarth NCI felt it might diminish their standing with the general public to be caught in the act of supplementing the rock pools.

Pengarth NCI had been formed in 2001 as part of a drive to develop the national network of stations along the British coastline and, as far as the local organisation was concerned, around the Cornish coast in particular.

The station manager and founding member of the Pengarth station was a retired naval officer who owned a thirty-foot cutter, which he kept moored in the bay during the summer and out of the water at Mylor for the rest of the year. But not many living in the area actually recalled seeing him sailing it at any time.

The rest of the watchkeepers were an eclectic bunch, varying in age from Darren, a thirty year-old electrician, to Thomas, still an active boat builder at seventy-two.

Robert Sinclair had been a schoolmaster for most of his active life, teaching English mainly to sixth-formers in Comprehensive Schools around the southeast of England. After twenty years the pressure and strain of the job had got to him and, on the verge of a nervous breakdown, he quit at the age of forty-six. His loving wife had taken a secretarial job, nursed Robert back to health and encouraged him to change direction completely. And by becoming a thatcher, that is precisely what he did, learning the trade mostly by observation and reading.

The Sinclairs and their two young daughters had moved down to Cornwall, bought a terraced house with the help of a fortuitous legacy and he soon found plentiful occupation in his new trade. That was ten years earlier, just before the invasion of the second home owners and the holiday cottage boom. And now in his late fifties Robert felt contentment in his life, a state developed from a combination of personal achievement and sound family structure. Apart perhaps from applying himself to writing a book, he could think of nothing more that he could ask for in his remaining years, so had decided to give something back to the community into which he had become happily embedded.

On the far side of the beach below he saw that Sadie was closing up the refreshment booth for the day and he looked up at the clock again. Ten to five. She usually opened for the season on the weekend of the late May Bank Holiday and then kept her own hours throughout the summer until closing in mid-autumn. He focused his binoculars on her as she pushed back the awning at the front of the hut and then pulled the shutter closed.

Most of the time she ran the Convenience Store in the village, but a small and efficient team of helpers did the counter and shelf stacking work for her. The refreshment hut was simply her sideline: opening when there were sufficient numbers of people on the beach to warrant the time and effort. Sometimes Robert stopped by for an ice cream and a chat at the end of a watch. Sadie was what he thought of as a handsome woman, a widow in her early forties, well proportioned in mind and body and sometimes he fantasised about making love to her in a hayloft. She had that sort of effect on men of a certain age. Robert had heard that Alf went further than fantasise, but that could just be village gossip and there were many local rumours concerning Alf.

He smiled at the thought of Alf and Sadie together and reflected that he would probably see the old reprobate in the Lugger that evening.

Promptly at five o'clock he reached for the telephone and pressed the speed dial to the Falmouth Coastguard Station. The answer was almost immediate.

'Falmouth Coastguard.'

'Hello Falmouth. This is Pengarth NCI, closing the watch for the day.'

'Thank you, Pengarth. Lovely day it's been.' The unidentified coastguard then chuckled. 'Lucky buggers soaking up the sun, eh?'

'I expect they'll be sorry in the morning. Anyway, we'll be opening shop again at nine-thirty tomorrow.'

'Right you are then. Goodnight.'

He went out into the early evening sunshine and as he looked up at the flag a puff of wind lifted the dark hair that hung lightly over his ears, while the top of his head remained untroubled. Hair had long ceased to grow on the upper reaches. Grasping the lanyard he began to untie the very un-nautical knot that one of the female watchkeepers had secured that morning. He then lowered the flag whilst humming a guttural rendition of the Marseillaise and for some reason thinking idly about Dijon mustard.

As he folded the flag he wondered what the Cornish national anthem was. It could be *Trelawny*, but he was not prepared to put money on it.

He made a closing entry in the log, switched off the VHF radio, locked the collection tin in the safe and put on his cap. A woman walking her dog on the coastal path gave him a wave as he was locking the outer door and he waved back.

He hitched his small rucksack onto his back and then strolled slowly onto the path that lead the half-mile back to the village. A passing gull mewed loudly and one of the grazing sheep raised its head suddenly at his approach.

The tide was on its way in and Robert watched kelp being brushed back and forth across the pitted rocks by the water's imperceptible rise. As he climbed over the style at the end of the field a buzzard left its perch on the top of a telephone pole and then eased itself lazily into the air.

He took in all these snatches of nature and felt an inner glow of contentment. There were worse places in the world to be.

At seven o'clock that evening Greg Treberthy came down the creaking back stairs of the Lugger, wiping his auburn moustache with the back of his hand and then taking his place behind what used to be the public bar. The brewery had knocked down a dividing wall and merged the two bars some years ago, but to long-standing regulars there was still an invisible barrier between saloon and public. He turned, nodded to Elsie and then belched quietly. Spaghetti bolognaise was still settling itself in his ample stomach and he regretted having followed it with a dollop of sherry trifle.

Greg rested his large hands on the counter and slowly scanned the clientele. Three NCI men sat at their usual table in the corner by the inglenook and were chortling about something, probably at one of Alf's bad jokes.

A man and woman, with *up country* written all over them, seemed to be analysing in hushed tones what they were drinking. No doubt Elsie had given them a pint each of Rufus Craggs XXX to let them know they were in Cornwall. Greg's stomach bobbed up and down in silent mirth.

At the end of the bar, no more than six feet from his elbow, a lone drinker sat on a stool with his eyes fixed on the beer mat in front of him. Eddy, the great thinker. He would only speak if spoken to first.

Finally, he turned to his left and through the open door into the games room he could see two of the village lads playing pool. One of them still owed him a fiver for breaking that flowerpot outside the pub front door.

The door in question opened at that moment and a shaft of evening sun spread across the beer-stained carpet. Greg looked up and then reached for one of the row of tankards that hung above his head.

Robert acknowledged the group in the corner and then shepherded his wife over to the bar.

'Hello, Greg.' Robert perched on one of the red seated bar stools. 'Been out in the boat?'

'Chance would be a fine thing,' the landlord growled as he pulled a pint of Rufus Craggs into the pewter mug. 'Still caulking last year's leaks.'

'Never mind, the summer's not yet arrived.' He turned to his wife. 'What're you having tonight, Binty?'

She had a pink oval face with pronounced cheekbones and the tips of her ears peeped through tufts of lightly greying blonde hair. Although her demure manner gave an initial appearance of quiet insignificance, anyone who knew her would vouch for the fact that she had the will and constitution of a thoroughbred racehorse. She was Robert's lifeline and he never allowed himself to forget it, in spite of idle daydreams about Sadie.

'Mmm.' She pursed her generous lips and then gave the landlord the benefit of a dimpled smile. 'I think tonight a long G&T would hit the spot. With ice and lemon please, Greg.'

'Coming up, my lovely.' Greg went to the upturned bottles on the wall behind him.

'And a bag of scratchings, landlord. My teeth are feeling lucky tonight.' Robert leaned against the bar and looked over at his NCI colleagues. Darren saw him, gave him the thumbs up and then there was another guffaw from their table.

Over on the public side of the room Alf rocked back in his chair and slapped his knee. 'That's not possible!' he boomed. 'Anyway you could be arrested for that.'

'Well, it seems in the right spirit of things,' Darren said with a straight face. 'If we're to save the world you have to resort to drastic measures.'

The pub door opened again and the newcomer glanced around the room before making his way to the corner.

'Hello there, young Mike.' Alf pushed a chair out from the table with his size twelve shoe.

'What's all the jollity about then?' Mike Nancarrow, a painter and decorator by trade, cheerfully took on any job in that line that came his way. Being largely self-taught and keen to maintain Cornish hours of working, most of his customers were up country second home owners and generally they only returned to him out of desperation. Nevertheless, he was a young man with a happy disposition, honest and keen to please.

'Well,' George Harris, the third man at the table, said in his slow laconic manner. 'We're listing the ways in which we can conserve energy and minimise waste.'

'Oh, you mean like turning off the stand-by button on the TV?' Mike sat down.

'No, no,' Alf snorted, 'that's too obvious. That's what the government tells you to do. What we're suggesting is the ways that they can't publish in a government leaflet.'

'Or a health and safety manual!' Darren the electrician added, to a chorus of groans. 'And why are you sitting down, young man, there's empty glasses yer.'

'You sit down, boy.' Alf rose to his feet surprisingly quickly for a big man. 'My round.' He slapped Mike on the shoulder on his way to the bar. 'And you think of some earth-saving measures by the time I get back.'

Alf Curtis stood just over six feet tall, with broad shoulders and a straight back. His short brushed-back hair was now completely silver, but traces of dark hair remained in his thick wiry eyebrows. What could be seen of his tanned face was surprisingly unlined for a man not many years off sixty and his intelligent grey eyes sparkled with mischievous good humour. The lower half of his face was well covered by a badly trimmed bush of a beard.

Alf came up behind Binty and rested his hand on her shoulder. 'How are you, m'dear?'

'Oh, hello, Alfie. I'm fine.' She patted his hand. 'Are you on watch tomorrow?'

'No, I'm too busy this weekend. I'm on next Saturday.' He looked across at Robert. 'Was that you waking up the district this afternoon, you hooligan?'

'Damned jet skier,' Robert took a sip of his drink. 'Didn't you hear him?'

'Had the window closed most of the time. Stocktaking. Heard your horn though. Good, isn't it?'

'Yes, but the blighter paid no attention until I used the megaphone.'

Greg came over to them.

'Four Rufuses, Greg.' He pushed the empty glasses across the counter.

'Parish council meeting on Tuesday, isn't there?' Robert asked.

Alf pulled a pained expression and then scratched his beard vigorously. 'Don't have to remind me, my old flower. And you can guess what's top of the agenda.'

'The road calming measures?' Binty arched her eyebrows.

'In the words of Roy Orbison, you got it.' He reached for the wallet in his back pocket. 'I'm hoping there'll be someone there from the Council or Highways, whatever good that'll do.'

'I think I can make it,' Robert said, 'but if I can't, good luck.'

'I hope you can, Rob. We need all the active support we can get.' He handed a couple of notes to Greg and held out his hand for the change. 'Right, back to the troops.'

Alf seized the four pints and manoeuvred his way back to the corner table.

'Right, lads, what've you got?' Alf plonked the glasses on the table.

'Cheers, Alf.' Mike took a long pull on his pint. 'What about peeing on the compost heap? That would save flushing and liven up the rotting process.'

'Come on, Mike,' Alf growled disparagingly and the others shook their heads in agreement. 'That's old hat. We need something original. Something the editor will ban from the Parish Magazine.'

'I know,' George leaned forward conspiratorially, 'night earth on the allotment. They do it in India.'

'Yes, that would be another saving on the flushing,' Mike added sagely. 'But how late would you have to stay up to do it. I got to get to work by eight.'

'That would be my problem too, Mike,' Darren added. 'Also, don't you have to be a vegetarian for that to work?'

'I don't see why.' Alf scratched his beard. 'Indians are curry eaters after all.'

'I can't eat curry.' George dipped his mouth. 'Gives me the runs.'

'Aha!' Alf stabbed a finger at him. 'That's the point! So much easier to spread around the allotment.'

A roar of coarse laughter burst from the corner table and the visiting couple looked startled. At the bar Robert smiled and secretly wished he could join the rowdy group.

'I've got another.' Mike was getting into the swing of the game. The others peered at him encouragingly.

'A generator to power the village street lights, powered by methane from George's chicken shit.' He leaned back, looking very pleased with himself, but George seemed sceptical.

'I've only got three hundred of 'em. Will it go that far?' he asked dubiously. 'Also, who's going to collect it all up and how d'you store the methane anyway?'

They all stared at Mike, who lowered his head and mumbled, 'Well, you'd have to start in a small way . . .'

The four men were pondering this problem when the door opened again. The up country couple were leaving and Sadie was coming in. She smiled at the couple and then went to the bar to greet Robert and Binty. Alf seized his pint and stood up.

'Excuse me, lads. Keep thinking.' The three exchanged knowing looks as he threaded his way past chairs on his way to the bar. Sadie looked up and saw him over Binty's shoulder.

'Get you a drink, Sadie?' Alf asked as he joined the trio at the bar.

'No thanks, Alf.' Robert's beaten you to it. 'What've you been up to?'

'Boring stuff, my flower.' He moved around to stand between her and Robert. 'Taking stock of me books. That and starting a sort of catalogue.'

'My God,' Binty exclaimed. 'That's a mammoth task, Alf. Why do it now?'

'You mean, after all these years of organised chaos?' He shrugged and his grin revealed even but slightly tarnished teeth looming like tombstones through the undergrowth. 'I don't know. Call it a spring clean . . . or a moment of madly inconsistent and uncharacteristic behaviour, if you like.'

'You do actually sell some of those books, don't you?' Robert asked with a twinkle in his eye.

'You're damned right I do. Virtually close down in winter. Just stock up from house clearances and the like. But, in the summer the emmetts flock in for their holiday reading. Prime position, you see.'

It was indeed a prime position. Alf Curtis had been a successful merchant banker for many years and had amassed a substantial amount of capital with the corporate takeover boom in the eighties and then had suddenly jacked it all in a few months before the Conservative Party ousted Margaret Thatcher. Having spent many happy holidays down in Cornwall, he made the momentous decision to settle by the sea and to spend the remainder of his days doing exactly what he wanted to do.

But, in spite of his bluff and open-handed manner there was a reticence when it came to his personal history. It was known around the village that he had been married, but he never talked about his wife and few were tactless enough to ask. Even Robert, who had known him for all the time he had been in Pengarth, plus some years before that, generally avoided the subject.

There was also a rumour that Alf had a child, or children, somewhere, but he was equally evasive on that score.

What was common knowledge was that in 1990 he had bought a terraced house at the lower end of Fore Street in Pengarth and then turned the ground floor front room into a bookshop. The first floor had been thoroughly renovated and that was where he lived and entertained visitors. The attic he had converted into a store-room for his ever-growing stock of books.

He found time at weekends to carry out coastal watch duties up at the lookout and, more importantly to the locals, he was Chairman of the Pengarth Parish Council – a position he had held unopposed for five years.

If he lived to be a hundred and twenty Alf acknowledged that he would never be a true Cornishman, but if questioned on the subject of status, he never hesitated to claim that he was a Duchy man by adoption. In his own mind he had quite simply and deliberately gone native.

'What sort of books do they buy then?' Sadie inclined her head and smiled her enigmatic smile.

'Raw sex and violence, my 'andsome,' he said in a cod Cornish accent and leered over his beer mug. 'Raw sex and violence.'

'No, seriously, Alf,' Binty nudged him in the ribs.

'Alright, seriously.' He adopted a serious face. 'All kinds from Almanacs to Zoological studies . . . plus raw sex and violence!'

Sadie chortled and her eyes disappeared under heavy eyelids hued with green mascara. Alf winked at her and then turned to Robert.

'Have you two eaten yet?'

'Yes, we had a quick salad. You?'

'No. I'm going back now to get my teeth into some game pie.' He slid his glass across the counter. 'So I'll wish you a goodnight, one and all.'

He turned to go and then, halfway to the door, paused and turned back to Sadie.

'Do you still need some help with that tax return, my flower?'

A flash of faint amusement crossed Sadie's tanned face before she replied. 'Yes, Alf, I'm not done with it yet. A bit of advice on the allowances would be useful, thanks.'

Alf Curtis nodded. 'Tomorrow perhaps. I'll stop by in the afternoon.'

George Harris looked up from the corner table and watched him leave the pub. He had thought of another energy saving scheme, but it could keep for another time.

Chapter Two

GREG, stripped to a T-shirt, shorts and leather sandals, looked up from his labours at the sounds of footsteps across the shingle. He shaded his eyes into the morning sun and stood up slowly with a groan as he pressed his other hand into the small of his back. Perspiration glistened on his moustache.

His stomach, as round as a football, betrayed the slackened muscles that twenty years earlier had been as tight as a drum skin. He had been a Gig rower of some note in the county, had run ten marathons and until quite recently had swum daily twice across the bay before breakfast. Now his only exercise was lifting beer barrels and sailing his beloved boat.

Greg wiped the sweat from his florid cheeks as his dark eyes focused on the person approaching along the beach. He pushed his peaked cap back to reveal a tuft of hair so white that it was impossible now to detect that it originally matched the rust colour of his moustache.

'Morning, Greg,' Robert stopped by the boat and tapped its hull. 'How much more work does she need?'

Robert's spaniel trotted up to one of the supports and cocked its leg. Greg scowled and threatened to throw a tin of caulk at it.

'Hello to you, Robert.' He glanced back at the boat. 'Another couple of days and she'll be shipshape, I reckon. You out for a walk?'

'Yes. Gave church a miss. Too fine a day to polish the pews with my backside.'

'Or wear out your knees.' Greg's stomach gave a couple of lurches with his soundless chuckle. 'Talking of church, is BK back yet?'

'No, he's still up country. Not back 'til Tuesday, I think.'

'In time for the Parish meeting, I hope.'

'I'm sure he will be.' Robert looked up as a seagull wheeled overhead and alighted briefly on the mast. 'We'll need all the big guns there. You going?'

'If I can get away from the pub.' He wiped his hands on a greasy rag. 'I feel as strongly about that road business as anyone. Could damage my trade as well.'

'It's already damaged my car and I bet the council won't pay for the repairs.'

'You're joking! The only way to get your money back is to withhold some of your council tax.'

'And then I'd end up in jail.'

'No problem there. Binty would bail you out.'

Robert looked at Greg dubiously and bent down to pat the dog. 'You reckon so?'

'No, maybe not. In which case, we'd have a whip round in the Lugger.'

'What a kind thought, landlord. Anyway, we'll see how it goes at the meeting. But I mustn't keep you from the good work. Be seeing you.' He gave a sharp whistle for the dog.

'Bye now.' Greg turned and smoothed his moustache before bending again over the split in the hull planking.

As Robert strolled away down to the sandy part of the beach, with the dog stopping regularly to sniff at each new and exciting aroma, Greg pondered his lot.

Like many others of his vintage in the village of Pengarth, he had chosen to change the direction of his life's path. He had been in Cornwall for most of his adulthood and, having a father who was born in the Duchy, he felt he truly had a claim to being a native.

From school he had gone straight into commercial banking and had ended up manager of a branch in Newquay. This had provided perfectly adequately for his family and he had begun to make plans for retirement when suddenly his cosy world collapsed around him. The branch had fallen victim of cost cutting and rationalisation by the parent company and he had found himself without a job at the age of fifty. There had been a modest redundancy payment, but no offer of another branch to manage, so he and his wife began to explore the options, deciding eventually to apply for the licence of a pub in the Roseland.

For a while he had been lucky. He was taken on by the local brewery, sent on a training course and eventually offered the Lugger in Pengarth. At that point it could not have been better, but then life turned sour once more.

Their son, their only child, had graduated from Exeter University with a geology degree and had decided to take a job with a mining company in Australia. Reluctantly the parents accepted that the parting was probably a useful career move for the young man, so they had seen him off to Sydney in the summer of 1999, on the eve of the sun's total eclipse over the UK. Unfortunately, in the eyes of his devoted parents, this proved also to be the eve of their son's total eclipse, because soon after arriving in Sydney he wrote home with the news no parent wants to read or hear.

Their beloved son had not gone alone to Australia. He had gone with the love of his life: an almond-eyed Thai boy called Pichai.

The shock was so great that Greg's wife, Suzy, sank into deep depression and Greg himself spent weeks in a state of frustrated anger, casting around for someone to blame. Such was the preoccupation with his own torment that he failed to notice that Suzy, normally an abstemious person, was beginning to hit the gin bottle in a stock-depleting way.

Then one day, after a bender at the pub in Poltock, she had driven her car off the cliff near the village's public toilets. It was forty-odd feet down, but at that point the rocks are unforgiving and the car's petrol tank had ruptured on impact. The coroner's verdict had been suicide whilst under the influence of *excessive alcoholic intake*.

Greg had been inconsolable and it came as no consolation to him whatsoever to hear at the inquest that the autopsy had revealed advanced intestinal cancer.

Greg's many friends had come to his aid, but for a long time there had been no way of easing his grief. He had taken compassionate leave from the Lugger and for a while considered visiting his son in Australia. But the boy had not attended his mother's funeral and Greg took that, together with his son's choice of partner, as being a final severance of their relationship. Thus he was left alone to suffer the consequences of having closed all doors to reconciliation.

Then, one wild late November afternoon, Greg had sailed out of Pengarth Bay with the intention of never returning. And that would have been the end of Greg Treberthy had George Harris not been on storm watch up in the lookout. He had just managed to make out the shape of a small boat through the gale-lashed window of the station, even though there was no navigation light on board and Greg's sail was a dark brown.

49

George had called Falmouth and given a bearing, but even then it was a close run affair. Ten minutes after giving the alarm, with the rescue helicopter on its way, George had lost sight of the boat completely. But, in the darkness, the helicopter crew had spotted it a mile off shore, had lowered the winch man and hauled a soaked and near-lifeless Greg off the swamped craft.

Already suffering from exposure, he was flown directly to hospital in Truro and then took three days to recover physically. The mental recovery took longer, but two things helped the process.

Firstly Greg became aware of the power of comradeship and how his friends old and new were able to impart to him their sincere concern and affection. And with that genuine care he came gradually to believe that there was something left to live for after all.

Then the boat itself, so nearly his coffin, became a powerful symbol for Greg Treberthy. Amazingly, a week after the incident, it was found upturned and with a broken mast on a beach three miles down the coast. This simple but unlikely discovery somehow had a profound effect on Greg and the boat thereafter became his therapy back to some kind of a normal life. It was now this same sailing boat that he lovingly caulked in preparation for another summer.

He looked over his shoulder at the sound of an outboard starting up and a few moments later an orange inflatable appeared from behind some rocks at the south side of the bay. A man in a green shirt sat at the stern steering the boat while a boy of about eight perched eagerly at the bow, a hand dangling over the side to catch the wave: Darren and his son going fishing.

Greg watched the scene for a while and then with a rueful sigh returned to his work. It had been seven years since he had seen his own boy and now he was not even sure where he lived.

Soon after midday he stood up, eased his joints, and then began to gather up his tools. It was time to clean up and relieve Elsie at the Lugger.

He checked that the boat was secure and then cast a final glance out to sea. The orange inflatable was sitting comfortably on a slight swell and puttering along at a couple of knots while the boy played his line over the side. Greg slung his denim jacket over a shoulder and plodded up the shingle to the slipway.

Chapter Three

AT twenty minutes to seven on Tuesday evening Alf Curtis slid off a stool on the public bar side of the Lugger and picked up a blue lever arch file from the counter.

'Well, Elsie my old flower, I'm off to do battle with the infidel. Wish me luck.'

'Parish meeting, is it?' Elsie, a tall heavy boned lass with pink-striped shoulder-length hair, carried on wringing a glass in a damp teacloth.

'Parish meeting it is.' Alf thought for a moment about relieving himself of the two swift pints he had downed and then decided it could wait. There was a bog in the village hall. 'I just hope there's a decent turnout, otherwise we're all wasting our time in there.'

'Maybe see you later then?'

'I should bloody well hope so,' he called back to her on his way to the door.

Alf walked slowly along Fore Street, past the Convenience Store and then took the cobbled alley that was a short cut to the hall. He had not yet decided exactly how to play this meeting. It could be a furious affair, or it could all end up a damp squib. A lot depended on who was there and what approach the Council's transport people took. All he had to do was to listen, prompt and, above all, to keep his temper. He was the chairman after all, he kept reminding himself. If there was to be a punch-up he was the referee and not one of the contestants.

He reached the side door of the hall, took a deep breath and went in. As soon as he rounded the corner of the passageway he saw BK sitting on his own at the head table, looking anxiously up at the clock. There was no sign of the Treasurer, the third member of the Council. Robert was Deputy Chairman, but he preferred to attend from the floor, unless Alf was unavoidably absent from a meeting.

Alf paused for a few seconds at the glass-panelled door before making an entrance. Someone had optimistically put out three rows of chairs, with about ten in each row. Normally, if ten people in all turned up for these meetings it would be a fair showing. The quorum of public attendees was only four, but on more than one occasion he had had to drag someone out of the Lugger to make up that number. Now there were a dozen whom he recognised, including Robert Sinclair and the vicar. Three of those he did not know wore the careworn pallor of Council employees.

Alf pushed the squeaking door open and made his way over to sit by B.K.Richards, clerk to the Pengarth Parish Council. The general murmur subsided for a moment as he sat down and then quickly resumed to its previous level. The Council representatives, two men and a woman, looked stonily ahead. Clearly their evening's entertainment had been disrupted.

'The Sarpanch has arrived,' Alf announced to the Clerk in his version of an Indian accent.

'The who?' BK asked, peering over his glasses at the assembly.

'Me, old boy. A Sarpanch is the elected leader of a village council in India. Read that this morning.'

'Ah, that accounts for the Welsh accent.' BK glanced at him with the trace of a smile and then went back to poring over his notes.

'No Hettie this evening?'

'No, there seems to be a family crisis over to Padstow.' BK took off his glasses and began to wipe the lenses vigorously. 'There's no Treasurer's report on the agenda, so it shouldn't matter.'

'Well, with Robert down there we have a quorum of Committee members anyway.' Alf opened his file. 'How was the trip up country?'

'Very successful,' BK said enthusiastically. 'Glenys and I bought an oak bureau in Exeter. Just what we were looking for to go in the blank corner of . . .'

The door opened loudly and Greg Treberthy came in, followed closely by George Harris. Greg nodded to Alf across the room, glanced at the Council people and then found a chair on the back row. George stood undecided until a woman tugged at his sleeve. He opened his mouth in a gap-toothed grin and sat down beside her.

'Sorry,' Alf turned back to the clerk, 'you were saying about the bureau . . .?'

'Doesn't matter.' BK's head went up towards the clock again. 'Now, about the agenda . . . shall we bring the road item forward . . . They . . .' He raised a finger in the direction of the Council people.

'They can stew,' Alf growled. 'We'll stick to the agenda that you prepared. You sent them a copy didn't you?'

'Yes.'

'Then they know they're here for item . . .' he put on his spectacles and peered down at the agenda. '. . . six. So, item six it is. Don't want them to think we're wetting our knickers over them.'

BK winced at Alf's metaphor, but nodded his agreement.

'And the minutes of the last meeting?' BK asked tentatively.

'Read 'em in full, as usual,' Alf said truculently and then instantly relented. 'No, wait. How long are they?'

'Three and half pages.'

'Bugger! Ok, a synopsis will do then.' He took off his wristwatch, let it fall heavily on the bare table and then looked at the audience.

Some continued to talk, so he rapped twice on the table and cleared his throat.

'Ladies and Gents, it's seven so we'll make a start to the meeting. Thank you all for coming out tonight.' He switched on his benign face and turned to the three visitors. 'And particularly to you folk from the Council for your attendance. Let's hope we can . . .'

The door at the back burst open so loudly that Alf was cut off in mid sentence. The benign expression was instantly replaced by a withering scowl as an equally belligerent looking middle-aged woman swayed across the room and found a seat. Alf had not seen her before and, from the expression on the faces of a number of locals, neither had they. There was no apology from the woman, who was now busily arranging the folds of her dress around an ample behind.

'It's alright, madam,' Alf said with thinly veiled sarcasm, 'we've only just started.'

She muttered something he could not hear, but George, sitting to her right, blinked a few times and plucked at an earlobe. Alf looked down at his notes.

'Right.' He turned to BK. 'We have a couple of apologies here.'

'Yes, and I have one from Liz Perkins.' BK shuffled some papers busily and then dragged the minute book closer to him.

'So, I'll now ask BK to give us a synopsis of the last meeting. I think reading them verbatim will take up too much time and we have a full agenda.' He scanned the room. 'Are we all in agreement?'

A murmur of assent and a few bobbing heads gave him the answer he expected, so he palmed an invitation to BK and leaned back in his chair. The clerk cleared his throat, fidgeted for a moment, and then began his précis.

B.K.Richards had lived in and around Pengarth for as long as anyone could remember and he had been known by his initials for just as long. In fact, most folk could not even recall what the 'B' stood for and Alf had never even thought to ask. His wife, Glenys, would know, but she also called him BK. Only their three children didn't and they called him Dad.

BK was a farmer. He had tried many disciplines of agriculture over the years, normally going with the flow of where the profits or the subsidies lay. He had raised beef cattle, had a milking herd, gone into arable and even had a couple of seasons specialising in vegetable crops. Then, five years ago, he had discovered pigs and had gone at the project with the enthusiasm of a teenager.

Initially Glenys had not shared this keenness and could only see the downside to everything porcine. Pigs were dirty, they stank, the people who worked with them were unapproachable, the pork market was unpredictable and there was a social stigma attached. But, gradually, she too had learned to live with and then to love the pigs and together they had built up a thriving business. They did this not merely in the conventional way, but also by specialising in rare breeds, making their own sausages and producing a new Porker Pasty, which initially they sold at farmers' markets in Truro. Now BK's Porker Pasty was consumed in vast numbers at university campuses as far away as Birmingham and Cardiff.

Although a very busy farmer BK still found time to involve himself in local activities and, apart from being clerk to the Parish Council, for which he was paid £250 a year out of the precept, he was also the Churchwarden of St Grace's Church. As Glenys sang in the choir and taught at the local primary school, altogether they made an admirable family unit and a boon for the village community.

BK finished his summation of the last meeting and pushed the book across to the chairman for his signature. Alf, who had been staring at the back of BK's head and pondering the mentality of a man who could devote his life to ham on four legs, ceased his reverie and brought his chair upright with a thump on the polished wooden floor.

'Does everyone accept that as being a fair summary of what went on at the last meeting?' Heads nodded. Alf put on his glasses, stroked his beard and then signed his name at the bottom of the page.

'Date?'

'Twenty-fifth of May.' BK wondered for a moment whether or not to tell Alf the year as well. One never could tell with him.

'Right,' Alf said loudly and glanced down at the agenda. 'Thank you, BK. Item two on the agenda is Planning Consents and this one is a retrospective application, Willy Carthew having knocked down a wall at the end of his garden and erected a shed. It doesn't say what Willy plans to do with the shed, but I assume it's a big one – yes we have the measurements here – and that it's not for some nefarious purpose like storing the cannabis that he's grown in his allotment.'

There were one or two titters, but BK put his head closer to his notes and groaned inwardly. Diplomacy, tact and – Heaven forbid – political correctness all seemed to have given Alf a wide berth and not for the first time he wondered how the man came to be elected chairman.

'Sorry, Willy, didn't see you there.' Alf pointed to the back row.

'S'alright, Alf, I didn't see you neither,' came the instant reply and there was widespread laughter.

And so the meeting progressed, until at last they reached the contentious item six.

'Item six,' Alf announced, 'Traffic calming outside the primary school on upper Fore Street. Now, as everyone in this hall no doubt recalls, after only short consultation the County Council decided to proceed with this project *in the interests of safety,* for the children crossing the road to and from school. This decision was made regardless of the opinions of local people and businesses and in spite of the fact that there has never in living memory been an accident involving traffic and schoolchildren on this stretch of road.'

There was muttering from the floor, so he paused and looked up. 'Dissent?'

'No, not really.' George Harris shuffled awkwardly in his chair. 'I just said to Mavis yer that in 1907 a cart knocked a boy off his bicycle outside the school. Penny farthing, I think it was.'

'Oh, for God's sake, George!' Alf's face creased in disbelief amidst general mirth. 'I said within living memory. You're not a hundred yet are you?'

One of the Council men turned to a colleague, raised an exasperated eyebrow and shook his head slowly. Alf saw the look and banged the table for order.

'The majority decision amongst villagers was that, if such measures were needed, then something like an illuminated sign and some road markings would be sufficient for the purpose. That was ignored or overruled by the Transport and Estates folk, who arranged for their subcontractors to lay the impediments that we suffer today.' He paused and looked over his glasses at the Three for a second. 'Now, several months after the road into our village has been blighted, we have called for a review of the situation. The representatives of the Council's Transport Division . . .' Some turned to look at them, as if for the first time. '. . . have come tonight to listen to our grievances and, I hope, to take those grievances seriously and go away, think about it, and then come up with an alternative arrangement.'

Perhaps he's not quite so hopeless after all, thought the Clerk.

'Now I have some formal written complaints to present to the meeting tonight and I would invite you . . .' Alf gesticulated towards the Three '. . . to take heed. I'll be giving you copies anyway, just in case you're not making notes. I happen to believe that most of these people have a justifiable grievance and good cause for wanting the impediments removed . . . or substantially modified.'

He turned to BK and made a whispered suggestion that he give his writing hand a rest as he had other copies of the letters.

'So, if no one objects, I shall read these out to the meeting and then invite parish members attending tonight to lodge their own opinions of the so-called traffic calming scheme.'

For the next quarter of an hour Alf read the letters of complaint; sometimes in full and sometimes, where they were too long, abusive or illiterate, he summarised. BK leaned back and watched facial expressions with a keen eye.

'. . . *and every time I mount the humps* (Alf paused as for a moment he had a fleeting vision of Sadie) *the scales fly off and my*

56

weighing mechanism goes out of alignment. This is causing considerable loss to my delivery business and frustration to my customers.' He put the letter down and slowly removed his glasses. 'Well, those are the reactions of some of the locals and that's only part of the story, but now I'll throw it open to the floor. Firstly, anyone here who approves of the road impediments?'

He peered over his glasses at the gathering and there was not a whisper of agreement, although one or two looked at each other. He was about to continue when there was a cough from the back and the middle one of the Three, the woman, began to speak.

'Chair, I would like to make a point regarding . . .'

'Who?' Alf's chin jutted forward and BK swore that he could see the beard moving of its own accord. 'Who did you say, madam?'

'Er, I was addressing you, the Chair.' She returned his stare, but at the same time appeared discomfited by Alf's bark.

'Madam, I am not a chair. I am a Chair*man*. A chair is what I sit on and I am not prepared to be sat upon by anyone. Although . . .' *Don't say it*, Alf told himself, but he did anyway, '. . . in your case I could make an exception.'

A coarse laugh came from a couple of the locals, but the vicar was shaking her head so much that her dog collar seemed in danger of springing loose.

Oh Lord, you've torn it now, thought BK.

'Really,' a high-pitched protest came from the smaller of the male Three, 'this is a most irregular way to conduct a meeting. My colleagues and I did not come here to be insulted.'

Alf held up his hands contritely and a beatifical smile spread over his face. He was prepared to eat humble pie to help the cause.

'I *am* sorry, madam . . . it is alright to call you madam? . . . It was not my intention to insult you. It was just a joke in poor taste. I am notorious for it and I apologise.' His smile broadened and his expression invited forgiveness. 'Shall we proceed?'

She dipped her mouth, nodded and then continued, 'I was going to make the point, Chair*man*, that it is probably not helpful to continue referring to the road calming measures as impediments. In the context of this debate it is a pejorative word and unlikely to . . .'

'What's *py-jorative* mean?' George asked his neighbour rather too loudly and was promptly hushed by the vicar.

'. . . unlikely to make proceedings run any more smoothly,' she ended lamely and looked down at her lap. Her colleagues nodded their heads in eager support.

'Madam, I refer to the humps and cushions in our Fore Street as impediments because that is exactly what they are. They impede the progress of vehicles and in some cases cause actual damage to them. That may not be the intention, but what is the difference between your humps and cushions and, say, dirty great potholes in the road? If there were potholes in the highway, any motorist would have legitimate cause to complain and in due course the Council would have them filled in. Your humps and cushions are inverted potholes and are therefore impediments, madam.' He stared hard at the woman, who, he noted for the first time, was not unattractive under the official veneer.

'Here, 'ere, 'ere,' George shouted and this time he received support all round. Even the vicar was nodding.

'Now,' Alf held up his hands, savouring the moment, 'any more constructive observations from the floor?'

Alf cast around for any personal experiences on the minefield of Fore Street and a hand shot up from the large blousy woman who had arrived late. 'Yes, madam.'

'I want to lodge a complaint about my rubbish collection,' she announced stridently and her jowls wobbled as she did so.

For a moment Alf was taken aback. *Who was this woman? Had she not been listening to the proceedings of the past half hour?* He closed his eyes for a moment and counted to three.

'Madam, we're still on item six to the agenda,' he stated patiently. 'I suggest that you raise your rubbish complaint under item eight, Any Other Business.'

She made a noise that sounded like a good old-fashioned harrumph, but said no more. However, she had effectively killed any further complaints and BK wondered idly if she was a plant from the Council. He certainly had not seen her around the village.

BK felt a nudge from Alf's elbow.

'Looks like all from the floor,' the Chairman whispered. 'Shall we put them on the stand now?'

BK glanced at his watch, looked over to them and then nodded.

'Well, that seems to be it from our side, for the time being.' Alf forced a smile. 'Would one of you like to comment on what you've heard? By the way, I'm very sorry but I don't know your names. Perhaps, for the record . . . ?'

They duly gave their names and BK scribbled them down. Alf was relieved to note that their spokesman was the one who so far had been silent. A few minutes of the squeaky-voiced one would surely drive him mad and the woman . . . anyway, it was a relief.

Rundle, the spokesman thanked him politely for inviting them to the meeting and for the opportunity to listen to all of their comments concerning the road safety measures. He then proceeded to give the official reasons for the existence of the scheme, heavily laced with local government jargon, and why after consultation with the Road Safety Audit team the Traffic Engineering Group still considered the measures to be appropriate. He was sorry if local people disliked these measures, but they had been devised in accordance within the prescribed criteria and with the health and safety of school children the paramount consideration.

It was a polished performance and, when he had finished, he folded his arms with an air of finality and smiled rather smugly at Alf.

That was a mistake.

'So, Mr Rundle,' Alf's response after a few moments' reflection was dangerously muted. 'Are you saying that is the Council's last word on the matter, in spite of what you have heard tonight?'

Rundle shrugged. 'There will always be complaints whenever something new occurs in a community, but the wider benefits have to be paramount, Mr Curtis. In time people here will get used to . . .'

'We've already lived with it for months,' Alf interrupted, 'and while we are largely dependent on visitors in the season the *getting used to* simply does not apply. Anyway, you can get used to living with a nail in your head, but it doesn't make life any better!'

'Come, come,' Rundle said tetchily, 'I hardly think that is an appropriate analogy . . .'

'Yes, it damned well is!' Alf's beard was twitching again. 'Those humps and cushions are *our* nail in the head, so you go back to your engineers and tell them to design something more suitable for this village. The school is only open for business for about a quarter of the hours in the year anyway and for the rest of the time we all have to suffer from the effects of the confounded impediments. You simply *cannot* . . .' he thumped the table for emphasis and his watch knocked against a glass, '. . . ignore the considered opinions and everyday needs of the people of this community, all for the sake of carrying out something that fits in with a drawing board plan. Real life cannot be plotted on a drawing board, Mr Rundle.'

To his surprise a ripple of applause came from the floor and he acknowledged it with a quick nod and a twitch of the lips. He had not been so pissed off about anything since the occasion when his car had slid into a ditch after skidding on slurry from Farmer Tremayne's trailer. And what was worse, all the excitement had put pressure on his bladder. Those two pints were needing to find porcelain, and soon.

'I'm sorry that you take that attitude, Chairman.' Rundle began. 'We have listened...'

'I really don't think you have, Mr Rundle,' Alf interrupted. 'But I would still ask you to take all of this back for serious consideration. At the very least . . . the *very* least . . . please smooth the edges off the impediments. They are simply too severe. This should cost the Council little, but would go some way towards making the scheme more bearable for users of the road in the meantime.'

Rundle seemed to reflect for a while and then turned for a few quiet words with his female colleague. She nodded obsequiously.

'We will certainly pass on our notes from this meeting.' He lifted his eyes to the ceiling for a moment as if rehearsing a speech and then carried on. 'I will also instruct the Area Manager for our contractors to investigate the situation you describe concerning the gradients for the cushions and ramps. If the manager then confirms that the situation is outside expected tolerances, the contractors will be instructed to rectify the works.'

'Whazzat mean?' George looked around for clarification.

'That's all I can promise.' It was obviously Rundle's last word on the matter.

'I have to say that your negative attitude is most disappointing,' Alf growled at the Three. 'Some might say obstructive and I have no doubt that the members of this Parish will not want me to let the matter rest there. I'm sure you'll understand that my personal views are largely irrelevant – I simply express the opinions of those who elected me. But, if you have no more to add at this time, I'll wish you all a very good night and thank you again for coming.'

Alf swivelled dismissively in his chair and bent towards BK's ear.

'Need a piss, old boy. Hold the fort by kicking off on item seven, would you?'

'Certainly.' BK grinned as Alf pushed his chair back. 'Don't hit any of them on your way out.'

'Bastards! I might at that. We may as well have been farting in a wind tunnel for all the notice they took of us.' He turned and raised his voice to the meeting. 'I'll be back in a couple of minutes, but BK will take the agenda forward in my absence.'

He strode down the side of the hall, squeezing past one of the chairs and heading for the inner swing door. The Council people were still gathering their papers together when the door closed behind him with a swish.

Alf savoured the pleasure of emptying his bladder, head back and eyes closed as the jet splattered against the urinal, gurgled past the chewing gum and then down the grill. He breathed deeply as he heard the murmur of voices, followed by the slam of the outer door. *Why do I let these bloody bureaucrats get to me every time?* He pulled up his zip and then, as he washed his hands, he stared at the angry face in the mirror. *Don't let the buggers grind you down, my old flower.*

As he went back into the hall BK was just reading the final paragraph of Constable Curnow's report on local felonies in the area. '. . . so, as the holiday season approaches please secure your fishing tackle and boating accessories.' BK put the paper down and removed the reading glasses from their precarious perch on his sinuous nose.

Alf landed heavily in his seat and turned to the clerk.

'Thank you, BK.' He looked up at the audience and grinned. 'I hope PC Curnow's next report doesn't include anything about bodies of Council workers being found at the bottom of the bay.'

There was a burst of laughter, which seemed to go some way towards clearing the oppressive atmosphere that had developed during the course of the previous discussion.

'So, if there's nothing more to be added on that subject, we'll move on.'

He turned to BK.

'Item eight.' BK prompted.

'Right, item eight, Any Other Business.' He suddenly remembered the blousy woman and caught her eye. 'Madam, you had something to say about rubbish?'

'Yes, I *do*.' She straightened her back and wiggled on the plastic seat of her chair. 'It's about the state of the . . .'

'Erm, if I may just interrupt for a moment . . .' BK was holding his Oxfam ballpoint pen in the air. 'I'm afraid I don't recognise you, madam. For the minutes I wonder if you would mind introducing yourself to the meeting?'

'Certainly, I'm Gloria Bush-Tyke and I've bought Lamorna Cottage at the top of Fore Street. I moved in . . .'

'Glorious Butch Dyke? What kind of name is that?' George Harris asked his neighbour in a stage whisper.

Someone in the audience snorted and Alf, who had also heard the comment quite clearly shaded his eyes and bit his lower lip. BK, who was a sucker for a pun, gave a sort of squeak and began to shake silently. Everybody, including the vicar, was now staring at the stranger with renewed interest.

'Gloria Bush-Tyke,' she repeated loudly and distinctly and then spelled it for good measure. 'B-U-S-H hyphen T-Y-K-E. Have you got that?'

'Yes,' BK said falsetto and then coughed. 'Yes, Mrs, er, Bush-Tyke.'

'Miss!' She retorted angrily and glowered at the clerk. 'Miss Bush-Tyke.'

'Of course.' BK lowered his head and began writing, but there was another prolonged snort from the floor. Alf could not be sure, but he thought it could have been Greg. In any event order would have to be restored rapidly.

'Thank you, I think we've got that straight. Now, what is your issue, madam?' He felt the table shaking and glanced to his left. BK seemed to be having a fit of some kind, so he gave him a sharp kick under the table and the trembling slowly subsided.

'As I was trying to say . . .' an exasperated expression settled across her features, '. . . for three weeks in succession the rubbish in my sacks have been scattered around my garden by vandals and as a council tax payer I am here to lodge a strong protest. I was led to believe that this is a peaceful and law-abiding place. That is why I came to live here!' She folded her arms and scowled at Alf.

He leaned over to BK and they exchanged a few words. The clerk had now recovered his composure.

'We are indeed a law-abiding community, Miss Bush-Tyke, as you will have heard from the constable's report. We only tend to have trouble when the emmets invade from up country. But, to address your particular problem . . . does this rubbish scattering happen on Mondays only by any chance?'

'Yes, on the day of collection. I put the bags out and in the morning it's all over the lawn.'

'When do you put the bags out?'

'On Sunday night, just before I go to bed.'

'Ah! Well, Miss B-T, you shouldn't do that. Rubbish bags should not be put out before six o'clock on Monday morning. It's one of the Council's regulations. And, do you know why?'

'No?' she said with a note of caution, wiggling a bit more on the chair and beginning to look less confident.

'Because of the white winged vandals, madam: gulls, which will rip a rubbish bag apart in minutes, devour the edible bits and scatter the rest far and wide while you still slumber.' He smiled indulgently at her, while she began to wither under an array of smug grins. 'And sometimes, when Mr Brock the badger fancies a trip to the seaside, he also will stop by for a snack.'

'Or George's old dog,' came a helpful suggestion from the floor.

'Oh, I see.' Her face twitched with embarrassment. 'Thank you. It never occurred to me . . .'

'Don't worry, Miss Tyke, you're not the first and you won't be the last.' Alf suddenly felt a thirst coming on and made a rapid decision to ignore any further business, in spite of a waving arm. 'Thank you everybody. I'll call a close to the meeting now. Date of next meeting BK?'

BK reached for his diary and in a couple of minutes they had agreed a date. Alf closed his file; people stirred, stood up and then began stacking chairs along the walls.

'Coming for a drink, BK?' Alf stretched and then caught Robert's eye, making a glass-raising gesture in his direction.

'Not tonight, Alf. Glenys wants me to move that bureau into position before we go to bed.'

Alf patted him on the shoulder. 'Ok, my old flower, orders is orders. Anyway, thanks for your support tonight. Oh, and I'm sorry if I embarrassed you – again!'

BK just laughed and shrugged his bony shoulders. He was accustomed to most of Alf's ways, but at times his chairman still had the capacity to shock.

'I'll lock up,' he called after Alf, who raised a hand as he headed for the door.

Four of them sat in conclave at the round table in the corner of the public bar section of the Lugger.

Alf had just bought another round and was wiping froth from his moustache. George Harris was laughing fit to burst at his discovery of Glorious Butch Dyke, Robert Sinclair was chuckling at the sight of George's merriment and young Mike was goading George along with ribald quips. The few at the bar occasionally glanced in their direction and threw comments across the floor to them, while Greg passed on to anyone who would listen what had occurred at the meeting.

'So, what're we going to do about the road impediments if the Highways people decide to sit on their hands?' Alf asked Robert above the din.

'Don't know what we can do, other than what you . . .'

'Cut it out, George!' Alf shouted. 'Can't hear what Sir Robert's saying.'

George's cackle gurgled to a sputtering halt. Still shaking like a startled blancmange, he picked up his pint and his stained green trousers soaked up some beer. Young Mike carried on sniggering, but turned his attention to Robert.

'I was saying we should follow your advice and take it to a higher authority.'

'Like God, you mean?'

'Shut it, Mike,' Alf rounded on the young decorator, 'this is serious.'

'Start with the County Councillor,' Robert continued. 'He lives in St Mawes I think, then, if that fails, write to the M.P.'

'And if nothing comes of that?' George had recovered his composure.

'Then it's time to call in God, maybe?' Mike tried again.

'Maybe.' Alf looked hard at Mike for several seconds. 'Yes, maybe, you're right, my young flower.' He turned to the other two and a wicked grin slowly widened his whiskery face. 'An act of God might be just what is needed. Well done, Mike.'

'What's going through your evil mind, you old devil?' Robert sat back and hooked his thumbs into his waistband.

'I'll give them time, but not too long, then we'll do something to draw their fire.' Alf stroked his beard. 'Something that will force attention to our cause.'

'What d'you mean, Alf? Like running naked down the aisle at the village pantomime?'

The three of them stared at George with degrees of incredulity written across their faces.

'No, George, that was not quite what I had in mind, although that might attract a column in the *Western Packet*.' He shook his head and then swallowed some beer. 'Good God, where do you get some of your notions?'

'Well it's like streaking, init? There's nothing like a streaker to liven things up when there's no action on the field.' George looked around for encouragement.

'Yes,' Robert said slowly. 'Yes, metaphorically, I see what you mean. If we do something outrageous to draw attention to the humps and cushions – within the law of course – then the whole profile of the wretched scheme will be raised.'

'What do you suggest then?' Mike asked eagerly.

'Well, certainly not streaking at the pantomime – that would really give Miss Butch Dyke something to shout about,' Alf mused.

Then quite suddenly he thumped his glass on the table and his dark eyes sparkled mischievously. 'I've got it! Do you remember that film with Kevin Costner, when the Confederates faced the Union army across a field and neither lot could decide what move to make next? What was it called?'

'Something about wolves?' Robert suggested.

'That's it. *Dancing with Wolves*.' Alf's enthusiasm was now in full spate. 'Anyway, the Costner character, lying in the surgeon's tent, sits up and pulls on his leg again and . . .'

'Pulls on his leg? You sure about that, Alf?'

'Yes, of course I'm bloody sure. Seen the film twice. Pulls on his leg, the one with the boot on, hops on his horse . . .'

'How many legs does the 'orse have?'

'Do shut up, Mike . . . hops on his horse and rides up and down the line between the two armies, shouting and waving his arms.'

'Bloody nutter,' George murmured. 'Get 'is head blowed off like that.'

'That's the point, my old flower.' Alf slapped George's knee and then instantly recoiled as he felt the soggy cloth. 'Forgot to pull down your zip, or something, old man?'

'That's beer before I drunk it, not after! And talking of beer I seem to be empty again.' He looked pointedly at Mike.

'Hang on, I haven't finished.' Alf protested.

'Ok, hint taken.' The young man jumped up and began gathering glasses. 'But don't go on 'til I get back, Alf, I want to hear what happens next.'

Mike hurried over to the bar and Greg saw him coming.

'Suddenly gone all quiet over at your table, Mike, what're you cooking?' Greg asked as he pulled a pint of Rufus Craggs.

'Nothing, Greg, just putting the world to rights.' Mike grinned and then felt around in his pocket.

'I always feel easier when there's a lot of noise coming from that table, that's all.' He pulled the fourth pint. 'Eight pounds forty.'

Mike winced and handed over a note. He took his change and then seized the mugs, two in each hand and weaved his way back to the others.

'Right, where were we?' Alf asked as Mike slid the pints across the table. 'It's like Listen with Mother, isn't it? Cheers, Mike.'

There was a pause as they all drank.

'Yes, so he rides up and down the line . . .'

'Without his leg dropping off again?'

'That's right, George. And that gets them shooting at him, but they all miss and while they're reloading the other side gets up and starts shooting back. This man's foolish act has broken the stalemate and that, my friends, is what we must do. We must break the stalemate. Draw their fire.'

There was a pause as they thought about the scenario and then George scratched his head.

'I still don't think you can be right about the leg though, Alf.'

'For Christ's sake, George, forget the bloody leg. The leg is not important. What *is* important is the parable.'

'Yes, so you mean we need to think of a stalemate breaker.' Robert struggled to subdue a surge of beer-induced wind. 'Any suggestions?'

There was a long thoughtful silence and Robert noticed Greg watching them intently, obviously now convinced that there was some plotting afoot. Then Alf suddenly slapped the table and some beer slopped out of Robert's glass.

'I've got it, men. If we want to draw attention to the problem, then we must highlight the problem in the most vivid way possible.' He picked up his tankard, looking very pleased with himself.

'Well?' Mike looked at him somewhat boss-eyed, a personal affliction brought on at about his fourth pint.

'Paint the buggers, Mike, and the brighter the better. Pillar-box red should do the trick. When that's done the Council will be forced to take some action.'

Robert looked sceptical and George stared at the ceiling, while Mike nodded his head as he gave the plan earnest assessment. Alf leaned back and looked from one to the other, with an expression of disbelief on his face.

'Well? What do you think? It's the best bloody way of drawing attention to those impediments and we might get more action than if we just sit around waiting for the Council to play games with us. This way they'll soon see we mean business.'

'But, Alf, you can't be serious,' Robert chuckled. 'It's been agreed at the Parish meeting that . . .'

'I *know*, my old flower, I know what's *officially* been agreed,' Alf said in the manner of a pantomime villain. 'But what goes on unofficially and what happens in the dead of night is another matter altogether, isn't it?'

Robert went on smiling indulgently as he quaffed more beer and some spilled from the side of his mouth. He brushed his shirt with the back of his hand and reflected that it was time to go home. Alf's fantasies tended to become more exotic with the quantity of beer he sank and with the level of encouragement from his audience. He drained his glass and then yawned.

'So you don't think much of the shock tactics, Rob?' Alf's enthusiasm seemed to be waning.

'I think it's a bloody good idea, Alf.' George had given the matter deep consideration and had decided to give the plan his seal of approval. 'Who's going to do it?'

'A very good question, George.' Robert stood up, stretched and tucked in a loose shirt tail. 'Probably not the Chairman to the Pengarth Parish Council, I think?'

'I damned well would if I were a few years younger,' Alf retorted indignantly.

Robert threw his head back and laughed, a short staccato burst of merriment at the thought of his fuddled friend daubing red paint on Fore Street in the small hours of the morning.

'I'm off, my friends. Thank you for your company . . . and for some interesting food for thought.' He threaded his way past two stray chairs and raised a hand to Greg on his way out.

'So much for genius,' Alf muttered and finished the last of his beer. 'Anyone for a refill?' he added glumly.

The other two shook their heads and George started humming tunelessly. Elsie arrived at their table with a few cheery words and gathered up the dead glasses. Alf recognised the moment and stood up unsteadily.

'To each his own, my merry men.' He belched discreetly and clapped Mike on the back. 'Our day will come and the foe will be vanquished.'

'I think it's a good idea, Alf,' Mike wailed after him as the big man lumbered towards the door. George just looked at him and shrugged.

Alf stopped outside the Lugger and took a deep breath of salty air before setting off slowly down the hill towards his home. The moon cast its pale silvery wash on the rippling waters of the bay, flashing like a thousand faulty fluorescent light tubes. The only sounds of the night came from rhythmic clinking of loose rigging and the hypnotic ebb and flow of wavelets on the harbour beach.

Across the bay beyond the lookout Shag Rock loomed black and sinister against the horizon, offering protection to the good folk of Pengarth against the wiles of the unseen Piskies. Alf paused in his slow deliberate stride and bowed to the barren island.

'You keep your counsel and I'll keep mine, you black devil.' His brief caustic laugh broke the stillness of the night and an unseen night bird flapped its wings by the boatyard roof. Alf gave his impression of an owl hoot and then resumed his plodding gait down the road.

Chapter Four

GREG lolloped down his back stairs grumbling to himself and by the time he opened the door into the pub yard the broken veins on his cheeks were glowing brightly. He flung the door open and the morning sun glinted off the silvery spikes of the two-day stubble that framed his moustache.

PC Curnow, looking contrite, was standing on the other side of the door.

'Sorry to disturb you so early, Greg.' With a professional eye the policeman took in the sight of the unshaven publican, who was wearing blue boxer shorts, a singlet and carpet slippers. 'Can I come in for a minute?'

Greg stood back and made a sweeping gesture with his left arm. Curnow nodded and went in.

'Is this a dawn raid, Roger?' Greg followed the constable into the saloon and then rested his backside against the brass bar rail. Curnow took off his cap and put it gently on one of the tables, making certain that it would not be sitting in a pool of beer.

'Not exactly dawn, Greg.' He glanced at his watch. 'Ten to ten. Still, I expect you had a late night last night.'

'What do you mean? Every night's a late night when you run a pub.' Greg rubbed his chin roughly. 'And last night was no exception.'

'Of course. Sorry.' Curnow reached into a pocket and withdrew a note pad. 'It's just that there was an act of vandalism in the village last night and I thought this would be a good place to start my enquiry.'

'Vandalism?' Greg's brow creased and he began unconsciously to scratch his right buttock. 'What kind of vandalism?'

'Rather odd really. No real damage in fact, but someone has painted the traffic calming cushions in Fore Street.'

Greg stopped scratching. 'Painted 'em? All of 'em?'

'Nearly all.' Curnow studied the landlord carefully for reaction. 'What colour?'

'Why do you ask that?'

Greg shrugged. 'No reason, but it might be an improvement if it's the right colour.'

'Bright red.'

'Oooh!' Greg winced. 'Perhaps not. When did they do it anyway?'

'Looks as if it was poured on at least eight hours ago. It's dry now, but an early riser's smeared some of it up Fore Street with their car tyres.'

'There you are, Sherlock. Match the tyre treads with the car and then ask the owner if he saw anybody. Could even be the culprit, if he's thick enough.'

'Would *you* have any idea who might have done it, Greg?'

'The Council, for all I know. Have you asked them?'

'The Council lodged the complaint just an hour ago, so I don't think it was them.'

'So, why the hell are you asking me, Roger?' Greg pushed himself away from the bar, suddenly conscious of the fact that he was in his underwear. He glanced down. And it was not particularly clean underwear at that.

'Because you know your customers, Greg. You see things and hear things in here. And if you don't know what's going on, then I expect you'll know someone who does.' Curnow began tapping his pad officiously with a pen.

'Can't help you, constable,' Greg replied resolutely with his jaw set firm. Curnow was a good man, the sort of fellow he might go fishing with, but Greg was not about to become a copper's nark: especially as he knew nothing about last night's events. He glanced up at the wall clock. 'And it's time I got dressed. We open in an hour and a half and I've not yet had my breakfast.'

'Sorry, Greg, but I had to ask.' Curnow put his pad away and buttoned down the pocket.

'Let yourself out, Roger.' Curnow watched Greg turn, walk out of the room and then mount the back stairs, chuckling to himself as he plodded upwards, 'Painted 'em red, eh! Red!'

'No joy here then,' the constable muttered as he left the pub.

Word of the road-painting episode had already spread around the village. It was being discussed in the shop, people were making suggestions as to who might have done it and others were peering at the scene of the desecration for clues. Two officials from the

Council had arrived and were taking measurements, while a photographer from the local newspaper was reeling off shots from every angle. Her colleague, the reporter, was busy with his tape recorder, stopping and interviewing anyone who had an opinion on the matter.

A Council official approached the reporter and began haranguing him for parking his car over one of the painted areas, while constable Curnow attempted to persuade the small crowd of onlookers to disperse and to go about their business. There was already a tailback up the hill where the officials were obstructing delivery vans and matters were not being improved by parents driving home after taking their children to school.

Further down the hill the Sinclair's telephone was ringing.

'Hello,' Binty said breathlessly, brushing a stray curl of blonde hair back with a floury hand. 'Yes, he's here, Greg.'

Binty put the telephone down and yelled for her husband. She heard the newspaper rustle next door and a few seconds later Robert ambled in.

'For me?'

'Yes, Robert, and I do wish you'd answer it yourself occasionally.' She handed him the instrument. 'I'm in the middle of making pastry.'

'So I can see,' he said looking at her hair. 'Who is it?'

'Greg.' She returned hastily to the kitchen.

'Greg, what can I do for you?'

Over the next few minutes Robert's face was like a series of rubber masks, expressing most of the known emotions, as Greg recounted the village story of the moment. By now the basic act of daubing red paint on some road safety humps had become embellished in the manner of galloping Chinese whispers, leaving fact to be far outstripped by imagination.

'Well, I'll be damned,' was all Robert could think of saying when the landlord had finished. 'Any idea who did it?'

A few seconds later he put the telephone down and his lips twisted slowly into a knowing smile. 'The old bugger!' he said quietly to the conch shell on the hall table and then went into the kitchen.

'I take it you haven't heard of the hoo-hah in the village this morning?' He perched himself on the edge of the table.

71

'No.' She carried on pounding with the rolling pin.

He told her and the pounding stopped abruptly.

'Do they know . . . ?'

'No, but I know a man who might.' He pushed himself away from the table and made for the back door.

'You'll be back for lunch, Robert?' she called after him. 'I'm making pasties.'

'I'll be back.' The outer door slammed and he was gone.

When Robert arrived at the bookshop Alf was standing in the doorway gesticulating in the way he always did when exasperated and a man in a tired pair of corduroy trousers and green jacket was on the receiving end of his tirade. Nearby a female with frizzy brown hair and denim skirt was taking photographs from various angles. Robert stopped a few yards away from the shop and chuckled quietly to himself.

'Ah, Robert,' Alf had spotted him, 'Come over here and tell these denizens of the third estate that I know nothing.'

'By the look of them, I think you mean the fourth estate.' Robert joined the group and nodded to the reporter. 'I think the third is something to do with the clergy.'

'Third, fourth, you know what I mean.' Alf's arms were still in windmill mode and his beard seemed to be reacting in sympathy. 'Anyway, I don't know what they're on about.'

Robert raised a staying hand to the press corps and took Alf by the arm, leading him just out of earshot. The reporter looked on intrigued while Alf's face went through the same routine as Robert's had a few minutes earlier. When the big bearded man turned back to face him there was a broad smile on his face.

'My dear chap.' He held out a hand as if meeting the reporter for the first time. 'Come in off the street. Why didn't you tell me the full story to begin with? I thought you were here about last night's Parish Council meeting.'

The two men went into the bookshop, followed closely by the photographer and Robert.

'Now, can I get you some tea, or coffee?' He made a rapid hand gesture to Robert behind the reporter's back, which the former interpreted as *put the kettle on*.

'Thank you, Mr Curtis. I'll have tea, no sugar, and Dorcas will have black coffee.'

Alf turned to stare at the photographer for a moment, as if doubting that anyone really could be called Dorcas, and then gave Robert his directions with a jerk of the head. Robert shrugged and then ambled into the large back room that was Alf's kitchen.

'Now, do sit down. Both of you.' Alf moved a few books and then struck a pose by the shop counter. 'Fire away.'

'Right.' The reporter took out his tape recorder. 'Do you mind if . . . ?'

'No, no, not at all.' The photographer flashed as Alf sashayed a magnanimous gesture through the air.

'Now Mr Curtis, what do you know about the red paint that was thrown over the road during the night?' the reporter began.

'Well, firstly, I presume you're asking me that question in my capacity as Chairman of the Parish Council?' The reporter nodded. 'In which case I can tell you all about the road impediments, the battle we're having with the County Council to have them removed, the outcome of the Parish meeting we had last night and the general feeling that these impediments have aroused in the community, but . . . what I cannot tell you is who was responsible for the daubing.'

The reporter lowered his head and his world-weary face registered disappointment, plus a tinge of exasperation. Were it not for the fact that a cup of tea was on the way he might have gone so far as to suggest to Mr Alf Curtis that his newspaper's time was being wasted, but then he took a sharp breath, lifted his head again and smiled indulgently.

'But, in your position, Mr Curtis, you must know a lot of what goes on here. For example, you were in the . . .' he glanced down at a pad, '. . . Lugger last night. Any rumours there?'

'Who told you that I was . . .' he began abruptly, but then caught Robert's eye as the latter carried a tin of biscuits into the room. 'I mean, yes I was there, but I can't say that anyone told me of their plans to paint the road red.'

With an admonishing glance at Alf, Robert left the room again as the kettle began to boil. The reporter reached out for a damp looking bourbon and then swiftly switched his allegiance to the garibaldi. He bit into the biscuit and then pressed Alf again.

'No, perhaps they didn't actually tell you anything, but . . .' he stopped to dislodge a mummified raisin from a troublesome molar with his tongue. '. . . I should think you have your suspicions.'

'The usual suspects, eh?' Alf grinned and lowered his head as if in contemplation. He looked up again. 'Well, there is a tearaway bunch of youngsters from the estate just off the road to Poltock. You know, all nose studs, nappy pins and tattoos. One or two of them were in the Lugger last night and they might have got hold of some red paint. Those humps don't do their motor bikes any good either.'

'I'm afraid I can't build a story around simple conjecture, Mr Curtis. If you have nothing concrete to go on . . .'

'Look, wait a minute.' Alf moved suddenly away from his perch and thrust his hands in his pockets, staring earnestly at the reporter. 'I have an idea. Why don't you use the story with the central issue being the locals' deep dissatisfaction . . . no, fury . . . at the so-called traffic calming measures in our village – I can give you the details, including all that has come up at the Parish meetings – and then the culmination will be the vandalism with the red paint and the question that will hang unanswered will be . . .' Alf removed a hand from his pocket and circumscribed an elegant question mark in the air. '. . . *What will happen next? Who is the phantom dauber of Pengarth?*'

He was warming to the theme and was about to build up to a suggested headline for the next edition of the paper, when Robert came in with a tray. Alf paused, arm still in the air, while Robert put the tray down and then began distributing mugs. There were murmurs of thanks from the press and then Robert made towards one of the chairs.

'Hey!' Alf's shout froze him in the act of sitting down. 'Not on that chair, old man, you've got something nasty on your arse!'

The press corps looked startled for a moment as they craned their necks to have a closer view of Robert's behind. Robert himself twisted his neck and then laughed.

'It's only flour.' He dusted his trousers off and turned to the reporter. 'My wife's baking.'

'You may sit down now, Robert.'

'Thank you, Alf.' He sat.

'I was saying, no, suggesting, how our friends here might present the story, Rob. There being no known culprit, the mystery and intrigue will be the story.' He turned eagerly to the reporter. 'What do you think?'

The reporter sucked his pen, swivelled his eyes to the photographer and then tightened his jaw. He was a sallow man of about forty, never going to work on a national at this stage of his life, but he was vastly experienced at what he did and he was not enthused by an overweight know-it-all Parish Councillor telling him how to present a story: if indeed there was any story here at all. On the other hand, if there was nothing more than a local fire, a park flasher or a sheep falling off the cliff this week, there were possibilities for making this one run for a while. He stopped sucking the pen.

'I'll bear your suggestions in mind, Mr Curtis, but first I've got to make a few more enquiries. I thought perhaps at the shop . . .'

'Good idea, I'm sure Sadie will have some useful suggestions.' Alf was still buoyed up by his inspiration on how to run the story. 'What headline will you give it? What about *The Red Hand Gang of Pengarth Strikes at Night*?'

'Too long, Alf. Anyway, if they'd been caught red-handed, then Roger would know who the culprit is.'

'Hmm, perhaps you're right. Anyway, I wonder if Roger has actually thought of that?'

'Thought of what?'

'Looking for someone with red paint on his hands, of course.'

'Or *her* hands. Let's not prejudge this.'

'No, you're right again. Could be a woman.' Alf turned to the reporter. 'Could be a woman, you know. Hadn't considered that. Jenny Whatsername drove over them when she was eight months pregnant. Nearly broke her waters.'

The reporter turned his recorder off and stood up abruptly. It was time to go. With a final disdainful look at the plate of biscuits and half finished mug of tea he headed for the door. The photographer, who had not spoken a word throughout, followed close behind.

A quick word of thanks and the pair were hurrying up Fore Street, heads close together in conversation. Robert and Alf, standing in the doorway, watched them go.

'Well, you wanted publicity, Alf, now you've got it.'

'Yes, bloody good show. Let's hope they present the story in the right way.' He turned slowly to Robert and, with a sly grin, asked, 'When did you do it then?'

'Do what?' Then Robert's mouth gaped. 'Oh, come on Alf. Me? I thought it was you! In fact I still do.'

'Not me, my old flower. I was tucked up in bed all night.'

'Well, it was your idea. I thought immediately . . .'

'Oh, Robert! That was only pub talk, idle conjecture, Rufus Craggs running amok. I'm too old for that kind of caper.'

Robert continued to look at him with disbelief written in his eyes. 'I don't know. I wouldn't put anything past you.'

'My dear chap, I *am* Chairman of the Parish Council, a responsible citizen. How could I actually sink to carrying out such an act of petty vandalism? Thinking of it and talking about it is altogether another thing.' His face brightened. 'But, having said that, it's bloody good publicity . . . as you just said. Just what we wanted.'

'I suppose so, as long as it doesn't all backfire on us.'

'Well, they say there's no such thing as bad publicity, eh?'

They both fell silent as they watched the press corps disappear into the Convenience Store.

The road jam had cleared now and constable Curnow was nowhere in sight. In the harbour a fishing boat's engine chugged into life as its crew cast off the moorings and a pair of seagulls swooped overhead mewing their plaintive cry.

Robert tapped Alf lightly on the shoulder and then turned for home. Alf, grinning with a fierce look of anticipation in his eye, went back into the bookshop rubbing his hands together. There was nothing like a spark of intrigue to spice up a day.

Chapter Five

ROBERT looked up and down Fore Street before going into the Lugger. Two youngsters were carrying their surfboards up from the harbour, heads lowered in conversation, and a couple of old Pengarth stalwarts were exchanging views in the shop doorway. Otherwise there was no one in sight.

It was just after half past seven in the evening two days after the red paint drama and Thursday's edition of the *Western Packet* had carried the story on page two. *Midnight daubers paint the town red*, the caption declared, and the story included excerpts from interviews and some mischievous conjecture as to whom the culprits might be.

Robert had reflected that it was a shame the local paper could not have produced a colour photograph for greater effect, but at least the reporter had heeded Alf's plea and included the reasons for the villagers' complaint about the traffic calming measures.

He pushed the door and eased past the burgundy velveteen curtain into the saloon. Greg was behind the bar and Elsie was collecting glasses from the public end. George Harris and young Mike were chortling over their beer at the corner table and, to his surprise, BK and Glenys Richards were at the bar. Two middle-aged women sat at the window table drinking white wine and poring over a map.

Robert came up beside Glenys.

'Hello you two, don't often see you in here.' Robert peered at their glasses. 'Would you like a drink?'

'Hello, Robert. No, we're alright, thanks.' Glenys put her hand over the glass, as if by magic it might suddenly be refilled.

If BK was a spare man, then his wife compensated with her fullness of frame. She was not exactly a fat woman, but one who had managed to have every sturdy bone of her body generously covered with flesh and then a bit more. To those who knew the family the intriguing fact was that their three children had each managed to balance the proportions of their parents equally and had turned out to be finely trimmed physical specimens. Certainly the elder two, teenaged daughters, turned heads in the village.

'We're celebrating a new contract for the Porker Pasties,' BK added modestly.

'Congratulations! Then you must have a drink on me. Greg,' he called across the bar, 'my usual please and one each for the entrepreneurs.'

Greg ambled over and began filling Robert's tankard, ignoring the Richards' half-hearted protestations. As the froth began to crawl down the side of the tankard he looked up.

'You playing on Saturday, Robert?'

'The charity match, you mean?' Robert fished in his pocket.

'Well, its not exactly a charity match, as such,' BK put in. 'It's a match between current and former Pengarth players to raise money for the church organ fund.'

'That sounds like charity to me, BK' Robert took his pint and then pushed the Richards' glasses over to Greg.

'Alright, but its for a good local cause. Anyway, are you putting on the gloves again?'

'Yes, I suppose so, if there's no one else,' Robert sighed, 'but I haven't told Binty yet. She thinks I've played my last game of cricket. She'll say I'm crazy when she hears.'

'It's in a good cause,' Glenys repeated.

'So your husband said, but then so is my health a good cause.' He pushed his money across the counter.

'You're a damned good wicketkeeper, Robert,' Greg said encouragingly.

'Used to be, old boy, used to be. The last time I played in a "friendly" it was three days before I could walk up the stairs. I'm too old to keep wicket. All those knees bends and diving down the leg side to wayward bowling!'

'Who else is on the crocks team then?' Greg asked.

'Let's see,' BK pushed his glasses back up the bridge of his nose and concentrated. 'I'm captain – for my sins – then Greg here, George, Alf . . .'

'No, not Alf. He's gone up country for at least two days,' Robert interrupted. 'He left after lunch today.'

'Oh, no, he told me he'd play,' BK's face twisted in dismay. 'Who'll I get at this short notice?'

'Not done a runner in the face of all the publicity, has he?' Greg asked.

'No, he's gone to a house clearance to buy up a few old books.'

'I thought he did his book buying through that e-bay thing,' Glenys chipped in.

'Mostly, but by the time he's made a successful bid there's little profit left for him in the shop. So, occasionally he goes to house clearances.' Robert was distracted for a moment by the arrival of three youths with surfers' blonde hair and Greg moved away to meet them at the far end of the bar. On the other side of the room George slapped his leg and guffawed at something Mike had said.

'Doesn't he also . . . ?' BK began and Robert lifted his tankard. 'I mean, I've heard there's someone he visits . . . oh, it's only gossip, I know . . .'

'I think he has a sick relative in Wiltshire who he visits occasionally,' Robert said quickly and then added, 'So, who else is in the geriatric eleven?'

BK took the hint and proceeded to list the players in the senior team, their past glories and their current ailments.

'Is Binty helping with the teas then?' Glenys raised her eyebrows hopefully.

'She might, when I summon the courage to tell her I'm playing.'

'Oh, come on, Robert, it won't be that bad. And anyway we have willing subs, if any of us falls apart.'

'God, that's reassuring, BK.' Robert drained his tankard.

'Have another?' BK turned and caught Greg's eye.

They talked on for a while about inconsequential matters that affect village life, while the pub numbers slowly increased until there was a comforting hum of voices in the place.

George and Mike were still at the corner table, but had now been joined by Sadie from the store. Her merry laughter, occasionally verging on the raucous, carried across the length of the two bars.

BK was in his churchwarden mode and was going on about the need for a new organ, the damage being caused by bats and the question of whether the infestation of anobium punctatum in the pulpit was live or not. Glenys was throwing in feed comments, but Robert merely nodded at appropriate moments. His mind was on Alf and his irregular trips up country.

'Well, what do you think, Robert?'

He focused, blinked a couple of times and realised BK had asked him a question.

'Eh, oh I'm sure you're right, BK.'

'You weren't listening to a word I was saying,' the lean man said accusingly.

'You were talking about having an organ replacement,' Robert said glibly. 'Which one?'

'Not him, Robert.' Glenys laughed and slapped his shoulder with a meaty hand. A dollop of beer slopped on the floor. 'The church organ.'

'I'm sorry, very rude of me, it's just something else on my mind at the moment.' He raised his tankard. 'Well, once again, congratulations on the new contract.'

'Thanks.' BK pushed his spectacles past the bridge of his nose. 'Er, Robert, just by the way, do you have any idea who threw that paint on the road?'

Robert grinned.

'In Pengarth one always has an idea who did what, but pinning it down to any one person . . . well . . . ,' he shrugged.

'So, what's your idea?' Glenys asked.

He rested his elbow on the bar, inclined his head towards the corner table and then turned back to face the enquiring faces of the Richards. 'Well . . .' he leaned a bit closer to them and whispered, '. . . it wasn't me.'

The first Saturday in June was a beauty. After rain on the previous day and much anxiety from the cricket match organisers, the morning had dawned heavy with mist and low cloud, which was good news for those who knew the local weather. *If it dawns fine, there'll be rain after nine:* or, something to that effect.

Sure enough, by ten o'clock the mist had lifted, the sea fret had dried off and the roller was out on the square. Darren and Mike heaved the rusty old thing up and down, passing monosyllabic comments between tinnitus-inducing squeals from the oil starved bearings.

At eleven BK was marking out the square and two small boys were pacing out the boundary and sticking in metal flags at appropriate distances apart. Glenys was in the pavilion, filling the trusty urn that had supplied countless generations of Pengarth cricketers with boiling water for their tea: the same urn that the vicar had tried to ban under health and safety rules, until Alf had laminated a notice beside it stating, CONTAINS BOILING WATER: NOT TO BE USED BY THE INEPT. The vicar had not attended a cricket match at Pangarth since that notice first appeared.

At about half past twelve several members of the two teams, principally Pengarth men and two women, were gathered with their kit in the Lugger for pre-match preparation. This involved lining the stomach with hot pasties, exercising the arms by the lifting of glasses and generally getting the adrenalin going by needling the opposition with proud boasts of past achievements.

'Young Malcolm's hotted up his pace by a few yards after winter nets. Reckon there's going to be a few bruises out there.'

'Hope they've got reinforced boxes.'

'He may be fast, but he couldn't hit a barn door at ten paces. We'll win on extras alone.'

'They say Alf's run away from this match, he's that scared.'

'Where's 'e to then?'

'Crossed the Tamar to make sure he's out of range.'

'You wait 'til you face our new spin bowler. He'll turn you inside out.'

'Shane Warne is it?'

'Bugger, how'd you find out?'

And so it went on, with sudden barks of laughter at each quip, a cheer whenever a newcomer appeared at the door, the merry clink of glasses and a general atmosphere of happy rural anticipation.

Soon before two o'clock the players and their acolytes began to drift out of the pub and meander up the hill to the playing field. The route took them past the Convenience Store, the school and the red-painted road impediments until the field entrance was reached near the top of the slope.

Over the years many had said it was a field too soon.

Even though it was near the top of the hill, and in spite of early attempts to reduce the gradient, the playing field was on a distinct incline. The square itself had almost been flattened by a century of rolling, scarifying and replanting, but someone had calculated that there was still a five-foot difference from the horizontal from one side to the other. This created a positive advantage for the home side, or to anyone familiar with the idiosyncrasy and this was exploited shamelessly in matches against neighbouring village teams.

The scratch team of old Pengarthians donned their cricket gear in the visitors' changing room. Like village cricket changing rooms throughout the land it harboured the heavy aromatic cocktail of linseed oil, stale socks, liniment and hoary old jock straps. But, to those who had played the game for years it was like nectar to the olfactory bulbs. The odour carried with it a reassuring sense of timelessness.

There were curses about ill-fitting trousers, boots with missing studs, pads with broken straps and strange mould-covered objects at the bottom of the kit bag. Taunts drifted across from the home team's changing room, cups rattled in the kitchen area and players' dogs drifted in and out of the pavilion, lured by the confusing variety of scents.

At twenty past two the captains went out to the middle and tossed a coin. One of them came back looking pleased with himself.

'Pad up, Robert.' BK said, looking around for the O.P.'s other opener.

'You won the toss?' Robert asked incredulously.

'Yes. Why?'

'And you chose to bat? You must be mad, skipper.'

'Why?' BK repeated, but now looking less self-assured.

'My dear chap, we'll probably be bowled out for twenty-five and then the whole match will be over an hour before tea. This is meant to be a special occasion.'

'Oh, do you think so?' BK looked around at his team and winced. 'Come on, Robert, what about the Dunkirk spirit.'

'I have to tell you, BK, that Dunkirk, in spite of what your history teacher might have told you, was a defeat. It was a rout.'

'Yes, but it was a heroic defeat.' He spotted Greg. 'Ah, there you are. Pads on, Greg, you're opening.'

'Opening what?'

'The innings, Greg,' he said with exaggerated patience and pointed through the pavilion window. 'Look, the umpires are going out, so you'd better get a move on.'

'Cannon fodder am I?' Greg asked in the manner of a man asked to go over the top from the trenches at the Somme. 'I've opened a few bottles in my time, but never opened a cricket innings.'

'Oh, heavens,' BK covered his face in his hands and groaned. 'I think I'll resign as captain.'

Robert, who already had one pad on, caught Greg's eye and winked. 'Come on, Greg, we can't have the skipper throwing the towel in at this early stage.'

Greg shrugged and then bent down to scrabble around in the team kit bag for a matching pair of pads. BK, sensing that the immediate crisis was over, relaxed and then began picking the rest of the batting order.

Five minutes later the home side ambled out to the middle and their captain, Darren, started to place his men.

Greg stuffed a well-insulated box down his trousers, pulled on his gloves and weighed up a couple of bats.

'Ready to do battle?' Robert pulled a battered cap over his bald head and grinned at Greg.

'Good luck, fellows.' BK called after them as his opening batsmen strode out of the pavilion on their way to the square.

'Shall I take first strike?' Robert asked halfway to the wicket and then realised that his fellow opener was not with him. Greg had stopped a few yards back and was tightening a pad buckle. Robert waited for him to catch up, before repeating the question.

'By all means,' Greg was still fiddling with the back of his pad as he stumbled to the wicket. 'You know they've given us all this ancient equipment on purpose. Today's pads all have straps with Velcro fixings.'

Robert patted him on the backside with his bat as he strode confidently to the striker's end. He felt far from confident, but it was part of the psychology of the game to appear in command. He took a leg guard and then began to look around the field. He knew this was a pointless exercise, because even if he hit the ball he did not expect to have much control over where it went. The passing years had taken their toll on his cricketing skills, but he was wily enough to know that giving the impression of being competent might fool the opposition for a while. The bravado should be good for a couple of balls anyway.

He tapped out his mark on the crease again and then prepared to face the first ball, but to his surprise Greg was advancing down the wicket towards him.

'No quick singles!' Greg hissed in his ear, nodded as if he really meant it and then shambled back to the other end. With this instruction firmly implanted in his brain, Robert crouched into position and peered up the pitch and beyond. To his horror the bowler was standing halfway to the boundary and, before he could shout that it was all a terrible mistake and that he was due somewhere else, the umpire said, *Play* and the bowler began his run up.

Surely that was nice young Sean, who helped Sadie in the shop occasionally and was always so polite to him, Robert thought wildly as the young man approached on his curving run. *Surely he wouldn't try to knock my block off? Bloody hell, I'm not even wearing a helmet, just a moth-eaten old cap. I'll step back and swing, that's what I'll do.*

Sean unleashed the ball, Robert stepped back with his right foot towards the leg side, closed his eyes and executed an elegant arc with his bat. There was a sickening clatter of wood behind him, a roar from the fielders, an ecstatic bowler and a crestfallen batsman.

83

Robert turned to look at the splayed stumps, hung his head and then set off for the pavilion. But, he had only taken a couple of steps when there was a groan from the wicketkeeper, followed by a disbelieving howl from the bowler.

The umpire's right arm was out horizontally. No ball. No one had heard his shout.

Sean swivelled on his heel and strode angrily past the umpire, brushing his white coat as he pointedly marked out his run again. The umpire, Geoff Uren, shouted over his shoulder, 'It's your boot over the line, young Sean, not mine.'

The square leg umpire trotted up to the stumps, straightened them and then replaced the bails.

Robert gathered himself for the next ball, muttering into his shirt. *You old fool, you've played this game enough times before, play down the line, don't back away, don't show him you're scared, play down the line, play . . .*

The next ball was on a good length and Robert played forward, right down the line, head over the ball, with a vertical bat. The only problem was that the line down which he played was the wrong one. The ball took off just outside the edge of his bat and thudded into the wicketkeeper's gloves.

'No!' Greg screamed from the far end and held up a traffic policemen's hand. Robert peered quizzically at him from the length of the pitch. Did he seriously think there was a run there, or was that what he meant by a quick single?

He took a walk out to square leg, still muttering, then came back to his crease and patted his bat gently against his right boot. Sean was on his way again. This ball was short and heading for the leg stump, but Robert was too slow to register these facts, so by the time his bat flailed down the leg side the ball had long gone. In fact, because of the slope, it carried on going legwards and the wicketkeeper's despairing dive was to no avail: four byes to the score.

Greg was slapping his bat at the far end just as eagerly as if Robert had helped the ball on its way. Robert himself was beginning to feel his confidence growing – his team had five runs on the board for no wicket and he was still there.

The fourth ball was a fast half volley outside the off stump. In his prime Robert would have planted his left foot to the pitch and scythed the ball past cover point for four, but his prime was another country. He saw the half volley, thrust his leg out on the off and swung his bat, but the ball was already past the stumps. He held the pose for a few seconds, rueing the missed opportunity, but also missing the significance of what was going on behind the stumps.

The keeper, perhaps distracted by the batsman's extravagant but ineffectual waft, had failed to gather the ball cleanly and first slip had deflected the rebound behind him. Greg, alert at the other end saw the possibility of a run to the misfield and, while Robert was still in a straddle position, yelled, 'Run!'

Robert looked behind, saw the overweight slip trundling after the ball, turned again and gawped at Greg coming towards him, pads a-flapping. Greg arrived in the middle of the pitch just as the slip reached the ball and Robert was still in his crease.

'Get back!' Robert shouted, holding both arms aloft.

Slip gathered the ball and, in the manner of a bull collecting itself to charge a matador, he wound himself up to throw to the bowler's end. Greg stopped, gaped at Robert and then slowly turned his bulk, rather like a tanker in mid-ocean.

Robert wanted to shut his eyes: Greg would never make it. The slip unleashed his throw, a low skimming effort, heading like a dart for the bull's-eye, while the bowler hovered over the non-striker's stumps ready to whip off the bails.

Greg ploughed on gamely, pads impeding his legs, bat out-stretched and head low. He was still two yards short of the crease when the ball passed him, but it never reached the waiting bowler. A split second after overtaking Greg it made contact with the edge of his lunging bat and re-routed itself towards the boundary. Greg dived, sprawled in an untidy heap and lay panting with his bat just over the crease, while the ball crossed the boundary line nearly fifty yards away. Four overthrows. Nine for no wicket.

'Obstruction!' the bowler shouted to the crouching umpire.

'Bollocks,' replied umpire Uren.

Greg, laughing heartily at his good fortune, stood up, brushed the dirt from his front and waved his bat cheerily at Robert, who was already striding down the wicket towards him.

They met in the middle.

'You said no quick singles!' Robert rasped through gritted teeth. 'There was no way I could have run that.'

'What are you complaining about, old man? I gained us four runs.' Greg was unrepentant.

'Yes,' Robert retorted, looking at his partner's shirt, 'but at the cost of a cleaner's bill. Come on, two more balls this over.'

'Three isn't it?'

'Oh my God yes. There was a no ball.'

They went back to their respective ends and it gave Robert a frisson of satisfaction that some members of the opposition already seemed to be a bit edgy. After only four balls of the match they were being made to appear sloppy.

He took guard again.

Ball number five was fast and straight and pitched well up to the bat, but Robert met it boldly in the middle. He stepped casually out of his crease to tap down an imaginary blemish in the pitch, while the ball was returned to the bowler. *That must have looked really good*, he thought. *It's all coming back.*

For good measure he repeated the defensive shot to the sixth ball, just digging out a yorker as it tried to creep under the bat.

The seventh and final legitimate ball of the over was short, fast and wide of the off stump. Robert, now full of confidence, executed an elegant drive, which was again completely unsynchronised with the pace of the ball. This time however the toe of the bat caught the ball on the rise and his follow through lifted it skywards. He felt the meaty contact, but had no idea where the ball had gone.

He was not alone. Several of the fielders, including the bowler and wicketkeeper, craned their heads like meerkats in search of it, while Robert waited anxiously for Greg's call. After what seemed to be an age, it came.

'One run!'

Still unaware as to which part of the field his shot had dispatched the ball, Robert ran to his partner's call. Greg, head down, ran as if pursued by a swarm of bees. The two fielders who *had* seen the ball also ran towards it, heads in the air, from fine leg and third man respectively. The batsmen had just completed their run as the ball reached the final few feet of its decent and four eager hands simultaneously grasped for the catch.

Too late the fielding captain shouted a name. Far too late. There was a sickening thud as the two met chest on at longstop position and the ball fell harmlessly to ground between them.

There were a few moments of stunned silence and then nine fielders and two umpires ran to the prostrate figures, who were now lying on the ground and groaning loudly.

Greg decided to seize his opportunity.

'Come on,' he yelled at Robert.

'No, no,' his partner called back. 'It wouldn't be sporting.'

'Bugger sporting,' Greg shouted back, forgetting the fact that there were young and female spectators on the boundary, 'this is war! Take every run you can.'

Robert gave him a glare and waved him back, while the girlfriend of one of the players ran onto the field with a first aid box. Robert put his bat down and went over to the scene of the collision. When he arrived the two were on their feet, but looking extremely groggy. One was holding his arm and the other was having blood wiped from his cheek. The girlfriend dried the cut and applied a sticking plaster.

'Go off for a bit, lads,' Darren said and then spotted a crestfall-en looking Robert. 'Not your fault, Robert. Bloody fools ought to have known better!'

'Do you need a couple of subs, Darren?' Robert asked as the wounded pair walked slowly off the field.

'Thanks. It'll probably only be for a few minutes.'

Robert signalled to the pavilion and BK got the message. In the true spirit of village cricket he sent out two of the OP's most inept fielders and the game soon resumed. One eventful over completed, with the score ten for no wicket. So far it had surpassed BK's wildest expectations.

Thereafter the OP's innings progressed very much along those lines. Greg got off the mark from his first ball, heaving a medium paced trundler over square leg for two runs and then somehow keeping the ball out of hand and stumps for the rest of the over.

In fact the first wicket did not fall until the sixth over, when Greg, perhaps losing concentration as his box slipped slowly down the inside of his leg, fell over his bat and was bowled for nine. He shambled off, cursing the state of the equipment he had been forced to wear, but was mollified at receiving a rapturous recep-tion from his team as he reached the pavilion. The score was thirty-three, with Robert not out fourteen.

Batsmen came and went at varying intervals. Some, like BK batting at six, stayed and doggedly nudged the score along, while others barely had time to take guard before they were dismissed back to the pavilion.

George Harris played a cameo innings of fourteen, which lasted five balls. Those who had remembered him in his playing days were familiar with his one scoring shot and he rolled back the years by executing this to perfection off his penultimate ball. The hoik over square leg, where the toe of the bat ends up nestling against the buttocks, made perfect contact with a short one from Sean and the ball disappeared through the pavilion door. There was a screech from one of the tea ladies inside as the ball clattered against the urn, but fortunately no one was hurt.

George probably tweaked some seldom used muscle in executing that shot, because in trying to repeat it on the next ball he lost his balance and fell on the stumps.

The two injured fielders returned to take up their positions at the end of the eighth over, but not before the substitutes had managed to drop three catches between them. In each case they made such dramatic attempts to cling on that Darren was heard to say bitterly they should have been awarded Oscars for their performances.

Then, half an hour before the scheduled tea interval, the last wicket fell. Robert had ridden his luck, but had also played some good shots and he was last out for a gallant thirty-eight from a total of one hundred and twenty-nine.

By the time he left the field with the OP's number eleven and the fielding team, all traditionally clapping each other, there was a fair gathering of village folk and other curious passers-by on the boundary. So, when BK patted Robert on the back he was looking very pleased with the situation. His team had made far more than any of them expected and there was a crowd to savour the occasion and to contribute towards the organ fund. It was after all a charitable event, as he kept reminding everyone.

At tea the situation was even better. The Pengarth team had lost a wicket to the wily bowling of none other than B.K.Richards. The secret of his cunning deliveries was that the bowler was as mystified as to what each ball was going to do, as was the batsman, and the one that took the wicket was a peach. It was the one that slips out of the back of the hand when the arm is at its zenith during delivery. It then soars over the batsman's eye line, above the height of the sightscreen, and then descends about a yard short of the batting crease. It is also very slow, so that the batsman has an age to decide which shot is appropriate for the occasion.

This opening batsman had never experienced anything quite like it, so was still in three minds when the ball arrived from above. At the last split-second he decided to treat it as a full toss and lunged out of his crease to sweep the ball, a là George Harris, over the boundary for six. But he played the shot a fraction too early. The ball hit the pitch after his bat had completed its parabola and, having no velocity behind it, trickled to a halt a foot on front of the stumps. The batsman, not seeing this and probably losing his presence of mind, kicked out behind him with his right leg in the belief that he had to stop the ball from hitting the stumps, but merely succeeded in booting it on its way again.

On contact with the leg stump, one bail wobbled and then obligingly fell to the ground. The OPs were ecstatic and some were even observed giving each other high-fives. Geoff Uren called, 'Tea', and removed the bails at his end.

Pengarth was twenty-two for one and the match was in the balance.

The two teams tucked into the traditional village cricket tea, prepared by three of the players' womenfolk. Some sat at tables in the pavilion, but most found a spot on the grass outside amongst their families, dogs and friends. BK had a hasty cup of tea and then began his tour round the ground with a begging box. Robert, sitting with Binty and two others, watched him and smiled. The Churchwarden had a winning way about him when he was further-ing one of his chosen causes.

For the OP team, that was the high point of their achievements for the afternoon. Two more wickets fell and one batsman retired, having been hit on the head by a wayward throw, but the Pengarth team reached the hundred and thirty runs required soon after half past six.

There was some disappointment amongst the former players, but the unanimous decision was that it had been a successful occasion. The OPs had notched up a reasonable score, the spectators had enjoyed the entertainment and had given generously to the cause and it had all ended in good time for a few drinks at the Lugger before dinner.

'It's a shame that Alf wasn't here,' Binty commented as she folded up the tartan picnic rug. 'He would have enjoyed it.'

'Yes, I'm sure he would have.' Robert paused for a moment and gazed thoughtfully towards the east.

Alf walked wearily through the reception hall and stopped in the evening sunlight just outside the main entrance to the red brick three-storey building and breathed in deeply. He felt drained.

His car, a ten-year-old Volvo estate, was parked a few yards away across the gravelled yard and he gazed wistfully at it. The vehicle was his magic carpet back to the sanctity of his home, but it was also the box in which he would have to sit for a very long journey to Pengarth.

He was just contemplating a walk around the grounds before setting off, when a short woman in blue uniform arrived quietly at his side. Alf turned and smiled down at her.

'Hello, Matron.' They still used old-fashioned titles at St Margaret's.

'Good evening, Mr Curtis, I was hoping to catch you before you returned home.' She was almost a foot shorter than Alf and she beamed warmly up at him, hands clasped in front of her uniform. 'I expect you'll be tired by the time you arrive home.'

'I'm tired already.' His shoulders sagged as if to emphasise the point. 'But, this has to be done.'

'Yes, I know that's how you feel.' She lowered her head for a moment. 'Even though she doesn't know you any more?'

'Yes, even then. I just . . .' he sighed and looked up at one of the mullioned windows. 'it's just the hope that one day she might . . . you know, some sort of recognition.'

She unclasped her hands and reached out to touch his arm. 'You've been coming regularly for so many years, Mr Curtis.' She narrowed her eyes as she peered into his. 'It may not be my place to say this, but it can't be doing you any good to see her like this every time. You know there will never be any improvement now.'

Alf scratched his beard fiercely and looked away from her.

'I know it's difficult for you to understand, Matron, but it's just something I have to do.' He wanted to say *she's all I have to hold on to,* but that was getting too deep and he wanted to be on the road home.

'I thought you might say that,' she said softly.

They smiled at each other again in mutual understanding and then Alf turned to go.

She shook her head sadly as the Volvo crunched its way down the drive. She knew he would be back again before autumn.

Chapter Six

'I THOUGHT you'd be 'round here.' Alf stood at his front door, his hair unbrushed, shirt held together by two buttons and a piece of toast in one hand. 'Come in, my old flower.'

'Thanks.' Robert stepped into the shop. 'Sorry if I'm too early, but I was passing and wanted to find out how you got on.'

'No, not too early. Had a bit of a lie-in after last night's journey.' Alf shut the door and checked that the *Closed* sign was still in place. 'Go on upstairs and I'll bring you a mug of something hot. It might even taste like coffee.'

He went up the uncarpeted stairs, taking care not to kick some carelessly deposited books on the way, while Alf slopped through to the kitchen.

Robert was inspecting a heavy leather-bound volume when Alf carried two steaming mugs into the room a few minutes later.

'That was a bit of a find.' Alf put the mugs down on his desk. 'A late nineteenth century encyclopaedia and in pretty good condition. I might get a good price for it on e-bay.'

'Fascinating how knowledge has advanced over the last century.' Robert put the book down on one of the untidy stacks. 'Or, perhaps it's simply the contemporary spin that is put on knowledge that has changed.'

'Oh, God, don't start getting deep at this time of the morning, Rob.' Alf dropped into a substantial armchair near the window. 'More importantly, tell me how went the cricket match.'

'Oh, that was great fun. And what's just as important, we old 'uns managed to make a match of it.'

'But you lost?'

'We lost, but only by seven wickets.' He chuckled. 'And we managed to injure three of the opposition.'

'Oh? How was that?'

Robert proceeded to recount highlights of the match, while Alf, legs stretched out before him, exploded with occasional bursts of laughter. The telephone rang once, but he ignored it, simply waving a hand in its direction until it stopped.

'So, you didn't need my skills after all?' Alf reached over to the desk, put his mug down and picked up an envelope.

'Well, your leggies would have added some variety to the attack, I suppose.' Robert saw the envelope and sensed that interest in the cricket match was on the wane. 'What have you got there?'

'Letter from the Transport people at the District Offices. Prompt, but not very edifying I'm afraid.' He opened the letter. 'I won't bore you with the details, but essentially they've produced their version of the proceedings at the meeting in the form of minutes then repeated what that pompous twit Rundle said at the end.'

'You mean the bit about asking the Area Manager to look into the situation, etcetera?'

'That's it. The trouble with these people is that they have too much time on their hands, too many resources and miles and miles of red tape to wrap us all up in.' He flung the letter over his shoulder onto the desk. 'They'll try to grind us down. Well, I'm buggered if I'll let 'em grind me down.' He thumped the sides of his armchair for emphasis and an eruption of dust particles now danced in the sunlight that somehow filtered its way through the grimy windowpanes.

'Hmm, none of us wants to be ground down, Alf, but most of us have other things in our lives to be getting on with.' Robert looked around the room and noted, not for the first time, how unkempt and dirty it was. Alf had probably not cleaned or aired it for months.

'And do you think I haven't got other things to be getting on with, eh? Bloody civil servants, they're barely civil and they're certainly not servants these days.'

Robert shook his head and chuckled. 'I sometimes think you live in a time warp, old boy.'

For a few seconds Alf stared at him in a strangely disconnected way and Robert wondered if he had unwittingly said something to cause offence.

'Perhaps I do,' Alf said somewhat distractedly, 'or bloody well wish I did, more's to the point. By the way, while we're on the dreaded subject, I drove over the impediments last night at about eleven and the paint's still there. Have they made any attempt to scrub it off?'

'A half-hearted attempt, I think. But there's some talk about burning it off. That may be the only way.'

'Well, if they're successful I for one hope the phantom red paint artist strikes again . . . whoever he is.' Alf looked at his friend quizzically.

92

'No, there are still no clues, but I have my own idea.'

'Probably the same idea as mine. We know who has access to a great deal of the red stuff, eh?'

'Exactly so.' Robert's face broke into a slow smile. 'Well, you'll be wanting to open the shop I expect, so I'd better be on my way.'

He stood up and then inclined his head towards the window. 'Do you ever open that for a bit of fresh sea air?'

'I probably would if I could, but both sash cords are broken.' Alf heaved himself out of the depths of the chair. 'When I do open it I have to prop it up with my trusty ruler.'

Robert's eyes scanned the mess on Alf's desk until he located the ruler. 'Ah, an old wooden twelve incher. Doesn't look strong enough for the job.'

'I'll fix the cords one day.'

Alf had started to move towards the door when Robert suddenly lifted a file on the desk and snorted.

'What the devil's this thing?'

'Ah,' Alf began, reaching out for the object, 'that is my paperweight. Isn't she a beauty?'

'Not exactly how I'd describe it, Alf. Striking perhaps, but not beautiful.' He looked more closely at the chrome-plated figurine of a naked kneeling woman. 'Isn't that . . . ?' he began.

'Probably not, but there is a striking resemblance I'll grant you. And I do call her Dolly.' He took the figurine from Robert, placed it on a loose pile of papers and patted it on the head. 'It was included amongst the items in the house clearance sale and I couldn't resist it. Come on now, bugger off, I've got work to do, even if you haven't.'

Robert left the room chuckling and he was still laughing when he stepped out into the street. It wasn't until he was well up the road that he realised he'd forgotten the other reason for visiting. He had meant to ask Alf if there had been any improvement in Lydia: but then it was probably just as well that he had not. Sometimes that was a subject best avoided.

When Robert wandered into the Lugger that evening he stepped straight into the arena of a fierce but good-natured debate.

Two old Pengarth locals were sitting quietly at the corner table in the public section, but they were the only people in the pub other than the group gathered by the bar, where B.K.Richards was expressing his views shrilly to the accompaniment of jerky arm movements.

'. . . but the trouble is that everyone has to believe in something. With a thinking human being you simply can't have a vacuum of belief. If it is not in a deity, then it is in something materialistic. Mankind always has to hold on to some kind of creed otherwise he's, he's . . .'

'. . . a nihilist?' Robert suggested as he came up from behind. He caught Greg's eye and made a tankard-holding gesture.

'Oh, hello, Robert. Yes, a nihilist, but even then he has a belief. He believes that there is nothing to believe in.'

'Oh, bollocks, BK' Alf snorted. 'You've just said a nihilist believes in nothing, thereby disproving your point. Nothing is zero.'

'No, no, Alf. There's a subtle difference between believing in nothing and having *nothing* as a belief.' BK looked pleased with himself. It was something he had remembered from *Thought for the Day* on the wireless.

'Too subtle for me, BK.' Greg pushed Robert's tankard across the counter and then rang up the till.

'What's this about?' Robert asked Sadie, who was quietly sipping a glass of white wine.

'Oh, Alf reckons that religious belief becomes weaker as people become more sophisticated. So, the more sophisticated we become in the western world, the more vulnerable we become to religious fanatics from the developing world.' She looked up at Alf. 'Is that about right?'

'Very succinctly put, my flower.' Alf looked at Robert and added, 'This all began because I said within the hearing of our good churchwarden that God is merely an intangible concept, born of superstition and fear. So, the less superstitious and fearful man becomes, so God fades in significance in his life. So, Man effectively becomes his own God. Seems logical to me.'

'Hmm, makes a limited amount of sense.' It was not the first time he had heard Alf express this homespun philosophy. 'But, why stir it up with our churchwarden? He might never come in here again. And he'll probably stop praying for your soul.'

BK smiled shyly and pushed his glasses back. 'I really only came in to collect the money from Greg's whip round after the match. But, I seem to have walked right into Alf's trap.'

'No trap intended, my old flower, I merely threw out a thought and hoped that you, as a man of God, might show me the error of my ways and set me on the straight and narrow path to salvation.'

'You're beyond salvation, Alfie!' Sadie laughed.

'And I,' BK shrilled to make himself heard above the hilarity, 'I am trying to convince this heathen that a person will always have a belief in something, even if it is not in God, the Creator.'

'Like what?' Greg leaned on the bar. 'I mean, if belief in God dies, what is it that'll take its place?'

'Well,' BK pressed his bony hands together and looked around the room, 'anything that he cannot explain, I suppose. For example, a gambler might believe that twenty-four is his lucky number. A sports fanatic worships his football club. A gardener might believe that if he doesn't plant his brassicas by the twentieth of March then his crop will fail.'

'Aha!' Alf thundered. 'My point is made! We're back to superstition. He may no longer believe that God will strike him down with a bolt of lightning for not attending Church on Sunday, but he still believes some mumbo-jumbo about plants and dates. It's redirected superstition.'

'Yes, I must say your analogy is a bit flaky there, BK,' Robert added.

'Oh, I'd better give up.' BK picked up his glass and his adam's apple jerked as he drained the last mouthful. 'But, I'll give you one last thing to consider. When the devout followers of Islam come swarming over the hill to meet the irresolute and effete lapsed Christians and other infidels, then there will be no contest. When that happens, your theories about superstition won't be worth a tinker's cuss.' He plonked his glass on the counter. 'With that thought I'll wish you all goodnight . . . and thanks again for the collection, Greg.'

There was silence as they watched the lean man pick up the blue cash sack with a bony hand and then walk to the door.

'Blimey,' Greg said eventually, 'that certainly is a thought. It's enough to drive you back to Church.'

'Not me,' Alf grunted. 'I may not have much time for God, but I'm not bloody effete, my friends. This infidel will go down fighting when they come.'

'How depressing.' Sadie pulled a long face. 'BK makes it sound like the Crusades in reverse.'

95

'That's probably exactly how the other lot see it too,' Robert said. 'I don't know much about Muslim teaching, but I expect the Crusades of eight centuries ago are fresher in their minds today than in ours. After all, the early Christians were just as fanatical in their attempts to conquer and convert as are your modern day Islamites.'

Alf grimaced. 'Yes, but we've moved on, Rob, and so should they. If my theory is correct and everyone achieved the same level of sophistication and shook off primitive superstition, there would be no more religion and fewer causes to fight for.'

They were all pondering this point when the outer door opened and Darren Dowrick came up to the bar.

'Ah, thank God for that,' Greg said across their heads to the new arrival. 'It was all getting a bit heavy in here.'

'Why, what have I missed?' Darren looked from one to the other in the group.

'Don't ask . . . you'll regret it,' Robert replied. 'What'll you have, Darren?'

'Oh, cheers Robert, I'll have a pint of Rufus please. Are you on watch this weekend?'

Robert nodded. 'Middle watch Saturday and I'm on reserve for Sunday. When are you on?'

'Third watch, Saturday. Weather looks as if it'll be blowing up a bit by then. Might make life a bit more interesting out there.' He took his beer. 'Good health.'

'I'm on first watch,' Alf stroked his beard. 'The way the glass is dropping I should think it'll be blowing well before you get on.'

The talk drifted on to coast watch matters and eventually, with some prompting from Sadie, the men were encouraged to recount some of their more amusing experiences from various duties at the Pengarth lookout. As more beer was consumed so the stories switched from amusing to amazing and then downright unbelievable. It became the NCI watchkeeper's equivalent of a fisherman's one-that-got-away series of tales and the men kept Sadie hooting with laughter for the best part of an hour.

People came and went around them, Elsie was constantly moving amongst the tables collecting glasses and exchanging banter, while Greg patrolled behind the bar in his unhurried manner. All thoughts of the fervent hoards sweeping over the hill to crush the effete infidel were forgotten and life in the Lugger proceeded as it had for generations.

A few minutes before Robert left the Lugger that evening, George Harris was taking his dog for an evening walk down Fore Street when a small blue saloon drew up alongside. The driver wound down her window, leaned out and asked him for directions to a place he had not heard mentioned for many months.

After his elaborate instructions she thanked him politely in an accent that did not seem to be quite English and then drove off.

'Funny that,' George murmured to his dog. 'Thought the old girl'd died a long time back. Why'd she want to go there this time of night?'

He and the old dog carried on slowly up Fore Street and the incident was soon forgotten.

Chapter Seven

THE paper delivery van was just bouncing over the last red-painted road cushion when Alf slipped out of the side entrance of the Convenience Store. He paused at the gate, tucked his shirt into baggy twill trousers, looked both ways and then strode off down Fore Street to his home.

The early morning was blustery as forecast and flecks of spume were being whipped around the rocks at the far side of the harbour. A flock of seagulls, seeming only partially in control of their flight, were screaming greedily around the mast of Ted Moss's boat as it pulled into the harbour with an early catch. Occasionally one of the birds would break away from the flock and dive towards the choppy sea for a morsel that had fallen from the boat. Up the hill near the top of Fore Street a flag of St Piran stood out erect from its pole in the Captain's garden as the gusting wind plucked at its fraying extremities. Pengarth was waking up.

Alf stopped at his front door, face turned to the harbour, eyes shut and breathed deeply. Apart from the faint chugging of the boat's engine, the mewing of the gulls and the tumbling of wavelets on the shore, there was no other sound to disturb the early Pengarth Saturday morning. It was how he liked his world: predictable, constant and orderly. He unlocked the door and went in.

Humming a Puccini aria he filled the kettle and put some bread in the toaster before turning on the radio to catch a news summary. He had a couple of hours before he was due on watch.

Some time later, still humming, he stepped under the shower and as the warm water cascaded over his head the hum metamorphosed into song. He had been on edge ever since seeing Lydia, but today he would put it all into a bin called *The Past* and bash on with the routine. The rough planking of life and raw meat of open emotional wounds caused stress and irrational behaviour, both of which he could do without.

By ten past nine, when Alf left by the bookshop door, the village was alive. Some up country visitors were leaving the store with provisions and newspapers, Ted Moss was at the water's edge

99

doing something to his crab pots, the postman was scurrying from door to door in his summer shorts and a buzzard was gliding aimlessly above the church.

Alf stood for a few moments checking his gear before setting off for the coastal path that led to the Coast Watch lookout. As he crossed the road he waved at the postman and shouted a cheerful greeting. Yes, today he would be in control again.

Visits to Lydia always put his emotions through turbulent water and, for a man who constantly sought the shelter of an orderly pattern in his daily life, it took a conscious effort to get back onto a comfortable tack.

The few sheep that had gathered around the lookout door scattered as he approached. Alf gave his version of a bleat and then paused to kick away their droppings from the step. He put down his rucksack and fumbled with the lock before clicking the combination into sequence. The wind-rusted old lock slid open reluctantly and Alf made a mental note to bring some lubricant next time he was on watch.

He pushed the door open and disturbed a swarm of flies that had settled on the windowpanes. Some flew out of the building, but the majority beat themselves frantically against the glass and he noted another item for the lookout: fly paper, or a damned good swatter.

Pulling back a cupboard door, with a loud click from his knee he crouched down and pressed the combination numbers on the safe lock. The door swung open and he removed the binoculars and the collection tin. He attached the binoculars to the pelorus and then flicked a switch to power up the VHF radio. Turning it on he peered at the knobs for a second before pressing the scan button. Immediately the digital numbers began their furious dance behind the radio's perspex covering and he was in contact with the maritime world.

He checked the wall-mounted weather station, noted the wind direction and then opened the log. The barometer reading was low at 1007, the temperature was eighteen degrees celsius and the wind was blowing five knots from the southwest. Alf made rapid entries in the log and then went to a drawer and took out the flag.

There were two Union Jack flags. One was smaller and very frayed and the other was full sized and smarter. For some obscure reason the National Trust, which owned the land where the lookout stood, had refused permission for the Cornish NCI to fly the flag of St Piran. Alf, being convinced that it was yet another warped interpretation of so-called political correctness, had reacted peevishly by promptly cancelling his membership of the Trust.

There was a rumour around Pengarth that Alf's underpants were made to the design of the Cornish flag, but if Sadie knew that for a fact she was not saying.

Anyway, the small and tattered Jack was only flown when the wind was blowing at seven knots or above, or if God was emptying his bladder. Today the visibility was good and the breeze stiff, but not enough to prevent the large flag being flown. Alf went outside, looped the rope over the flag's toggle and ran it up the pole. He secured it, hummed a few bars of the National Anthem, saluted and then went back inside.

Just after half past nine he called the Falmouth Coastguard and reported that the Pengarth Watch was open for business. Receiving a brief word of thanks, he replaced the receiver and then spread out the chart and ordinance survey map.

There was a light swell running and the sea was verging on rough, but nowhere bad enough to cause any problems to a sailor who knew how to handle his boat. Alf did not own a boat, nor did he do much sailing, but he had lived long enough in Pengarth to understand the sea and to know all of its moods. He could also recognise expertise in others and tell from intercepted radio messages and sightings whether or not a boatman was competent in handling his craft.

Out to sea now he could detect with the naked eye a freighter heading for Falmouth, a naval supply vessel, two fishing boats over to the east and a solitary Bermudan rigged yacht. He opened the page of the daybook and noted these vessels, before scanning the horizon with his binoculars. For a while there appeared to be nothing more above the wavy line where the sea met the sky, until a long low smudge on the horizon told him that there was a tanker between eight and ten miles out. Alf put the binoculars down and craned his head forward to look up the coastline.

NCI watchkeepers had a brief to observe what was going on along the coastal path and on the beaches as well as activity at sea. This early in the morning, with the weather cool and June still in its infancy, it was unlikely that there would be any swimmers, but early morning walkers were not seasonal. They came at all times and in any weathers: some of them totally bonkers, Alf thought.

He sat down on the high stool and unscrewed the top of his thermos flask. From there he could see in both directions up and down the coast, watch the sea birds working the air currents, mentally name the small salt-toughened flowers that tufted between the rocky outcrops and listen to the rhythmic flapping of the flag above him. It was, he reflected as he took a sip of coffee, a useful exercise in co-ordinating one's senses: a sort of orchestration of all five.

He was checking the tidal flow an hour later when the telephone at his elbow bleated. It was Poltock with their buddy call. The two watchkeepers exchanged a few observations and then he made an entry in the log.

At eleven o'clock the VHF radio suddenly came alive. There was a diver down somewhere up the coast and Brixham Coastguard was dealing with the situation. VHF traffic on the incident held his attention sporadically for nearly an hour as he continued to scan the bay.

Soon after midday he left the lookout and made his way down the rocks to where he would be obscured from the path, unzipped his fly and turned his back to the wind. He was just completing this operation when he heard a dog bark from somewhere between the lookout and the road. Heaving his frame back up the rocks he saw a yellow Labrador bounding along the path, apparently excited by the sight of a few sheep that were grazing a little way up the rise in the field. A few yards behind the dog a woman was waving a lead and shouting at it to stop.

Alf reached the lookout and stood at the door, hands on hips and drawing heavy breaths. *Bloody people who couldn't control their dogs!*

She spotted him and gave her dog a more urgent yell, just as the sheep were beginning to show signs of breaking into a blind headlong run. Alf remembered an occasion when one of the flock had fallen halfway down the cliff and had to be rescued by the emergency services. It was not something he wished to have repeated on his watch.

The urgency of the woman's shout obviously did the trick, because the dog stopped, looked around and then trotted down towards Alf at the lookout door. The sheep went back to grazing, as if nothing had happened.

He bent down and stroked the dog's head as it lapped eagerly at the water bowl by his feet. The woman however stayed a fair distance away, standing contritely with the lead dangling at her side. He remained bending over the dog, but raised his head and smiled politely in her direction, thinking perhaps that she might be discomfited by the uniform's air of authority. A friendly gesture should give reassurance and perhaps even help fund-raising if she were to venture down to his door.

She returned his smile, but came no closer. Instead she gave him a tentative wave and call out, 'I'm sorry, he doesn't normally chase sheep.'

'So they all say,' Alf growled softly, but waved back in acknowledgement, still appraising her as best he could from a distance.

'Bruno, come now,' she called and the dog stopped lapping.

'Go on, dog,' Alf commanded and pointed towards his mistress.

She whistled and the dog turned and ran back up the field to meet her on the path. After attaching the lead to his collar she glanced back at Alf, as if for a sign of approval. He simply nodded and then watched them carry on up the path, the dog pulling rather too much for a trained animal.

Alf stood and watched for a while, scratching his beard and speculating. She was well dressed in smart country clothes, which seemed at a distance to be too warm for the time of year. She wore no scarf or hat, so the gusting wind blew her dark shoulder length hair freely and occasionally she grabbed at her skirt to stop it lifting. Even at that distance he had noticed that her face seemed pale, as if not recently exposed to the sun, but long legs – what he could see of them – bore her steadily along the uneven path, suggesting that she was quite fit. Taking all that together, plus the slight intonation in her voice, Alf concluded that she was probably a foreigner on a visit to the Duchy.

As the woman and dog approached the gate leading into the adjacent field he turned and went back inside the lookout. It was nearing the end of the watch and she had been the only visitor he had greeted all morning and not a penny had been dropped in the collection box by the door.

He picked up his pen to make an entry in the daybook and then drained the last drops from his flask. It was ten past twelve and Robert would probably be setting out at any moment to relieve him.

Then there was a sound. A sharp unfamiliar noise.

Alf's pen hand froze just above the log and he turned his head slowly towards the open door. It was the unrelatedness of it that first alerted him. This sound had jarred with the routine noises that surrounded the lookout. *Was it a cry?*

The wind was whipping around the radio aerial and the door occasionally creaked on its hinges, but those were usual noises. No, there was something else just then. He was certain of it.

Going to the door he closed his eyes and concentrated all attention on a repeat of the sound.

Nothing.

For several seconds, nothing but the wind.

Then suddenly there it was again. It *was* a shout or cry, some way off, out of sight. No doubt about it this time.

'Damn!' He dashed back into the lookout and grabbed his binoculars. Outside again he scanned up and down the path and the beach as far as he could see. '*Where the hell's it coming from?*'

There was no one on the path, no one walking up from the village and only three youngsters playing harmlessly on the beach a quarter of a mile away.

Then the cry came once more, only for an instant, before being rubbed out by the wind. But he had the direction this time. It was from over the brow to the north of the lookout. For a moment he paused as he rehearsed the rules in his mind, but only for a moment.

'Sod it! I have to bloody well go, there's no one else.' He pulled the door closed behind him and set off up the path at a trot, with the binoculars thudding against his chest.

Wheezing and gasping he reached the crest of the rise and then looked desperately about. At first he neither saw nor heard anything, except for a gull that wheeled overhead, squawking agitatedly.

Then he saw the dog.

The yellow Labrador was clawing its way through the gorse from the cliff side of the path, with its lead trailing behind. Alf ran over to the frightened animal and grabbed the lead before it could run off. It had a cut over its left eye, a claw dangled from one paw and it had broken gorse tangled in its coat. He crouched down beside it.

'What've you done with your mistress, eh dog?' he said urgently and then he heard another cry from the far side of the gorse. It was fainter, but there was no mistaking it this time.

Knowing how treacherous that part of the cliff was, he tethered the dog to a post before cautiously squeezing through the gap in the undergrowth. The cliff edge was only about six feet beyond the path at this point, but an unfamiliar walker would not be able to see this over the dense growth on the cliff side of the track. Apart from tangled gorse the ground cover consisted of lethally barbed short blackthorn bushes and clumps of coarse grass, which tended to obscure the many deep rabbit holes from view.

There had once been sheep fencing there, but all that remained now were a few broken posts and treacherous wisps of rusty barbed wire. It was indeed a place fit only for rabbits.

Sweating freely now Alf inched his way towards the edge, trying not to think of the vertical drop to the rocks and the sea below. How steep was it? Fifty, maybe sixty feet down at that point? He could not remember.

Alf pulled out his handkerchief and wrapped it around his left hand before seizing the firmest looking bush and then leaned out over the cliff edge. Fragments of loose shale broke away and fell with a clatter as he pushed his right foot as far forward as he dared, while gorse thorns spiked through the cloth and into his hand.

He took a deep breath, leaned out just a little further and then saw her. She was lying just a few feet beneath him on a small rock ledge that looked as if it had been home for a seagull's nest and it appeared that only a single flimsy bush was preventing her from going all the way down. Her left leg was twisted at an unnatural angle and a thin trickle of blood traced its way down the side of her face.

At first he could not tell if she was conscious and he did not want to startle her by calling out. Then he noticed feeble movements from the fingers of her left hand as she tried to grip on to a rock on the cliff face and it was at that point he realised he had no choice. The drop to the serrated rocks and the sea below was sheer.

'Don't move! Don't pull that rock or the whole cliff face might come away. Please, just stay very still and I'll get help.' He heard more shale spraying out from below his foot. 'Did you hear? Just keep very still and we'll have you up again.'

He thought he saw a slight movement of her head and he certainly noticed that the fingers had stopped clawing. Very gingerly he pulled himself back from the edge and then reversed through the gap in the gorse.

'Come on you bloody dog.' He unhitched the animal, which was licking its torn claw. 'I bet this is your doing.'

He loped all the way back to the lookout, with the dog bounding joyously by his side, tethered it and then took a few deep breaths before picking up the telephone. His chest still heaving, he pressed the speed dial button.

'*Hello, Falmouth Coastguard.*'

'Hello, Falmouth, this is Pengarth NCI.' He paused to take another deep breath before continuing as calmly as he could. 'We have a casualty over the cliff here and perched on a ledge.'

'*Alright, Pengarth,*' the cool voice replied. '*Please let me have your name and then give me a location bearing.*'

'NCI watchkeeper Curtis,' Alf replied, putting on his glasses to see the lookout bearing at the top of the chart, cursing quietly as perspiration spilled over his brow onto the lens. He wiped it away and then read out the bearing.

'*Is the individual in immediate danger of falling further?*'

'In my estimation, yes, in imminent danger of falling. The cliff's about fifty feet high at that point and quite insecure.'

'*And can you tell if the person is injured?*'

'It looks as if her leg is broken.' He kept glancing anxiously up the path, as if expecting some kind of activity there.

'*Alright, Mr Curtis,*' the measured voice continued, '*stay where you are in case we need to make further contact. I'll contact the Pengarth mobile coastguard and they should be with you very soon with full rescue equipment. Meanwhile stand by the phone.*'

'Right, Falmouth, I'll wait for your call.' Alf replaced the receiver and began to fret.

Two minutes passed before the telephone rang again. He scooped it up.

'*Mr Curtis, sod's law I'm afraid. The mobile's out on a call further down the coast at the moment and can't be with you inside half an hour. You say she's in imminent danger of falling?*'

'Yes, yes it's a very narrow ledge and there's only a small bush stopping her rolling over. Half an hour's too long.'

'*One moment.*' There was the sound of a muffled conversation before the voice resumed. '*Right, in the circumstances we'll be scrambling the rescue helicopter now and it should be with you in less than a quarter of an hour.*'

'That's good, but I'm afraid even that may be too late. I don't know how she's staying on that ledge as it is.'

In spite of his training Alf was agitated and the coastguard at the other end probably picked this up from his voice, no doubt thinking, *these NCI fellows do a good job, but they're inexperienced amateurs when it comes to an incident like this and I've got to keep him thinking clearly.*

'*Mr Curtis, I have to ring off now, but please stay at your lookout,*' he repeated calmly. '*The pilot might have to contact you by radio and I also need you there. Do you understand?*'

'Yes.' Alf clenched his jaw and peered up the path again. 'Which channel shall I set the radio to?'

'*Probably six seven, but I'll contact you again very soon.*' The line went dead.

Alf stood very still for a minute and fought a battle between what his training said he should do and what he knew he should do as a human being.

His eyes dipped to the cupboard below the ordinance survey map and slowly a wildly defiant look crept over his face. He was just about to open the cupboard when the telephone rang.

'Pengarth NCI,' he said brusquely.

'*Falmouth here, Mr Curtis. The helicopter is about to take off and will be there with a rescue team in just over ten minutes. Stand by. They'll contact you on VHF if necessary.*'

'Thank you.' Alf put the phone down.

His mouth was dry and he felt the perspiration trickling down his neck. In his imagination he could see the plant breaking and the woman slipping to her death on the rocks below. Those jagged uncompromising rocks were reaching up like rows of serrated broken teeth, just waiting to impale their victim. If she died it would be his fault and all because he obeyed the rules. How could he live with himself if she fell while he sat and waited by the radio?

The deliberation only took a few seconds more before suddenly he knew what he had to do. He turned swiftly and crouched to open the cupboard door below the bookshelves.

'Now, what the hell do I need?' he murmured. 'Rope, gloves – damn, no gloves – first aid kit . . .'

He found the coiled length of hemp rope and prayed that it was long enough. Then he unhooked the first aid kit from the wall and removed his dark uniform tie. He scribbled a hasty note for Robert, had a quick look around and then he was out of the lookout and setting off up the slope again at a rolling jog. Inside the lookout the dog barked a couple of times and then settled down again to its licking.

Alf reached the spot, dropped the box on the ground and began uncoiling the rope. He found the nearest post to the gap in the gorse and tested it. It rocked slightly, but seemed otherwise to be sound and deeply planted. He wound one end of the rope three times around the base of the post and then knotted it firmly. This was going to be her lifeline and possibly his too.

Alf played out the line and at the other end he formed a noose, again testing it with a couple of firm tugs. Before crawling back through the gorse he scanned the path in both directions and cursed. Of all days for there to be no walkers in sight. He closed his eyes and for a moment remembered what BK had said about God. *If He exists, He certainly would be welcome here right now,* Alf thought.

He began to ease his way once more towards the cliff edge, holding firmly on to the knot he had tied in the rope. When he reached the unstable rim of the cliff the rope went taught behind him and he gave it another testing pull.

Above him the gull still wheeled and mewed like an anxious parent whose young are being threatened – which probably was the case.

'Just my luck if I'm dive bombed by a bloody gull,' he said through gritted teeth as he reached the edge.

She was still there and seemed to be in the same position. *Good girl,* he thought, and then it occurred to him that she might have passed out. *God, that really would make things tricky.*

He tried to summon a little saliva into his mouth and then called out cautiously, 'Hello there, I'm back and I've brought a rope.' There was no response, so he tried again. 'Can you hear me? Move your hand if you can hear me.'

Nothing happened for a few moments and then he saw the fingers of her left hand move. Alf closed his eyes and he breathed out slowly. *Thank God for that much. Now comes the hard part.*

'Listen, this is not going to be a picnic, but I must ask you to help.' Still hanging on to the knot with a sweating hand, he began to lower the noose. It was only about six feet down to the ledge, but at that moment it seemed to him to be twenty. 'I'm lowering a rope to you now and when you feel it touch you I want you to do something very brave. Can you still hear me?'

The fingers moved and then suddenly he could see that her one visible eye was open.

'I know this will hurt you, but you must get the noose over your head and under your arms.' The rope brushed her face and she flinched. 'Do it very very slowly now.'

At first she did not move and he thought his worst fears were being realised. She was frozen through fear. What now? That bush, which looked a mere twig, would surely snap soon whether or not she moved and the ledge was clearly unstable. He could see bits of it flaking off all the time. It was surely only designed to hold a family of seagulls.

'You must do it, my flower, it's your only chance,' he said urgently. 'Left arm first, very slowly. Loop it through the noose without moving your body, if you can.'

He thought he heard a whimper and then, oh joy, he saw her arm begin to move. It lifted from the ledge in slow motion and he manoeuvred the rope to make it easier for her.

'That's right, that's the spirit,' he encouraged.

First her hand, then past the wrist and up to the elbow the rope slid. He let out more slack so that the noose would broaden. His left hand was growing tired and he could feel the strain on his arm socket, but he kept his concentration on what his right hand was doing.

A small slip with his foot sent a shower of stones and earth tumbling down and bouncing off her back on its way to the sea. Alf paused to steady his stance.

'Good girl. Now try to raise your body and bring your right arm round and through the loop. I know it's not easy, but . . .' He stopped in horror as part of the twig snapped and then bent out over the abyss, quivering in the wind.

Neither of them moved for several seconds. Then, above the swish of the wind through the gorse, he thought he could hear the sound of rotor blades and his mind came alert again.

'Go on, try it. Even if the plant goes you've got the rope to hang onto and it's firmly tied up here. Please try.'

The helicopter sound had gone again. Had it been his imagination, or perhaps it was some other aircraft? No matter, she was moving again. She had raised her torso sufficiently to loop her right arm through the noose and now she just had to get it properly over her head.

'Well done, well done.' He longed to be able to rest his left arm, to wipe the salty perspiration from his eyes, to turn off the wind that was whipping gorse against his legs, but at the same time he was feeling an immense sense of achievement. Once that noose was under her armpits she would be safe, even if the entire ledge crashed into the sea, she would dangle there until the rescue helicopter arrived. *Where was the bloody thing anyway? Ten minutes they said.*

Her head lolled forward as she let out a cry of pain, but she had done it. The rope was round her torso and under her armpits. But maybe that cry also contained a tiny element of relief or triumph at the monumental task she had just performed.

'That's brilliant. Brave girl.' Then a sudden and almost irrelevant thought struck him and he called down, 'Your dog's safe, by the way.'

He shouldn't have said that.

The thought of her dog and its welfare must have momentarily caused her to forget her own predicament, because she twisted her body slightly onto her right side. The sudden movement sent shock waves down her broken leg and she screamed. At the same time the gnarled little twig that had been her saviour lurched over, displaying all its spindly roots, and a chunk of the ledge fell away.

Alf humped into action, taking a step back, digging his heels into the soil and taking the strain on the rope with all his weight.

More of the cliff crumbled as the tightened rope cut into the unbonded fabric of its edge, but the sudden deadweight that Alf had braced himself for did not happen. He was now a yard back from the side so he could no longer see her and for a few desperate seconds he remained taking the strain and wondering what to do next. Practically in despair he decided to shout instruction and hope that she could hear.

'Hello, I'm still here!' he yelled. 'Can you hear me?'

Above the wind he heard a faint response.

'Thank the Lord,' he sighed and then shouted again, spacing out his words, 'I don't know if you can get up on your good leg if I help by pulling. I think it's the only way.'

He waited, but there was no reply.

'I can't let the rope go slack for a moment, so it's up to you.' His back was hurting now and he felt that he would not be able to trust his grip much longer. 'Yell again if you think you can get onto one leg.'

Again there was a shout. *God, the woman had guts.*

'Terrific! I'm going to count to three. On three I'll pull like hell and you try to stand. Keep your foot as close to the cliff face as possible now.'

Alf risked removing his right hand from the rope for a second to dry it on his trousers and then braced his body.

'One...two...THREE.' He heaved, but at first nothing happened. *Christ, I can't do that again!*

He held the strain and then, just when he thought he would have to slacken off he felt a movement from the cliff end of the rope. There was a piercing cry, but at the same time the rope eased and he felt himself going backwards. He dug his heels in and heaved again and again until the rope went tight. He was now in the thick of the gorse and only two yards from the retaining post. If he could secure the rope more tightly to the post then she could remain in that position until . . .

There was a sudden movement behind him that had nothing to do with the wind.

'Alf! What the hell are you doing?'

Alf twisted his neck to look over his shoulder. It was Robert, looking aghast.

'Fishing, you bloody idiot! What d'you think? Come on, Rob, give me a hand here. We've got to pull her up.'

At that moment he did hear the helicopter.

There could be no doubt about it now and suddenly he knew he had to finish what he had started before the professionals arrived. Robert stood there rather foolishly with his mouth open, looking skywards.

'For Christ's sake, Rob, grab the rope. She's tied securely and she's only six feet down the cliff.' He turned back to the job in hand with his face set grimly and prepared to pull for life: his or hers, at that moment it didn't matter to him. Behind him Robert jumped into action and grabbed the rope.

Pulling together it took them only a minute or two to raise the woman from what remained of the ledge, up the cliff face and then onto flat ground. As soon as that was achieved they pushed back through the gorse and then lifted and carried her gently back to the path. Mercifully for her, at that point she was in a dead faint.

In those final minutes Alf was hardly aware of the helicopter hovering above, its rotors flattening the coarse grass and raising loose soil from the path. It was not until he and Robert had settled the woman on the grass that he looked up and saw one of the crew gesticulating from the open door forty feet above. Alf pointed vaguely to the top of the incline and gestured for it to land.

Robert turned urgently to him and grabbed his sleeve.

'Now, quickly, before the shit hits the fan, tell me what's gone on here.'

'Her dog . . . you saw it in the lookout? . . . pulled her off the cliff. I called Falmouth. They sent that,' he pointed to the helicopter and caught his breath, 'and I made an executive decision that they would be too late. End of story.'

'I'm afraid that's where you're wrong, old boy.' Robert put his pullover under the woman's head and then started to straighten her torn clothing. There was little he could do with her broken leg. 'You shouldn't have left the lookout.'

'I know the rules, Robert, but I had no choice. She'd be a broken doll on the rocks down there by now if I'd left it to those boys.'

Robert looked at him for a few moments and then shrugged. The helicopter was landing a few yards up the path and, as often happens on such occasions, as if by magic there were suddenly a few spectators.

'Do you know who she is?' Robert asked.

Alf, who was gradually recovering from his ordeal, began to remove gorse thorns from his hand. The adrenalin was subsiding and he suddenly felt physically and emotionally exhausted, but he had not yet started shaking. He glanced up at Robert.

'No idea. Why don't you search her for a clue?'

Two of the helicopter crew were running from their craft with their heads lowered under the blades, calling on the spectators to stand back as they came down the slope with a stretcher.

Robert looked down at the woman and noticed that one of her jacket pockets was ripped down the seam. He reached over, pulled back the loose flap of material and saw the corner of something maroon protruding. He took it out.

'It's her passport,' he exclaimed and flipped it open. 'Her name's Rowena Fischer, British citizen.'

Alf remained sitting on the grass picking at his hand and did not look up. With his job done he seemed suddenly to have lost interest in the woman whose life he had just saved. He did not even seem to notice when she moaned and opened her eyes, or when the helicopter crewmen arrived on the scene. It was Robert who

112

greeted them. He slipped the passport back into the woman's pocket and stood up.

'Afternoon, gentlemen. Which one of you made the call to Falmouth?' The crewman stood there calmly, looking from one to the other, while his colleague got down on his haunches to attend to the woman.

Alf still did not look up, but paused in his picking to raise his right hand.

'You Curtis?'

Alf nodded and then seemed slowly to focus on the situation. He stayed on the ground, but turned to Robert.

'It's your watch, Rob, you'd better get on down there. I'll sort this out here and then come down, do the incident report and write up the log.' He was trying hard to conceal the fact that he was beginning to shake.

'Alright,' Robert replied dubiously and shot a glance at the crewman before turning and setting off for the lookout, collecting the first aid kit on the way.

'And check the dog, I think its torn a claw,' Alf shouted after him.

With the crewman still watching him closely Alf rose slowly to his feet. He felt his legs quivering and for a moment thought he would fall over. The crewman stepped forward to steady him, while his colleague replaced a syringe in his medical case. Rowena Fischer was quiet again.

A blanket was put around Alf's shoulders.

'Yes, I should think your report will make interesting reading,' the first man said flatly with a sideways glance as he helped settle the woman securely onto the stretcher.

Alf stared at the rope attached to the old post and his ordeal started to come back to him in subliminal flashes. The wind was dropping now and he could hear the metallic and dismembered voice of the VHF radio coming from the helicopter. He cocked his head and turned his eyes to the woman. It was really a rather flimsy rope and she was no featherweight. Was he mad? What made him do it?

With the red blanket still around his shoulders, Alf began to coil the rope while the crewmen carefully lifted the stretcher. They were a well-trained and experienced team, not needing to speak to each other as they worked. By the time Alf had completed coiling the rope and untying it from the post they were ready to carry her up the slope.

The pilot saw them returning and prepared the helicopter for take-off.

Alf removed the blanket from his shoulders and draped it over the stretcher.

'Will you be OK, mate? You don't look too steady.'

'Yes, I'll be fine now.' Alf suddenly put a restraining hand on the crewman's arm. 'Look, I'm sorry I wasn't at my post, but I did what I thought was necessary at the time and I'd probably do the same again. And I really don't mind if you put that in *your* report.'

'Well,' the man inclined his head towards the cliff edge and managed a reluctant smile, 'if it's any consolation, it looks as if you might have saved her a fall.'

'It's every consolation, thanks. And I might have to quote you on that.' The men looked at each other and then turned to leave.

'Where'll you be taking her? A&E in Truro?' Alf called after them.

'She's going to A&E, but we'll not be taking her.' He bent his neck towards the helicopter. 'This bird's going back to its nest. We're taking the stretcher as far as the lane, where an ambulance should be waiting.'

Then right on cue they heard the dipping wail of an ambulance as it threaded its way along the narrow lane towards the field entrance. The two men lifted the stretcher and began to march briskly up the field, while the helicopter pilot started the rotors moving. As far as the crew was concerned for all practical purposes the incident had been dealt with satisfactorily and it was now time to return to Culdrose.

Alf watched them and for a moment a pang of guilt crossed his conscience. But only for a moment.

He was still standing there when the helicopter eventually rose from the field, turned out to sea and then set off back to its base. He slung the rope over his shoulder, cast a disapproving eye at the three onlookers and then made his way down to the lookout.

By the time he reached the door he found to his relief that he had stopped shaking, but he felt the need of a strong drink.

Without a word to Robert he took a pen, reached for the incident report file and began to make his entry. Robert respected the silence and continued to scan the horizon through binoculars while Alf carefully selected what he considered to be the appropriate words.

When he had completed the entry Alf breathed a heavy sigh and slammed the file closed.

'Now for the log,' he growled and Robert passed it over without a word.

It was not until he had completed the formalities that Alf squared up to Robert and gave him a lopsided grin.

'Thanks for your help, my old flower. Probably couldn't have finished the job without you.'

'Damned lucky for you that I went up there at all. I nearly missed your note.' Robert put the binoculars down and gave Alf an appraising stare. 'You're not going to be flavour of the month with the authorities, you know.'

'I know, but I wonder what you, or any of the others, would have done in my place, eh? All that stood between that woman's life and death was a spindly little plant that had no right to be growing there in the first place. I simply weighed up the situation and decided that the plant would go before the chopper came.' His bearded jaw signalled defiance and he added with quiet conviction, 'I had no choice, Robert.'

'Well, it certainly was very brave, I'll give you that.'

Alf laughed and clapped him on the shoulder. 'Your tone implies *stupid*, not *brave*. Well, maybe it was, but I didn't allow myself to think about it at the time. I'll probably go home now and shake like a jelly.'

'I suggest you go home, have a hot bath and a strong drink and then call the Captain, before he calls you. I think pre-emption is a good idea in this case, don't you?'

'Hmm, maybe you're right there.' The telephone rang and Robert picked up the receiver.

'Yes, sorry, Poltock.' He raised his eyebrows at Alf. 'We had a bit of an incident here and I forgot the call. Yes, all's well now.'

Alf picked up his possessions and winked at Robert before leaving the lookout and heading for the path back to Pengarth. He smiled to himself as he trudged wearily along the narrow track. *A bit of an incident, ha, you could say that again!*

When he arrived home there were two people staring through the bookshop window and he paused to ask them if they were looking for anything in particular. One said that he was after a particular Simenon for a holiday read and Alf said that he had the very book inside. He unlocked the shop and they went in.

By the time he had found the book, sold the man's companion another and then discussed literature generally, Alf had become completely sidetracked from his intended course of action. As soon as he had taken their money and they had left, he replaced the *Closed* sign on the door and went upstairs to have a hot shower.

The Captain was forgotten.

After bandaging his hand, he poured a large whisky and retired to his office. The shaking had begun again.

Some time and a couple more whiskies later the ringing telephone failed to wake him from his armchair slumber, so he missed a terse message from St Margaret's Psychiatric Hospital being recorded on the answering machine.

Chapter Eight

CAPTAIN Petroc Williams RN Retd. seldom went into the Lugger
for a casual social drink. He preferred to take his evening snort or
three of gin and tonic on the veranda of his small but comfortable
house on the hill above the bay.

He and his wife Hilda had lived there since he had retired from
a Bristol insurance company ten years earlier. He had taken a
senior administrative job at the company soon after terminating a
distinguished naval career. His last two years at sea had been spent
on a Broadsword Class frigate and he had then completed his final
lap at a shore-based job in Portsmouth.

He was a short man, but very broad, with a florid face and one
eye that appeared to operate on independent suspension. Strangely
this did not seem to disrupt his vision in the slightest, but it did
disconcert others with whom he was holding a conversation. In the
NCI lookout and from his eyrie he used an old brass telescope,
which he held firmly to the non-roving eyeball and not much that
went on in the bay and beyond escaped his attention.

Soon after arriving at Pengarth he had identified the need for a
regularly manned lookout and had persuaded the NCI Trustees that
he was the man to set it up. Next he bullied the National Trust into
agreeing to let him convert the disused coastguard station above
the bay. Terms were agreed, a contract drawn up and signed, and
soon after that Captain Williams set about mustering his crew.

He had trained the initial half dozen volunteers along the lines
of HM Coastguard's Memorandum of Understanding, plus the
necessary basic competences, and then the local organisation was
up and running. The only disappointment, as far as Petroc Williams was concerned, was that with just ten trained members the
lookout could only be manned at weekends.

In spite of pleas in the Parish magazine, notices in the store
window, occasional press gang forays into the Lugger and Hilda's
coffee mornings, their numbers remained stubbornly at ten. And
those were not always fit for action at the same time.

Tonight's Lugger foray however was not for recruitment purposes.

117

Petroc pushed the pub's door open, swept past the curtain and marched straight up to the bar. A few curious faces turned to see what had suddenly burst into their midst and conversation paused until Petroc dropped anchor in front of the row of beer handles. At the corner table George looked at Darren, nodded meaningfully and held up five splayed fingers: the length of the Captain's stride provided ample scope in the village for impromptu wagers.

'Evening, Captain, G & T?' Greg, ever alert to his customers' needs, reached for a glass.

'Well, no thank you, Greg.' Petroc's cheeks were more rubicund than usual and Greg guessed that he had already downed a couple at home.

There was an awkward silence as Greg remained poised with the glass and Petroc seemed for a moment to dither uncertainly.

'Well, actually, yes, I will dammit, but it'll have to be a swift one.' Petroc flicked the landlord a twitch of a smile, clearly delighted by his own decisive change of heart. 'I'm on a bit of a mission. Trying to find Alf Curtis actually. I've been bangin' on his door with no response at all.'

Greg took the tab off the tonic can, popped a slice of lemon on top of the gin and put the glass in front of his agitated customer.

'He's not been in here tonight, Captain.' He turned to look down the length of the bar, where Robert was deep in conversation with Sadie, and raised his voice. 'Robert, do you know where Alf is?'

Robert looked up. 'Who?'

'Alf.'

Robert frowned and then had a quiet word with Sadie, before coming over to Petroc's end of the counter.

'Alf? Didn't he contact you this afternoon, Petroc?'

'No.' Petroc took a large gulp of his G&T. 'In the circumstances I wish he had.'

'Well, I know he intended to. At least that's what he told me when he left the lookout.'

The Captain plonked the glass down on the bar and exhaled hugely from his barrel chest. 'I expect the entire village knows more about what went on this morning than I do, but from what I've heard it was not handled in a very professional manner. I would have thought . . .'

Robert seized Petroc by the elbow, gave Greg a meaningful look and then guided the Captain away from the bar. Petroc had the presence of mind to grab his glass before moving across the room to an empty table by the window. They sat down and Robert began to explain his version of what had occurred earlier and also what he understood to be Alf's reasons for acting as he did. This little conference had not gone unnoticed and the hum of conversation in both bars seemed suddenly to change gear as a result.

At the end of it, Petroc drained his glass, stood up and announced loudly enough for everyone to overhear, 'Well, I'll try his house again. Maybe throw a rock through the window this time.'

'Try painting his doorstep red while you're at it,' came a voice from the public end and amidst general laughter it added, 'that ought to bring him running.'

Petroc frowned and cast a disapproving eye in the direction of the unwanted comment. His face already pink seemed to go a shade darker. In spite of all his years out of the Navy he still found insubordination hard to take: there had been a serious breach of the rules and it was not a matter to be taken lightly, even by some tipsy lout in the Lugger. With the merriment ringing in his ears he marched out of the pub and on down Fore Street to the bookshop.

This time, seeing a light on in a back room, he went through Alf's side gate and banged on the door. Through the frosted glass he could see movement and then after a few seconds Alf's silhouette loomed ghost-like from within the kitchen. There was a click of the lock and the door swung open.

Alf still had on his dark uniform trousers, but he had changed his shirt for a loose fitting T-shirt bearing the image of a blonde woman in the act of swallowing a microphone: or so it seemed to Petroc. Apart from that he wore only carpet slippers with broken down backs.

'Come in Petroc,' Alf stood back and Petroc caught the sickly sweet aroma of whisky as he stepped into the kitchen. 'I intended to speak to you earlier, but after all the excitement I just zonked out in the chair. Only woke half an hour ago. Some bugger banging on the door.'

'That was me.' Petroc's face still held its look of general disapproval.

'Oh. Anyway, come on upstairs, it's more comfortable there.' He paused with one foot on the stair. 'Would you like a G&T, by the way?'

'No, Alf, this is not a social call.'

'Oh, shame, I'm having a whisky. Sure you won't change your mind?' Alf went over to a cupboard in the kitchen, his face holding a whimsically expectant expression.

'Ah, well, if you are, maybe a small one,' Petroc said as if to refuse might cause offence, but at the same time attempting to retain his officious demeanour. Alf, with his back to the captain, grinned as he removed the cap from the Gordon's: *round one to me.*

He plopped some ice into the glasses, put them on a tray and trudged upstairs, with Petroc in his wake.

'I don't think you've been up here before, have you?' When they entered the room Alf waved a free hand at one of the less comfortable chairs and Petroc stared critically at the cushion before lowering his broad beam gently onto it. Alf handed him the drink and then settled himself in the other chair.

'Good health.' Alf raised his glass, but did not drink. 'Now, Petroc, I don't know what you've heard about this morning, but I do know that you are due a full explanation.'

'Robert gave me the outline of it in the . . . er . . . a short while ago, but obviously I need to hear your version.' He took a quick sip. 'You know that this will have to go up to the Regional Manager?'

'Only if you wish it to, old boy,' Alf said smoothly over the top of his glass.

'No, that's where you're quite wrong, Alf. Dammit, the rescue services were called out, the RN helicopter, the coastguard, so it's naïve to think that the RM won't know what's gone on down at Pengarth.' Petroc ran stubby fingers through his thinning sandy-white hair. 'Make no mistake, we'll be under the grill after this little incident, so I'll need every detail of your story.'

'My report's already in the log, but I'm going to draft a longer version for you tomorrow. And the formal station incident report will also be with you shortly.' Alf winced. 'Oh, and I nearly forgot, so will the bloody Health and Safety accident report.'

Petroc looked at him for a while without saying anything. He knew how to deal with insubordination from lower ranks, how to hold his own with peers and how to swallow his pride and be diplomatic with superiors, but here was a different situation. Alf Curtis fell into none of those categories. Curtis had never been a serviceman, but he was an intelligent mature individual, a bit of a maverick, as well as being Chairman of the Parish Council. Also, the NCI, with all its rules and regulations, was a volunteer organisation and he could not afford to lose any members through disaffection. Continuing to stare at Alf, he bought some time by taking another swig.

A spring was attempting to penetrate his left buttock and he adjusted his posture in the uncomfortable chair.

'I know you'll do all that, Alf, but I would still like to have your own unexpurgated verbal version.' Petroc, turning the glass thoughtfully in his hand, had settled on a conciliatory approach.

'The no-holds barred, unofficial version, eh?'

'Yes.'

Alf stroked his beard and looked out of the window. From that angle he did not have a view of the sea, but he did have a clear picture of the lookout and, at that moment, even of the seagull perched on its flagpole. At least, it would be a clear picture if the windows were cleaner. But then the sun *was* setting. He made a mental note to deal with them tomorrow as well: *Dreckly*, as the Cornish say.

So, the swivel-eyed old salt wanted an unofficial, unexpurgated version of what he had done up there that afternoon. He turned back to focus on the captain.

'Alright, Petroc, I'll tell you honestly and off the record.' He paused to glance out of the window again. 'I took the action I did because it seemed to be appropriate for the situation and that's the simple unglossed truth of the matter. Call it instinct, if you like.'

Petroc started to speak, but Alf held up his hand.

'It would have been easy to follow the regulations and stay in the lookout, by the telephone, as the written instructions dictate. I know that a watchkeeper is no use to the coastguard if he can't be contacted during a rescue operation. I know all the rules, so there's no point in you, or the Regional Manager, haranguing me with them. But, I also know that if I had done what those rules said I should do, the helicopter would have been too late and the woman – Mrs Fischer – would have been smashed like a rag doll on the rocks by the time it had arrived. I knew that when I contacted Falmouth and I know it now.'

'You can't have known for certain.' Petroc's brow knitted above his florid features and Alf was reminded fleetingly of a wrinkled tomato. In other circumstances he would have felt like laughing, but now was inappropriate. Right now he was rapidly becoming pissed off.

'It's called judgment, Captain. Judgment, based on instinct.' Alf put down his empty glass and clenched the arms of his chair. 'Rules and regulations are fine for purposes of accreditation, but they will always be put to the test in a real live situation.

'In my judgment the ledge on which that woman was precariously balanced would not have held her for the quarter of an hour it took the chopper to arrive. For God's sake man, the downdraft from the blades would probably have dislodged her. I did what I knew to be right to save her life. And what is more, I'd do it again in similar circumstances.'

'And what about your life?'

Alf was not expecting that. For a few moments his mouth remained half open as he struggled for an answer to the question he had not yet asked himself. It had indeed been a frightening experience, but he had not at any stage contemplated his own demise. Nor had he asked himself if he would have done such a foolhardy thing if the victim had not been an attractive woman who had smiled at him only minutes earlier.

'Well,' he began tentatively, 'that wasn't something I considered at the time. As I said, the circumstances demanded immediate action.'

The captain had temporarily taken his wind.

'So we might have lost a watchkeeper and a walker in the same afternoon.' Petroc stared balefully into his empty glass. 'And that is probably what would have happened if Robert hadn't turned up when he did.'

For some reason that he could not analyse or define, that observation touched Alf on a raw nerve and he bridled.

'I'd have got her up, with or without Robert's help. By the time he'd arrived she was secured by the rope! Look, I've told you why I took the action I did and, unless you want to make an inquest of it, Petroc, that's all I have to say.'

'All right, Alf.' Petroc put up both hands as if in a vain attempt to stop a charging bull. 'No inquest, at least not from me. I just need to be prepared for questions from on high. Just in case there are suggestions of disciplinary action.'

Alf drew in his breath sharply, his eyes blazed as he sat upright, glowering at the tomato-headed sea captain. Stress, whisky and now this pompous little prat with the roving eye had all combined to try his fragile patience to the limit. *Disciplinary action! Who the hell did the man think he was, to sit there in his own domain and issue threats?* He took a few deep breaths before replying.

'I think enough has been said for this evening.' Alf could almost hear his own teeth grinding as he spoke. 'If you want me to quit as a watchkeeper, then just say so, Captain, and I'll oblige, but never threaten me with anything such as disciplinary action. I've been around too long for that.'

Both men then stood up as if on an invisible signal and Petroc now found himself staring into Alf's beard from an uncomfortable distance. He coughed in what he hoped was an authoritative manner and stepped around the big man to place his glass on the untidy desk.

He froze for a moment as his eyes fell on the chrome-plated statuette, before coughing again and turning to face an angry Alf Curtis.

'There's no question of me requiring you to resign, Alf, and I am certainly not threatening you with anything. I'm simply trying to pre-empt what position the RM might adopt.'

When Alf simply stared back, Petroc shrugged and turned for the door, pausing with his hand on the knob when he reached it. 'I'm sorry that you've taken it this way, Alf. You really ought to appreciate that as Station Manager I'm merely attempting to gather all of the facts. But,' he paused and coughed again, 'as a friend, I was going to add that your actions, right or wrong, were that of a very brave man.'

He turned swiftly and went down the stairs, while Alf remained staring thunderously at the darkened void of the doorway. A full minute passed before his expression gradually melted into one of self-doubting bemusement.

It was several hours later, on returning from the Lugger in a state of advanced inebriation, that he noticed the green light flashing on his telephone answering machine. He stood over the machine for a while, staring at it and swaying, until finally walking away to his bedroom.

'A brave man, my Captain! A brave man, bollocks.' Alf shouted as he stood over the lavatory bowl, steadying himself on the towel rail, while his urine splashed erratically around the rim. 'What does the Captain know of Alf Curtis, eh? There's not an ounce of bravery in that shitty worthless lump of humanity. There's nothing he's ever finished that he's started and there's nothing he's ever started that's worthwhile.'

He flushed the lavatory and went to throw some water on his face.

'Except once . . .'

As he fumbled with a packet of salts, dropping his tooth mug in the basin, alcoholic tears of self-pity began to mingle with the water on his face.

'Except just once . . . and even then I managed to cock it up.'

Chapter Nine

ROBERT was sitting in the small conservatory just off the Sinclair's drawing room reading the sports news when the call came. He carried on reading, knowing that Binty was in the house and would answer it. No doubt it would be for her anyway.

A minute later she came down the step into the conservatory pointing the portable phone at him like a loaded weapon.

'St Margaret's,' she said as he took the phone from her.

'Oh, Lord.' He looked quizzically at her, but she just shrugged.

'Hello,' He held her gaze as he attempted to fold the newspaper with one hand. 'Robert Sinclair here.'

She watched him as he went through a series of grunts, facial expressions and sympathetic noises.

'Well, thank you, Matron, I appreciate your call . . . yes . . . yes, I'll certainly let him know as soon as I can and I'm sure he'll be there . . . yes . . . goodbye.' He switched the telephone off and looked up at his wife.

'Lydia?' she asked.

'Yes. They tried to contact Alf yesterday, but there was no reply.'

'What's the problem?'

Even as she asked the question she realised the absurdity of it. Lydia herself had been the problem for years. Not her fault, poor thing, but a perpetual burden to Alf nevertheless.

'She's been taken ill. Physically ill, I mean.' He stood up and cast a rueful eye at his cooling cup of coffee. 'I'll have to go round to Alf. I don't understand why they weren't able to get through to him.'

Long before he reached the bookshop he could see that he was not Alf's only visitor that morning. Two men and a woman stood outside talking between themselves and occasionally knocking on the door. As he approached, he recognised one of the men, even though this time he was wearing a pale linen jacket.

'Aha, the man from the *Western Packet!* I'm sorry I don't remember your name.'

'Tony Gibbins. And you're Mr Sinclair, aren't you?'

'That's right. Good memory, but then I suppose that goes with the job.' Robert craned his neck to peer up at Alf's office window. 'You and your colleagues not having any luck here?'

'We're not actually colleagues, Mr Sinclair. These two,' Gibbins waved a dismissive hand at them, 'are from the *Guardian*.'

'Goodness, you're out in force, and all for our little village road problem.'

'It's not about the paint this time,' the woman from the *Guardian* said in a surprisingly deep voice. 'It's about the cliff rescue yesterday.'

'Ah!' Robert looked at the second man, who had two cameras slung around his neck. 'You obviously keep tabs on the coastguard activities. Listen in on the VHF transmissions, eh?'

'Mr Sinclair!' Gibbins looked genuinely shocked at the suggestion.

Robert just smiled at him and then wondered what to do next. Alf was obviously keeping his head down, but he did need to talk to him urgently.

'So, no movement from inside then?' He shaded his eyes and tried to see through the gloom of the shop and into the kitchen beyond.

'Not so much as a twitch from the curtains,' the photographer volunteered and Robert guessed that he would be an expert at twitching curtains.

'How long have you been here?' Robert looked at his watch.

'Only about fifteen minutes.'

'Well, it's not yet ten o'clock and I can tell you Mr Curtis is not an early riser. Why don't you go up the hill and knock on Captain Williams' door. He's the NCI station manager and should be able to give you a story. Then if you come back at about eleven you might find this door unlocked.' Robert's guileless expression invited them to accept his suggestion.

'This Captain Williams,' Gibbins began, looking hopefully up Fore Street, 'where exactly does he live?'

'Top of the road, turn left by the post box, carry on up and his house is the one perched on the hill with a veranda overlooking the sea.'

'Thanks.' The *Guardian* reporter seized her photographer by the elbow and they set off, while Gibbins hesitated. He was about to say something more, but changed his mind, turned and hurried after the other two. Robert grinned and then slipped through the side gate.

'Come along, Alf, open up,' Robert shouted through the letter-box. 'They've gone and I have something important to tell you.'

It took another session of banging and shouting before eventually the key turned and the back door eased open. Robert stepped into the kitchen.

'My God, you look awful,' Robert exclaimed to the red-eyed being before him.

'What, worse than usual?' Alf shuffled over to the sink and ran some water into the kettle.

'Yes, far worse than usual.' Robert turned on the ceiling light and Alf flinched. 'The trouble is that you're now going to have to sober up faster than usual.'

'Why? To talk to the carrion crows outside?' Alf rubbed his eyes with the heel of his hands and then sat down heavily.

'No, not them, they can wait. I've sent them off to see Petroc.'

'What?' Alf suddenly came alive. 'That buffoon will blacken my name!'

'Don't worry, they'll get your side of the story before they go to press on Thursday. Now listen, this is far more important.' He waited to make sure that Alf was concentrating. 'Less than an hour ago I had a call from St Margaret's.'

Alf stopped and stared at him. 'Lydia?'

'Yes. They tried to contact you yesterday, but you were either out or refused to answer.'

Alf frowned at a vague recollection of seeing the flashing light. 'Too pissed more like,' he mumbled.

'Whatever the reason, it doesn't matter now. What is important is that Lydia's been taken ill . . . I mean physically ill . . . and she's quite poorly.'

'Christ, what sort of ill?'

'I don't know the details, old man - I'm just passing on the message. Matron thinks it would be a good idea for you to get up there as soon as possible.'

'Yes, of course. I'll give her a ring right away.' But he didn't make a move.

The kettle began to boil. Alf looked at it vaguely, rose slowly and then began to go through the motions of making coffee. 'So no details . . . Bugger . . . I have a bad feeling about this, Robert.'

Robert looked at his back, but said nothing. However well one knows a person, there are times when words are superfluous: an intrusion. There was a long silence between them, broken only by the sound of a spoon clinking against china.

Alf finished stirring and placed the mugs on the table.

'Would you like to come?' He sat down again and cast Robert a pleading look through tortured eyeballs. 'She's your cousin, after all.'

'No, Alf, there'd be no point. She wouldn't even know me.' He stared down into the dark steaming liquid. 'But, I'm prepared to keep you company on the journey if you want . . . or perhaps drive you there . . . if you're not up to it.'

'No, I'll be alright, I suppose.' The mug disappeared into two large hands and he blew into the steam. Then the glimmer of a twinkle appeared as the corner of his eyes creased. 'On the positive side I could give the press the slip for a day or two.'

'Yes, you would, but I thought you wanted them to hear your side of the story.'

Alf waved a dismissive hand. 'That's not important now. Anyway, I'll be back before the story goes to bed and then I'll be able to check what old tomato-head's told them.'

'Tomato-head!' Robert's shoulders gave a lurch and he spilled some coffee on the table. 'I've not heard that one before.'

'That's how he struck me when he came here last night to read me my rights.'

'Did he now? You know he was looking for you in the Lugger?'

'No I didn't, but it's nothing to worry about. I think we both know where we stand now.' Alf took a few sips of coffee and then got up and eased his back. 'I'll go and make that call now. Do you want to hang on?'

'No. You can tell me about it when you get back.' Robert also rose, made for the back door and then paused with a hand on the knob. 'Oh, you'd better be off before eleven. That's when I told the press you'd be up.'

'Thanks for the tip.' Alf grinned back at him. 'I'll be gone before then.'

'Are you sure you'll be fit to drive?'

'Yes, my old flower, I've had worse hangovers.'

'Well, good luck. And I hope it's not as bad as it sounds.' Robert grinned encouragingly and then slipped out of the door, relieved that his friend was beginning to look slightly more human.

Alf wasted no further time in calling St Margaret's, getting the latest report on Lydia and then preparing himself for the journey up country. His head began clearing after a second cup of strong coffee had broken through the fur barrier and it was just after eleven when he slipped out of the back door carrying an overnight bag. He glanced up and down Fore Street before crossing over the road and into the alley that led to his lock-up garage.

He turned his head away as he drove past the press corps, who were making their way purposefully down the hill, and accelerated out of the village after passing over the last of the traffic impediments. The red paint had dulled down over the past few days, but he was pleased to note that attempts to remove it altogether had failed.

Half an hour later he was on the A30 and heading out of Cornwall.

He slotted in a CD in an attempt to subdue unheralded thoughts that kept surging to the surface of his mind. To a certain extent Mahler's Resurrection Symphony achieved that aim, although the finale also threatened to resurrect an anvil at the back of his head. He lowered the window and let the air jet strake his hair for a few miles.

Another symphony, two sets of road works, a brief comfort break and a suicidal pheasant later the Volvo crunched over the gravel drive of St Margaret's and came to a halt beside an Age Concern van.

Alf sat for a while with his eyes shut before he opened the door. By now he had convinced himself that today he would be saying some things for the last time. If Lydia's condition was as bad as they had described, it was likely he would not have another opportunity to empty his conscience to her.

He opened the car door, eased himself out and stretched. When he turned towards the dark red brick building with its mullioned windows and fussy gables, Matron was standing on the top step, waiting for him. She must have seen the car from her office window.

He strode across the gravel to greet her.

'Matron, good afternoon to you.'

'Mr Curtis.' The small woman took his hand and smiled in a way that conveyed understanding and yet authority at the same time. 'What a long journey for you.'

Alf followed her in, smiling also, because she always said that. She led him into her office and gestured towards a chair.

'Would you like some coffee, or tea?'

'No thank you. Perhaps a glass of water a little later.' Alf gave the room a quick appraisal while she shuffled a few papers on her desk. He was studying a print of Vermeer's pearl-eared girl above her head when she spoke again.

'Lydia has pneumonia.' She folded her hands on top of the papers and her clear grey eyes held his over the top of her spectacles. 'Two nights ago, when it was pouring with rain, she left her bed and wandered into the garden and it was a few hours before anyone noticed that she had gone. In fact it might have been longer had not one of the staff gone into her room after another patient had caused a disturbance. We alerted the night staff and anyone else we could find and scoured the house and grounds for nearly an hour before we found her.'

She looked down at her hands and her eyes closed for a few seconds. Alf, whose brow by now had creased into furrowed rows, opened his mouth slightly as if to speak, but she was talking again.

'She was dancing in the mud along the side of the duck pond, soaked through and quite delirious.'

'Doing what?' Alf practically whispered. 'I mean . . . how did she get outside?'

'This isn't a prison, Mr Curtis,' her voice seemed to hold a note of regret. 'We watch them all during the day and at night their windows are barred, but the doors are not locked. They'd have to get out in a hurry if there's a fire, you see? So, if one of them decides to get out and is resourceful enough, it can be done. It's rare, but it can be done.'

'I see.' Alf smoothed his beard thoughtfully with both hands. 'So, is she in hospital now?'

'Normally she would be, but we are equipped with oxygen and other necessary equipment, so we've kept her here. The doctor's attended to her, of course, and she has a room on her own. She's as comfortable as can be expected.'

'But, the pneumonia . . .'

'It's a severe case.' She removed her glasses and began wiping the lenses.

'How bad?' He thrust the question at her and she blinked, taking a few moments to reply.

'In a younger person and one who has the will to fight it there would be an excellent chance of a full recovery. Your wife has been in here for a very long time and her body has become institutionalised, thus reducing its ability to fight back. Also,' she added softly, 'as we both know, her rational mind went a very long while ago. All in all, not a good recipe for strong resistance, Mr Curtis.'

'No, I suppose not.' Alf's mouth was dry, but the hands that gripped the plastic arms of his chair were clammy with perspiration. He felt the old helplessness overwhelming him again and he wanted to be somewhere else, far away from this establishment. Suddenly, spontaneously and harshly he demanded, 'So you don't expect her to live much longer? Is that what you're saying?'

'In the circumstances, I . . . would be surprised . . . if she recovered.' Her last word trailed away as she lowered her head.

'I'd like to see her, please.' He stood up quickly, as if every minute counted, and she followed suit, more sedately.

'Of course. Come with me.'

They went out into the corridor and Alf trailed after the Matron. He paused to glance into the communal room where he had often held his meetings with Lydia and had conducted one-sided conversations about matters of little or no consequence. Invariably there had been an audience.

She would rock gently, staring but seeing nothing out of the window, while he told her anything that came into his head. Occasionally, very occasionally, she would stop rocking and turn to him with a radiant smile and an expression of infinite wisdom and understanding and for a moment he liked to believe that she knew him. And all the while the other inmates carried on with their meaningless existence; watching television, trying to do jigsaw puzzles, knitting shapeless objects that no one would ever wear or just staring at the lines on their hands.

On every visit he lived with the hope that his Lydia would suddenly escape from her secret world and show that she was not one of these zombies, but it never happened, not once. And now, it probably never would.

Matron was waiting for him at the end of the corridor, so he moved on after her.

The room was small, with a single bed, two straight-backed chairs and a bedside table littered with medical detritus. Lydia was lying on her back in the bed, slightly raised and with an oxygen mask attached to her face. Her hair, which now appeared greyer than he remembered, was fanned out on the pillow and her bare arms lay outside the blanket. Her chest rose and fell in gasps as if being pumped by an external force, but at least her breathing seemed to be regular.

He noticed that the veins on her thin hands were very blue. In fact much of what he could see of her appeared to be blue. He turned to look enquiringly at the Matron.

'You can stay as long as you like.' She touched his arm and turned to leave.

'Thank you. Oh, might I have that glass of water now?'

She smiled. 'Of course, I'll send it along.'

The door closed softly and he was alone with Lydia.

He stood looking down at her for a long time, trying to see her through someone else's eyes. Whose eyes? It could have been a young man of twenty-five, not long graduated from university, enthusiastic, handsome, keen for adventure and feeling that the world was waiting for him to arrive. Was it such a man? Or was it a misanthropic and cramped individual, who suffered from unfulfilled ambitions and half remembered dreams? Or again, was it simply the person she had always wanted him to be, before her imperfect mind finally lost a grip on reality?

My God, Lydi, he thought, *I tried and I still try. There were so many times that you had good reason to loathe me, to say that I had let you down, or that I had changed from being the man you'd married. No, I didn't change, my dear, I've always been a selfish bastard. It's just that for a while I tried to be someone else and for a while I succeeded and we were almost happy.*

But, deep down within me the restless serpent of distraction kept hissing its siren message, there is another way, there is something better, seize it before it's too late. But since you left me for your other world, I've paid the price. No one knows, but I pay every day . . . in the darkness of my room . . . when I stand over you like this . . . even when I try to forget through the futile railings of my drunken buffoonery.

He pulled a chair up to the side of her bed and sat down.

So, is this to be the end? After all these years will this now be your release? My release? He reached out slowly and rested his hand gently on the pale, almost translucent, skin of her forearm.

'I'm sorry Lydi, I didn't have time to tell Catherine,' he murmured close to her ear. 'In fact I haven't heard from her since Christmas and I'm not a great letter writer myself, so I'm not even sure that she's at the same address in Sydney. What went wrong there, I wonder? I did my best to be a good father. She was always closer to you, but that's true of any mother and daughter, isn't it? I was working so much of the time . . . I know . . . and spending unnecessary time away from home . . . but I provided for her and we gave her a top class education and a great wedding.'

He paused to look out of the window.

'No, I know that's not all it takes . . . you don't have to remind me.'

He looked back at her and cocked his head, but the sound of her shallow breathing had not changed its rhythm. For some terrible reason he almost wished it would. A voice whispered deep inside his head, *please either get stronger or stop altogether.*

'I'll write to her, no phone her, as soon as I get back. It's not right that she shouldn't know.' He smiled suddenly at the recollection of the photograph. 'Did I tell you that we have another grandchild? A boy, Gareth, named after your father. He was born last November and they sent me a photo. Hell, I must have told you that before. I would have brought the photo, but . . . oh God, you're so cold, Lydi.'

It was many years since he had called her *darling* and in any event he had always regarded that as a superficial endearment. Friends of theirs had continued calling each other *darling* right up to the week before their divorce. Now he had no one to call by that overused epithet, even if he had wanted to.

He stared at Lydia's immobile face. He had loved her in his own fashion, but perhaps she had just never been the sort of person one calls *darling*. No, Lydia had come uninvited from the shadows, when he had been vulnerable and unprepared for her love and then life had just moved along from there.

'It's no good having regrets at this stage, Lydi, I know that, but you deserved better with your life. *I* could have made it better, if I'd been less self-centred, or perhaps if we'd had another child. But then you probably would have . . .'

The door made a small squeak as it opened and Alf looked over his shoulder. A slim young woman wearing an apron over her dress held out a glass of water.

'Sorry it's been so long.' Her face creased into a dimpled smile.

'Thank you.' He took the glass, but did not rise. The girl glanced at Lydia and then backed towards the door, still holding the smile.

He stared at Lydia again for a long time without speaking and then, very slowly, moved his hand away from her arm, extended his forefinger and lifted a loose lock of hair from her cheek. Even then, he hoped to be surprised by some kind of a reaction, but nothing changed: only the sun's rays had shifted and they now glinted off the oxygen apparatus above her head.

'Oh, Lydia, I never did tell you the full story, did I? But maybe that was at the root of all our differences from the beginning. Maybe that . . .' He grunted and a sardonic grimace played on his lips. 'No, it's all too late for that now, my flower. Far too late. Just try to accept that I did my feeble best to be a decent husband to you, riddled with flaws as I am. There was always something just out of reach, wasn't there? Our marriage was always a notch or two short of the perfection that I was looking for . . . but that was never your fault, Lydi. It was mine.'

He fingered his beard distractedly and raised his eyes to the window. How long should he stay? If this were to be the last time, what else should his final words be to the mother of his child, his wife of thirty years? Certainly nothing portentous: Lydia had always been a straightforward sort of person, scornful of frills or embellishments.

So, after staring at her frozen face for a while longer, he decided to make his farewell monologue conversational, as if he were coming back tomorrow for another chat. That way seemed to him to be appropriate and kindly.

'Something out of the ordinary happened at the watch yesterday,' he began and glanced down at the plaster on his hand. 'My God, yes, it was only yesterday. A woman went over the cliff and I did a daft thing for an old bugger. I slung a rope over and hauled her up. Robert helped me on the last bit . . . by the way, he sends his love . . . and she . . . the woman . . . was carted off in an ambulance. Bit of stink with the coast watch authorities because I broke the rules, but I did the right thing. I know I did.' His eyes narrowed and he leaned closer to her face. 'You do think it was the right thing to do, don't you? No, perhaps not. You never understood most of the things I did and that's a fact. Well, old girl, I did save her life and for a short time I didn't care a toss about mine. How about that, eh?'

His fingers strayed to a loose flap of sheet at the side of the bed and as he fiddled with it, he realised that he suddenly felt emotionally empty. The lack of response and the rhythmic pulse of her forced breathing had combined to suck him dry. There was nothing more to tell her – or that he was prepared to tell her – and it was time to go.

He stopped toying with the sheet, reached out for the water glass and drained it, before pushing himself up from the chair.

His timing was good, because the door opened behind him as he stood looking down at the helpless being on the bed. A nurse slid past him and bent over Lydia and he stepped back to give her more space. The nurse straightened and then turned to him.

'Are you going now, Mr Curtis?' It almost sounded like a request.

He hesitated. To leave now would be final, but to stay would benefit no one: certainly neither himself nor Lydia. But there might be regrets later if he left her now.

Alf swallowed hard, looked past the nurse at the pale inert figure of his wife and nodded.

'I'm going,' he said hoarsely, followed by a whispered, 'Bye, Lydia. I'll see you tomorrow.'

He left the room. The door closed behind him and he leant against the wall with his eyes closed. He was still there when the girl came out into the corridor a few minutes later.

'Are you alright, Mr Curtis?'

He opened his eyes and forced a smile. *My wife's dying in there, so yes, of course I'm bloody all right,* he thought, but he said, 'Yes, I'm okay, but I'd like to see Matron before I go.'

'I'll take you to her.'

He followed.

Matron was in the staff common room, but came out the moment she heard Alf was waiting.

'I'll be off now, Matron,' he managed to say it in a matter-of-fact way with little hint of pent-up emotion. 'I'm booking into the Golden Lion in town for the night, but I'll be here again at about nine tomorrow. I wonder, if anything happens in the night, would you . . . ?'

'Of course, I'll let you know.' She hesitated. 'Er, does the Golden Lion have extension lines to individual rooms?'

'No, you're right, probably not.' He reached into a pocket for a bookshop business card. 'My mobile number is there. I'll leave it on.'

She took the card and they parted.

Alf had a solitary meal in the town's only hotel and then spent an hour drinking whisky sodas at the small bar beside the lounge. For some of the time he had to suffer the monologue of a salesman from Leeds, who had a mission in life to convert everyone to solar panel home heating. Fortunately for Alf he was not required to contribute anything other than shake or nod the head at appropriate times.

Eventually, after the man slipped him his business card (Polar To Solar Limited – *Save with the Sun*) the salesman apologised for having to deprive Alf and the barman of his company and went upstairs. Alf caught the barman's eye and wordlessly pushed his glass across for a refill.

The mobile did not ring during the night, but his alarm went off at half past seven. He slid out from under the duvet and sat for a few minutes on the edge of the bed, exercising his toes on the carpet and staring in an unfocused way at a Monet print on the far wall. He had not slept soundly and now he just yearned to get back to his own little shed in Cornwall.

A hot shower and full English breakfast improved his mood to somewhere slightly below par and at a quarter to nine he was settling the bill at the reception desk. The Volvo took a few turns of the key to fire into action and he thought about checking the battery back home. It would prove to be another abortive mental note.

He parked the car on the familiar gravel drive and sat for a while listening to the news headlines whilst studying the grotesque shape of a lightning-blasted cedar. Anything to postpone what he now regarded as the inevitable.

Matron was not at the front door when he went up the steps, but there was no reason for her to be. She was a busy woman with dozens of deserving cases to attend to, plus a business to administer.

He stood in the middle of the entrance hall, looking about and wondering where to go next. On other occasions, when no one had met him, he had gone directly to the patients' commonroom to see Lydia.

He was about to set off for her room when he saw someone coming along the corridor towards him with a purposeful air about her. Alf recognised the rounded figure and moon face of the Matron's deputy, Angela Swift.

'Good morning, Mr Curtis,' the woman said without smiling.

Alf did not return the greeting, but stared at her bleakly for a few moments before stating bluntly, 'She didn't last the night, did she?'

'Well, actually she did,' she said as if announcing a great feat of endurance. 'But not much longer than that, I'm afraid.'

She rested a chubby hand on Alf's arm. 'Your wife obviously had a very strong heart, but sadly she lost her fight about a couple of hours ago.'

They were still standing in the middle of the hall. Alf lowered his head and Miss Swift raised her hand to his shoulder as if to steady him.

'However much you're prepared . . .' he murmured into his beard.

'I know. Please, come and sit down in Matron's office and I'll bring you a cup of tea.'

Alf allowed himself to be guided down the corridor and then be seated in an armchair by the window. He looked up at the sympathetic moon face.

'Matron's not here?' he asked.

'No, she's been called away this morning I'm afraid, so I'll deal with what's necessary.' She hesitated and then fiddled with something on the desk before turning back to him. 'Do you want to see her . . . Mrs Curtis, I mean?'

'No.' Alf forced a lop-sided smile. 'We said goodbye yesterday.'

'I see. Well, I'll be back with a cup of tea in a few minutes.'

She rustled out of the room and pulled the door closed behind her.

Alf sat very still for a while and then tipped his head slowly back, opened his mouth and drew in a long despairing breath. It was over. For both of them the long agony was over.

After she returned with the tea Miss Swift was very quick and efficient, having already been fully briefed by Matron. St. Margaret's final account had already been prepared and there was a form to sign as next of kin. Alf confirmed that he did not want to see Lydia's body and then they talked for a while about the funeral arrangements.

Lydia had not left a will – she had no material possessions to leave – but Alf knew she preferred cremation. She used to say that she feared being sealed alive in a box and then waking up underground. So cremation it was to be and Angela Swift gave Alf the names of two undertakers in the district.

Then, at the end of the formalities, she reached below Matron's desk and lifted up a cardboard box, about the right capacity to hold a pair of size twelve shoes.

'These are all of her personal bits and pieces that we could find. They're mainly letters and photographs, I think.' She seemed apologetic, as if it were her fault that Lydia had left the world with so little.

'Thank you.' Alf dragged the box across the desk. 'Now, about her clothes . . .'

'There aren't many of those either.'

'What do you usually do? They're no use to me.'

'Charity, or we could use some for our own patients, if they're in good repair.'

'That would be fine. Would you mind if I left that to St Margaret's?'

She nodded and two deep lines creased her dumpling cheeks. 'Of course not.'

'So that's all then?' He was about to stand up when a thought struck him. 'Will there have to be an inquest? I mean, in the circumstances . . . ?'

'I don't think so, as she was under regular medical supervision. Unless of course anyone wants to lodge a formal complaint against St Margaret's?' A slight frown appeared below her fringe as she said it. 'In which case there might have to be a disciplinary investigation.'

'Well, there won't be any complaint from me.' He rose decisively and picked up the box. 'You and the staff of St Margaret's have looked after Lydia for many years and I know you couldn't have done more for her health and comfort.'

'Thank you, Mr Curtis.' The frown disappeared and she also stood up. 'The certificate will be prepared after the doctor has formally certified cause of death. He should be here any time now, if you would like to . . .'

'No, I'll be on my way now.' He turned to open the door, keen to be out of the place. 'I'll let you know about the funeral arrangements as soon as we're sure there'll be no complications.'

'I'm certain there won't be any.'

Unlike Matron, she didn't stand at the entrance to watch him go. Alf reversed the Volvo with rather a heavy foot on the accelerator and gravel clattered against the wheel arches. He grated into first gear and the car went off with a lurch and a further spray of gravel from behind. It was not going to be a co-ordinated sort of a day. But then, he thought, his was not always a co-ordinated sort of a life.

A light Cornish mizzle greeted him as he crossed the Tamar. It was a welcome if not happy return to his adoptive county, but his mood lifted as he approached the bleak and barren beauty of Bodmin Moor. Another thirty miles to home: to the magnificent claustrophobic cocoon that was Pengarth.

Pengarth's was a modest unassuming community, but the village offered him the mundane certainty of a life without the emotional crevices that could so easily upset the equilibrium of his daily existence. He could handle the humdrum wrinkles of parochial co-habitation that occasionally disturbed the ozone-soaked tranquillity, but anything beyond that tended to raise the stress levels above the acceptable. And the avoidance of stress was his reason for living where he did.

Alf drove unnoticed into the village in mid afternoon, put the car into the garage and then reached for his suitcase and the cardboard box. Hoping to make it to his house without being observed, he used the alleyway and hugged the wall along Fore Street until he was opposite the bookshop. Young Mike, carrying a ladder and a bucket hailed him as he crossed the road: no one goes undetected for long in Pengarth. He shouted a greeting to the decorator as he put the case down and fumbled for his keys.

Inside the house he left the case at the back of the shop and went to the kitchen. He dropped the box on the table and then turned on the ceiling light. The back of the house usually benefited from the evening sun, but today it was overcast with intermittent rain and the interior held an aura of gloom.

Not having eaten on the way back, he now felt a gnawing in the cavities of his stomach and he went to the fridge to pull out a large pasty. He set the microwave, then went upstairs to check his office and found his answering machine flashing.

It was a terse message from Captain Petroc Williams.

'Alf, this is just to let you know that I've had a discussion with the Regional Manager and I expect you'll be relieved to hear he's decided not to pursue the matter any further.' A pause. *'On the other hand, perhaps you couldn't care a damn either way.'* Cough. *'Anyway, just thought I'd let you know. Goodbye.'*

'Well, that *is* a weight off my mind, dear old Tomato Head.' He deleted the message.

There were no other messages and the microwave was pinging, so he went down again. He dropped the hot pasty on a plate by the box and scuffed over to the far side of the kitchen to pour a large whisky. *What the hell, it was getting on for five o'clock.*

The shoebox was still unopened on the kitchen table the next day. Alf had prowled around it like a suspicious dog every time he went into the kitchen, but he had decided not to touch it for a full day after returning home. It was as if it were still too hot to handle, or it was disrespectful of Lydia's memory to delve into its contents when she was less than a day dead. Something inexplicable like that.

In any event he had stayed indoors all day, mostly working in his office, not answering the telephone and ignoring knocks on the door. It was not until early evening that he finally sat at the table and slit the string that secured the box lid.

Then for the next two hours he pored over the contents of the box, sorting, discarding, brooding and sometimes pausing to reminisce.

He had decided to mark the back of every identifiable photograph with a brief narrative and to send Catherine any that might be of nostalgic interest, perhaps keep a few for himself and then throw the rest away. He would then be completely ruthless with the paraphernalia; the old theatre programmes, wedding invitations, restaurant menus and the like. Why she had hoarded so many of those he had no idea and now he was not even interested as to whether or not they even belonged to her. They would go. And so would the few trinkets of cheap jewellery.

Then, finally, there were the letters. He decided to look at these in greater detail, because there might just be something of Lydia's happier past that Catherine would cherish and perhaps pass on to her own children. Alf tended to disclaim any latent sentimentality in his nature, but he did admit to an element of romanticism under the crust, vehemently denying that the two were the same emotion. Yes, he would review the letters with care.

They were in haphazard order and the dates varied widely. Some were from him and those were mostly sent long after she had forgotten the name of the sender and certainly after she had ceased to remember him as being her husband. Although fully conscious of that fact he had nevertheless felt the compulsion to keep on trying. To stop writing would have signalled a final defeat, a severance, a coward's way out. It was a masochistic duty that he had set himself and to which he had adhered all the way through to the very end.

After re-reading the one in which he had told her about their first grandchild he pushed his chair back noisily and went to pour another whisky.

The telephone began warbling before he sat down again, but he let it ring.

He gulped some whisky and then took up a couple more letters. These were short ones in an unformed hand from the grandchild he had never seen and as he read them he felt a tightening in his throat.

Then, as he picked up another letter, a narrow slip of paper dropped out and fluttered onto the table. It was a four-line verse in her hand, which read,

> *The evil lurks in all of us,*
> *the beastly demon's rage.*
> *We fear the key that turns the lock*
> *And lets it from its cage.*

He read it again and then closed his eyes in an attempt to search into Lydia's head.

Was this piece of doggerel her own composition? Was she trying to express something she had foreseen? Might she have known what was happening to her? And, if so, what would that have done to an already disintegrating mind?

With a sudden movement he screwed up the paper and threw it across the room. *It didn't matter now! It simply didn't matter!*

Alf gulped at his drink again and returned to the diminishing pile. There were some letters from abroad, a few from her mother, some from people he did not know and even a couple she had started and abandoned about fifteen years earlier. One of those was to Santa Claus.

He shook his head.

141

Then, unexpectedly, just as the telephone began ringing again soon after seven, he came across a sealed envelope. There was no address on the front, just the initials BC written across it in pencil.

He looked at the envelope for a long while, irrationally nervous at what he might find inside. All the other letters had been opened and many were crumpled. This one was in pristine condition, as if ready for posting, but missing a stamp and an address.

The telephone eventually went silent.

Alf turned the envelope over and over, held it up to the light and even sniffed at it. There was a faint odour of a perfume she used to wear. He reached across the table and picked up a paper knife, inserted it cautiously and then paused. Turning the envelope over again he adjusted his glasses and examined the BC once more. It was printed, but he was certain it was her hand, because of the flourish on the letter C.

With a quick jerk he slit the envelope.

There was a single A4 sheet inside, folded twice. He opened it up, turned it over first and looked at the signature at the end. *With all my love, Lydia.* Turning back to the beginning, he noted the date. Nearly sixteen years ago.

He turned to the script.

When he saw the addressee's name at the top he gave an involuntary gasp and raked a hand through his hair, while the letter trembled in the other hand.

Then he began slowly to read the letter and as he did so he felt his nerve ends going numb, as if they were being subjected to an all-enveloping deep freeze. He was being drawn into a weird state of shock, a condition brought on partly by what he was reading, but also by the uncanny sensation that the writer was watching him. He even imagined he could hear her voice, just as if she were reading it aloud.

Alf reached the end, drained the glass and then forced himself to read it again.

It seemed that the letter had been written by a woman who was almost hysterically aware of her reason slipping away. But she was one who also needed desperately to divulge everything from the heart, before the door closed permanently on her sanity.

And yet, in spite of the impression of urgency in every sentence, it was clear that Lydia had never had the courage to deliver the letter. So, it had remained for all those years in limbo, in a time warp, its despairing cry entombed in a sealed envelope and hidden in a shoebox.

Lydia's letter had in effect become a mummified soliloquy of despair.

But if the letter's tortured contents were not sufficiently heart-rending, it was the first three words that polarised Alf's attention, constricting his throat and leaving him practically struggling for breath. Alf read them once, twice and then again for good measure.

When he finally fell onto his bed that night, partially dressed, befuddled and bemused, those three words were still flashing at him in neon lights.

She had started the letter, *My Darling Brendan . . .*

Chapter Ten

'ROBERT, I've decided, I'm going up to Smugglers' Cottage to see Mrs Fischer.' Binty was wearing her determined face. 'Are you coming?'

Robert removed his spectacles and dropped the invoice he was scrutinising onto the kitchen table. He had a desk and a filing system, but he preferred to spread his business papers across the ample pine table, which was a convenience for him and an annoyance for his wife. Now he sat back and scrunched his face as if wrestling with a difficult decision.

'I was rather hoping that Alf might be the first to pay her a visit. She's his rescue after all.'

'Don't be daft, Robert, it's not as if she's someone else's prize. She's not a salvage claim, you know.' She propped herself against the table while pulling on what she called her driving shoes. 'That poor woman's been out of hospital since yesterday and no one's been to see her yet.'

'How do you know?' Robert challenged. 'Do you have your spies up there already?'

He ducked her swipe and chuckled.

'Well, I'm going right now, so make up your mind.'

'Any point in giving Alf a ring, d'you think?' He stood up and looked ruefully at his untidy pile of papers. 'We ought to find out about Lydia, if nothing else. I've been putting off calling him for the past couple of days.'

'It's only ten o'clock. Give him a bit longer.' She grabbed a light plastic raincoat and her car keys. 'Call him when we get back.'

'Ok.' He gave his papers a final glance and then followed her out of the front door.

Like Alf, the Sinclairs owned a garage in the narrow lane that ran parallel with Fore Street and as they passed his lock-up Robert glanced through a crack in the door.

'Well, at least he's back.' Robert looked at Binty and shook his head. 'I wonder what the poor old bugger's been doing.'

Smugglers' Cottage was a mile out of the village, down a farm track off the road to Poltock. Whether or not it had actually been used for smuggling in an earlier era was beyond even village folklore, but it was admirably situated for the purpose. It did not take much imagination to envisage swarthy Cornishmen trudging up the narrow path from the secluded bay below, bearing kegs of rum or sacks of sugar on their shoulders in the black of night. The cottage could have shone a light as a signal without anyone else seeing it and there was even a small cellar for overnight storage. Goods would have been well on their way up country before the customs men were anywhere near the place – unless of course they were lying in wait following a tip-off.

Sometime during the latter part of the nineteenth century, the neighbouring farmer had acquired the cottage and for nearly a hundred years agricultural workers had occupied it.

When they were not working the land and struggling to make a living, those folk would have enjoyed one of the finest sea views in the Duchy. Recognising that fact and after reducing the number of his permanent employees, the landowner had sold the cottage and a quarter acre of land in 1965 to a doctor and his wife.

After a few years of contented occupation the doctor unexpectedly ran off with a young Spanish woman he had met by chance whilst picking mushrooms in an adjacent field. Their relationship had been nurtured over glasses of cold cider in various pubs during the summer of 1971 and his wife had had no inkling of what was going on. After he debunked she never saw her husband again and no one in the area ever knew for certain whether or not they had subsequently divorced, but she had remained on at Smugglers' Cottage.

What the locals did know was that poor jilted Mrs Crabtree locked herself away from the world from the day the doctor left. People saw less and less of her and those who did commented on her increasing eccentricity. George Harris in his undiplomatic way used to say, 'Old mother Crabtree's marbles are rolling down the cliff one by one.'

So, when the postman reported back to Pengarth that mail had been stopped to Smugglers' Cottage and that it looked shut up, it was assumed that the old lady had died. As few people had spoken to her in recent years, it never occurred to anyone to check on what had happened. Everyone just seemed to be waiting for the inevitable For Sale sign to go up, followed by another Four-by-Four bearing a family from east of the Tamar.

Now there was a new unexpected mystery. A woman with a foreign accent, who Alf Curtis had pulled from off the cliff edge, had moved in.

The Sinclair's small green estate car bumped along the rutted track, avoiding the worst of the potholes and the most mountainous of the cowpats.

'Perhaps we should have rung first,' Robert said as the breath was punched out of him by a particularly severe hole.

'I don't suppose the telephone's been reconnected yet.' Binty swerved as a pheasant ran across the lane. 'We don't know how long she's been in, or how long she intends to stay.'

'We don't even know what she's doing there at all, my love.' He smiled at her. 'And that's the real reason why we're going, isn't it?'

'Oh, Robert!' She cast him a sidelong glance. 'How uncharitable.'

The tall Cornish hedge suddenly revealed a gap and at the end of a short drive they saw a blue car parked outside the cottage door. Binty pulled up behind it, switched off the engine and turned to him with a sudden thought.

'You weren't planning a job for this morning, were you?'

'If that's a question rather than a statement, the answer's no. I'm trying to finish off the Trebell's cottage later this week, but today was to have been paperwork.' He looked pointedly at her. '*Was* to have been.'

'Well, you should have said . . .'

'Oh, come on, we're here now.' He opened the car door.

They walked across the weed-infested gravel and then stood self-consciously at the cottage door. Robert was searching for a knocker or bell push when suddenly it opened and Rowena Fischer appeared behind an enquiring smile.

Robert's recollection of her was of a woman in distress, with torn clothes and barely conscious. In those circumstances her features had made little impression on him, so it came as a surprise now to see a handsome woman with immaculately groomed dark shoulder-length hair, lightly streaked with grey, a white cotton blouse and knee-length navy skirt. On one foot she wore a flat-heeled suede shoe and on the other a sock, which covered the lower part of a plaster cast. Her face had the pallor of city dwelling, but was remarkably unlined for her age and her bluish grey eyes exuded intelligence and a hint of humour.

It was Binty who stepped forward and held out her hand.

'Hello, I'm Binty Sinclair. I'm sorry to disturb you unannounced, but we couldn't find a phone number.' They shook hands. 'Oh, and this is my husband, Robert.'

'Ah, my rescuer.' Her smile broadened as she greeted him. 'I'm Rowena Fischer, as you probably know already. Please come in.'

'Actually, I'm only a co-rescuer,' Robert said to her back as they went into the cottage and followed her into a bright room with a panoramic sea view. 'Alf Curtis has the right to the title of rescuer.'

'Ah, yes.' She leant on a walking stick and at first did not make any move to sit down. 'I'd like to meet him properly – when it's practical to do so.'

Robert noted that not only was her accent tinged with a European inflection, but also her phraseology was oddly formal and involuntarily he found himself becoming intrigued.

'Um, Alf's going through a bit of a bad time at the moment. Some personal problems. But I'm sure he'll make every effort to come up here soon.'

'I see.' She looked down at her bad leg for a moment and then suddenly seemed to remember they were still standing. 'Oh, please sit down. There aren't many chairs, I'm afraid, but . . .' She waved an arm at the sparse selection of furniture.

Binty caught Robert's eye with a look that sent him a message. It wasn't her place to suggest refreshment in a stranger's house, but as their hostess was incapacitated . . . Robert frowned at her and then turned his attention to the view. Binty opened her mouth to make her offer, but she was too late.

'I feel I owe you an explanation.' Rowena, who was now sitting, stretched the broken leg out gently and then placed her hands demurely on her lap. 'This cottage belonged to my aunt, Dora Crabtree – you probably knew her. She went into a nursing home just before last Christmas, after she became unable to look after herself any longer. She died about two weeks ago and I came over for her funeral. She and my uncle had no children – or, at least, none that survived them – and, to my surprise, I found that she had left me this place in her will. She left my sister most of her other possessions, but for some reason I got the cottage. I arrived in the village last week, after dark.' She paused with a rueful smile. 'I'd not been here for many years, so had to ask a villager the way. He was very helpful, but even then it took me ages to locate the place. Then, of course, it was all locked up and a bit spooky.'

'Not very nice for you,' Binty said sympathetically.

'No, but I managed, even though the electricity was still off at the time. And I did have Bruno for protection.'

'Ah, yes, the dog. Is he yours?' Robert asked.

'I suppose he is now. He belonged to my aunt, but he's been with the Menears since she went into the home. Do you know them?' The Sinclairs nodded. 'Well, then you'll know their farm is adjacent to this cottage . . . my nearest neighbour. Anyway I collected Bruno on the morning of the cliff business. We weren't used to each other I suppose and he was keen to run around. He slipped away from me into the gorse, after a rabbit probably, and rather foolishly I followed.' She shrugged. 'Stupid of me, but my mind was on other things and I had no idea the cliff was so near.'

'You were very lucky. If Alf hadn't been there . . .' Robert let the sentence hang.

'Yes, very lucky indeed. By the way, I hope he's not in any trouble over the helicopter . . . ?'

'No, I'm sure not. There was a bit of a fuss over the fact that he left the lookout, but that seems to have died down. Anyway, Alf can look after himself,' Robert added lightly.

'Good, I'm glad. I don't remember much detail, but I know he was incredibly brave. And he managed to keep me calm.' She smiled again and a dimple appeared in her left cheek. 'Let's hope he isn't sent the bill for the helicopter's outing.'

That produced a short burst of laughter from Robert and a demure chuckle from Binty. Rowena looked from one to the other and seemed surprised at the reaction to her joke. She also seemed to have decided that she liked these people, because, when the mirth had subsided she asked, 'Would you like some coffee, or tea?'

'Oh, no thank you, we only came to see if there's anything we can do for you. Robert works part time – he's a thatcher you know – but I have plenty of time if you need anything from the shops, walk the dog, or any other help at all . . .'

'That's very kind and I might take you up on the offer.' Robert noted regretfully that she did not press the offer of coffee. 'The car's automatic, so I can drive a bit, but Bruno might need a walk when I get him back from the Menears again. Meanwhile, I must hobble around and get this place in a decent living order and have the telephone line restored for a start. My husband will be wanting to contact me and he only has my mobile number.'

She must have noticed Robert's eyebrows rise, because she added, 'Yes, I do have a husband. He's a banker and our home is currently in Geneva. Although he's French we've lived in many European countries over the past thirty years. That's probably why I keep being mistaken for a foreigner every time I come back to England. Too much French speaking.'

'That sounds most interesting. Do you have children?' It was a question only a mother could ask and Binty found the response rather surprising.

'Non,' she said quickly and apparently unconsciously in French. 'We never did and maybe they would have been an encumbrance with our lifestyle.'

'Yes, I suppose so. So much moving about . . .'

An awkward silence followed and Robert looked at his watch, while Binty found something to brush off her slacks.

'Anyway,' Rowena continued with slightly forced enthusiasm, 'I'll probably be here for a week or two, until we decide what to do with this place. My husband's in the middle of an important business transaction at the moment, so he won't miss me a great deal, and in any case the hospital says I shouldn't move around too much too soon. They wanted to keep me in for longer because of possible delayed shock, but I discharged myself. I'm not fond of hospitals.'

'I expect they wanted you to sign a disclaimer,' Robert muttered.

'Yes, they did and I was only too happy to oblige.'

'It's to protect themselves you know . . . nothing to do with your best interests.'

'My husband's very cynical sometimes,' Binty added hastily with a half smile and Robert grunted.

'I'm just a realist my dear.' He stood up and then tapped Binty on the shoulder. 'These days you seem to pick up worse diseases in the wards than the one you went in with. Come along Binty, I'm sure Rowena has a lot to do.'

Binty followed his lead and stood up. 'Yes, of course. Well, I'm so glad we've met and we'll certainly give Alf a report on your progress.'

'Please don't get up,' Robert said, but Rowena was already on her feet.

'Thank you both for coming and I'll remember your offer.'

She limped behind them to the front door and stood there until their car disappeared round the bend in the lane.

'Did she remind you of anyone?' Binty asked after a few minutes' reflection.

'Not particularly.' Robert was behind the wheel for the return journey and was concentrating on avoiding the deepest of the holes. 'Do you mean to look at, or her voice?'

'Her features. I know I've never actually met Lydia, but she reminded me a little of an older version of that photograph Alf used to keep in his office.'

Robert turned to glance at her and dipped his mouth, but made no comment. *Lydia*, he thought, *is quite probably with us no more. Alf would have called if nothing had changed.*

Alf watched the last of the flames die down in the bottom of the rusty incinerator in his back yard and dusted his hands off.

It was late afternoon and he had not decided what to do after that act of posterity termination. He had selected what he had wanted to keep, but had ruthlessly destroyed the rest. It was symbolically the cremation of Lydia's darkest years. Next it would be her body and then he would be free, with his duty completed up to her last breath.

There would be a sense of loss for a while, but certainly no lasting grief. He had done that emotion to exhaustion a long time ago and it was now a spent force.

He turned away from the smouldering remains and went back into the house, a dull ache still throbbing between his eyes.

Free for what? It was impossible to go back and he was uncertain how to go forward – if indeed he had the will to go forward in any purposeful manner at all.

He wandered through the house, picking up a jerkin as he went and then left by the front door, swinging the *Closed* sign round before stepping onto the pavement. Life would probably just carry on as before. He would resume the mask of good old Alf, the bluff, outspoken old soak, who enjoyed a laugh with the lads in the Lugger and occasionally pursued an ambivalent dalliance with Sadie. He would continue getting up the noses of petty authority, even though he was meant to represent petty authority himself, and he would carry on like this because it was expected of him. He was Alf Curtis, the character, the amiable buffoon, the rather wobbly pillar of Pengarth society.

Above all else, he would try to put out of his mind the *Darling Brendan* letter. That belonged to Lydia's past. It would do no good now, after all these years, to waste any thoughts on the agonised words she had spilled onto the pages of that epitaph to sanity.

A seagull left its perch on a chimney above him and then also left a well-directed deposit on Alf's shoulder as it headed out across the bay, but he did not seem to notice, or to care. A small boy did notice and giggled as he passed by with his parents, tugging at his father's sleeve and pointing.

Although June was not yet halfway through, emmets were increasing daily in number, but that morning they were not registering on Alf's malfunctioning radar.

He carried on down towards the harbour.

'Alf!' A voice came up to him from beyond the slipway and he looked up to see a burly figure standing with hands on hips.

Alf took a deep breath, forced a smile and waved back. It was Greg Treberthy, a hundred yards away and working on his boat. Alf ambled over to him.

'How's she coming on, my old flower?' He steadied himself against the hull as he knocked some seaweed off his shoe.

'Almost seaworthy. Just putting a final lick of varnish on the decking, then she'll be ready for the water.' Greg put the brush down and wiped his hands on a rag. 'I've been looking out for you.'

'Oh, why? Haven't I paid my mess bill?'

Greg laughed and his stomach bobbed about in tempo. 'No, you're paid up. I just wondered if you'd like to come out with me?'

'No thanks, you're not my type.'

Greg exploded with laughter again. 'In the boat, man. Come out in the boat. I can manage easily enough without a crew, but I thought it would do you good to get some sea spray down your tubes.'

Alf hesitated.

'Yes, I'm game, if you'll allow for the fact that I'm a hopeless landlubber.'

'There's nothing to it in this old boat.' Greg slapped its side. 'Anyway, you've crewed before. I've seen you.'

'Must have been for a bet. Anyway, you're on. When d'you have in mind?'

Greg looked up at the sky and squinted. 'I think the weather should be settled for a few days and the barometer's still high enough, so what about the day after tomorrow?'

'I'll check the diary, but if there's nothing else on, I'll shut the shop and bugger the customers.' *Good old, coarse old Alf*, he thought. *I'm getting back into the role, no trouble at all.* 'What time of day? And shall I bring a fishing line?'

'Tide'll be running out in the morning, so seven o'clock?'

'Seven! That's before the bloody cock crows, Greg.' His face crumpled under the beard at the thought, but then he relented. 'Oh, well, I guess it'll just have to be an early night before to compensate. Just be sure to kick me out of the Lugger before eleven.'

'I will. And don't bother with the line – you'll be too busy for that.' Greg chuckled and then put his head on one side, adding cautiously, 'You've had a bit of a rough time these last few days I hear. Hope things are looking up now.'

'Yes, fine now,' Alf replied carelessly and focused on the horizon for a moment, before turning back to the florid landlord and smiling. 'Absolutely fine, my old flower. See you tonight.'

He turned and strode purposefully back up the beach to the slipway. *Alf Curtis was back and barking.*

Chapter Eleven

PC ROGER Curnow fought hard against his instincts and drew even harder on his training. *If this situation persists*, he thought, *I'll be tempted to call for back up*.

Two people from the Council, wearing grim faces and Day-Glo jackets, were taking notes, photographs and measurements and firing occasional questions at him. A reporter from the *Western Packet*, whom he recognised from the previous incident, was also asking questions of anyone who would listen to him, while his paper's photographer strolled around doing her job from every angle.

An uncontrolled dog was running around the still-wet paint and leaving paw marks all over the place and a growing group of rubberneckers was getting in everyone's way. On top of all that the traffic was building up and drivers were losing patience.

It had happened again.

The difference this time was that words had been crudely written across the now dull red on the humps and cushions in Fore Street and the colour was emerald green. Obviously done under the cover of darkness and presumably without risking artificial light, the perpetrator had written, TAKE THEM OFF; each word on a different impediment. The individual letters were ill aligned, but perfectly readable both ways, because the wordsmith had very thoughtfully painted his instructions on each side of the humps and cushions for the benefit of traffic in either direction.

If there was a funny side to this incident, PC Curnow did not see it.

'Come along citizens, please move along, you're not helping the situation by standing around.' He held his arms out as if attempting to move cattle into a pen and then spotted George Harris in the group of onlookers. 'Haven't you got a job to go to, George?'

'This beats work, my 'andsome,' was George's immediate response and the good folk of Pengarth joined in the hilarity. 'Anyway my hens can look after themselves.'

Tony Gibbins, with a nose for who is on the inside track, elbowed his way over to George. At that same moment a delivery van driver lost patience and began to mount the pavement on the other side of the road.

'Oy!' Curnow yelled and held up his hand. 'I didn't say you could come through yet.'

The driver wound down his window as the policeman approached in the measured tread of a man in control of a situation. At least, that was what he hoped it looked like.

'If I don't get these loaves down to the shop soon they'll be stale, constable.'

'Your loaves are the least of my concerns at the moment,' Curnow said steely-eyed a couple of feet from the driver's face. 'Now back off the pavement, stop there and wait for me to tell you to go.'

'But I'm past the obstacle now,' the man wailed, 'why can't I go on?'

'Do you want me to check your MOT, driving licence, tax and . . . ?'

'All right, all right.' The driver grated into reverse gear and lurched back onto the road, forcing a cyclist to take evasive action. He then switched off his engine, folded his arms and stared straight ahead like a petulant schoolboy.

Curnow turned and went back to deal with the others.

'Constable, do you know where I can find Mr Curtis?' Tony Gibbins was still putting himself about.

'Is the *Western Packet* so short of news this week that its ace reporter needs to waste time on a little green paint?' It was a long sentence for Constable Curnow, but he was beginning to feel a little frayed at the edges and the cattle were being slow in returning to their pen.

'I'm not actually here for the paint. I came to see Mr Curtis about the cliff rescue, but it seems it's my lucky day,' Gibbins retorted slyly.

'Well, I have no idea where he is.' He turned away abruptly to wave furiously at the van driver. 'Proceed on down the hill now!'

'He went sailing with Greg this morning,' George said helpfully. 'Should be back by now.'

Gibbins saluted George and set off down the hill to the bookshop. The silent photographer followed like a tame dog.

156

Greg and Alf had moored the boat and furled its sails half an hour earlier and were sipping at a hot coffee laced with rum, when Gibbins knocked on the shop door. Alf cursed, looked at the kitchen clock and then put his mug down.

'Can't they read? It says *Closed* on the door.' He stumped out of the room and into the shop. 'Back in a minute, Greg.'

He raised the roller blind on the door, groaned when he saw who it was and then pulled the door open.

'Mr Gibbins of Grub Street,' Alf announced with an exaggerated flourish.

'I appreciate the alliteration, Mr Curtis, but wasn't Grub Street the home of hack writers and their ilk?' Gibbins stepped into the shop uninvited, his sallow features reflecting a hint of sardonic amusement.

'Ah, no slur intended, my old flower.' He looked over Gibbins shoulder. 'And Dorcas too! Come in, come in, we're just warming up in the kitchen.'

They trailed him into the back room and Gibbins nodded at Greg, who greeted them with a twitch of his forefinger.

'Greg Treberthy, landlord extraordinaire, Tony Gibbins the scribbler, Dorcas the flashbulb.' Alf waved his arm around and headed for the kettle.

'Not for us, thanks,' Gibbins said hastily, still remembering his last experience of Alf's brew and biscuits. 'I was just wondering if you could spare a few minutes to let us have your version of the cliff rescue.'

'And if you can throw any light on the green paint job?'

They all stared at Dorcas, but for different reasons: Alf, because he had never heard her speak before, Greg because he wanted to know what she meant by green paint job and Gibbins because it was not her place to speak without being invited to do so.

'What's the green paint job?' Greg was the first to recover.

'Never mind about that now, sir,' Gibbins said testily. 'We'll come to that later.'

'No, no, come to it now, what's happened?' Alf looked from reporter to photographer. The latter, now looking abashed, was fiddling with her camera.

'It's more paint on your humps and cushions,' Gibbins sighed, glaring at Dorcas. 'Slogans in green paint.'

Alf turned to Greg. 'Did you know about this?'

Greg projected his lower lip and shook his head.

'Well, I must go and see!' Alf made a move for the back door, but Gibbins seized his arm.

'Please, Mr Curtis, we go to press in a few hours and I must get the cliff story written up. The paint won't go away in a hurry.' He let go of Alf's arm.

While Alf hesitated, Greg put his mug down and moved away from the dresser he had been leaning on. 'I'll go and look, Alf, and leave you to help Mr Gibbins with his report.' He patted Alf on the shoulder as he walked past him. 'Thanks for crewing this morning. It was good to have the old girl back in the water.'

'Thank *you*, Greg, it was most exhilarating. And you were right. Just what I needed.' He watched the landlord leave and then turned to Gibbins. 'All right, you win. Let's get down to it then.'

For the next half hour, still resisting Alf's offer of refreshment, Tony Gibbins scribbled in his notepad as he prised the cliff rescue story from Pengarth's reluctant hero, while Dorcas took a couple more photographs.

At the end of it all the reporter flipped his notebook shut and stood up, looking satisfied with the situation.

'Now, I don't suppose you know anything about the green paint, sir?' Gibbins actually smiled as he asked his question.

'Nothing whatsoever. I went to bed early last night and got up early this morning for a sail round the bay. What could be more virtuous than that?' He eased the two towards the door just as the telephone began to ring. Gibbins hovered by the doorway as Alf picked up the kitchen extension. It was Robert.

'Rob, my old flower, hold on a moment. I've got the press on the premises.' He put his hand over the receiver and looked enquiringly at Gibbins.

'The lady – Mrs Fischer – do you know how I can contact her?'

'No idea. I don't know if she's out of hospital yet.' He held up his hand. 'Robert, they want to talk to Mrs Fischer – do you know where they can contact her? . . . Oh, I see. Right, I'll tell him. Hold on again.'

He cupped the receiver once more and spoke to Gibbins. 'She's out of hospital, but would you drop by Robert Sinclair's house – you know where that is? – and he'll give you directions.'

Gibbins mouthed his thanks and left.

'Now, Robert, we need to catch up on a few things. I'm about to open the shop – yes, a rare event these days – so why don't you come down here as soon as you've dealt with Gibbins? Good man, see you in a few minutes.'

Rowena Fischer's second visitors of the week were not as welcome as the first. For a minute she considered pretending that she was not at home, but the two people who got out of the van with their newspaper's name on the side would have seen her car in the drive and also heard the dog barking from the hall.

She sighed and then hobbled to open the door at the second knock.

'Mrs Fischer?' Gibbins proffered his business card, which she glanced at but did not take. 'We're from the *Western Packet*. I wonder if we could ask you a few questions about your ordeal on the cliff last week?'

'How did you find me here?' She stood in the doorway and folded her arms.

'Pengarth is a small village and word soon gets about.' He looked pointedly over her shoulder.

Reluctantly she stepped aside and gestured for them to enter. Gibbins wiped his feet energetically and looked about him.

'Nice little place. Been here long?'

'Come this way please.' Ignoring his question, she hobbled into the back room She had already decided that there would be no offer of refreshments. Dorcas padded along the short corridor after her, staring at the plastered leg.

'I'm really rather busy sorting things out here, so I'd be grateful if you'd be quick with your questions.'

'I'll certainly try to be,' Gibbins said, sitting down uninvited. 'Do you mind if Dorcas takes a few photographs?'

Rowena looked at the photographer sternly for a few seconds before replying, 'All right, if you must. I suppose you'll want my leg in the shot?'

'Yes, standing and sitting please,' the frizzy haired Dorcas replied, manoeuvring herself to find the best light. 'I think two or three shots will be enough.'

Rowena sighed again and waited for instructions from the photographer, while Gibbins flipped his notepad open and pulled a pen from his jacket. When that ordeal was over she sat and stretched out her leg. The retriever came trotting across the bare floor and flopped at her feet, resting its head on her foot.

'Ah, that's a nice touch.' Dorcas crouched down and began clicking again.

'Yes, I take it that's the dog that caused all the trouble?' Gibbins asked.

'It is.' She bent forward and patted the animal on its head. 'But I won't be suing.'

Gibbins' staccato burst of laughter was a signal of his relief that she had a sense of humour after all. He was beginning to think this was going to be a blood-from-stone assignment: well, perhaps it still could be, but now there was some hope. He twisted in the chair to find a more comfortable position, while Dorcas melted into the background.

'Now,' he began, 'we've heard Mr Curtis's side of the story. Could you tell me what you remember of that afternoon?'

'What I remember?' She flicked her hair back. 'What I remember is that I was walking along the coast path. I stopped for a few words with Mr Curtis at his lookout, went on up the path, the dog pulled away through the gorse, I followed, lost my footing at the cliff edge and went over. Is that the sort of thing you want, Mr Gubbins?'

'Gibbins.'

'Mr Gibbins, I'm sorry. Is it what you want?'

'Well, as a thumbnail sketch, that's fine, but could we flesh it out a bit?' Gibbins raised an eyebrow hopefully.

For the next ten minutes he coaxed the flesh out of her, but it was plain that she was reluctant to indulge in any show of emotion regarding what had undoubtedly been a traumatic experience. Gibbins soon realised that he would have to do a great deal of reading and writing between the lines to bring the story to life: it certainly would not be the first time.

'So, have you seen Mr Curtis since he rescued you?' Gibbins crossed his legs and Bruno lifted his head at the sudden movement.

'No.'

'Not at all?' he asked incredulously.

'No,' she replied more emphatically.

'Does it seem a bit strange to you that he didn't visit you in hospital?' He began slowly to rake the pen through his hair and a few particles of dandruff floated to his collar.

'Not really. I think he had to go up country, as I believe you call it, so it wouldn't have been possible anyway.'

'And not since he returned?'

'Mr Gibbins, when I said no, I meant no,' she said firmly, but with a slight smile playing around the edges of her mouth.

'Oh, well . . .' *Time to change tack, Tony*, he thought. 'I detect a hint of a foreign accent, Mrs Fischer. Are you German, by any chance?'

'I don't see what that has to do with the story, but, no, I'm not German.' She inclined her head with an expression that said, *keep guessing*.

'English, with European intonation, possibly French,' Dorcas interjected, spoiling the game with her keen ear for accents. It was a skill that had won her many a bet.

'Correct!' Rowena looked at her, clearly impressed. 'My husband is French and we've lived away from England for most of our married lives.'

'So, you're over here on holiday?'

'Sort of.'

'Is your husband not with you?' He glanced vaguely around the room, as if the Frenchman might be lurking nearby.

'No.'

'Do you have family?'

'No.' She frowned and bent to pat the dog's head again.

Gibbins scribbled for a while before looking up and grinning at her. 'Well, thank you for your time, Mrs Fischer, that's all very helpful. The story should be in tomorrow's edition, if I get back to the office in time.' He stood up.

She gave him a wan smile. 'Do you mind if I don't get up? The leg's throbbing a bit just now.'

'Not at all, we'll see ourselves out.' He nodded to Dorcas and then looked through the window, as if for the first time. 'You've got a cracking view here.'

'Yes, we have.'

Gibbins paused at the door for a moment and then abruptly turned back to face her. 'Do you intend to meet with Mr Curtis again? Perhaps in more congenial circumstances?'

'It's entirely up to him.' The pale smile remained. 'Goodbye, Mr Gibbins.'

Out on the driveway Tony Gibbins slammed the van door, started the engine and glanced back at the cottage. 'She's a cool one, that Mrs Fischer. There's an element of mystery about her, don't you think?'

Dorcas snorted. 'Why, just because she speaks with an Anglo-French accent?'

Gibbins shrugged, but did not reply. He put the van into gear and prepared for the jolting drive back to the main road. *You have to have a nose for these things*, he thought, *and I have a nose while most photographers only have lenses*.

Chapter Twelve

THREE days after the *Western Packet* ran the story of Alf's cliff top rescue the man in question put his head under the pillow and cursed B.K.Richards, for no doubt it was he at the end of the rope that rang the bell at St Grace's.

Alf had not been a regular churchgoer since Lydia used to try to make a Godly man of him and that was about two decades ago. Her attempts had failed and the more God continued to deal him duff hands, the less he felt inclined to offer God anything in return. It never seemed to occur to Alf that perhaps if he paid more heed to God then He in turn might start dealing out aces. But Alf never had been one to compromise. Not even with God.

The cracked bell of St Grace's that now called the faithful to worship merely tugged at what fragment of conscience remained on the subject, but still failed miserably in raising him from his Sunday lie-in.

Why in any event, he wondered, *did the faithful need to be summoned?* Those who intended to go to church would have set their alarm clocks the night before and those who did not were unlikely to change their minds at the sound BK was making with that impaired lump of cast iron. The whole rigmarole struck him as an anachronism – or, as George Harris sometimes called it, a *knackerism.*

Eventually the bell stopped and Alf removed the pillow, turned and lay with his arms folded behind his head. There actually *was* something he intended to do today, but it did not involve church.

It was something he had been putting off for several days and, yes, it was also about conscience. It was time to pay a courtesy call to Mrs Fischer, but exactly how to play it remained an undecided issue in his mind. He was not going in order to have her gratitude heaped on him, nor was he going out of curiosity to discover more about the woman.

If he had been around when she had been in hospital it would have been simpler and more natural, but now that she was on the mend and so much time had passed, the visit might well seem contrived. Or at least that was his own interpretation.

163

In the end he decided simply to play it straight. He would go along unannounced – no choice there because the telephone had still not been connected – and enquire how she was faring. Perhaps he might also take a copy of the *Western Packet*, to have a chuckle over their shared adventure. Yes, that should break the ice a bit.

So, what might be good timing for the visit? Would she be at church? Probably not: too much attention from gawping locals. Did she have Sunday lunch and, if so, should he offer to take her for a meal at the Lugger? They did an excellent roast beef and three vegetables for about five quid. No, that would be too soon and too forward. Dammit, he was health visiting, not courting!

He heaved himself out of bed and plodded off to the bathroom.

As he stood in front of the bathroom mirror snipping a few wayward tufts from his beard he came to a decision.

He would wait until the church service ended at eleven, walk slowly up to the car and then aim to arrive at half past. That would be ideal: too early for lunch, but after the church service was over. He could trim his visit to about thirty or forty minutes, thus causing minimum interference to her day, but still allowing him to get on with his afterwards.

Alf pulled on his trousers and paused in buckling the belt. But, suppose she was out walking the dog when he arrived? A shame, but no real problem. He would take along a business card and write a short note on the back. Good. Another potential problem resolved.

After spending some time checking his e-mails and putting in a few e-bay bids, Alf clumped downstairs and grabbed his jerkin.

A short time later the old Volvo was tackling the rutted lane, emitting squeaks and groans as it progressed. Alf winced every time he was forced to go through a pothole, fully expecting to hear a vital part of his trusty chariot clatter to the ground.

On reaching the turning into Smugglers' Cottage he braked sharply at the sight of two cars in the drive. The blue saloon was probably hers, but the other was a shiny new silver BMW with up country plates. His planned visit had not allowed for a third party and there was no option C.

He twisted to peer over his shoulder to left and right, but could see no obvious place to turn the car. Also, the track ahead petered out with a closed farm gate a few yards ahead. The choice seemed to be either to reverse up the lane until he could turn into a field entrance, or to go into the cottage forecourt and turn beside the BMW. The former he reckoned to be a very tricky manoeuvre in his estate and the latter carried a strong risk of being spotted.

He banged his fist against the steering wheel in frustration and accidentally hit the horn.

'Bugger! You stupid oaf.' Alf crunched the car into reverse. 'No bloody choice now.'

The car had only reversed by a few feet when he made the mistake of glancing back at the cottage. She was standing at the open front door.

Alf stood on the brake.

'Oh, well,' he sighed and slid the car back into first gear.

He pulled up behind the blue car and got out.

'Sorry about the horn,' he announced as he walked over the unkempt gravel to greet her. 'Hit it accidentally. I saw you had a visitor, so was about to push off again. Should have come days ago, but . . . anyway, I'm . . .'

'Mr Alf Curtis, I presume,' she said, smiling, and held out her hand. 'Please don't apologise, I know you've had a few of your own problems to deal with.'

'Oh? Who told you that?' He felt her soft hand's momentary grasp slacken and he let go.

'Robert Sinclair said you had some matters to sort out, that's all.' She flicked back her hair and he noticed a red mark on her right cheekbone. 'Please come in.'

'But, your visitor . . . I would have phoned, only I understand it's still not connected.' He hesitated at the door.

'Oh, that's only my husband.' She gave a strange little laugh and then added, 'He's out on the cliff path walking Bruno, the dog.'

'Your husband?' Alf had stopped again. 'I thought he was in Geneva, or some such place.'

'He was, but he's managed to take a few days off to check on me.' Did he detect a slight barb in the last phrase? 'Do come into the sitting room. Would you like coffee?'

'Thank you.' He followed her in and the first thing he saw was a copy of the *Western Packet* on a table. He had left his in the car.

Alf stood and admired the view with the semi-professional eye of a trained NCI watchkeeper. The sea was calm with a slight swell and he guessed that the wind out there would be no more than force three, a gentle breeze. There were four sailing boats between two and three miles out: two sloops and a cutter, both with Bermudan rigs, and a schooner with its two foresails. With the naked eye that vessel on the horizon looked like a container ship and possibly a naval supply vessel over to the south. An inflatable with outboard motor was flying across the water from Pengarth direction and . . .

'Do you take sugar?' she called from the kitchen.

'Yes, please, one spoon.'

Because of the rise in the land to the right and the dense growth of small twisted oaks one could not see Pengarth from the cottage, but a mile to the left he could clearly identify the farmhouse that overlooked Poltock Bay. Alf guessed that would be her nearest neighbour.

He stroked his beard and speculated on the current value of this little gem of a property. Too lonely for him and obviously hopeless for his business, but it would suit many a person simply trying to escape the twenty-first century.

Alf moved away from the window and tried to widen his scope of vision by leaning up against the wall to the right of the bay window. As he did so, his shoe pressed down on a hard object and he heard something snap under the sole. Lifting his foot he saw that it was a piece of glass and he bent down to pick it up.

He was about to rise again when his eye caught the corner of a picture frame jutting out from a chair near the window. He pulled it out and stood up.

Placing the fragments of glass on the window ledge, he then began to study the photograph in the frame. There were two young women with their arms around each other standing by a flowerbed, with a large stone house in the background. They wore what looked like Edwardian clothes, as if for a fancy dress function. Both were laughing and their wide-brimmed hats obscured most of their features, but he assumed one of them to be Rowena Fischer. There was a penned note across the bottom of the print.

'It is a beautiful view, isn't it?' She came in and put two cups on the low table in the middle of the room.

'Yes, its always changing and always stays the same. It's part of the reason I do coast watch actually.' He held out the frame. 'I found this on the floor. The glass has been broken.'

For a second or two she seemed stunned, but then recovered quickly and took it from him.

'Thank you. The wind must have blown it off.' She put it face down on the coffee table and forced a smile. 'A pity about the glass.'

Alf glanced back at where he had found the frame. Other than the window ledge itself there was no surface within six feet of that chair. He found himself looking again at the mark on her face.

'Please sit down, Mr Curtis.' She already had.

'Alf. Everyone calls me that.' He sat and then inclined his head towards the local paper. 'I see you've bought the *Western Packet*. Did they do the story fairly, do you think?'

'Yes, not bad for a local paper.' She leant over and handed him a cup. 'A bit heavy on the drama, but then there's much of it I don't remember, so maybe it's true. Anyway, let me now thank you formally for your heroic and selfless act.'

She smiled warmly at him and unconsciously rubbed the knee of her plastered leg.

'It's kind of you to say so, Mrs Fischer, but at the time it seemed the only thing to do. I've been called a BF since, but I reckon I'd do it again. Once a BF, always a BF, don't you know?' Alf's eyes twinkled as he looked at her over the rim of his cup.

'It's Rowena. Not my choice of name, but it's the one I'm stuck with.' She inclined her head and a whimsical smile played around her lips as she added, 'Anyway, I hope you didn't get into hot water for breaking the rules.'

'No, that's all sorted out now. It was only a few job's-worth types waving the health and safety rule book under my nose, that's all.' He thought he heard a dog bark in the distance and she seemed to hear it also, because her eyes flicked aside for a second. He noted the nervous reaction and went on quickly, 'I should have gone to see you in hospital, but I was called away on . . . an urgent matter.'

'I quite understand. Anyway, I probably wasn't in any kind of mood to welcome visitors then.'

'No, I suppose not.' There was an awkward pause. 'So, how are the injuries coming along?'

'Oh, very satisfactorily, so the doctor says. I'm moving around the house without a stick now and most of the bruises have gone.'

'But not that one.' He touched his cheek.

She hesitated and then her hand mirrored his action. 'Oh, no, that's something else. I . . . I walked into a door this morning. Maybe I put the stick away too soon.'

For some reason he could not explain he felt embarrassed at the discomfort she was now trying to conceal. It was as if he had accidentally discovered a closely guarded secret or caught her unawares in compromising circumstances. Inexplicably and uncharacteristically her discomfort had transmitted itself to him.

167

'Yes, maybe you're right. About the stick, I mean,' he said hastily.

It only lasted an awkward second or two, but in those few moments a shadow passed over her blue-grey eyes. He gave her a quick reassuring smile. After that they talked for a while longer on matters of little consequence and as they talked the aura of tension about her gradually lifted.

Alf was just thinking that he should be going when suddenly there was a sound at the back of the house and Rowena blinked rapidly. The dog, Bruno, ran into the room and rested its head on her lap and immediately the shield went up again.

'My husband's back,' she said crisply and then looked down at the dog. 'Oh, Bruno, you're dirty!'

She pushed the dog away and began to pull herself out of the chair just as he appeared in the doorway.

'Hello?' It was an enquiry rather than a greeting and delivered in an unmistakable French accent.

'Jacques, this is Mr Curtis.' She stood awkwardly with her fingertips on the arm of the chair for balance. The dog had retreated to the kitchen, from where they could hear loud lapping. 'He's the one who rescued me from the cliff.'

'Ah, Mr Curtis, of course.' Jacques Fischer advanced across the room and held out his hand to Alf, who by now was also on his feet. 'You have my sincere thanks. You are a very courageous man.'

He pumped Alf's hand with both of his, while Alf murmured a few platitudes. The Frenchman was a few inches shorter than him, with black hair swept back from his temples. He had a straight nose above a neatly trimmed moustache, dark brown eyes and a cleft in his chin. His skin was sallow, as if its one-time tan had been allowed to fade under too many boardroom lights. Alf disliked him instantly.

'I did what I had to, M'sieur.' Alf released his hand and saw Rowena looking at him curiously over her husband's shoulder. 'Did you arrive here recently?'

'Last night. I drove down here directly from Exeter Airport.' He gave a Gallic shrug. 'Your roads . . . I had forgotten how awful they are!'

'We like it that way,' Alf replied with a fixed grin. 'It helps keep undesirables on the other side of the Tamar. Will you be staying long?'

Fischer seemed to spend a couple of seconds digesting Alf's quip before replying, 'Rowena and I will be leaving for France as soon as possible – maybe even tomorrow.'

'Oh? Forgive me, but I was under the impression that you were intending to stay here for a while, sorting out the cottage and so on.' He addressed his comment directly to her, but she looked down at the floor.

'Then your impression is incorrect, Mr Curtis. I can spare only a few days away from my work and when I go my wife will be accompanying me back home.' He gave Alf a lopsided grin and a curt nod for emphasis.

'I see. Pity.' He hesitated under the Frenchman's stare. 'So, does that mean you'll be selling the cottage, Rowena?'

'I really don't see that is any concern of . . .'

'Jacques!' she interjected sharply.

'Actually, in a sense it is my concern.' Alf felt his chest swelling, the same way it did the last time he punched a man on the nose. 'You see, I'm Chairman of this Parish and I need to know about things like planning consents, empty properties and troublesome neighbours.'

The white lie seemed to work, because Fischer shrugged and then bared his teeth in a smile that did not synchronise with his eyes. He turned to his wife, but addressed Alf. 'So. Chairman of the Parish. Yes, we will be putting this house on the property market. It has no place in our future plans.'

Alf stared hard at Fischer for a few seconds and then switched his gaze back to Rowena, trying to read something in her expression. Her jaw was set at a defiant angle, but the eyes betrayed nothing. Alf merely grunted, not trusting himself to speak for the moment. The man was quite right, it was after all no business of his.

'I see. Well, I wish you both good luck. And,' he turned to Rowena, 'it was delightful to meet you, even if the circumstances were unusual.'

He turned to head for the door, but Jacques Fischer beat him to it. The Frenchman spun remarkably lightly on the balls of his feet, moved quickly down the corridor to the front porch and then opened the front door with a flourish. At that point he summoned all his charm as he beamed warmly at the departing guest.

'It was so kind of you to come and enquire about Rowena's health,' he gushed. 'And we shall never forget your courageous act.'

'Thank you,' Alf said abruptly and then looked over Fischer's shoulder. 'It's a shame that Pengarth couldn't hold you any longer, Rowena.'

'Yes, it's not quite as I planned, but . . .' The sentence tailed off.

Alf accepted Fischer's formal handshake, stepped outside the door but then turned back swiftly before it could be closed again.

'By the way, that photograph . . . was that your sister standing next to you?'

She seemed taken aback for a moment and her hand went unconsciously up to her bruised cheek. 'Yes, it was. How did you . . . I mean . . . ?'

'There's a family resemblance, that's all, my flower.' Alf smiled at her. 'Au revoir.'

He caught the flared nostrils indicative of Fischer's disapproval at his apparent familiarity, but Alf continued to smirk as he strolled back to the car. The cottage door closed firmly behind him.

As he negotiated the holes up the lane Alf searched his mind desperately for the reason why he cared whether she stayed or left. What the hell! He had pulled the woman back up a cliff and then only just met her properly for the first time and then they had talked for only a few minutes. Was it because he felt proprietorial towards her as a result of his rescue act? Did he really care whether or not old Smugglers' Cottage fell into the hands of property sharks? Or was it that he had formed an instant dislike for that slimy shit of a Froggy husband? He had no answer.

This was new territory for him, or at least, territory that he had not visited for very many years.

He reached the end of the lane and stopped to let a tractor pass before turning left onto the Pengarth road. This was a situation that called for a second opinion and he knew the man to ask.

It was a long while before anyone came to the Sinclair's door and when it opened Binty stood there looking dishevelled and clutching a trowel.

'Hello, Alf.' She pushed some loose hair away with the back of her hand. 'I was in the garden, digging weeds.'

'Sorry to interrupt the good work, my flower. Is the old man in?'

'No, he's finishing the Trebell's job in Grobally. Some of us still have to earn a living, you know.'

'Even on a Sunday? Never mind, I'll come back later.' He turned to leave.

'Can I help? I was just coming in for a spot of croust anyway.'

He hesitated and then thought for a moment. 'Yes, Binty, perhaps you can. May I come in?'

She beamed at him and stood back from the door. 'Go into the kitchen and help yourself to a beer, while I wash my hands.'

He was pulling the tab off a tin of bitter when she came back.

'Like to join me in some cold pie?'

'Don't think we'd both fit, old girl.' He snorted at his feeble joke. 'Yes, why not, if there's enough to go round.'

'You don't change, Alf.' She shook her head, smiling as she took the pie out of the fridge. 'And thank God for that. We need some real people around here.'

He sat down on the window seat and looked at her, while she cut the pie into slices.

His best friend's wife at first glance was a homely woman, with unruly blonde hair, too much flesh around the waist and a bosom to keep a drowning man afloat. But her full face was always animated and the startlingly pale blue eyes radiated wisdom and humour in equal measure. Alf knew for a fact that she had carried her husband and their children through hard times, with very little external support or money, and that to Robert and their children she was a woman in a million. She was the one he should be talking to, not dear old Robert.

He got up from the window seat and pulled a chair away from the kitchen table.

'Funny you should say that, Binty.'

Something in his voice made her stop and look up.

'Say what?'

'About not changing . . .' His eyes narrowed as he struggled to find a way to begin. 'You see, I think I need a bit of advice . . . from the sage of Pengarth.'

'Well I told you, Alf, he's not here.' She reached for two plates.

'I know that, my flower.'

'A sage, Alf, is a wise old *man*.' She stuck out her lower lip at him.

'Oh, all right, sagess then. I need to ask your advice about something. For once old Alf is stuck.'

'Go on then.'

While she served up the pie with a hunk of Yarg cheese he began describing his dilemma regarding Rowena Fischer and the fact that her husband was about to take her back home, seemingly against her will. It was not easy for him to open up, even to someone he knew well, for the simple reason that he never normally did that kind of thing. Alf Curtis was incisive; a man who knew and spoke his mind; a man who *gave* opinions and rarely sought one. He was a man who did not believe in compromise.

When he had finished talking she stared at him for a while and then looked down and cut off a slice of the cheese.

'You know it's none of your business, Alf? Saving her life doesn't give you the right to organise it thereafter.' She popped the cheese into her mouth.

'I know and I never intended to do that kind of thing . . . until I met the Frog. The bastard hit her, you know.'

'No, I don't know that, and neither do you,' she said quietly.

'Dammit, Binty, all the signs were there. The broken picture frame, the bruise on her cheek that was nothing to do with her fall, her reaction when I mentioned it, his overbearing manner . . . it's all there.' He raised his arms for emphasis.

'You don't *know* he hit her,' she repeated.

'Yes, I do. I may not be able to prove it, but the bruise is on her right cheek and he's left handed!'

She laughed. 'Oh, Alf, are you playing detective now?'

'Now you're laughing at me.' He gave her a hangdog look. 'Maybe I should have seen the sage after all.'

She reached across the table a placed a chubby hand on his arm. 'I'm sorry. So, what do you want to do about the situation?'

'I was rather hoping you might have a suggestion. I can't stop her going, but if we could create a set of circumstances that might . . . persuade her to stay . . . at least for a while longer.'

'But, why do you want to interfere? Even if her husband is a bully, it's something she must have lived with for a long time and if she stays on here it'll only be delaying the inevitable.'

He forked in the last of the pie, pushed his empty plate away and leaned back. That question was the one he could not rationally answer.

'You're right, of course, but I just see it as unfinished business. And, yes, I do have a vested interest in her welfare, because if I hadn't pulled her up that cliff she would very likely have had no future, let alone welfare.' He thought about what he had just said and then nodded. 'Yes, unfinished business is what it is. I don't like loose ends.'

'So, how can you help her by delaying her return to Europe with her husband?' Binty stood up and took his plate to the sink.

'Maybe not at all, but for certain sure we won't ever be able to do anything if she goes tomorrow. Look, I know she wants to stay a while longer, because that's what she told Robert.'

She leaned against the sink and thought, while Alf watched her and waited. After a while she opened her mouth and then closed it again. Then suddenly the pale blue eyes came alive and she clicked her fingers.

'Her state of health! She's not fit to travel yet. She's still not recovered fully from the shock of the fall and if she travels too soon she's likely to have a relapse. And there's the leg itself to consider.' She gave him a wide grin, showing pink gums above her even white teeth. 'How about that?'

'That sounds brilliant, my flower.' Alf exclaimed, slapping the table. 'But, we'll have to get that to come from a quack. We can't just put the idea into her head.'

'Yes, you're right. How well do you know Phil Julyan?' she asked, referring to Pengarth's general practitioner.

'As well as any of his patients I suppose. Hardly ever go to him professionally, talk to him in the pub from time to time and played cricket with him a couple of times in the past. Why?'

'Well, I know him much better than that. You remember I helped him out for several months when he was looking for a receptionist at the surgery and he's been here for dinner a few times. I'll see if he'll return a favour.'

'Binty, you have the makings of a star performer.' He pushed his chair back noisily and went over to plant a kiss on her cheek. 'If Phil plays along that should surely work. If the Frog cares anything at all for his wife he won't go against medical advice. You'll have to act fast though.'

'Why? When do they leave?'

'Could be as early as tomorrow.'

'Then I'll go to see him this afternoon and hope he's not out with the family. If he'll agree to the plan, without compromising himself professionally, then he'll have to contact her for a consultation right away.'

'Their phone's still not connected.' Alf frowned. 'Phil will just have to be persuaded to go along uninvited and then hope the Frog's not whisked her away already.'

'Right, I'll put that to him.'

They spent a few more minutes finalising the scheme and then Alf prepared to leave. He felt his spirits lifted in the way that a small boy's are when he hears his best friend is coming to play.

173

He was about to say goodbye when he suddenly stopped on the doorstep and winced.

'Blast! What am I thinking about? I won't be here on Tuesday. I'll be at Lydia's funeral in Wiltshire.'

'Well, that shouldn't be a problem, Alf. If Phil persuades them that she can't travel yet, that decision will be made before Tuesday.' She chuckled. 'You don't have to be here to apply a ball and chain you know.'

'You're right . . . again.' He took a step onto the pavement and then stopped once more. 'Er, Binty, do you think Robert will want to come . . . to the funeral, I mean?

'I'll ask him, but so far he's not said he intends to. Lydia was only a distant cousin and he hasn't seen her since . . . well, you know. But if you . . .'

Alf looked down at the ground and nodded slowly. 'No, that's fine . . . that's . . .' He pursed his lips and then added quickly, 'Anyway, if you could just put it to him . . . ?'

'I'll do that, Alf. He may well decide to go just to keep you company.'

'Thank you, my flower. And thanks also for the advice, the pie and everything else.' Alf flashed her a farewell grin and then set off down the hill.

He stopped outside the Convenience Store, looked up at the bedroom window and shrugged. *This might be an entirely appropriate afternoon*, he thought, *for sampling some of Sadie's saffron buns and a cup or two of tea.* What was needed was a diversion from recent happenings.

Chapter Thirteen

ONE way and the other, Tuesday proved to be a long way off, in terms of what happened between Sunday afternoon and Lydia's funeral.

Binty had waited for Robert to come home before going up the hill to see Dr Julyan. She had telephoned the doctor earlier and he had agreed to talk to her for a few minutes after he had brought his daughter back from her riding lesson. While Robert soaked in a hot bath, clutching a sponge to his chest, she had outlined the plan to prevent Rowena's abduction by the Frenchman. He knew better than to interrupt, but at the end of her discourse he fired off a number of questions, most of which she and Alf had already covered. Eventually, he had simply shrugged, sat up in the bath and started scrubbing vigorously. Binty usually knew what she was doing, even if Alf did not.

Dr Julyan was instinctively reluctant to be a pawn in any scheme that involved interfering in someone's private arrangements, and strangers at that. But gradually Binty managed to arouse his professional interest and eventually he found himself agreeing that it was too soon for Rowena Fischer to be travelling any distance from Pengarth. Apart from the fragile state of her leg, there was the consideration of possible trauma as a result of delayed shock. No, he certainly could not recommend that Mrs Fischer travel abroad for at least another week – and that had nothing to do with Binty's request. He told her that he would call in at Smugglers' Cottage first thing on Monday morning.

Greg Treberthy had taken the sloop out after closing the Lugger at three and waved at Darren up in the lookout at Pengarth Head as he sailed past. Two fishermen were casting off the rocks below and he gave their floats a wide berth. He lifted his face to the sky and blinked as spray from the bows splattered his ruddy cheeks. Two canoes approached on the starboard side, their occupants paddling rhythmically with an air of dedication, rather like the aquatic version of that absurd exercise called power walking, he thought. Never mind, each one to his own, and his own was exactly where he was now: cutting through a slight swell before a gentle breeze on a sunny June afternoon.

Alf returned from his visit to Sadie in the late afternoon and forced himself up to his office to attend to business matters, which for various reasons had been neglected of late. He planned to work at his desk until half past six and then go up to the Lugger. Binty's pie had been tasty, but inadequate to stoke the boiler for more than four hours and Sadie's saffron buns had merely whetted his appetite.

After high tea B.K.Richards, Glenys and the three children put on their stout farm shoes and set out for the coast path, which was half a mile and two fields from their home.

This was a regular event in their busy lives, but an important one. Church attendance on Sunday morning, followed by a commune with nature towards the end of the day was part of the Richards' regime. It was a time to blow away cobwebs of frustration and anxiety and for the family to be together under God's sky. The only thing that varied from week to week was the direction they took once they reached the path.

On this Sunday, after consultation and a vote, they went left towards Poltock.

The Richards children went ahead with one of their young Border Collies, while BK and his wife strolled in more leisurely manner, hand in hand, a few paces behind. They had walked a mile along the path when Glenys was the first to see a figure approaching the style up ahead. She shaded her eyes to get a clearer view and then squeezed BK's bony hand.

'Look, surely she's not going to get over the style with that leg.'

'No, you wouldn't think so.' BK quickened his stride. 'But, she'll need some help if she's going to try.'

'Isn't that the lady who's moved into Smugglers' Cottage?' Glenys struggled to keep up with him. 'You know, the one Alf rescued from the cliff?'

'You could be right.' The children and dog had reached the style and were milling around uselessly as Rowena stood on the other side of the obstacle in a state of indecision.

BK cupped his hand to his face and shouted, 'Wait there, Miss. I'll give you a hand.'

'She's a missis,' Glenys hissed.

'Ah, right.' He arrived at the style and moved one of the children aside. 'Now, you can't be climbing over that style with a leg in plaster, can you?'

'No, I suppose not. Stupid of me even to try really . . . and with a walking stick too.' She appeared to be making light of the situation with a laugh, but Glenys noticed the smudges under her eyelids. 'I never thought of styles when I set out.'

'Well, I suggest that you don't get over now, because there may not be anyone to help you back when you return home,' BK said logically. 'Have you come far with that leg?'

'Just from Smugglers' Cottage.' She pointed up the hill, although the house was out of their view from where they stood.

'Ah, then you must be Mrs Fischer,' Glenys came forward and held out her hand. 'I'm Glenys Richards and this is my husband, BK, and these are our children. We farm at Cargarth.'

'How d'you do.' She gave them a communal smile and then looked down at her encumbered leg.

By now even BK had noticed the red rims around her eyes and he also saw the bruise on her cheekbone.

'Are you all right, Mrs Fischer?' he enquired solicitously. 'None of my business, but this is rough ground for a broken leg and you're a fair way from home. All up hill too.'

There was a long pause while she seemed to be trying to recover her composure. Her arm rested heavily on the style as if relieving pressure from the injured leg and some untethered hair hung carelessly against her cheek. BK had seen the quick nervous glance in the general direction of the cottage at his mention of her return route and wondered if something else might be causing her upset.

Rowena lifted her head and smiled at the kindly man with the lean face and prominent Adam's apple. 'Of course, you're right. It was foolish of me to go out so soon. I just . . . needed air, that's all. The question now is, how do I get back?'

'We'll carry you!' the youngest of the girls volunteered and the adults broke into spontaneous laughter.

'I think I'm too heavy for that.'

'I could get the quad bike down here,' BK said pensively and stared back up the track. 'But that would take a while.'

'What about the air ambulance?' came another youthful suggestion.

'Oh, no!' They'd not come out for me again. Not twice in a fortnight.'

'BK you could help Mrs Fischer up the hill. If she leaned on your arm . . .'

'Yes, that's the answer.' BK climbed over the style and stood beside Rowena. 'I reckon we could manage that way, don't you?'

'Well, I . . .'

'He's much stronger that he looks,' Glenys laughed.

'Yes, he can lift two piglets at once,' a young voice piped up and there was more laughter.

Rowena's lips held onto a grim smile as she reviewed the family, but Glenys could see the beginnings of tears pricking her expressive eyes. It seemed as if she were summing up the situation before making any kind of commitment. The five anxious faces waited patiently until at last Rowena, with a nervous toss of her hair, came to a decision.

'You are very kind,' she said emphatically, 'and I accept your offer of a prop up the hill. I really don't have much option.'

'Good. Let's get to it then.'

Glenys and the children climbed over the style, while BK and Rowena worked out the most efficient and comfortable way to support her. In the end it was decided that she would put her weight on his shoulder, so that the broken leg would take as little pressure as possible and they would rest every few minutes.

And that was how they managed it, with the children watching on anxiously, the dog diving into bushes after rabbits and Glenys bringing up the rear, occasionally asking Rowena questions.

Eventually, when they reached the gate at the end of the track by the cottage, Rowena uncoupled herself from her human crutch and leaned against a post.

'Thank you all so much. I really couldn't have managed without you. And I'm so sorry to have disrupted your family walk.' She was breathing heavily from the exertion, but Glenys wondered if there was something else that might be causing her anxiety. She could see the bonnet of an expensive car in the drive.

'You sure you can manage from here?' BK asked.

'Yes, absolutely sure. I'd ask you all in for tea, but I don't think we have enough to go round now.'

'Oh, don't you worry about that, my dear.' Glenys thought she had spotted a movement behind one of the cottage windows and added with a note of concern, 'Now, are you certain there's nothing more we can do for you this evening?'

'Certain, Glenys. Don't worry, I can take care of myself now.'

The Richards family watched her as she hobbled up the track and into the cottage driveway. Then, reluctantly BK turned his brood away and back down the hill, glancing over his shoulder once before eventually the dense vegetation obscured the cottage from view.

'She'd been crying,' BK said after a while.

'I know, and I don't think it was because of the leg either.'

'What makes you think that?'

'Wrong kind of crying.' She smiled at him. 'We women have an instinct for these things.'

'She had a bruise on her cheek too.'

'I saw that also.' Glenys sighed and pushed back a branch that jutted out over the path. 'Poor woman, I think she's very unhappy about something.'

They were quiet for a long time after that, each buried in thoughts concerning Rowena Fischer, while their children chattered carefree around them.

At five o'clock Darren called through to Falmouth and informed them that he was about to close the watch. It had been an uneventful afternoon, with little activity out at sea, a few people on the beach and a dribble of walkers along the path.

He switched off the VHF radio, locked the weather station and took down the flag, before making his closing entry in the log. He carried out a quick visual sweep, then put on his cap, slung his binoculars round his neck and left the lookout.

Darren did not own a boat, but occasionally went fishing for mackerel with his son in a friend's inflatable dingy. The coast watch duty did not therefore come from a deep love of the sea, but more from an innate respect for it. He had known many who had suffered accidents whilst out on the water and some who had lost their lives, so to him the regular vigil was a form of obeisance to the power and mystery of the deep waters and the elements. Mercifully it was rarely exciting, but it was often interesting and it afforded an opportunity to do something completely different from his day job as an electrician.

He secured the lock and then turned to trudge along the path back to the village. By the time he reached home and changed his clothes his sister would have his tea ready: maybe grilled mackerel tonight. Then he would go up to the Lugger and spend a pleasant couple of hours before retiring for an early night.

Darren had been married, but the union that had produced his only child had not lasted long. His wife had fallen for the lead singer in a local band and they now lived together in Camborne. In the circumstances of the separation Darren had been granted sole custody of the boy.

From time to time a local girl took his fancy, but he had no immediate plans to settle in with anyone else just yet. He was still only thirty-two and he was keen to build up his business before there was to be any further commitment. His sister, four years younger than him was the flighty one, but until she went off with someone permanently, the mutual dependency suited them both, especially as their parents had emigrated to Australia five years earlier.

His shower, change of clothes and meal followed in rapid succession and then he was out of the door again after listening to his boy's news.

Much as he had enjoyed Louise's grilled mackerel, he was now paying for eating it in haste. It weighed heavily on his chest as he went down Fore Street and on reaching the pub door he paused to ease off a loud belch.

'Cor, that's better,' he muttered and pushed the door open.

It was quiet inside and Greg looked up as Darren came round the corner of the velveteen curtain.

'Hello, Greg, where's all the customers then?' Darren settled onto a barstool.

'Heard you were coming,' Greg said deadpan as he pulled a pint of Rufus Craggs. 'Have a good watch?'

'Very quiet out there too. Yours was about the only boat to go past the lookout on my watch.'

'That'll soon change, when the emmets start arriving.'

'Yeah, I reckon so. There'll be no room in the water then.'

Darren took a draft of ale, wiped his mouth with the back of his hand and the two men fell into a quiet period of contemplation. After a few minutes Greg looked up and sauntered over to a customer at the end of the bar. When he came back Darren's glass was half empty.

'By the way, Darren, talking of our dearly beloved emmets, does your sister still muck out for the holiday home owners?' Greg asked as he dried a glass.

'Yes, she does. Doesn't spread it around too widely mind, but she has a selected few she does for. Brings in quite good money. Why?'

'Well, Mrs Fischer up at Smugglers' Cottage was in here yesterday – you know, the woman Alf rescued – and she's looking for someone to give the place a thorough going over. Do you think Louise would be interested in it as a one-off?'

The door opened and George Harris clumped up to the bar, winked at Greg and slapped Darren on the back.

'Well, I can ask her. She's not too busy at the moment. Do you know what sort of job she wants done?'

'Come back to you in a minute, Darren. What'll it be, George? Pint or half a litre?' Greg reached for a glass.

'Ask a silly question.' He nudged Darren. 'Good evening to you, young gentleman.'

'We're talking about that Mrs Fischer,' Darren said, pushing his empty glass across the counter. 'Greg says she's looking for someone to clean the place.'

'Oh, yer? Better hurry up and do it then.'

'Why's that?' Greg began filling Darren's glass.

''Cos she's going tomorrow, that's why.'

'How do you know that, George?' Darren asked.

'There's not much goes on around here that George Harris doesn't know, Darren.'

'I was talking to the farmhand – what's his name? – who works up at the Menears' farm. He says the husband's turned up and they're going soon after this weekend.'

'How would *he* know that?' Darren demanded.

'Because the husband asked if the Menears would take the dog back tomorrow, that's how.'

'I wouldn't have thought she was fit enough to travel yet.' Greg said thoughtfully.

'Dunno about that. She's was seen out walking this afternoon.'

'Is there nothing that escapes your notice, George?' Darren laughed.

'Nothing, my 'andsome.' George observed his companions furtively. 'But I only tell the half of it.'

'I'm sure that's true, but going back to what we were talking about before the town crier arrived . . .'

'Oy, watch it! Town crier indeed!'

'. . . would you ask Louise if she might consider going up there to do the job? And, by the sound of it, the sooner the better.'

181

'Yes, I'll ask her, but it sounds as if it'll be a big job. Doubt if the place has been cleaned since old Mrs Crabtree moved out. When was that, last Christmas?'

'Something like that. Anyway, they're not on the phone, so if she wants to know more about it she better go up there as soon as she can.'

'Sounds as if tomorrow morning won't be too soon an' all.' Darren peered into George's glass. 'How are you getting on with that one, George?'

Doctor Philip Julyan, a youngish man with sandy hair and very pale eyes, had been the sole practitioner at the Pengarth surgery for five years, having brought his family down from Warwickshire around the end of the millennium. He was a busy man, but found his work around the parish rewarding and varied. In his short time in the village he had made many friends and had vastly widened his experience of general practice.

Village life by the sea had also provided him with enough human stories to fill a book and the scene that greeted him when he turned up at Smugglers' Cottage that Monday morning might have warranted a chapter of its own.

His surgery was not due to open until ten o'clock, but the visiting nurse and his receptionist were there at nine to deal with what he called routine traffic. This gave him an opportunity to visit deserving cases round Pengarth and also provided an hour or so for malingerers to think twice before taking up his valuable time.

On this Monday morning he had called in on David Menear's mother who was bedridden at the farm, having suffered a series of strokes. She was a tough old bird of eighty-six and might well go on for another five years. On the other hand the next stroke could result in the curtain coming down permanently on her show. As a result, she was one of Julyan's deserving cases.

He stopped the car suddenly in the Smugglers' Cottage drive-way, rather as Alf had done the previous day, and took in the scene at the front of the cottage. A tractor stood unmanned near the end of the lane, a police car was parked next to a very new looking BMW and a small blue saloon was over to the right by the hedge. The front door to the cottage was wide open and an excited golden retriever kept going in and coming out again, as if being sum-moned and dismissed alternately by different controllers.

182

Julyan might have missed the broken pane of glass had it not been for the corner of a net curtain that protruded from between the shards and flapped feebly in the gentle breeze, as if someone inside were waving goodbye in the old fashioned manner.

With all the other vehicles around there was little room for his Jeep, so he nosed it up behind the saloon. He turned off the engine, reached for his bag and then got out cautiously. From inside the cottage he could hear voices. Several voices. Some loud, some more controlled and occasionally one female.

He was just beginning to wonder at what point he should intrude on the drama within, if at all, when he heard the clanking of a bicycle's mudguard approaching from up the track. He closed the car door and waited, like a member of the audience at an Agatha Christie play, to see which actor was coming in stage left.

The bicycle rounded the corner.

'Hello, Louise, come to join the party?' he said as soon as he recognised the cyclist.

Louise Dowrick pulled up alongside the doctor and slid off the saddle, looking puzzled.

'What party, doctor? What's all these cars doing here?'

'I've no idea. I've only just arrived myself. Came to see Mrs Fischer. Professional visit.'

'Oh, so have I.' She smiled at him. 'But not quite as professional as yours. Darren says she wants to have the place cleaned. He said she's going back soon.'

Julyan raised his eyebrows and nodded slowly. 'Did he now?'

'Yes, might even be today.'

At that moment the shouting began again, the female voice said something quite distinct and unladylike and then a door slammed. Phil Julyan looked at Louise and inclined his head.

'I think it's time we went in and found out for ourselves if our services are still required. Come on.' He strode off towards the front door, while Louise found somewhere to prop the bicycle and the dog came tongue-lolling to greet them.

Julyan did not knock but went in ahead of Louise.

The first person he saw as he entered the sitting room was PC Roger Curnow, who appeared to be trying to take notes and to control a situation at the same time. David Menear was standing beside him and he did not recognise the third man. He did however recognise a head wound when he saw one and the man was dabbing it now with a bloodstained dishcloth. There was no sign of the woman.

The cameo froze as they all turned to stare at him.

'And who the 'ell are you?' The stranger was the first to come to life and the French accent was unmistakable.

'Hello, Roger,' Julyan said calmly, ignoring the Frenchman. 'What have you got here?'

'Hello, Doc.' The relief in Curnow's voice was unmistakable. 'I'll tell you in a while, but Mr Fischer here could do with some immediate attention. 'Oh, hello, Louise! You too? I won't even ask . . . at least, not yet.'

'Morning, David.' Julyan had taken the spluttering Fischer further into the light and prized the cloth away from his head to inspect the cut. 'I've just come from the farm. Your mother's holding her own pretty well.'

'That's good to hear.' David Menear, in his brown working overalls, was wearing his cloth cap pushed back on his head at an angle that somehow matched the look of bemused incredulity on his weathered face.

'Louise, get some hot water in a bowl please and you, sir, sit down and keep still until I get a clean bandage on this cut.' Julyan turned to the constable. 'How did this happen, Roger?'

'Well, this is Mrs Fischer's husband,' Curnow began by way of introduction. 'I was on the way to Truro this morning when I got a call from Dave that there was some kind of disturbance at Smugglers' Cottage, so I turned round and came back.'

'I was taking the tractor into that field,' Menear took up the story, 'and I got off to open the gate, when I heard this screaming and yelling and things breaking like. Sounded like all hell had broken loose. Had my mobile on me and I remembered Roger's number – had to call 'im only last week about a stray cow, didn't I? – and told him there's a fracas going on at Smugglers' Cottage. Didn't want to go in, so I just sat yer and waited for 'im to arrive.'

Curnow stopped tapping his pad and resumed. 'Seems there'd been a domestic here, doctor. Pots and pans flying, window broken, blood flowing. I was in the middle of sorting out their stories when you came in.'

'And where's Mrs Fischer now? It was she I came to see.'

Louise had located the kitchen and now came back with a bowl of hot water. He immediately began mopping the congealing blood from Fischer's scalp and searching for fragments of foreign objects that might have remained embedded. Fischer winced, but remained calm and quiet.

'She's in the bedroom, over there.' Curnow pointed. 'I'll have to go over her story again. It's a bit confused so far.'

'I see.' Julyan reached into his bag for a bandage. 'Now this is only temporary until we can get you into the surgery for a closer examination.'

'I can't spare the time to go to a surgery,' Fischer exclaimed, nearly yanking the bandage from Julyan's hand with the sudden movement of his head. 'I have a flight from Exeter in four hours and we have not yet finished packing.'

'I think you'd better forget the *we*, Monsieur, until I've had an opportunity to examine your wife's leg,' Phil Julyan said calmly, suddenly appreciating the context of the Sinclair's anxiety and pulled tightly on the bandage to stifle any repost from the Frenchman.

'I got the impression that's what this is all about, doctor.' Curnow looked hard at Fischer as he spoke. 'I don't think she wants to go . . .'

'This is absurd . . .' Fischer began, but then decided any further protestation at that point would be wasted.

'You can do what you like, Mr Fischer, but I would strongly recommend that you have this head wound further examined before you travel. You could have concussion. By the way, what did the damage?' He fastened the bandage and stood up.

Fischer glowered, but did not reply.

'It was a saucepan,' Curnow said with the straightest of faces, but Julyan caught Menear's lopsided grin. This was Cornish pantomime to the life. Curnow glanced at his notes. 'Apparently she threw it because he tried to hit her with the dog's lead.'

'That is not true!' Fischer exploded again. 'You are only listening to her side of the story.'

'I will take a full statement from you, sir, as soon as you're ready, but up 'til now I have to say that your approach to this situation has been less than helpful. Now that the doctor has patched you up perhaps we can begin again more calmly.'

Julyan caught the constable's eye and with a slight head movement called him to a corner of the room.

'Will either of them be pressing charges for assault?' he whispered.

185

'Too early to tell, doctor. I'm still trying to get some coherent statements out of them.'

'I see.'

There was a cough from the doorway and they looked up to see Louise standing patiently.

'Does this mean I won't be needed now?'

'Ah, I think that's up to Mrs Fischer, Louise.' The doctor turned to Curnow. 'She was asked to come up here to clean the cottage.'

'I can wait a while if you like,' she said rather too eagerly, hoping that she might be around to witness the next act in the play. What she had seen and heard so far would surely put all other village gossip into the shade for a long time.

'Yes, perhaps you'd better wait until we all know who's going where and when.' He closed his bag and turned to the constable. 'Will that be all right with you?'

'Yes, fine. You can go now, Dave, if you want to get on. I've got your statement.'

'Right-ho then, Roger.' He grinned at Curnow. 'What a to-do, eh? Oh, by the way, Mr Fischer, about Bruno, I'll come back for him later . . . when I know for sure that you and Mrs Fischer is going.'

Fischer raised his head, looked at Menear bleakly and just nodded.

The farmer paused for a moment and then left the cottage, returning to his tractor in the lane. Spraying had been set back for a while today, but on the whole it had been worth it to be part of this charade.

Louise took the bowl with the bloodied water back to the kitchen and Curnow pulled up a chair alongside the Frenchman to get another take on his story, while Doctor Julyan crossed over to the bedroom.

He knocked softly and waited. There was no reply, so he turned the handle and was relieved to find that it was unlocked. He went in and closed the door quietly behind him.

She was sitting very still on an upright chair gazing through the window at the sea. Her hair was tousled and there was a stain of some kind over the shoulder of the pink blouse she wore. Clothes were strewn in and around a suitcase that lay open on one of the unmade single beds and only one of the curtains had been drawn back. Altogether the scene was one of suspended chaos.

'Good morning, Mrs Fischer.' He could see the profile of her face only by looking into the dressing table mirror. She wore no makeup.

She did not turn around but moved her head slightly so that she could catch sight of him in the mirror. 'Good morning, Doctor Julyan, I wasn't expecting to see you today.' Her tone was flat, but not unfriendly.

'Well, this is a small community and I got word that you were planning to return home fairly soon.' He put his bag on the floor and went over to pull back the other curtain. 'I really couldn't have you do that before I give you a proper check-up.'

She sighed and then turned to face him with a wan smile.

'That's very thoughtful of you, doctor, and I'm sorry that you've walked in on all this. I believe the police call it a domestic disturbance.'

He found another chair nearby and pulled it over to sit next to her. She wore a long skirt, so he could only see the plaster from halfway up her calf.

'It might surprise you to know that I see quite a lot of it, even in this quiet spot. But, I do understand that you might find the situation embarrassing.' He drew the chair a bit closer. 'Now, if you could just turn this way a bit more I'll be able to examine the leg.'

She did as he asked and pulled the skirt up to her knee. He bent forward, tapped in various places, moved her toes gently, uttered the sort of grunts that are peculiar to his profession and then sat upright again.

'Any pain?'

'Occasional twinges, but no real pain. Sometimes there's cramp in the foot, but that's all.'

'And no doubt an excruciating desire to itch under the plaster.'

'Yes, that too.'

He looked directly at her for several seconds without speaking and just long enough for her to blink under his stare.

'Do you want to go back to Geneva with your husband today?' he asked softly and there was no immediate reply. 'Mrs Fischer? I'm asking you that question in a professional capacity, because if you are going under duress so soon after suffering pain and shock, there could be adverse repercussions.'

She met his gaze and seemed to be trying to connect with his line of thinking. Her hand went up and combed its way through the unkempt hair and he noted the darkening bruise on her cheek.

'What sort of repercussions?'

187

'One can't tell with delayed shock. In fact, ideally you should have seen a therapist soon after the leg was reset. I just had no idea that you were contemplating returning to Europe so soon.'

'Doctor Julyan,' she sighed, 'I was not contemplating anything of the sort myself. Going back to Geneva now is my husband's idea.'

'So, I come back to my original question, do you want to go back with him today?'

She turned to look out to sea and he waited patiently, studying her profile. It was a strong face, with good cheekbones and well-defined lips. *She must have been a stunner in her youth*, he thought.

Eventually, when she turned back to face him, her lips had curved into a wry smile.

'Who put you up to this, Doctor Julyan?'

It was his turn to be taken aback. It was *his* job to listen, to ask questions and to diagnose. But his mask slipped for only a second.

'I can't imagine what you mean, Mrs Fischer.' He managed to look stern and puzzled at the same time. 'Any recommendation I make to you is strictly professional and based on the conditions as I see them. I am not put up to things, as you call it.'

'Of course not.' She looked down, still smiling.

'Please answer my question. If you want to travel with your husband, then there's nothing I can do to stop you. But, I warn you that if you are going to travel under stressful conditions then . . .' He raised his hands and let her guess the outcome.

'Very well, doctor, I'll be straight with you.' She clasped her hands together on her lap and looked at a point above his head. 'Before my husband arrived a couple of days ago I fully intended to stay here for several weeks. Now he wants me to return with him and for us to sell this cottage. I made it quite plain that I do not wish to do either of those things and it was over that disagreement that we fought. But, as you can see, this time I won the round.'

'The round maybe, but not necessarily the war.' He arched a sandy eyebrow. 'I know this is a policeman's question, but will you be pressing charges for assault?'

'No, doctor. My husband and I have been married for many years and I know him rather well. He may be a bully sometimes, but like all bullies he is also a coward. He will return to Geneva on his own, tail between his legs, and in due course I expect I will join him. He will be all contrite and shower me with gifts and we'll carry on until the next round.' She paused to examine his expression. 'Don't look so surprised, doctor, many worse things happen in a marriage.'

'Yes, I know, but mostly those marriages don't last.'

'Believe me, this one lasts in name only. You see, I have no children to turn to, no settled home and only one sister in England. We've been on the move for so long that it's now part of my life and I don't know how to escape . . . But, please understand, there have been good times too, you know . . . it's not all been unpleasant . . . a lot of the high life, interesting people and places . . .' She hung her head for a couple of seconds and then raised it again with defiance in her blue-grey eyes. 'And then, out of the blue, Smugglers' Cottage came along.'

'Your bolthole at last?'

'Exactly.'

In the stillness that followed Julyan could hear the murmur of voices in the next room as Curnow coaxed a statement out of Fischer. A gusty breeze had picked up from the sea and a few gulls careened around above the overgrown garden, seemingly tossed at the fickle whim of the wind. The cottage was too far from the sea actually to hear the waves against the shore, but sight and imagination were senses enough to compensate for that small deficiency in the idyll. He could understand perfectly why this peripatetic woman in an apparently loveless marriage needed to hold on in this spot, even if for a short period of time.

'Then it is my advice to you that it would be unwise for you to travel any distance from this place at least until the plaster has been removed from your leg. And I give that opinion for psychological as well as physiological reasons.' He pushed the chair back and stood over her. 'The nurse who attends my surgery drives past your lane on her way to and from work and I shall ask her to visit you every other day for the next week. This afternoon she will stop by to give you something that I am prescribing to help with the stress that has clearly been brought on by recent trauma. Obviously I'll explain all of this to your husband before I go. Now is there anything else that I can help with while I'm here?'

Rowena rose stiffly. She felt as if she had been sitting for a long time and the tensions of the past couple of days had permeated through to her muscles. But Julyan noted that those in her face appeared now to have relaxed somewhat.

She placed a steadying hand on the dressing table.

'No, Doctor Julyan, you've done everything you can and I'm really grateful.' She took a step forward and smiled warmly at him. 'And, like a good patient, I shall follow your advice to the letter.'

'Splendid.' He picked up his bag, headed for the door and then turned back abruptly. 'Oh, by the way . . . Louise is here . . . the girl from the village to do your cleaning. I do recommend that you take her on as from now . . . there's obviously a great deal for her to do here, so I expect she'll still be at it when your husband leaves for his plane.'

'Oh, that is good news.' She had picked up his nuance. 'Perhaps you'd ask her to come in here and I'll tell her what needs to be done.'

'I'll do that. Goodbye for now then.' He smiled at her. Now for the Frenchman.

Julyan had no way of knowing what had been said between Fischer and Constable Curnow, but the Frenchman was now quite subdued and compliant. The policeman had finished carrying out his duty and was talking on the mobile phone, so the doctor took the opportunity to explain briefly to Fischer his diagnosis and recommendation regarding his wife. Again the man accepted the situation and appeared more anxious now about catching his flight from Exeter.

Once satisfied, Julyan went to the kitchen and asked Louise to go through to Mrs Fischer to discuss terms.

'I think it's all calmed down now,' he murmured to her, 'but please don't leave the house until Mr Fischer's driven off.'

'So, she wants the cleaning done after all then?'

'Oh yes.' He smiled and patted her shoulder. 'Lots of proper job cleaning and dreckly too!'

Doctor Julyan gave Curnow a nod as he left the cottage. *There would be quite a queue at the surgery by now*, he thought, *but there was no question that he had already done a good day's work at this place.*

Chapter Fourteen

ALF reached the A30 and put his foot down.

He had left Pengarth later than he had intended and now he was in danger of missing the start of the funeral at half past two. If there were no traffic hold-ups he should make it, but if not . . . he cursed himself for spending too long chatting to the Sinclairs.

He had gone round to their house early to hand over the spare keys to the shop and somehow the conversation had drifted on to the happenings at Smugglers' Cottage the previous day. Once Louise Dowrick had returned from her morning's cleaning at the cottage the news had spread round the village like fresh cream on a hot scone.

PC Curnow had stayed on for a few minutes after the doctor had left, just to ascertain, Louise thought, that neither party would be bringing charges. She had gone into the bedroom to be formally employed and instructed by Mrs Fischer and had then begun her work.

Shortly after that Mrs Fischer had taken the dog out for what she called a hobble round the next-door field while her husband had packed his bags in the bedroom. He had left in the BMW without a word to his wife or Louise, speeding up the lane oblivious of the potholes. After that, everything in the cottage settled down quietly and Mrs Fischer had seemed to be more at ease.

So, Alf thought, *Rowena Fischer was due to be around for a couple more weeks at least.* For an inexplicable reason he found himself feeling ambivalent about that prospect, even though he had been the main instigator of her remaining on at the cottage. And that ambivalence in itself he found unsettling.

Lydia's funeral was to be held in the chapel of the crematorium nearest to St Margaret's. There had been no traffic problems on the way and Alf arrived in time. In fact he had to wait near the gates while the mourners' cars from a previous service had snaked their way out of the grounds.

He parked the Volvo and watched for a while as undertakers and their attendants cleared away flowers that had lain on display for barely an hour. Very shortly his own floral tribute would no doubt be set out on the same spot. Would there be any others, he wondered? Poor Lydi, about to leave this world unobtrusively on a conveyor belt.

Circumstances beyond Lydia's control had forced her to give up church attendance years earlier and the vicar of their Parish was long gone to his own eternal rest, so Alf accepted that the pastoral function at today's funeral would necessarily be an impersonal one. He felt a pang of remorse at this and then found himself again wishing that he had persuaded Robert to accompany him.

On cue the hearse came through the black wrought iron gates and wound its way at a respectful speed up the drive to the crematorium portico. A single vehicle followed it. Alf got out of his car and wandered across to greet its occupants. The Matron from St Margaret's, a nurse he recognised and an old man got out of the car as he approached.

Four black-coated pallbearers went to the rear of the hearse and began to run the casket out on well-oiled bearings.

'Matron, how good of you to come.' Alf held out his hand and wondered if she did this for all of St Margaret's departed.

'It's a sad ending, Mr Curtis. I've known your wife for many years, through her good times and bad.' That seemed to Alf to be a fair assessment in a sentence.

He greeted the nurse and then turned to the old man with a quizzical expression.

'I can't remember if we've ever met,' the man said with a surprisingly strong voice and held out his hand. 'I'm Lydia's Uncle Charles.'

'Good heavens, so you are!' Alf exclaimed as he took the age-spotted hand. 'As a matter of fact we did meet, but I don't blame you for not remembering. You were at our wedding.'

'Oh, I'm so sorry. Shocking of me not to recall. Of course we were. Lovely occasion it was too.'

'You live in South Africa don't you?' Alf asked hastily in an attempt to cover the old man's embarrassment.

'Did. Came back a few years ago, when my wife died. Live in a dreadful hotel in Worthing now, full of dribbly old people.' Uncle Charles rocked back with a staccato guffaw at the thought of those less fortunate than himself and Alf saw the undertaker frown. Presumably dribbly old people were the lifeblood of his business, especially when they dribbled their last.

'I see. How did you come to hear of your niece's death?' For some obscure reason Alf could not bring himself to personalise Lydia to the old man. Perhaps if he had sought her out and visited her himself . . .

'Saw it in the *Telegraph*,' he said, as if it were the most obvious thing in the world.

'Of course.' Alf looked up and saw the priest trying to catch his eye. 'I think it's time we went in . . . the conveyor belt is about to roll again.'

Charles laughed once more, but Matron drew in a sharp breath and cast a sideways glance at Alf. A moment later the pallbearers hefted the coffin onto their shoulders and the four mourners followed it into the dim interior of the chapel.

Alf and the other three moved to the front row in the small chapel and, after settling the coffin on the launch pad to oblivion, the pallbearers slunk like deferential vampires to seats near the rear.

He looked around with distaste. There was no sign of an organ, but reedy piped music whined through the building's homogenised atmosphere from a hidden source, almost drowning the sinister hissing that came from the other side of a heavy maroon curtain. Everything was sanitised, polished and phoney. Even the candles were fakes, giving off forty-watt glows rather than naked flames. It was the kind of place that would make any sane person, whether or not in mourning, want to run out screaming into the open air. It was the sort of place where butterflies died.

The Chapel door closed with barely a sound and the priest stepped forward from the gloom to begin the service. After a brief introduction and a prayer he invited them to sing a hymn that had once been a favourite of Lydia's. *Oh God our help in ages past, our hope for years to come . . .*

Alf launched lustily into the hymn in his unpretentious baritone, aware that only some of his notes were in key, but anxious to ensure that someone should show they cared a damn for the deceased. As a result of his defiant paean neither he nor anyone else heard the chapel door open, nor saw a figure slip discreetly into a pew near the rear.

The eulogy would have been embarrassing had it not been so brief. The priest had never met Lydia as a whole person, so had no idea as to her true character, nor any record of her history. She was just another one who had passed away from St Margaret's – the only difference was that this one was younger than most of the others.

As he sat with his head bowed, Alf felt a wave of guilt wash over him. *He* should have given the eulogy, or at least primed the priest. For too long he had been going through the motions with Lydia, visiting by rote, saying the right things and all for what? To salve his conscience so that he could return to Cornwall and continue wasting his life without the encumbrance of a prematurely senile wife?

Then, as the priest closed the book that hid his crib sheet and invited them to pray, the situation regarding Lydia ceased to be an opaque blur to Alf and came suddenly into sharp focus. For him Lydia had not died last week, she had died many years ago and they were now simply cremating her mortal remains.

Nevertheless, there was no question that he, Alf Curtis, *should* have recognised that it was his job today to reconstruct her as she had been in good times, so that he could send her off to eternity a complete person. But he had failed to grasp that vital point and now it was too late.

He had not identified what was required until after the final lap of her race had been run, simply through his own introspection. He had failed Lydia in that simple humane task, as he had failed so often before, and now it was impossible to make amends. Once again he had been too late to do what was right and proper, as demanded by the circumstances.

Alf knelt, screwed his eyes shut and clasped his hands so tightly together that the knuckles turned white. He listened to the priest's words and said a loud Amen in the right places, but he was finding it impossible not to lace the liturgy with self-derision.

They remained kneeling as the curtain parted for a moment, a button was pressed and the coffin rolled slowly out of sight. There followed an awed silence as the curtains closed silently again and that was that. She was gone.

The service ended and the priest wafted his way down the aisle as the canned organ music signalled their time for departure. Next please, it seemed to be saying.

Five pews back Robert stood up and waited for Alf to turn around. The music was Bach's Air and unconsciously in his head Procol Harum's words strung along with the melody. *And so it was later, as the miller told his tale, that her face at first just ghostly, turned a whiter shade of pale* . . . In spite of the occasion he smiled nostalgically at that half-forgotten anthem from the summer of love.

Alf stood up stiffly and prepared to shuffle out with the others. He raised his head and then blinked disbelievingly when he saw Robert. Easing past the nurse and grinning broadly Alf went up to his friend with both arms outstretched.

'My dear old flower.' Alf seized Robert's hand as if they had not met for years. 'So good to see you in this place of gloom and despair. What made you change your mind?'

'Conscience, I suppose,' Robert replied diffidently. 'Should never have considered letting you go through this on your own.'

'Well I appreciate it, old chap, I really do.' Alf glanced quickly behind him into the light of the doorway. 'Give me a couple of minutes, Rob, I must say goodbye to those folk.'

Alf went almost joyously into the sunlight, the heavy mood of the occasion almost physically rising from him into the summer air. He caught up with Matron, shook her hand and thanked her once again for all she had done to make Lydia comfortable. He smiled warmly at the nurse and then wished Uncle Charles a safe journey back to Worthing.

'You must look me up one day,' the old fellow said earnestly, knowing the chance of that happening to be extremely remote.

'If I'm ever in Worthing, you can bank on it,' Alf responded, knowing that Worthing was as far off his compass as Wyoming. 'What's the name of your hotel?'

'Hotel Deffoe, but we all call it Hotel Death Row. Ho ho ho, get it?' The old chap began laughing so much that his hat nearly fell off.

'Not near the dead centre of town, by any chance?' Alf stoked the fire.

Matron seized the paroxysmal Charles firmly by the elbow and ushered him quickly to the car before he had a seizure of some kind. She did not relish the thought of this one in her care. Alf left them and wandered over to the priest, thanking him for a very *sincere* service: the poor man had done the best he could in the circumstances.

Robert was waiting patiently beside his car.

'My God, you must have belted the poor beast up the A30 to get here.' Alf patted Robert's ageing vehicle on its bonnet. 'When did you leave?'

'Probably about an hour after you. And you're right, I did push the old girl rather hard. Perhaps you'd better stay with me on the way back, in case I break down.'

'Yes, of course.' Alf looked hard at his friend and shook his head in wonderment. 'I still can't believe you actually did this . . . I can't tell you how much I appreciate your being here.'

'Well . . . poor Lydia . . . I just knew that I'd always regret it if I didn't make the effort.'

Alf looked across the lawn and saw the hearse sliding away and then observed the beginnings of a gathering by the crematorium gates. 'Time to move off, I think. They're dropping like flies around here. It might be catching.'

'Are you going straight back?' Robert asked as he walked around to the driver's door.

'No, that service has given me an appetite. Look, there's a nice little hotel just off the A303, about ten miles from here. Let me treat you to a very late lunch.' Alf didn't wait for an answer, but set off for his car. 'Follow me.'

For a few moments Robert stared after him, amazed at Alf's ability to switch his emotions so readily. Was this insouciance a blessing or a curse, he wondered? Whichever, it seemed to Robert to make Alf somewhat lacking in the tender side of humanity.

He shrugged, got in and started his car.

They pulled into a recess in the drive and allowed the next cortège of mourners to pass by and then carried on through the gates. The Volvo spat out a puff of grey smoke as Alf put his foot on the accelerator and from that point Robert tagged along in his wake. They left the A303 at Mere and a mile down the road Alf turned into the car park of a mock Elizabethan hotel called The Cockspur.

Robert got out of the car, looked at his watch and called over to Alf, 'It doesn't look like the sort of place that serves lunch at three-fifteen.'

'Not the main restaurant, no.' Alf hitched up his trousers as he made for the front door. 'But there's a little bistro thing at the back where they'll rustle up something any time of the day. Broken my journey here many times.'

196

To Robert's surprise Alf was greeted cheerily by name as he went past the reception desk and he threw back a light-hearted quip to the receptionist before leading the way into a room at the rear of the building. An elderly uniformed waiter appeared from nowhere and hailed Alf with a polite but gap-toothed grin beneath a neat shiny moustache. The man led them to a table by the room's only window and left them a menu each.

'You've obviously made an impression here.' Robert glanced around the dark green room.

'Story of my life, old boy, I seem to make an impression everywhere I go, but not always for the right reasons.' He prodded the menu with a forefinger. 'I recommend the duck. It might be straight out of the freezer and into the microwave for all I know, but I've always found it very succulent.'

'Right, I'll go with the recommendation.' Robert closed the menu and looked over Alf's shoulder at the only other occupied table in the room. Two young women were in earnest conversation over their cappuccinos.

'Good. Now where's Gaston?' Alf craned his neck in the direction of the kitchen door.

'Gaston?'

'The waiter.'

Robert snorted. 'I don't believe it!'

'It's his name all right. Or so he says.' Alf waved the menu.

'You're joking. Only waiters in French farce are called Gaston.'

'Well, you tell him that. He's coming over now.'

The aged waiter wafted his way over to their table as if walking along a narrow plank.

'Gentlemen? You are ready to order?' he asked deferentially, a napkin draped over the sleeve of his dark jacket. Robert looked closely at him. His small moustache appeared to be waxed.

'Yes indeed, Gaston, but first my friend has a question to ask you.'

The waiter shifted his attention from Alf to Robert, rather in the manner of a tortoise moving its head under the shell, one eyebrow arched enquiringly.

'Oh, ah, yes, er, Gaston.' He shot a furious glance at Alf. 'If the bar's still open I'd like a lager please . . . and one for Mr Curtis.'

'Certainly, sir.' Gaston gave a curt bob of the head. 'And for your meal, gentlemen?'

'Two duck please, Gaston, with all the trimmings.' Alf handed him the menu and gave Robert a lopsided smile. The waiter bobbed again and then left.

'Bastard!' Robert said as Alf started chortling. 'I hate to think what you were like as a schoolboy.'

'You daft bugger, you know perfectly well what I was like as a schoolboy!'

'I know I do, but I still hate to think what you were like.' Robert grinned back at him. 'But I suppose it's now far too late for you to change.'

'I hope so. I intend on being lowered into my grave with people saying *that was Alf Curtis, that was, cantankerous old bugger, but a man known and loved far and wide.*' He suddenly frowned and added sombrely, 'Not like poor Lydia today - unknown, unloved and soon to be forgotten.'

'Now don't start getting morbid, Alf, none of it was your fault. You couldn't help it turning out the way it did.'

'That's what I keep telling myself, my old flower, but somehow it doesn't often work.' Alf flapped his napkin open and dropped it on his lap. 'Nothing I'd have liked better than to have a close loving relationship with my wife – like you and Binty, for example.'

'Well, we've had to work on it at times, you know. It's not always been easy.'

'I know that, but Binty's been your rock to cling to in stormy seas.' There was a long pause before he added demurely, 'I'm not much good at being a rock.'

Robert pursed his lips and stared at Alf under his eyebrows while his friend fiddled with the cutlery.

They had known each other on and off since their teens, but only rarely had Robert seen what lay under the shell of the man who now sat opposite. And on those rare occasions he was unfailingly surprised by the sensitivity and apparent vulnerability of Alf's persona beneath the crust. It was a startling and almost shocking contrast to the bluff and self-assured being that he presented to the world.

It was at times like this that Robert took to pondering about his friend's contrary character.

Gaston returned with two cold lagers and placed them with infinite care on the table.

Alf looked up at him and smiled broadly. The crust had closed over the core once more. The waiter turned like an arthritic old ballet dancer and Alf clamped a large fist around his glass.

'Remind me again, Rob, was Lydia your first or second cousin?'

'Neither, actually,' Robert replied with a quick laugh. 'She was the daughter of my father's sister's husband's brother, if you can get your head round that.'

'Good lord, no wonder I could never remember.' Alf tipped the glass back and left froth on his moustache.

'A simpler way to look at it is that she was my first cousin's first cousin – so really no relation at all.'

'No, I suppose not. Fancy that, all these years and I thought you were proper cousins. Life's full of surprises.' He wiped his upper lip. 'She had a sister, as you know. Lives in New Zealand. Surprised not to have heard anything from her, especially as they used to be quite chummy years ago.'

'You told her, I suppose?'

'Oh yes, but not a word back. Maybe moved on somewhere else.' Alf winced at some memory and then changed the subject. 'By the way, did you see the old man at the funeral today?'

'The one who seemed to think the whole affair was a huge joke?'

'Yes, that's the fellow. Well, it turns out he was Lydia's uncle. He was at our wedding for heaven's sake, but neither of us knew the other. Shocking how the years can change a person.'

'Hardly surprising, Alf, it was about thirty years ago and you've grown a beard since.'

'I know, and he's grown old, but still . . . there are chaps I can meet today from school or university and not seen them since, but I'd know 'em instantly. Yet take another bloke and he's changed out of all recognition. I suppose it's a matter of hair loss, girth, specs and that sort of thing.'

'And beards.'

'And beards . . . but not usually for women.' He looked quickly over his shoulder at the two women and mused, 'Do you think women change less than men over the years? I mean, they can't grow beards and they seldom suffer hair loss.'

The kitchen door creaked and Gaston emerged backwards, carrying a tray.

'Women certainly change with age, but in different ways.' Robert, anticipating Gaston's arrival, made room for him to lower a bowl of steaming vegetables. 'Take Rowena for example . . .'

'Rowena Fischer?'

'Yes.'

'Why her?'

'I don't know really. First person I thought of, I suppose, and because she's still a handsome woman for her age.'

'Hallo . . . you don't fancy her do you?' Alf pointed a knife at him and leaned back in his chair, grinning.

Gaston settled the bowl to his satisfaction and then trudged off again, his face a picture of discreet inscrutability.

'Of course not, but there's no harm in looking at the menu, as they say. The point I'm making though is that I . . . or you even . . . might have fancied her when she was younger. Whereas, she, looking at *us* now, could never imagine even looking twice in our direction at any time, because we've changed so much.'

'Hey there! Speak for yourself, baldy! I am still much sought after.'

'Is that what you like to think?' Robert decided that it might be unfair to bring Sadie into the discussion. 'Anyway, to return to my point, with a good-looking older woman one can always tell from the features whether or not she was a stunner in her youth.'

Alf peered at him impishly. 'My, I didn't know you still studied form.'

Robert dipped his mouth and shrugged.

'So, you're an expert on this subject, are you?' Alf probed.

'Oh, I give up.' Robert slapped his napkin against the table and rocked back in his chair. 'I don't have to be an expert in order to express an observation of . . . ageing differences between the genders.'

'Sorry, old man, only jossing.' He looked up. The waiter was returning. 'Ah, Gaston, the canard at last. You're a champion. I'm looking forward to this.'

The waiter arranged their plates with meticulous attention to detail, bobbed his little bow, and then retreated.

'They don't make 'em like that any more,' Alf listed his head in the direction of the departing Gaston. 'Do you think he was a looker in his youth?'

'Impossible to tell now . . . and that's my point. Now, if Gaston had been a Gastina . . .'

'Gastonella is more likely.' Alf shovelled some vegetables onto his plate. And what if he had been *born* a Gastonella and undergone a gender change . . . what price your theory then?'

'Ah, I think you've got me there.'

The two young women left their table and one of them gave Robert a toothy grin as she passed on her way to the exit. He smiled back and wondered if their inconsequential banter had been overheard. Alf appeared too engrossed in dissecting his duck breast to notice.

'So, Alf, are you telling me that Rowena Fischer has made no impression on you?'

Alf finished chewing and took a swig of beer before replying. 'Of course she's made an impression, but not necessarily because of her feminine allure, old boy. If you've helped pull a woman off a cliff ledge then a kind of bond is bound to develop, but it doesn't have to be sexual. Anyway, she's too old for me.'

'Too old? Why, how old do you think she is anyway?'

'Must be at least . . . oh, I don't know . . . fifty-six?'

'She's fifty-two.'

Alf paused with his knife halfway through a carrot, blinked a few times and then stared at Robert. 'How do you know that? Have you been cosying up to Mrs Fischer on the sly, Robert?'

'I saw her passport - remember? She was born in March 1953.'

To Robert's surprise Alf's face seemed to undergo a steady contraction as a frown deepened across his brow as very slowly he rested his cutlery on the side of the plate. A quizzical expression shaded his eyes as he gazed intently across at Robert.

'1953? Are you certain?'

'Yes, it was there plainly in her passport. Why, what's so important about her age?'

'Oh, nothing really,' Alf's lips twitched as he picked up the cutlery again, but the shadow of a frown remained. 'Just shows how wrong I can be about women's ages. In fact come to think of it she actually looks much younger . . . I should have said forty-nine . . . not fifty-six.' He hastily pushed a forkful into his mouth and stared at his beer glass as he chewed.

Robert looked down at his plate and prodded at the duck as if making sure that it was dead and then peered at Alf from under his eyelids. He made an incision in the meat and cleared his throat. The silence screamed out to be broken.

'Have you ever studied the shags and cormorants from the lookout . . . how they just sit there on the rocks doing damn all for most of the time? They dive around for a while looking for fish and then, when they've got what they need, they go back to the rocks and hang their wings out to dry.'

'What about it? That's the role nature designed for 'em.' Alf did not look up, but carried on attacking the duck.

'Well, don't you think we're rather like that in Pengarth . . . we old bits of flotsam in the lee of Shag Rock? Just doing what we have to do, then sitting around drying our wings for the rest of the time until the next meal.'

Alf stopped chewing, put his cutlery down and looked quizzically at his companion, but said nothing.

'That is until something unexpected comes along to disturb them . . .'

Alf's jaw began working again and a small droplet of gravy caught the overhead light as it bobbed around on his beard, but still he remained silent, staring at Robert.

'Has something come along to disturb you, old man?' Robert asked quietly.

Alf reached out for his beer, gulped down a mouthful and then pulled his napkin roughly across his mouth. 'I'm not a fucking cormorant . . . or a shag,' was all he said before eating again.

There was little conversation after that and Robert made no attempt to force it. He should never have been so crass as to bring Rowena into the conversation, he thought, especially on the day that Alf had buried his wife. And as for cormorants and shags . . . he winced.

All sign of the earlier levity had disappeared and Robert continued to wonder and to juggle with improbable thoughts all the way back to Pengarth.

By the time he crossed the Tamar Alf's Volvo was out of sight, some miles ahead of him. But then, he mused, Alf had always been ahead of him in nearly everything they did.

Chapter Fifteen

A FEW days after the funeral Alf rose early and settled behind his desk to clear a backlog of orders, invoices and correspondence. From time to time he jumped up and pulled a book from a shelf or a catalogue from the filing cabinet. The computer breathed its mechanical drone on the corner of his desk and outside the June day gradually heated up.

He had not been to visit Rowena Fischer again, but he had heard that the Frog had returned to Geneva without much fuss and that she had settled into a routine at the cottage. Louise Dowrick had arranged to go up to the cottage daily, sometimes to do domestic chores and sometimes just to take up some goods from the Convenience Store. There was still curiosity in the village about Rowena and gossip continued to spread in increasingly distorted versions regarding the flare-up with her husband. Alf thought about her from time to time, but kept putting off a second visit. There would be time enough for that.

The telephone trilled and he answered it, rising from his chair and then walking slowly to the window as he listened to the caller. It was a subject of little interest to him and he stared idly up Fore Street through the salt-encrusted glass as the caller pressed on.

He rubbed the pane to little effect and squinted with his face pressed to the glass to get a clearer view. Something was going on up the road and he could not make it out.

There was a sudden silence from the other end of the telephone and Alf realised that the caller was waiting for a reply. He moved away from the window and brought his concentration into focus.

'Yes, I'm sure that will be very interesting, Mrs . . . Ah . . . but I'll have to consult my diary and get back to you . . . what? Oh, my diary's under a pile of papers here somewhere and I don't want to take up your valuable time looking for it now. Yes, I'll get back to you . . . if you'd just leave your number . . .'

Alf scribbled the number on a paper block, put the phone down and went back to the window. He undid the catch and heaved at the sash.

'Bloody sash cords!' he grunted and let go.

The sash, although heavy because of the broken cords, was surprisingly free between the beadings and it came down again with a solid thump, rattling some of the panes. Alf cursed once more and went over to his desk to find the twelve-inch ruler.

He sifted through the papers that he had so recently put into a semblance of order, lifted a couple of files, opened drawers and even looked under the cushion on his chair, but the ruler was nowhere to be found. He stopped the search abruptly and put his hands on his hips, staring disconsolately at the mess on his desk.

Suddenly his eyes opened wide with the triumph of discovery.

'My old flower, I knew you'd come in useful one day!' He seized the chrome-plated female effigy that was his paperweight and went back to the window.

Balancing Dolly carefully on the narrow window ledge, he pushed the bottom sash upwards to about the height of the statue. She was just over half the height of the ruler, but he estimated that that should be enough for him to poke his head out and have a good look at what was happening.

When he was confident that the statue was secure he knelt down and eased his head sideways through the gap. There was definite activity further up Fore Street, with a Council contractor's lorry and a few men in Day-Glo jackets, but a badly parked van was preventing a complete view. He was just contemplating going downstairs to get a better view from the street when there was a shout from directly below.

'Oy, Alf! What you doin' there?'

Alf's head automatically shot up and the sudden movement not only crushed his ear against the underside of the window, but also disturbed Dolly's precarious equilibrium. Before the pain from his ear had had a chance to register, Alf saw his paperweight topple and he tried to make a grab for it.

He was too late.

Dolly teetered for a moment on the sloping sill and then went over. At the same time the window came down, but not before Alf had the presence of mind to remove his head, thus preventing further damage to his ear. However, in his haste he overlooked the position of his grabbing hand, which remained outside, and the sash descended firmly on his wrist. Not surprisingly, the Chairman of Pengarth Parish Council roared an oath that must have been heard from the harbour to the Convenience Store.

'You orright there, Alf?' came the same voice from below, once the bellowing had ceased.

'Of course I'm not all right, you blithering idiot,' Alf shouted as he struggled to raise the window sufficiently to release his hand.

Having achieved that feat, he staggered over to his desk, clutching his wrist. He could feel a trickle of blood from his ear approaching his shirt collar and remembered that somewhere in the bottom left hand drawer he kept some sticking plasters. He yanked the drawer open and the first thing he saw was the twelve-inch ruler jutting out from under some papers. Forgetting the injured ear and throbbing wrist, he seized the ruler and stomped back to the window.

Once more he heaved it open and then shoved the prop between sill and casement.

This time there was enough room for him comfortably to get his head and chest out over the frame and he now glowered down at the cause of his misfortune.

'What the devil do you want, George Harris? You might have killed me, shouting out like that!'

'Sorry, Alf, but the door's locked and I saw your head pokin' out like.' George stepped back so that he did not have to bend his neck so acutely and squinted up at Alf. 'Your ear's bleeding.'

'I know it's bleeding, George, thank you kindly. I was just about to stick a plaster on it . . . unless you want to come up and do it for me.' Alf glanced down as a crimson drop fell onto the sill.

'Can't do that, Alf . . . 'ealth and safety.'

'What, you think you're going to catch AIDS or something?'

'No, I'm not a trained first aider, my 'andsome.' George grinned broadly from the safety of the road. 'Anyway, what's that dropped out of your window?'

'That's Dolly, my paperweight. Did she make a hole in the pavement then?' Alf leaned a bit further out of the window and then immediately spotted the vulgar object, glinting mockingly in the sunshine. 'Oh, hell and damnation!'

Dolly had gone straight down onto the narrow canvas awning above the shop window. It was a taught strip of material about eight feet above the pavement and six feet below the windowsill. The paperweight had obviously been heavy enough to create minimum bounce on impact and had lodged against the awning's metal frame. Dolly now lay on her back, with her knees and her other two prominent features pointing to the sky.

'What now?'

'She's stuck on the awning, George. Can you see a stick or something to knock her off from below?'

George did not move, but looked casually to left and right. 'Nothing like that here, Alf, but I could go down to the harbour. Might be a stick down there.'

'No, don't worry about that, I've had an idea.' Alf pulled himself back into the room and went to a cupboard in a far recess past the bookshelves. There he found a fishing net, attached to a long pole. He reckoned if the net was strong enough it would be just the ticket for the job in hand.

He passed the pole through the window and carefully followed it up to his waist. Then, looking down, he saw to his surprise that a small group of people was beginning to gather around George, all staring up at his window.

'You selling tickets down there, George?' Alf asked as he manoeuvred the pole into position.

'I think they'm just waiting for you to drop out of that window, Alf.' George chortled.

'I should think you folk have had enough excitement in the last week or two, wouldn't you?' The net closed over Dolly and he twisted the pole slowly to get the wire rim underneath her bottom. Another spot of blood landed neatly beside the first. 'What were you yelling at me for anyway, George?'

'Oh, I nearly forgot.' George turned to look over a couple of heads at the action up the road just as Dolly tumbled into the mouth of the fishing net.

'Gotcha!' Alf exclaimed and then began to raise the pole back to the horizontal. 'Forgot what?'

'To tell you that the Council are working on the road humps. They're burning the tops off and the foreman says they're lowerin' 'em.'

'What!' Alf, momentarily forgetting his delicate operation, turned his head sharply to peer up the road and his shoulder nudged the underside of the sash. This in turn gave a slight upward lurch of the sash, but the sudden fall back was too much for the old wooden ruler.

In an instant the twelve-incher became two six-inchers, which now both spun like large sycamore seeds to the pavement. But, before they completed their journey, two other things happened in rapid succession. The window, now completely unsupported descended on Alf's back, just above the belt, and at the same instant it caught the end of the fishing pole. The jolt to the pole sent a shockwave to the net end and Dolly once again leapt joyfully to her freedom.

Alf was in no position to see what happened to her immediately after that, but George watched open-mouthed as the heavy lump of burnished metal cart-wheeled through the air and landed at the feet of a woman standing a few feet away from him.

The entire scene froze for several seconds.

The woman stared aghast at the object at her feet, Alf's face writhed into a pre-explosive expression, George's dentally-challenged mouth continued to hang open as he gaped up at the window and half a dozen bystanders stood wide-eyed at what they had just witnessed.

'Mr Curtis!' The woman who had narrowly escaped being crowned by a chromium-plated nude paperweight was the first to recover. 'What is that?'

Alf's face was turning a dangerous shade of red and the blood-spattered beard bristled as his mouth attempted to form words appropriate to the occasion. To his credit however he said nothing immediately, but with difficulty he raised his torso to glare at the woman.

'Aha, Miss Bush-Tyke! Just the person to have around in a crisis, I'm sure,' he growled down at her. 'What is what, may I ask?'

A few more people were arriving for the morning's free entertainment and speculative murmuring began, interspersed with the occasional snigger.

'This thing at my feet.' Gloria Bush-Tyke shuddered visibly. 'It's disgusting.'

'Oh, that. It may look disgusting to you, madam, but it's a valuable objet d'art from the neo classical era Dollia Partona,' he retorted and then turned his attention back to George. 'Now, Mr Harris, as you are largely responsible for getting me into this undignified and somewhat painful position, may I suggest that you do something about getting me out of it . . . and right away!'

'Like what do you suggest, Alf?' A number of faces turned away from George and then skywards to hear the reply from the Chairman of their Council.

'You've tried the front door, so why not try the back door now?' he enunciated with exaggerated clarity. His back was beginning to

207

hurt from the extraordinary position he had been forced to adopt and as far as he was concerned the last drop of humour had been extracted from this farcical situation.

The faces were now looking again towards George.

'Good idea, Alf, I'll be with you in a jiffy.' George strode importantly up the path, through the gate and up to the side door. He was back a few seconds later and now the faces did not know which of the two to watch and some older necks were beginning to ache.

'What are you doing back here, man?' Alf demanded.

'Sorry, Alf, that's locked too,' George said sheepishly. 'What now?'

'Bugger!' Alf roared in a voice that could be heard across the still waters of the bay.

He had overlooked the fact that he had not left the house that morning.

'Oh!' Miss Bush-Tyke exclaimed and her hand flew to her bosom. 'And he's the Chairman of the Council too.' She turned and after a final furious glare up at the window she stormed back up Fore Street.

'You've driven off old Butch-Dyke,' George called up to him. 'That's a vote lost.'

'Never mind that. I'll probably resign soon anyway. Get a ladder please, George.' He cast an eye around the gathering. 'Would someone amongst you please help George Harris bring a long ladder to this window?'

'Can't do that, Alf.'

No one had moved.

'Why the hell not?'

''Ealth and Safety, Alf. We'll need scaffolding at that height.' George's grin almost split his face.

'What are you talking about, you daft bugger? It's less than fifteen feet off the ground.' Alf focused on George's expression and then noticed that a few of the others were beginning to nudge each other's ribs and to snigger. 'George Harris, you're enjoying this, aren't you? When I get down I swear I'll strip you to your string vest, tie you to Greg Treberthy's mast and hang a pilchard from your privates!'

'Then I think you'd better find someone else to get you down, Mr Curtis,' George shouted above the general laughter, ''Cos I don't fancy that kind of reward.'

At that moment a car drew up as close to the pavement as the crowd would permit and the driver wound down the window. A few peered curiously at the driver and Alf attempted to see over their heads. His own was beginning to throb.

'Oh, God,' Alf murmured as he saw Rowena Fischer ease herself out of the car. 'That's all I need to complete my humiliation.'

She stood there for a few moments, taking in the scene of Alf's predicament. The crowd made way for her as she limped onto the pavement and squinted up at him.

'This may sound a silly question, but are you all right?' she asked tentatively.

'Yes, Rowena, it is a silly question. Can't you see that I'm just hanging about touting for business?' He instantly regretted the sarcasm and bit his lip.

'Well, then I'll be on my way, shall I?' She was smiling at him. 'Seriously, is there something I can do to help?'

'Yes please, my flower,' Alf replied contritely. 'This bunch is totally useless. If you have a mobile phone on you would you call the Sinclairs and ask Robert to come down with my spare key? The number's five three one after the Pengarth code.'

'Or you could call the fire brigade,' suggested an anonymous voice.

'Don't you start, or I'll string you up with Harris.' Rowena keyed in the number and Alf added, 'George, if you aren't already, you could make a mint selling tickets down there. Might as well get something out of the morning's entertainment.'

'Better still, you could sell your story to the press.' George pointed up the road. 'Because, they're on their way now.'

'Oh, Christ, no!' Alf craned his neck and made out the shambling figure of Tony Gibbins coming down Fore Street with Dorcas in tow. 'What's he doing here?'

'I told you, Alf, the Council's working on the road. He's come down to see if there's a story . . . and by crikey, it looks like he's hit the jackpot today.'

'I can't get a signal here, Alf, it's too close to the water,' Rowena cut through Alf's muttered curses. 'It's not far. I'll drive up there.'

'Won't be necessary, my 'andsome,' came another voice from the crowd. 'That's Robert's car coming down Fore Street now.'

'Thank God,' Alf breathed. 'Let's hope he's brought the key.'

He twisted his head to see Robert overtake Gibbins a hundred yards short of the bookshop and then pull up behind Rowena's car. Robert jumped out and triumphantly held a bunch of keys aloft. A spontaneous cheer broke from the gathering as he passed between them on his way to the front door.

'I told you to get those sash cords mended,' Robert shouted up to the window as he turned the key. Rowena was right behind him and a few strides to her rear and closing fast was Tony Gibbins.

'Don't let that man in!' Alf yelled. 'He already has my life story.'

'Only up to last week, Mr Curtis.' Gibbins shouted back. 'Looks like there's a whole new chapter this morning.'

Alf heard the shop bell tinkling as his rescuers pushed the outer door open. To his relief Gibbins was still on the pavement when he heard it slam shut again. Then there were urgent footsteps on the stairs and a moment later his office door swung open.

'Not much of a chapter for you, Mr Gibbins.' Alf called down, with the confidence of a man who is about to be let out of jail. 'You'll just have to make something up.'

'Oh, I don't know . . . interesting angle to the cliff rescue, don't you think. *Rescued woman returns the compliment, rescues rescuer.*'

'You'll have to do better than that,' Alf laughed as Robert came up behind him and hooked his fingers under the window casement. 'Sounds a bit clumsy, even for the *Western Packet.*'

Another cheer and some clapping came from the watchers as Robert heaved the sash up with a grunt. Rowena, somehow not far behind Robert, grabbed Alf's belt, just in case he should topple forward and he winced at the sudden pressure on his stomach. Then, with exquisite timing the ubiquitous Dorcas stepped forward, pressed her shutter button and the moment was frozen on her camera's disc. Gibbins beamed up at them gleefully and executed an extravagant bow.

'Damnation!' Alf exclaimed as Robert eased him gently back into the room, where he collapsed heavily onto the floor.

'Thank you, Mr Curtis,' Gibbins called from below to the now closed window, 'I won't need that story now . . . a picture paints a thousand words.'

'And a thousand turds to you,' Alf muttered from the floor. He beamed up at his rescuers. 'What a fool I am.'

Alf held out an arm and Robert pulled him to his feet. He uttered a sharp yelp as he tried to straighten his back and they helped him over to a chair. As he sat down slowly Rowena studied the side of his head.

'That's a nasty cut on your ear. Where do you keep the first aid stuff?'

'Show her, Rob, there's a good chap. Oh, and please bring something for my splitting head as well.'

He held the offending head between his hands and shut his eyes. Down below the onlookers were slowly dispersing and returning to their interrupted businesses. They now had ample fuel for ribald discussion in the shop and in the Lugger for many a day to come.

Robert returned, while Rowena gathered the items she needed from the bathroom.

'Someone phoned through to Binty with news of what was going on down here,' he explained. 'I would have come earlier, but I was outside seeing what the Council blokes were up to.'

'That's all right, old man. I'm just glad the car was outside your house at the time.' Alf stopped massaging his temples and looked at Robert through half-closed eyes. 'And what is the Council doing? George Harris – bloody man – said something about shaving off the tops of the humps.'

'That's right. It's the only way they can remove the paint and they're grading the ramps at the same time. Probably a sop to us to make sure it doesn't happen again. So, it's a sort of victory for us I suppose.'

Rowena came in and put a bowl with hot water on the desk.

'It certainly is, my old flower. We'll have to drink a toast to the phantom paint dauber in the Lugger tonight.'

'Hold still, Alf.' Rowena began to dab the damaged ear with a warm sponge. 'It's not too bad, but head wounds always bleed a lot.'

'You experienced in this sort of thing?'

'First aid? Yes, I've done the course . . . many years ago.' She dried the wound and then reached for a plaster. 'I'll leave you to wash the blood out of your beard, if you don't mind.'

'I think I'll leave it there . . . might make me look even more fearsome.' He turned his head and grinned at her.

'Keep still.'

'Yes, ma'am.' He caught Robert's eye and winked. 'Long time since a lady ministered to me.'

'You don't deserve it.' Robert checked the time. 'Look, I have to go now that you're in good hands. I've got a job to finish and I'm already an hour later than I told them.'

211

'See you in the pub tonight?'

'Maybe.' Robert turned to leave, but stopped suddenly at the door. 'Oh, by the way, that thing . . . the one that was the cause of all the trouble . . . it's on the counter downstairs.'

'What? Dolly?' Alf said indignantly and Rowena pulled his head back into position. 'Thing indeed! She's a masterpiece.'

But Robert had already gone.

Rowena stood back to study her repair job and then began to pack away the first aid equipment.

'Thank you, nurse.' Alf touched the sticking plaster on his ear. 'Good job, but would you finish the ministration by bringing me a glass of water and an aspirin please?'

'They're right beside you on the desk.' She smiled at him as she zipped up the first aid bag. 'I think you can manage that on your own.'

Alf raised an eyebrow and reached out for the glass.

He was swallowing the pills when she limped back into the room.

'What were you doing down at the bottom of Fore Street anyway?' He stood up gingerly and went to look out of the window. Everyone had gone and life in Pengarth had returned to normal, except for the Council's Day-Glo boys working further up the road.

'I just came down for some groceries and then saw the gathering outside the bookshop.' Then she added with a mischievous grin, 'Thought perhaps a celebrity was doing a book signing here.'

'That'll be the day,' he laughed. 'Anyway, now you're here, please stay a while and have some coffee with me. Unless of course you've got something melting in the back of the car.'

She hesitated for a moment, glanced at her watch and nodded. 'Thank you, that would be nice. I'm not in a great hurry.'

'Right, sit you down . . . that's the most comfortable chair . . . and I'll be back in ten minutes.'

'Are you sure you're up to it . . . your head, I mean . . . ?'

'Nearly better already.' He set off down the stairs to the kitchen and on the way down called back to her, 'Have a look at the books if you like.'

So she did.

They were all over the cluttered room. Most were on shelves in the conventional manner, but dozens were stacked laterally as if awaiting cataloguing or removal to the shop below. She picked one up and then another and then a third, glancing at titles and authors' names. There was no order and no obvious connection between any of them. They were just books great and small; learned and trivial; leather bound and paper backed.

When he returned with a round metal tray bearing coffee mugs, biscuits and sugar he noticed that she was looking into an early countryside guidebook. He put the tray down.

'That one's in very good condition. Picked it up at an executor's house clearance last spring. Do you take sugar?'

'No thank you.' He handed her a mug, wondering if perhaps he should have offered china cups. 'Those old countryside books are becoming very popular. Nostalgia for the good old days, you know . . . if there ever was such a thing as the good old days.'

'Well, I suppose that's what's caught up with me. I've spent so little time in this country as an adult that I'm now trying to hold on to what I remember.' She closed the book. 'How much are you selling this one for?'

'Why, do you want it?' He sat down and waved a hand inviting her to do the same.

'Yes, I'd like to buy it.' She stroked the spine with an index finger.

'Then it's yours, no charge and no argument.'

'Oh, but I can't . . .'

'I said . . . no argument,' he repeated firmly.

'Well, that's very kind indeed. Thank you, I'll treasure it.'

'Don't just treasure it, my flower, read it as well. Books are for reading, not just for covering wall space or coffee tables.' He stroked his beard for a moment and then stopped suddenly when he felt the remains of congealed blood. 'My theory on books is that if you start one and it's rubbish, then stop reading it and throw it away. If it's good, then cherish it and read it again and again.'

'Sounds like good advice.' She put the book on her lap.

'Any particular part of old England that takes your fancy?'

'Hmm, I'm a southern girl, only having been north of Watford twice, so I'd have to say that the area around Hampshire holds most nostalgic memories for me.' She sipped her coffee, with a wistful look in the grey-blue eyes.

'Any particular part of Hampshire?'

She did not reply for a while and a thin line on her brow suggested that she was attempting to recollect. Alf sat patiently, studying her well-structured face and finding himself increasingly intrigued by Mrs Fischer. There was an indefinable sense of inscrutability about her that . . .

'There was a small village, a few miles south of Andover . . . I always have to think . . .'

It was a long time before Alf discovered what it was that she always had to think, because at that moment the telephone began to ring.

'Excuse me.' He got up and went across to the desk, irritated at the interruption. 'Hello! . . . Oh, Matron, good morning.' His tone softened instantly. 'Yes that's right . . . that's what I told them . . . Yes . . . well, how kind of you . . . I do appreciate it.'

After a few more words he rang off and then stared pensively out of the window, almost as if he had forgotten about his visitor.

Rowena sat very still, studying his shaggy profile until suddenly he drew breath through his teeth and turned back to her.

'That was the matron from my wife's nursing home. The undertaker's engraved a plaque in her memory and they're going to fix it in place tomorrow.' His lips twitched in an attempted smile and then he added gruffly, 'She's very kindly chosen the spot for me.'

She looked away and made no attempt to speak. There had been no need for him to confide in her and now she did not trust herself to say anything that might sound trite. When Alf moved away from the window and sat down again he was the first to break the silence.

He wore an untroubled and open face as he asked, 'Have you heard from your husband?'

'Yes, he phoned soon after arriving back in Geneva. He's happiest when he's stuck into his work, you know.' Her eyes strayed down to the book on her lap, as if wondering how to complete what she was saying about Hampshire. She had remembered the name of the village.

'So, no further recriminations about you staying on?' Lydia had slipped back into the shadows of Alf's sub-conscious again.

'No, he's accepted that . . . for the time being.'

'Good. And how long might the time being be?'

Her sudden peel of laughter was as spontaneous as it was surprising. Alf certainly saw no reason for the outburst of merriment and he cocked his head in the manner of a faithful dog reacting to a mysterious foible of his mistress.

'God knows. It all depends on his patience and how much he needs me. But for the present he's busy and I'm happy enough here.'

'Does that mean you'll not be selling Smugglers' Cottage?'

'I told Doctor Julyan that Smugglers' Cottage is my bolthole. I have no intention of selling my only refuge.'

'I'm sure that we'll all be very pleased to hear that.'

'We?'

'The people of Pengarth. We like to adopt those who adopt the village . . . and we're not so keen on up country incomers who use the place and put nothing back. You know, there are many cottages here that are empty for most of the year.'

She nodded her appreciation of the compliment and then stared at him for a few moments, before asking, 'You're not Cornish, are you?'

'Only by adoption. I've been here a long time and, being a kind of human chameleon, I've absorbed the local colour.' He folded his hands behind his head and flinched as he touched the ear. 'In fact, if you scratch the surface, you'll probably find a mongrel.'

'So, where did you grow up?' she probed gently.

'Oh, all over the place. My parents were peripatetic . . . rather like you.' He unfolded his hands in a sudden movement and leaned forward. 'Would you like some more coffee?'

She blinked and shook her head, regarding him with an enigmatic smile.

So, Mr Alf Curtis doesn't like to talk about himself, she thought. She began speculating that perhaps he had recreated himself in this small Cornish village to such an extent that memories of the past were not now permitted to intrude, and certainly not in front of strangers. So, even the *my old flower* was an affectation. Almost endearing once one became accustomed to it, but an affectation nevertheless.

Rowena drew in a quick breath and changed the subject.

'Er, that photograph on the shelf behind you . . . is that your daughter?'

'Yes, she lives abroad now. I contacted her after her mother died of course, but I knew she wouldn't come over for the funeral.' He turned to look out of the window. 'Doubt if she'd turn up to mine.'

'Oh, surely she would. Anyway, that event must be a long way off. Perhaps she'll be closer to you by then.' She almost bit her tongue at the clumsy string of platitudes.

Alf grunted and stood up suddenly, walking over to look into the street. He reached up and idly flicked at one of the broken sash cords. Spots of his recently shed blood lay dried and dull on the sill.

'You said you didn't have children?' He did not turn around.

'No, we never did. We thought about adoption a few times, but it wouldn't have worked out with our lifestyle.'

'What a shame.' He looked over his shoulder and appraised her. 'You'd have made a good mother.'

'Oh? What makes you say that?'

His mouth dropped open and he turned sharply to face her, his eyes expressing shock. 'I'm so sorry, Rowena, that was a presumptuous and impertinent thing to say. I just meant that you seem to have all the qualities . . . Please forgive me, that comment was quite out of order . . .'

'That's all right, Alf, I'm sure it was meant as a kindly observation. No offence taken.'

'Still, I shouldn't have . . .'

At first her lips twitched in a faltering smile of reassurance, but then, after a pause, a frown appeared. Her head drooped and as she stared at the book on her lap the words came stumbling out of her mouth. It was as if she wanted them to stop but was incapable of doing so.

'Actually, I nearly was a mother once, but I was very young . . . far too young . . . and I couldn't keep it . . . and then . . . and then there wasn't to be a second chance. I suppose it was nature's way. How are we to know?'

He stared at her, uncertain of what to say or do. Here was a woman he barely knew who, without warning or prompting, had divulged to him what was possibly her most intimate secret. If he had been the tactful Robert he would have known how to react, but he wasn't and he had no idea of how to receive this revelation. All he could manage now was just to close his mouth and try not to look stupid.

A gull landed noisily on the window ledge and strutted from one end to the other before taking off again.

Slowly she raised her head and then, as her eyes met his, she recognised his state of confusion.

'Oh, now it's my turn to apologise, Alf,' she said with a wan smile. 'I really don't know why I came out with that. It's many years since I've mentioned it to anyone. But I know that it won't go any further. I would prefer . . .'

His brain suddenly came alive. 'No, of course not. It's none of my business and I'll simply put it out of mind.'

'Thank you.' Rowena nodded a few times, as if putting a seal on his assurance.

There was another awkward pause before she suddenly turned her attention to her watch and then got clumsily to her feet before he had a chance to assist.

'I've taken up too much of your time already.' She smoothed her skirt down and gave him a lopsided grin. 'It's been quite a morning, one way or another.'

'It certainly has.' He went over and guided her to the door. 'I set out to do a full day's work too.'

'Well, there's still over half the day left. Don't come down, I'll see myself out.' She paused. 'How's your head?'

'It's fine now. Made of coconut shell you know.'

She laughed. 'Well, thank you for the coffee.'

'My pleasure. And please be careful on those stairs. They're rather steep.' He watched her go down and when she had reached the bottom he called out, 'Rowena, would you flip over the *Open* sign on your way out. You never know, I might have some customers.'

'Will do,' she called back and then he heard the bell tinkling as the door opened.

I'll simply put it out of mind, he had said, but he found he could not. He went back to his desk with the intention of resuming his work, but the question that kept rising to the surface was, *How old was far too young?*

Chapter Sixteen

PREDICTABLY, the main picture on the front page of the *Western Packet* that Thursday was the one that Dorcas had scooped outside the Pengarth bookshop. The picture was hers, but the caption was pure Tony Gibbins. It read: *Pengarth Chairman in the Frame.*

The story began, *In a strange reversal of roles, Rowena Fischer was on hand to assist in rescuing Alf Curtis, Chairman of Pengarth Parish Council, from an embarrassingly awkward situation earlier in the week. On a visit to the village to follow up the Pengarth painted road humps mystery, your reporter . . .*

It took all of Alf's bravado to step into the Lugger that evening and he did so to the spontaneous accompaniment of a raucous cheer and ribald laughter. He strode across the floor treating the company to a regal wave and a sickly smile. His photograph, with Robert heaving the window up and Rowena clutching his belt was pasted to the mirror behind the bar and he winced as he saw it yet again. The expression on his face was that of a man straining to break wind and there was Mrs Fischer immediately behind him.

'Some people will do anything for publicity,' came a shout from along the bar.

'Frightened the mackerel out of the bay you did, Alf,' from another.

'Butch-Dyke b'aint stopped runnin' yet,' George Harris's voice boomed out.

He leaned across the bar to the phlegmatic Greg. 'Pull me a pint of Rufus, Greg, and then turn the hoses on this mob.'

Gradually the din subsided and decorum resumed amongst the locals, leaving the few visitors looking bemused. Alf settled himself on a stool and took a long pull on the beer.

'Good evening, Alf.' He did not need to turn his head to recognise B.K.Richards' soft Cornish burr. 'Good result, eh? Just shows if you keep pushing these bureaucrats something will eventually give.'

'Hello, BK.' It was a great relief that here was a sensible man who had not come to mock him. 'Yes, indeed, it almost looks like a victory, from where I sit.'

'No doubt about it and that's part of the reason I'm in here.' The lean man eased himself onto the stool beside Alf. 'Do you think we should hold an extraordinary meeting just to summarise to the people what the position is now?'

'I don't know. Do you think it's worth it? Would anyone turn up?'

'Well, we know from the last meeting how strongly a lot of the villagers feel about the traffic calming issue, so I think we owe it to them to explain exactly how the matter's been resolved.'

'You think it's been resolved then?'

'I certainly think we've got them to change as much as they'll ever change, Alf, so to that extent . . .' BK toyed with an empty glass as he spoke.

'Here, let me fill that for you.' Alf reached over, but BK placed his hand on the top.

'No thanks, Alf, I'm not stopping. So, you don't want a meeting?'

'Look, my old flower, I'll be guided by you, the Clerk to the Parish Council. But first, tell me exactly what concession we've got from the County Highways people.'

'Well, it's not arrived yet, but the top man in Highways has promised to let me have a letter next week summarising what they've done and why and also the further minor adjustments they intend to carry out.'

'Do you know what these other adjustments are . . . and when do they intend to do the job?'

'I think it'll be an illuminated speed limit sign either end of the cushioned area and the removal of that daft build-out just before the school. Those are the major things. They plan to do it before the beginning of the school holidays.'

'I'll believe that when I see it! They haven't got the time for it now.' Alf drained his glass. 'Anyway, let's have a brief meeting when the letter arrives. Ok? In all probability only you, Hettie and I'll turn up, but at least we'll have made the effort.'

'Ok, Alf, I'll let you know.' BK slipped off the stool and then hesitated before giving Alf a sly look and asking, 'Are you all right now? I mean your injuries . . . ?'

'Yes, old man, I'm fine. These days I seem to have so many aches and pains I hardly notice a few more.'

Alf smiled reassuringly, but it was a lie. There were bruises to his back and wrist and the cut on his ear still smarted, but there were unseen mental bruises as well, the sort that he hid with the Good Old Alf routine. It was not merely an ego issue, but something that was more complicated than that. Like the Earth's ozone layer, his outer crust was cracking and he was not sure how to seal it up again.

BK left and for a while Alf fiddled with the beer mat beside his elbow, trying to make a face or recognisable form out of the abstract pattern on its damp surface. Then, he looked up suddenly and saw Greg studying him thoughtfully.

'You know what you need, Alf?' Greg asked casually as he wiped the counter.

'A skinful of Rufus Craggs, landlord.' Alf's face cracked into a broad grin and he pushed his glass across. 'That's what I need.'

'No, that's not what I had in mind.' Greg pulled the pint and cast a professional eye around his kingdom. 'When you have something pressing on your mind, or the world has turned sour on you, you need to get out to sea. It's saved my sanity many a time.'

'Also damned near took your life too, my old flower. I'm sure you don't forget that.'

'Maybe, but that little episode also *saved* my life and gave it purpose.' Greg's burgundy cheeks were set firm and Alf could see from his eyes that the man was in deadly earnest. 'So, what I'm saying to you is that you need to come out in the boat again . . . soon.'

Alf stared at Greg for a while as he considered the proposal and then began to nod slowly. 'All right, Greg, you're on. I enjoyed the last outing and I don't think I made too much of a fool of myself.'

'You handled the old boat competently.' Greg moved aside as Elsie brushed past him on her way to the far end of the bar, where Darren was waving two glasses.

'Good of you to say so. When did you have in mind?'

'Is tomorrow too soon for you? The tide's right at about three in the afternoon.'

'Three will suit me just fine. Or, if it doesn't at this moment, I'll make damned sure it does by then.' He picked up his glass and gave Greg a lopsided grin. 'You've made me feel better already.'

'Good man.'

'But, Greg . . .' He raised his eyebrows and looked over the landlord's shoulder at the mirror. 'Do me a favour . . .'

The landlord winked and reached behind him to take down the newspaper cutting.

Alf stood up and prepared to join the reprobates' table across the room. He suddenly felt fortified for anything they could throw at him and furthermore he needed to shake young Mike by the hand.

He chuckled to himself as he manoeuvred his way across to the public end of the room. The red hand of Pengarth needed to be congratulated.

The following afternoon found Binty Sinclair out walking her old dog near Poltock Head.

She stopped a few yards short of the cliff edge, checked the ground for rabbit droppings and then sat down on a firm dry tuft of coarse grass. She drew her knees up close to her chest and folded her hands around them. A gentle breeze blew off the sea and ruffled her hair and a turned up shirt collar flapped lazily against her neck. This was one of her favourite places on the coast.

It was also a place her ageing collie knew well, but his days of running around chasing sticks and trying to catch seagulls were over and he now lay placidly at his mistress's feet.

From where she sat Binty had a wide view of Pengarth Bay to her right and of the houses at the top end of Fore Street. She could also see the roof of the Coast Watch lookout, although it was not usually possible to make out which of the watchkeepers was on duty.

The left arm of the bay was guarded by Poltock Head and a craggy rock stood like a full stop to its comma just fifty yards offshore. That was Shag Rock, a haven for gulls, cormorants and the eponymous shag.

About twice a year a fool would swim out to the rock and then become stranded, fearful of swimming back against the tide. Robert had spotted a fellow there from the lookout once. He had seen the man waving a shirt and, from closer observation through the binoculars, it appeared that he was one leg short of a pair. When the rescue services eventually hauled him off, that observation proved to be correct. They were not impressed when he told them without shame that he had had to prove to himself that he could do it. His insurance company was not impressed either when he claimed for a new artificial limb. While he was on the rock the tide had come in and the shifting sand had buried his tin leg. It was never seen again.

Binty could also see the beach round the point to the left of Pengarth Bay itself. There were a number of people on the sand, playing games, strolling or just lying, and a few were in the water. The Gulf Stream would not take effect for another month or two and the hardier youths had yet to arrive for their summer holidays. Nevertheless, two windsurfers were out there in the shelter of the bay tugging at their masts in an effort to catch the breeze, their sails fluttering like disconnected butterfly wings above a slight swell.

From where she sat the land sloped gently down to the cliff edge, so the border of gorse, scrubby blackthorn and fern did not obscure any of the view. Sometimes sheep were put to graze in this field, but at present the occasional pale cluster of droppings suggested that the flocks had not been moved down again since spring. As a result, the fresh growth of grass had become a haven for clumps of pink thrift, red campion, delicate spring squill and, unusually for the south coast, a few long-necked cowslips.

There were only three sailing boats in sight, all making light work of a gently rippled surface. The furthest out of the bay looked like Greg's sloop, but with the naked eye she could not make out who was aboard.

The dog instinctively raised its head as Binty reached into a pocket for a biscuit. She tossed it to him and he caught it with practiced ease and then immediately turned his attention to movement from the path further up the field behind his mistress.

Binty twisted to look over her shoulder and a frown line appeared on her forehead. This was *her* place for solitude and contemplation and she was loath to share it with anyone so soon after she had arrived.

'Stay down,' she said to the dog and then turned to look again. The person had left the path and was walking down towards where she sat. Even before the limp gave her away Binty saw that it was Rowena Fischer. She waved.

'May I join you?' Rowena asked as she approached, breathing heavily and leaning on a stick. 'Or, is this quality time on your own?'

'No, not at all, find a clean tuft to sit on.' Binty smiled warmly up at her and patted the grass.

'Thank you.' Rowena bent to stroke the dog and then found a suitable patch to sit on.

'Where's your dog?' Binty asked.

'Oh, Bruno's at the vet this afternoon. He's having an overhaul. Too long on the Menear's farm, I think.' She settled herself and then stared out to sea. 'What a gorgeous view from here.'

'Isn't it. There's always something happening out there.'

'Mmm. Is Robert working today?'

'Yes, but he doesn't often come up here with me anyway . . . unless it's with a bottle of wine late on a summer evening after all the other chores are done. He feels that he gets his fill of sea views from his stint at the lookout.' She looked at Rowena's bad leg, which was now concealed inside a pair of pale blue slacks. 'How's the leg progressing?'

'Oh, Phil is pleased. He says the plaster can be changed next week.'

'That's good news.' Binty noted the use of Dr Julyan's first name. 'I suppose that means you'll be getting ready to leave us soon?'

'Trying to get rid of me?' Rowena cast a teasing smile and then added, 'No, I'm in no hurry and Jacques is up to his neck in work. But, the day will come . . .'

'And how's Louise working out . . . in the cottage, I mean?'

'Oh, she's delightful and we're getting on fine. It would actually be quite difficult at times to manage without her.'

'Good, I'm glad to hear that.'

The two women, having temporarily exhausted the small talk, now both gazed out to sea. The breeze was picking up a knot or two and the flowers danced on their slender stalks. The dog gave a low moan of contentment and stretched its neck out on the grass and a gull, hopeful of a scrap to eat, strutted in the grass a safe distance from them.

'Is that Greg Treberthy's boat out there?' Rowena asked, breaking the silence.

'The one with the dark sail, yes.' Binty looked at her. 'Are you interested in sailing?'

'No, I don't sail. Never been that close to the water. I used to ride a lot though.'

'Well, when the leg's better you could get a hack around here. There are plenty of bridleways.'

'Oh, that was years ago, Binty, mostly when I spent some time in Hampshire.' She plucked at a tuft of grass. 'Do you sail?'

'Robert drags me out to crew sometimes, but I usually end up getting in the way.' She laughed. 'I think I'm the wrong build for that kind of activity.'

'So, what are your kinds of activity?' Rowena continued to watch the boat with the dark sail as it tacked into the wind.

'Mainly sedentary I'm afraid . . . WI, flower arranging, cooking for local functions . . . that sort of thing. But I do like walking . . . as you can see.' Binty suddenly felt that she had given away enough of her limited lifestyle. 'How did you know that's Greg's boat?'

'I didn't really. I heard he was taking Alf out this afternoon and I just guessed.'

Binty cast a furtive glance at Rowena as she continued to stare into the distance. *My*, she thought, *Mrs Fischer already knows how to tap into the Pengarth grapevine.*

'So, Alf's out there now?'

'Yes, I suppose so, unless he changed his mind.' Rowena looked down at the rough grass by her side and then began to run her hand lightly over the stubbly blades. Without looking up, she asked, 'You know Alf pretty well, don't you?'

'I've known him since we've lived here . . . that's about fifteen years . . . but I don't think anyone really knows him that well. He tends to keep a lot to himself. Why do you ask?'

Rowena did not reply for a few moments, but continued to tickle the palm of her hand. Then she stopped abruptly, looked up at the boat with the dark sail and said with a careless shrug, 'He saved my life, so I'm just curious . . .'

'Well, if you want to know more about Alf Curtis, the man to ask is my husband. Robert's known Alf for longer than any of us. They went to school together.'

'Really?' Rowena turned and stared wide-eyed at Binty. 'They go that far back?'

'Actually, it's a case of yes and no. After school they went to different universities and then lost contact, until they met up here again about twenty-five years later.'

'So, that was a co-incidence?'

'Pure co-incidence. It even transpired that Alf had married a distant cousin of Robert's and neither of us even knew that for years.'

'That would be Lydia?'

'Yes, Lydia. Poor Lydia.' Binty blinked as she tried to read Rowena's expression in the dazzling light. 'I never actually met her, you know . . . but, it's a funny thing, from early photographs I've seen of her, she looked not dissimilar to you. I said as much to Robert soon after we first met.'

'Oh? And what did Robert say to that?'

'He didn't say anything actually.' She shrugged and added with a little chuckle, 'But that's not unusual for him. My husband's a deep thinker.'

Rowena stretched her leg further out on the grass, twisted her torso so that she was taking her weight on her left arm and raised her face towards the sun.

Binty cast a sidelong glance at the profile of her companion's face.

There was a guilessness about Binty's manner that made her warm and approachable, but underneath the bland chubby façade there was also a steely quality. She had no intention now or ever of revealing a confidence that might betray a friend, but her instinct led her to suspect that at any moment she was about to be put to the test.

'What similarities did you see?' Rowena asked casually and Binty's lips twitched imperceptibly.

'Oh, it's hard to say,' she answered lightly. 'You know how it is with photographs. You can see one of your mother and say, goodness, doesn't that look like me at that age, but with another snap of the same person there will be no similarity at all. I suppose the photograph I saw of Lydia . . . the one Alf always kept in his sitting room . . . just captured an expression that I saw when we first met.' Her cheeks lifted and creased as she smiled sweetly at her companion. 'That's all really.'

'If Alf invites me in again I must have a look at that photograph,' Rowena said lightly. 'Perhaps I have a double.'

'I'm afraid that won't be possible, my dear. Alf took it down some time ago.'

'Oh, pity.'

'Mmm.' Binty saw that Greg's boat was now returning to Pengarth harbour and one of the men was lowering the mainsail. She turned back to Rowena and thought carefully before adding, 'You must understand this much about Alf, that he kept Lydia's illness very close. Still does. In fact there's many in the village who didn't even know he'd been married before word finally got out that she'd died. He certainly never abandoned her, but also he chose not to talk about her . . . not even to his friends. Lydia was a closed book in the private part of Alf's world and the few of us in the know always respect that. Even now that she's gone I suspect a pain still burns deep inside him . . . whatever the outward appearances.'

'But why should there be a pain? It wasn't his fault that . . .'

'I've said all I intend to say on the subject, Rowena. I'm just warning you in case you accidentally say something that might cause him . . . distress.'

It was clear that the subject was closed and the point was further emphasised by Binty suddenly pointing towards the village. 'Look, they're back.'

'So they are.' Rowena began the awkward business of rising to her feet. 'And so must I be going back. I've got to collect Bruno from the vet before they close.'

'I've enjoyed our chat.' Binty beamed a smile up at her. 'Perhaps we can walk our dogs together before you leave us.'

'Thank you, Binty, I'd like that.' As if on cue, the collie sat up, yawned and began scratching its ear. Rowena laughed and then turned to begin the climb back up the slope. 'Well, 'bye for now.'

Binty gave a little wave and then called the dog over to her side. As she stroked its matted fur and dodged the occasional friendly foray with its tongue, she thought about Rowena Fischer and wondered why she harboured the uncharitable hope that her stay in Pengarth might not be too much longer extended. Likeable as Rowena was, there was also an aura about her that suggested she might be the cause of disruption in the ordered running of Pengarth society.

Chapter Seventeen

THE calendar flipped over and suddenly it was July.

The Sinclair girls were down from university, together with their plans for meeting up with friends at Newquay for surfing, just as soon as mother had dealt with their dirty laundry.

Binty and Rowena had begun walking their dogs together twice a week. Rowena's original plaster had been removed and replaced with a less cumbersome one. Initial medical reports on the leg were favourable and she now walked with greater ease. But, just as an added precaution, she still carried the walking stick.

The Council's Highways Department had sent a letter to the Clerk to Pengarth Parish Council explaining at length that they had reached the decision to shave fifteen millimetres off the road calming humps in order to comply with specified measurement as laid down by the Highways Authority. BK had run off several copies of the letter and had gleefully popped one through Alf's letterbox.

There had also been a considerable amount of local excitement in the last week of June, when Customs and Excise officers had chased a van up the A30 and eventually caught it on Bodmin Moor. At the back of the van, in boxes marked *Cornish Pilchards,* they had found bags of cocaine with a street value of over a million pounds.

This highly satisfactory outcome had started after a tip off from the St Furda chandler, a Pengarth resident, who had been suspicious at the amount of cash being spent on boating equipment by two strangers. And by cash, he meant notes in large denominations. He had contacted Falmouth coastguard immediately, who had alerted the local Customs people and an immediate watch had been set up on the main arterial road, more in hope than expectation.

It was widely known that cocaine smuggling was a continuing headache for the authorities in Cornwall. Boats, mostly from Spain and Brittany, land their cargo in small coves near villages like

Pengarth and then, after the pay-off, the drugs are mostly driven straight up country to major distribution centres in the Midlands and further north. In the main the couriers are hardened criminal incomers, some resident in Cornwall under government re-housing schemes, and Customs officials in the Duchy find themselves stretched to their limits in trying to catch them.

It was unusual for middlemen to launder their gains so soon after a drop, but on this occasion they were either careless or in a hurry, so thanks to the sharp action of the astute chandler, the Customs men got lucky.

It was a huge haul and also a big story for the *Western Packet*, not to mention the national papers. Alf Curtis, whose mood since the sash window incident had tended to fluctuate between brooding and bellicose, had been relieved that for a change he was not responsible for making the headlines.

Then, on the first Saturday in July Pengarth co-incidentally had a second link with St Furda in the form of a home cricket fixture.

After his success with the Pengarth veterans team Robert had been persuaded to play for the village team in the absence of their regular opener, although he refused resolutely to keep wicket. St Furda was a very competitive team and long before strapping on his pads Robert was having misgivings about his decision to play; a decision that Binty had scathingly described as weakness in the face of blatant flattery by Darren Dowrick.

The afternoon of the match was cloudy with a light breeze off the sea, but it was warm enough to sit out on the grass to watch the cricket. At tea St Furda had notched up a formidable one hundred and sixty two for the loss of eight wickets in their allotted overs and Pengarth knew they had a battle ahead to overtake that score.

Robert collected his tea and a plate of sandwiches and then strolled over to join Binty on a tartan rug that she had laid out near the heavy roller. Their old dog lifted its head as it caught a whiff of ham and cress, which hung over the edges of thin-cut white bread.

'Ahhh,' Robert lowered himself onto the rug and balanced the teacup on a biscuit tin. 'Had yours I see.'

'Yes, I couldn't wait 'til you lot came off.' She gripped his knee. 'How are the old muscles holding up?'

'Fine, but I've only been standing at slip all afternoon. It'll probably be a different matter when I bat though.'

'Don't worry, you probably won't be in that long.'

'Thanks very much.' He looked over towards the pavilion. 'Ah, here comes Alf.'

'He's not playing, is he?' Binty looked horrified at the thought.

'No, he's umpiring. And gave one dodgy decision too. Riled the St Furda boys no end.'

'Hello, Sinclairs. Mind if I join you?' Alf squatted as gracefully as a man can whilst holding a full cup of tea and a plate full of cake.

'I was just telling Binty about that chap you gave out caught.' Robert bit into a sandwich.

'Well, he *was* caught! No doubt about it, a clean catch by the 'keeper. Don't know what the buggers were moaning about.'

'They were moaning, Alf,' Robert swallowed an intransigent lump of gristle and flinched, 'because you should have called a no ball.'

'What? The bowler's foot wasn't over the line. I may have many deficiencies, but deaf and blind I am not.'

'That may be so, old boy, but I'm afraid one of your deficiencies appears to be inadequate knowledge of the current laws of the game.'

'Eh?' Alf cast Robert a challenging look and scratched at his beard.

'The ball was above the batsman's shoulder when it reached him. In fact it was above his head. The law says that's a no ball and you should have called it.'

'You're joking.' Alf's mouth hung open. 'Are you saying that bouncers are no longer legit?'

'Not when it's the third one in the over.'

'Well, damn me . . . none of you blighters told me that, and I gave the poor sod out on forty-nine. Why didn't you tell me?'

'Because you're the umpire, Alf.' Darren said as he joined them and settled himself next to Robert. 'And, more important, we needed the wicket.'

They all laughed and the *poor sod* who had failed to notch up a half century was soon forgotten.

'Good tea, this,' Alf said to Darren with his mouth full of cake. 'Louise make it?'

'Yeah, she and two others. She'll be coming over to join us in a minute.'

There was a clatter of plates from the wooden pavilion and a raucous outburst of laughter from the few who were having their tea inside.

A couple of opportunistic gulls had flown onto the ground and were now strolling around in the hope of picking up a discarded crust from one of the groups gathered on the grass. In the distance the sound of the ice cream van's discordant chimes reminded them that the holiday season would soon be in full swing, but apart from that the only sound beyond the ground was a tractor silageing in the field adjacent to the track.

Alf suppressed a belch and leant back on his elbows, letting a brief ray of sunshine bathe his face. Darren peered at him for a while and then asked, 'Ever thought of shaving that fungus off, Alf?'

Alf opened an eye and swatted at a fly. 'Certainly not, my old flower. We don't want to frighten the horses do we? Anyway no one would recognise me.'

'I'm sure it would take years off you, Alf,' Binty added, now also studying Alf, as if for the first time.

'What is this, a conspiracy to have me buy razor blades again?' Alf opened the other eye and raised his head. 'Ah, hello there, young Louise. Sit you down on a corner of this fine Sinclair tartan.'

Louise giggled and then, with a sigh, sat with her back to the roller.

'Finished in there, or would you like some help?' Binty asked.

'We've finished serving the teas, but some help with the washing up would be nice, thanks.'

'You're a busy lass these days,' Robert commented as he retied a shoelace, 'what with Smugglers' Cottage and all your regular work.'

'Oh, it's not too much, really.' Louise glanced at her brother and ran a hand through her curly brown hair in a self-conscious gesture.

'That's not all she's doing,' Darren said proudly. 'She's also part of the Wrappers for Sappers team.'

'Oh, Darren, that's nothing . . .'

'No, it's not nothing, Louise.' Binty interrupted. 'It's a wonderful thing to be doing for our boys over there. It's so easy to forget what they're going through.'

Alf sat up. 'What's this? What've I been missing?'

'Tell him, Louise,' Darren urged.

'Well, a group of us heard that one of the things our lads out in Iraq like most . . .' Louise began.

'. . . other than what they can only get on R & R . . . !' Alf interrupted.

'Shut up, Alf.' Binty frowned at him. 'Go on, Louise.'

'. . . other than letters from home, are sweets. Not chocolate, because that melts. So we decided to get together and send some wrapped boiled sweets. At first we posted it to an Engineer regiment, so we called it Wrappers for Sappers . . . bit of a silly name really . . . but now we send sweets to all of them in Iraq, and to Afghanistan too.'

'Don't they get pretty sticky before they arrive?' Robert asked as he threw a crust to one of the gulls.

'I expect they're a bit tacky when they actually reach the men, but they travel out in sealed containers. Anyway we've had letters back and they really seem pleased to get them.' Louise stopped with a shy smile and glanced at her brother.

'Bravo,' Alf said. 'I bet they are. Good for you. Robert, what was it that our generation used to send to the US army in Vietnam?'

'Did you send things? I don't think I did.' Robert looked thoughtfully at his bat. 'It wasn't our war, so . . .'

'No, I know it wasn't but I got very caught up in the anti-war propaganda at the time. Didn't you? No, perhaps not. You never were much of a rebel.' He turned a wistful gaze over towards the pavilion. 'Yes, it certainly was an age of rebellion . . . flower power, protest songs, marches, banners, and all that sort of thing. It may be hard to believe it looking at me now, but I used to join those anti-war marches, shouting slogans with all the rest.'

'What stirred you into doing that?' Binty gave him a lopsided grin.

Alf was pensive for a moment and then snapped his fingers. 'Jane Fonda! Yes, it was Jane Fonda who moved me to take action, no doubt about it. My God, I had a crush on that girl! Did you ever see *Barbarella*?'

They all burst out laughing at that and perhaps also at the thought of the young Curtis marching in protest with the hippies. The gulls took off in fright and Darren shook the dregs from his empty cup onto the grass, while a wasp settled unseen on the remains of a cup cake.

'There's not the passion for that sort of thing today,' Robert mused. 'This is an age of cynical acceptance . . . more's the pity.'

'It's not all cynical, Robert,' Darren said. 'People still march in protest when they want action taken. And it's not just the young either.'

'All right, they do, but it's usually out of self-interest. That wasn't the spirit of the anti-Vietnam War protests. People who marched then believed they could change the world with good intentions.'

No one said anything for a while as they pondered that opinion. Louise shook her head gently, but was too diffident to express her thoughts on the matter. Binty peered down the neck of her thermos flask and then screwed the top back on. Alf waved the wasp away and Darren idly prodded at some cake crumbs on his plate.

Then Alf cleared his throat.

'I can't be sure now what my intentions were back then and I certainly can't remember what we sent to Vietnam in the sixties . . . if anything at all . . . but I can tell you that the GIs used to send souvenirs back to the USA.' He sat up and drew a knee to his chest. 'I had an aunt, married to an American, living in Pennsylvania, and she used to collect some of the stuff they sent back home from the war zone. She gave me a few of these souvenirs on a visit to the UK. I remember one thing in particular - it was a beautiful silk map of an area in North Vietnam – probably a place they later napalmed out of existence - and apparently these maps became popular in the States as headscarves. Actually even I found that a bit inappropriate at the time, but I've still got it in the back of a drawer somewhere.'

Darren looked up at the pavilion and saw the other umpire begin his walk out to the middle. The tea break was over.

'Mrs Fischer has a memento from the Vietnam War,' Louise said softly. 'She keeps it on her dressing table.'

They all turned to stare at her and a blush began to rise up her neck from sudden embarrassment at having revealed what her employer kept in her bedroom. But it was too late now to retract.

'What is it?' Alf asked as he brushed crumbs from his trousers. 'A Gook's jockstrap?'

'Alf, really!'

'Sorry, Binty.' He slapped his wrist.

'It's a shell.'

'I've got to pad up,' Darren looked at Robert. 'You're in six. Come on, Alf, the fielders are heading out.'

Alf groaned and began to get to his feet.

'What, a sea shell?' Binty asked.

'No, not that kind of shell. It's actually a shell casing, shiny, about so tall.' She held her forefinger and thumb apart. 'She keeps mascara brushes and things like that in it. Quite pretty really, if you forget what it was used for.'

Robert noticed Alf's reaction before the others.

He had frozen in the action of pulling on the umpire's white jacket and now he was staring down at Louise, his eyes like headlamps under cascading eyebrows.

'A shell casing? You sure?'

'Yes. She told me.'

Slowly he resumed pulling the jacket over his shoulders.

'What colour is the shell casing, gunmetal or brass?'

Louise seemed perplexed at the intensity in his voice. She dipped her mouth and gave a little shake of the head. 'I . . . I'm not sure I can remember exactly.'

He stood over her, his expression unchanged, mechanically securing the coat buttons. 'Was it brass, Louise? Think, girl.'

'Brass. Yes, polished brass.'

Alf did not reply, but blinked rapidly and drew his lips tightly together. He stood very still for a few moments, looking away and staring intently into the distance. Then he turned abruptly and plodded off towards the square.

Louise looked anxiously at Binty, who raised her eyebrows and shrugged.

Binty turned to her husband. 'What's got into him?'

'God knows.' Robert watched Alf reach the square and then carefully replace the bails on the stumps. 'Who can tell what gets into that man these days . . . or why?'

'Blimey, he quite gave me the creeps just then.' Louise shuddered and then began to collect cups and plates. 'I wonder why the colour of the shell matters so much?'

'Don't worry about it, dear.' Binty rose and eased her shoulder muscles. 'We all have to live with Alf's funny ways. I'll come and help with the washing up.'

Robert continued to stare pensively across the field, rolling and unrolling the top of the rubber grip on his bat.

Pengarth's last wicket fell at ten past seven. They had failed by twenty-four runs to beat St Furda and Robert had failed by thirty runs to match his heroic performance for the Veterans earlier in June. Not for the first time in his village cricketing career he swore that that was his last game.

The Pengarth cause had not been helped by some further inexplicable umpiring lapses from Alf Curtis. He had called two five-ball overs, given Darren out LBW off a ball clearly going down the leg side and been too late in getting out of the way of a hook shot that would certainly have crossed the boundary. The ball had ricocheted off his boot and then along the ground and into the grateful hands of the square leg fielder. Alf had hopped around for a bit, but showed no sign of being amused by the incident. The furious batsman had tried the same shot off the next ball and had merely succeeded in top edging to the wicketkeeper.

However, all of these mishaps were soon forgotten or forgiven by the time the players, duly showered, sprayed and powdered, all met up at the public bar end of the Lugger. All, that is except for Alf. He had muttered an apology to Darren and had slipped away immediately after stumps had been drawn.

Robert, pulling off his grass-stained whites in the pavilion, had watched him walk away with the demeanour of a man who had been condemned to be hanged.

Later that evening Binty, seeing Robert about to accept a third pint, dragged him away from his discussion with Greg on the merits of the last season's Beaujolais nouveau and then out of the pub. As they stepped into the clean, warm, salty air of Fore Street, Binty linked arms with her husband and they began a slow stroll up the hill to their home. They did not speak for a while and gradually, as they walked, the sounds of merriment from the Lugger faded and gave way to those of high tide waves thumping onto the harbour rocks.

They reached their front door and Binty uncoupled herself from Robert, reaching up to pluck a few dead petunia flowers from their hanging basket.

'I expect we'll have to take this down again soon.' She threw the dead heads into the gutter.

'When the season starts properly, you mean?'

'Yes. How many times was it vandalised last year? Must have been three or four.'

'Young hooligans. I don't know why modern youth can't hold its drink.' He pushed the front door open and went in. 'Hello, anyone home?'

'The girls are clubbing in Truro, dear. I lent them my key.' Binty closed the door and took off her shoes. 'I don't suppose they'll be back before we're in bed.'

'Clubbing! That's what cavemen used to do to their women.' He grunted. 'Who's bringing them home?'

Binty stopped and gave him a disbelieving look. 'Robert, put the brain in gear . . . we lent them the car.'

'Ah yes, so we did.' He tapped his forehead and wandered into the kitchen. 'Like a nightcap?'

'Of the milky variety, yes please.'

'Right, I'll join you.' He poured some milk into a saucepan and put it on the hob. 'Now, where do you keep the chocolate?'

'In the usual place. That cupboard on the left.'

She sat on the padded seat under the window and watched as Robert pottered around, finding utensils and ingredients, whilst keeping an eye on the simmering milk.

'What's the matter with Alf, do you think?'

'The matter . . . ?' He dropped the top of the chocolate tin on the floor and cursed.

'Wipe that off before you put it back on. There's dog hairs on the floor.'

He raised his eyebrows, but did as he was told.

'What makes you think there's anything the matter with Alf?'

'Well, it's the way he's been lately . . . moody, snappy and generally unpredictable.'

'Alf's always been unpredictable.' He poured out the milk, stirred it and then handed her a mug before sitting down at the table. 'Anyway, he's had a rough time emotionally in the last month. He's only human, you know. He'll get over it.'

'I don't think it's just Lydia, Robert. Something else is gnawing away at him and, perhaps I shouldn't say this, but I think it's connected with Rowena Fischer somehow.'

'Rowena? What on earth can she . . . ?' He laughed and ran a hand over his bald pate. 'Is this your famous woman's intuition again?'

'Call it that, if you like, but all I know is that his odd moods crop up whenever Mrs Fischer comes on the scene.'

'Are you referring to the cricket match this afternoon?'

'Yes, that's the latest instance.'

'But she wasn't even there, old girl.' He recoiled as the hot liquid burnt his lip and a few drops fell onto the table.

'Don't be obtuse, Robert. I know she wasn't there physically, but that odd business about the shell casing . . . or whatever it was Louise saw . . . had a most peculiar effect. You saw him.' She leant across to the draining board and seized a dishcloth, which she then threw over to him. He dabbed at the spill. 'And when have you known Alf not join us all in the pub after a game?'

Robert did not reply, but clutched the mug in both hands and stared at a point somewhere behind Binty's head.

It was true. Even by Alf's erratic standards his behaviour since the day of Rowena's rescue had been mercurial. Nevertheless, old friend or not, Robert did not see it as his place to interfere in what was going on in Alf's head. He was old enough to sort it out for himself. If there was a problem and it was somehow connected with Rowena Fischer, then he had no clue as to what it was about, or how he could do anything to help. On the other hand, if . . .

'Well? What do you think?' Binty cut into his musing. 'You know him better than any of us.'

'My instinct is to leave well alone. If he asks for advice, I'll give it to him, but meanwhile . . .' He put the mug down and held her gaze.

'Fine friend you are, Robert Sinclair . . . if that's all you have to offer.'

'All right then,' he said tetchily and pushed his chair back from the table, 'what would you have me do? It's all very well conjuring up this . . . this . . . impression of a soul in torment, but when it comes to shove, I bet it's me who's expected to do the shoving and not you! What would you have me do, eh?'

For a few seconds Binty was taken aback by this sudden outburst. In the third phase of his life Robert had become a placid and cogitative soul, rarely given to displays of emotion or anger. She blinked and drew in a breath.

'No, I expect you're right, dear,' she said calmly, staring at her mug. 'It's none of our business. It's just that I'm fond of Alf and . . . well . . . he has no one else now . . . not that he even had Lydia during the past fifteen years or so . . . but now he's completely on his own, except for his friends. That's why I thought we ought . . .'

'Stop!' She looked up to see him smiling raggedly at her. 'You win. You wily wheedling women always win in the end. If you really think it's that important I'll find an excuse to go and see him tomorrow and try to persuade him to get whatever it is off his chest. Is that good enough for you?'

Binty treated him to a beatific smile.

'Thank you, dear, I'm sure that would be the right thing to do.' She blew him a kiss. 'Wouldn't it be awful if Alf did something terrible and we had just stood by and never tried to help?'

'What on earth are you suggesting? Being a bit melodramatic, aren't you?'

'Maybe, maybe not. I just want to make sure we're not ignoring a friend in need, that's all.'

He nodded at that, then looked at the wall clock and yawned. 'I'm on first watch tomorrow, but I'll go and see him right after I hand over at noon.'

Asleep in bed, Binty did not hear their daughters creep in through the back door an hour later, but Robert lay with his eyes open, staring at the chink in the curtains through which a three-quarter moon shone silvery-white. He could not erase Alf's face from his mind: it was the face of a man who had seen a ghost. If that were the case and Binty was right about his state of mind, now might indeed be a good time to begin a little exorcising.

Chapter Eighteen

MIKE Nancarrow, the decorator, crouched low to squeeze through a narrow gap between the gorse bushes. It was a tricky business and he knew that he would end up with several scratches and probably a sore back, but he expected the reward to make the pain worthwhile.

Ever since he had been a nine year-old boy he had been snaring rabbits along these paths. He used a wire loop system taught to him by his father, a man well known to successive gamekeepers on the two local estates. Mike's dad was still alive, but now lived in a small flat in the Poltock almshouse and kept a seat warm in the local pub, regaling all who would listen with stories of his past exploits. Nancarrow senior had handed down many of his skills on to his only son and some of them were actually legal.

Mike's father had taught him rabbit snaring at an early age and as a result the boy had acquired a liking for their meat. Preparing a rabbit was a bloody business, but he considered it fully worthwhile once the creature was bubbling away in the cooking pot. It was a point of strong disagreement between Mike and his girlfriend, Rose, but she had learned simply to be out of the house when the operation was taking place.

Mike now lay flat on his stomach and unhitched the wire handle from its wooden securing stake and reeled it in. There was a fat one on the end, garrotted and glassy-eyed, but still fresh and intact. Sometimes, when he was not early enough to his traps, he would find that badgers or foxes had been the beneficiaries of his kill and that always made him resentful. One should be permitted to enjoy the fruits of one's labours. Creatures of the wild should follow nature's calling and make their own kill, rather than deprive him of his. So went his logic.

He unhitched the loop and put the rabbit into a hessian bag he had dragged in behind him. Next he wiped the loop and wound it up carefully. He never set a trap in the same place after a kill, owing either to a superstitious notion or to a suspicion that rabbits might just be more intelligent than was generally imagined.

Mike completed winding the wire, slipped it into one of the large pockets of his brown overalls and then prepared to reverse out of the undergrowth. This was his favoured hunting ground and he had set five traps in the area the previous day. He now still had three more to check, the first having yielded nothing.

It still gave him a schoolboyish thrill to think that he knew secret places and tunnels in the rough areas off the coastal path into which no other human had ventured: at least, not since his father had been active in the pursuit of the poor man's venison, as he liked to call it. Rose sometimes said that that was why he was still so small – all that tunnelling around had stunted his growth. But, then she had to admit that there might be something in the rabbit juices that made up for his lack of height in other ways.

Mike backed off as far as he had to before reaching a point at which he could turn around. He preferred not to be spotted emerging onto the main path at any time, but to be seen coming out backwards would be both undignified and embarrassing.

The early morning sun slanted like a hundred laser beams through the tangled undergrowth as he reached the last bush before the path, dragging his sack behind. He was about to emerge when he sensed rather than heard footsteps from the upslope. A quick assessment told him they were coming in his direction, so he pulled himself back in and froze a couple of yards from the track.

These were not the casual footsteps of a Sunday rambler. There was something urgent about them. A heavy tread, the odd stumble on a root and the middle aged pant of an unfit male. Mike slowly shrank back into his warren and then remained still and alert.

There was the tiniest of gaps through which he could see the pathway, but it was enough to get a snapshot of the walker – or the lower half of him. A few strides and the man had gone past, breathing heavily. Mike saw a flash of dark brown trousers tucked into socks, brown leather shoes and a walking stick. Not much to go on, but he thought there was something familiar about the brown trousers.

When the walker had passed, Mike scrambled forward to get a complete view of the hurrying figure. He emerged from his tunnel and pushed back a branch of gorse, but he was a second too late. There was a bend in the path and the walker had disappeared around it. All Mike got was another snapshot of a dirty brown shoe.

He turned to cast a cautious glance along the path to make sure that there was no one else coming and then emerged. Curiosity had now overridden his original mission and he set off immediately in pursuit of the walker, brushing earth and gorse particles off his overall as he went. He paused at one of his known tunnels and slung the hessian sack as far as he could into the dense thicket, before trotting on up the track. Then, scampering on he rounded another bend and saw the man in full outline.

It was Alf Curtis.

Mike nearly laughed out loud. Alf Curtis on an early Sunday morning hike was as unheard of as George Harris eating a vegetarian pasty. He stifled his urge and sank back out of view. Something about Alf's body language told him that now was not the time to reveal himself, so Mike stalked on.

Alf had reached a fork in the track. The main route was to the right and followed the coast all the way to the Tamar. The left fork was less used, other than by locals or people doing a circular walk back to Pengarth. After hesitation and a backward glance, Alf turned left and then set off at the same lumbering gait.

Mike followed in pursuit, hugging the side of the path and only slowing when he reached the fork. But when he got there Alf had disappeared and he muttered an oath. He knew that one way the path tapered into a narrow strip between wizened little trees, bracken and scrub, until eventually it widened onto one of farmer Menear's field tracks. That track then widened out and ran adjacent to Smugglers' Cottage before joining the Pengarth road. But, just before the field track there was an even narrower fissure in the scrub that wound around to the back garden of the cottage. He used to go up there as a boy, pretending that he was a smuggler carrying his contraband up from the coast. One day, old Mrs Crabtree had spotted him and chased him off with threats of unleashing the dog.

Because Alf had disappeared so quickly along the straightest part of the path, Mike guessed that he had taken the smugglers' route and so that was the path he now followed, until the rear of the cottage came into view.

Squeezing between the trunk of a stunted oak and a large pitted rock, Mike found a vantage point from which he could clearly see the back of the building. He pressed himself against the rock – which was the size of two hay bales and home to small ferns and lichen - and tried to see where Alf had gone.

He was just beginning to think that he had been wrong about his quarry's destination when, about thirty yards from his position, he saw one of the gorse bushes move and then the top of Alf's silvery head appeared.

Alfie boy, Mike whispered to himself, *what are you up to?*

Mike wriggled along the side of the rock until he had found a more comfortable position and then waited. He had the time to kill, there being nothing on until cricket at Falstones that afternoon.

It was unusual for Pengarth to have two fixtures on the same weekend, but this had been an exception and he had volunteered to make up the numbers. Darren had promised to pick him up at ten to two, but apart from collecting his rabbits, having a bite to eat in the Lugger and getting his gear together, he had all the time he needed to wait for Alf Curtis's next move.

Suddenly the silence was disturbed by the sound of St Grace's old cracked bell wafting up from the village on the morning breeze. This seemed to be the signal for action down below, because Mike saw a hand part the gorse as Alf squeezed his bulk towards the overgrown jack-and-jill hedge at the end of the cottage garden. Once he reached that point he paused again and then, apparently satisfied there was no one about, he found a foothold and heaved himself up. Once more he stopped, perched on top of the wall, and then dropped over the other side with a grunt that carried back to Mike's rock.

Mike, observing this charade with amazement, shook his head and muttered, 'Alf, you certainly ain't no James Bond.'

Alf crouched low and, giving a passable impression of a geriatric kangaroo with piles, loped across the rough cut grass and up to one of the cottage windows. Mike looked on in amazement as Alf pressed his face to the windowpane, shielding his eyes from the sun's glare as he did so.

Then, Mike heard the car.

It was approaching the cottage slowly, but Alf did not seem to hear it for several seconds. When he did, he stepped back from the window and cocked his head as if to locate where it was coming from, but there could only be one direction. Someone was driving up the lane from the road and, even as Alf was reacting, the car turned into the cottage driveway.

Alf crouched and ran to the wall by the lane and, to Mike's astonishment, with the aid of his stick almost vaulted it. The car pulled into the drive, the engine was cut and a few moments later a door slammed shut.

She came around the side of the cottage holding a bunch of flowers just as Alf rose from the other side of the wall and started to walk nonchalantly along the lane towards the road. He nearly made the cover of the garage, but she had spotted movement out of the corner of her eye. Instinctively, Mike shrank back against his rock and a piece of fern poked him in the ear.

'Hello,' Rowena called out from the middle of the garden, the bunch of flowers by her side. 'Good morning?'

It was a startled response, as if another person was the last thing she expected so see at that time of the day. Her unexpected arrival had obviously also shocked Alf, who had nearly been caught in the compromising act of snooping through her window, and Mike, from the safety of his rock, was left wondering how these two disorientated people were going to resolve the situation.

After what seemed a long while, Alf emerged at the other end of the garage and then stopped suddenly as if just seeing her for the first time. His face expressed surprise and he waved his stick in a friendly greeting.

'Rowena!' he hailed. 'Good day to you.'

'This is early for you, Alf?' Again the questioning inflection. 'Are you out for a stroll?'

'Yes, this is my way of communing . . . not being a churchgo-er,' he shouted back.

'I would normally be in church, but . . . not today.' She looked down at the flowers, hesitated and then seemed suddenly to come to a decision. 'Why don't you come in? There's a gate just there . . . by the garage. It's a bit overgrown, but it does open.'

'Ah, yes.' He went over to it and fumbled with the catch. 'Well, not for long, I've got a lot to catch up with.'

That was the last distinct word that Mike heard from either of them. When Alf met Rowena Fischer in the middle of the garden their voices dropped and he was only able to follow the gestures that accompanied the murmur of their voices.

Alf pointed to the bunch of flowers. She hesitated and then indicated a corner of the garden, talking without looking at him. Alf pulled himself upright and folded both hands over the crook of his stick. While he listened his eyes were transfixed on her face and his entire body went as still as Lot's wife on a salty day. When she had finished talking, she raised both arms in a gesture of futility, like a stricken bird that has accepted its inability to fly.

Alf remained motionless, whilst her gaze stayed locked on the same spot in that unkempt corner of the garden. Mike craned his head forward and squinted in an effort to see what was the focus of their attention, but there was nothing obvious. All he could see were two rotting stumps of what might once have been legs of a garden bench.

Then Alf suddenly came out of his trance and, robot-like, reached out tentatively as if to touch her arm. But, he pulled out halfway and his hand fell back by his side. He might have said a parting word of farewell, or he might not, but after the failed gesture he turned and plodded back to the side gate by the garage.

She did not at first seem to notice that he had gone, but proceeded to the place where the two stumps stood and reverently placed the flowers between them. For several seconds her head hung low as if she were saying a prayer and only then did Rowena look over her shoulder to see that Alf had left the garden.

She turned abruptly and then stood and stared after him until he had rounded the corner in the lane. Then, after a swift backward glance at the flowers, she made her way around to the front of the cottage.

The stage was bare, the actors had gone and only the props remained.

Mike eased his body away from the rock and stared up at the sky, his mind in confusion. He had no doubt that he had witnessed some kind of human drama, a mimed performance of great emotional significance, but any kind of explanation was completely beyond his powers of analysis.

He came alive with a start as he heard the back door opening. Crouching low, he slipped back along the path just as Rowena let Bruno into the garden.

Three dead rabbits, one in a hessian sack, made a badger family an excellent meal that night.

Robert knocked once more on the back door, having already hammered on the front, but still there was no answer. He looked at his watch. A quarter past twelve.

He stood there in his NCI uniform wondering what to do. He had handed the watch over and now he was growing hungry. Binty was cooking a roast leg of lamb, which he knew would be ready by one o'clock, but she was aware that he was calling on Alf at the end of the watch. It had, after all, been her idea. Now Alf appeared to be out and Robert was loath to break up his Sunday afternoon by having to return later.

He went round to the front of the bookshop again and peered up at the office window. It was closed, but that probably meant nothing, as Alf almost certainly had not yet mended the sash cords. In the end he shook his head, shrugged and turned to walk up the hill. It was quite possible that Alf was genuinely away from home and not just lurking out of sight.

He walked in through the open front door and called out, 'Binty, I'm back!'

There was a muffled reply from the rear of the house and he carried on up to the bedroom to change out of his uniform.

'Couldn't find him,' Robert announced to Binty's back a few minutes later as he walked into the kitchen, armed with a schooner of dry sherry. 'He must be out.'

'Hello, dear.' She finished what she was doing and turned around. 'Couldn't find who? Alf?'

'Yes. I did all but rouse the dead at his house, but no joy.' He bent down and peered into the oven. 'Lunch nearly ready?'

'Ten minutes.' She dried her hands. 'You're not leaving it at that, are you? You'll try again after lunch?'

He sighed, having expected this response. His wife did not give up that easily once her course was set.

'Oh, I expect so. Where do you suggest I try next then?'

'The Lugger would seem to be an obvious place. I'm surprised you didn't pop in on your way back.'

'I thought about it, but then I'd have stopped for a pint and been late for lunch.' He fumbled around in a drawer for cutlery. 'Hungry work up at the lookout you know.'

'How was it today? Any excitements?'

'No, thank God. A couple of walkers stopped for a chat, that's all. Barometer's dropping though, and the wind's picking up. Could have some rain later.' He stopped and inclined his head. 'Where are the girls? All I can hear is the sound of silence.'

'They've gone to the yacht club for lunch with friends.'

'Not taken the car again, I hope.'

She laughed as she removed her apron. 'No, don't worry, they were given a lift.'

Robert grunted and then went to turn on the radio. Binty completed her preparations and a few minutes after that they sat down to eat their meal.

They did not have much to discuss and in any event Robert's mind had switched back to the unanswered question of Alf's whereabouts. His friend was never the most predictable of men, but at least ubiquity had always been one of his qualities. He was the sort of person who one noticed by his absence and Alf had now been absent for several hours.

Robert was almost relieved when the meal ended. He gave Binty a hasty peck on the cheek, apologised for abandoning the washing up and then left the house, heading for the Lugger.

He pushed past the velveteen curtain, stepped aside to allow someone to pass, then went up to the bar. Elsie saw him and came over.

'Yes, Robert, what can I get you?'

'I can't stay, Elsie, but can you tell me . . . have you seen Alf today?' A cursory scan of the clientele had drawn a blank.

'Not in here today, nor yesterday for that matter.' She reached for a glass. 'But Mike saw him this morning . . . out walking.'

'Walking? Alf?'

'Yes, so he said. Along the coast path I think.'

'When was that? Did he say?'

'Early, I think. Mike was out . . . well, you know.' She opened her eyes wide.

'I see. Do you know if he's at home now?'

'Who? Alf?'

'No. Mike.'

'No, he's due over to Falstones playing cricket.' She looked up at the clock. 'Darren should be picking him up about now.'

'I'll try to catch him.' Robert turned on his heel and hurried to the door, causing a temporary disruption in the flow of conversation.

Mike lived in a small rented house with Rose up a cobbled lane near the top of the old village. Beyond that there were modern houses in what was always known as the new village. Many of those houses were holiday homes, with names like *Driftwood* and *Sea Vista* and price tags that put them beyond the financial reach of most born and bred locals. Mike had the use of the yard at the back of the house, where he kept his paints and the other tools of his trade in a timber shed and where there was just enough room for him to park his van.

The van was there when Robert arrived, out of breath and perspiring, but there was no answer to his knock. He went round to the back and put his face to a window. No sign of occupation. Darren must have come and gone.

He cursed and set off down the hill again, pulling out his mobile as he went.

'Bints, it's me. I'm going to have to drive over to Falstones. . . .Yes, I've been to the Lugger, but it seems the only person who's seen him today is Mike and he's playing cricket over there . . . I don't know . . . maybe an hour, maybe two . . . What? . . . No, I don't know his mobile number. Look, I might call you later. 'Bye.'

He reached his lock-up and checked through the crack in the next-door garage to see if the Volvo was there. It was. He swung his garage door open and then checked his pocket for the car key.

A couple of minutes later he was driving into Fore Street.

A camper van with a Welsh sticker on the rear door held him back as he wound his way out of the village and he thumped the steering wheel in frustration. Once they joined the main road going north he executed a risky overtake and received a horn blast from a frightened oncoming motorist.

'Calm down,' he said angrily to himself and slowed as he approached the outskirts of Grampound Road village.

For most of the way to the A30 the route was a narrow snaking road with high hedges and flashing glimpses of cultivated fields and far-off china clay waste tips. It was, in normal circumstances, an attractive drive, until one reached Cornwall's main arterial road, but the countryside's charms offered few distractions for the man at the wheel.

The car curled round the sharp bend at the junction with the main highway and then accelerated for a mile before turning off again onto the Newquay road. As Robert slowed to take the left turn he noted busy leaf activity in an ash copse by the verge. The wind was picking up.

He had never been to Falstones, but he knew exactly where the turning was, having passed it many times on his way to Newquay airport. Finding the cricket ground was another matter.

He stopped and asked three people, one of whom was a foreigner, before he was able to get precise directions. It was up a rutted lane behind a former Methodist Chapel, which was now a children's nursery.

'*I hope to God he's not fielding*,' Robert prayed as the car bounced along the track. '*At least if he's batting I won't have to wait long.*'

He pulled up alongside a row of cars that strung out from a faded weatherboarded pavilion and studied the individual fielders. None was familiar and he gave a sigh of relief. Pengarth was batting, so Mike should be in the pavilion. He got out of the car and went across.

'Darren,' Robert hailed Pengarth's skipper who was approaching from a stroll around the boundary, 'how's it going?'

'Oh, hello, Robert. Fancy seeing you over here.' He looked out at the square and then back at Robert. 'Fine, so far. Only one wicket down and twenty odd on the board. Having a change of heart about playing then?'

'No chance of that.' Robert shaded his eyes. 'Mike Nancarrow's not out there is he?'

'No, he's not in for a while. You looking for him then?'

'Yes. In the pavilion?'

'Should be.'

'Thanks.' Robert began to move off.

'See you later in the Lugger?'

'Maybe,' he called back over his shoulder and then hurried on.

The familiar cocktail of liniment, foot powder and stale sweat hit him as he entered the changing room. Mike was hunched forward on a bench screwing a new stud into his boot and appeared not to hear him come in.

'Hello, Mike.'

'Blimey!' Mike jumped and almost lost his grip on the boot. 'Robert! Didn't half make me jump, creeping up like that. What're you doin' here?'

Robert smiled apologetically and sat down beside him. 'Looking for you actually. I'm hoping you can help me find Alf.'

'Alf?' Mike looked at him cautiously and gave the stud key a final twist.

'Yes, you seem to be the only one who's seen him since yesterday afternoon. He's not at home and I've looked in the Lugger.'

'Could he be on watch?' Mike asked hopefully, now pulling on the repaired boot.

'He's not on watch this weekend. When did you see him . . . and where?'

Mike hesitated for a time, his concentration fully on tying the bootlace. Eventually he sat upright and leaned back against a dirty pair of flannels hanging from the hook above his head. He planted his hands on his knees and stared out of the dirty glass of the pavilion window.

'I don't like telling tales, Robert . . . specially if it's about someone I have a regard for.' He turned then to meet Robert's gaze. 'But, you're a friend of his and I expect you've a good reason to want to know where he's to.'

'I do have a good reason. I think he could be in some kind of a fix and I want to help him sort it out.' Robert patted his bald pate and sighed. 'But first I need to find the old bugger.'

'Ok then . . . I saw him this morning, round about when the church bell was ringing, up at Smugglers' Cottage.' Mike watched keenly for a reaction to this information.

'Smugglers'?' Robert frowned. 'Mrs Fischer's place? Did you see him go in?'

At that moment they were distracted by a concerted shout from the square and a few audible groans from outside the pavilion. A wicket had fallen.

'No, he didn't go in. It looked like he didn't want to be seen and she came back while he was looking through the window.'

'What? You mean . . . looking through one of the cottage windows?' Robert stopped and looked up as a Pengarth man came in to put on his pads.

'That's right. Then he heard the car coming and he scarpered. She came round the corner . . .'

'Hold on, Mike.' Robert lowered his voice and leaned closer to him. 'Did you notice which window he was looking through?'

Mike looked puzzled and scratched his head with a nervous gesture. 'Does it matter?'

'It might.'

'Dunno, Robert, I . . .'

'Was it on the left or right side of the cottage . . . from the back . . . I assume you were somewhere at the back when you saw them?'

'Yes, I was in the bush at the back . . . I'd been rabbiting.' His face then contorted as he tried to recollect. 'It was a window . . . on the right.'

'On the right. I see,' Robert said softly. 'So, what happened next?'

The dismissed batsman came storming into the changing room and flung his bat into the kit bag. There was a dark stain down one trouser leg. 'I was never run out. Bloody umpire needs a guide dog.'

'Hard luck, mate,' Mike said and then returned his attention to Robert.

'Alf had hopped over the wall and was trying to look as if he'd been out walking, but she saw him and called him over. She was holding a bunch of flowers.' He knew that the next bit would be difficult, because he did not understand it himself. 'They got talking, but I couldn't hear what they were saying. I think she was upset, because she didn't seem to notice when Alf just sloped off. Then, when he was out of sight up the lane she just . . . just laid the flowers in a corner of the garden.'

Mike stopped and waited for Robert's reaction. For a few seconds there was none, because he was trying to picture the strange scene and to put it all into some kind of perspective. The aggrieved batsman, having tossed his box into a corner, left the room, still muttering.

'What did you do then?'

'I left. Went straight back home. Even forgot to pick up my rabbits.'

Robert's lips tightened and he tugged distractedly at an earlobe. For a few seconds he appeared to have forgotten that Mike was sitting beside him. Then, with a sigh, he turned back to face the young decorator.

'Thanks for that, Mike. At least you've given me a clue where I should start looking.' Robert started to get up from the bench and then had a thought. 'Have you told anyone else about this?'

'No . . . except to say in the Lugger I'd seen Alf out walkin'. Didn't see anything to be gained by goin' into details.'

'No, you're right, there's nothing to be gained by gossip.' He stood up and toed a loose bat back into its kitbag. 'But I think it would be a good idea if you continued to keep this to yourself . . . at least until I've found Alf.'

'You can count on me.'

'I know.' Robert smiled grimly down at him. 'Don't worry, he'll probably turn up with a simple explanation and we'll all have a good laugh in the Lugger tonight.'

'I hope so.'

Robert tapped him on the shoulder, turned to leave the changing room and then paused in the doorway to allow someone in. He glanced out at the sky and then back at Mike. 'I hope the rain holds off for you.'

He gave Mike a thumbs-up as he left the pavilion and exchanged a passing word with George Harris before going back to his car. Pengarth were thirty-eight for two.

Halfway back from Falstones Robert pulled into a lay-by just past the locked gates of a sand and aggregate dump.

The countryside across and below the hedge was far from pretty and certainly did his adoptive county no justice. The A30, a malignant grey viper a mile distant, cut its intrusive way through meadowland and on towards Penzance, while on the other side of the road a giant pylon bestrode the ground like a conquering marauder alongside a tawdry stucco-walled house. Through a gap in the hedge he could see the corpse of a rusting car, abandoned to creeping ivy and untamed brambles.

The traffic, audible just as a low moan through the car window, was an incessant flow of hectic self-important bustle, completely oblivious of the timeless tranquillity that lay within yards of its tarmac boundary.

As he watched the vehicles speeding in both directions it occurred to Robert that even an analogy with worker ants would be pretentiously inaccurate. Ants, carrying their heavy loads, were fulfilling nature's purpose and pursuing a worthwhile activity for their community, while most of those below him had possibly never considered what purpose they served as they polluted the atmosphere with their emissions, noise and unnatural haste. And what useful purpose was he, Robert Sinclair, serving now, driving around trying to find someone who possibly did not wish to be found anyway?

Robert reached into the door pocket and took out a half-filled plastic bottle of water and, staring into the distance as he took sips of the lukewarm liquid, wondered why he was feeling so frustrated, helpless and disturbed.

Alf Curtis's problems were no concern of his. No one was more his own man than Alf and no one would be more irritated than he to know that anyone, even Robert Sinclair, was hunting him down in order to ask intrusive questions. Whatever the man had been up to that morning was his business and his alone.

Robert had no reason to doubt that Mike's account was accurate and although it aroused in his mind all kinds of conjecture, the matter was still none of his concern. And perhaps, he reasoned, that was why he felt disturbed. His was an impotent frustration born of uninformed confusion.

A heavy lorry rumbled past the car and rocked it with an impact of side wind. He blinked as if suddenly waking from sleep, drained the bottle and then dropped it into the passenger well. He started the car and pulled back out into the road, not at all sure what to do next.

He turned on the radio and tuned into Radio Cornwall.

There had been an occasion in the past when he had intervened in trying to sort out someone else's problems, but through misunderstanding it had all backfired badly and he had lost the trust of a friend. *This*, he told himself, *would not happen again, even if Binty badgered him to go on searching.*

Robert stopped at the crossroads with the busy A3058 and focused his attention on the traffic. It looked like an unbroken stream in both directions.

But, if Alf needs help . . . just if . . . what should he, Robert, be doing now?

He was still asking himself that question when he parked the car in the garage at Pengarth, not knowing if he would be needing it again that day. Before going back home he did another check on Alf's garage, but the Volvo had not moved.

As he made his way down the steps towards the alleyway known unpretentiously as Side Walk, a thin drizzle began to fall and he held onto the pipe railing as he trod cautiously over the damp cobblestones. By the time he arrived at the Convenience Store in Fore Street the pavement was properly wet from a steady rainfall.

He wiped his feet and looked around.

'Is Sadie in, love?' he asked the young shop assistant, whose name he could not remember.

'She's upstairs, Mr Sinclair. It's her afternoon off,' she answered protectively.

'On her own?'

'Yes.' She gave him a lopsided grin. 'I think she's doing some painting.'

'I see. I don't suppose you've seen Alf Curtis today?' Robert picked up a small loaf of bread and pushed it across the counter. He felt as if he were buying information.

She thought for a moment, while she rang up the till. 'No, not today. Well, not while I've been here.'

Thanks anyway, Julie.' Her name had suddenly come back to him. 'Oh well, into the rain again.'

'Would you like to have a . . . ?' she called after him, holding out a plastic bag, but he was already going up Fore Street at a trot.

Binty looked up with a start from reading a newspaper as Robert blundered in through the front entrance, uttering minor expletives.

'This has come earlier than expected,' he shouted from the hall.

'Well, you said the barometer was dropping, dear.' She peered over the top of her glasses as he entered the room. 'Any luck with Mike?'

'Yes and no, I suppose.' He puffed as he brushed water from his sleeves. 'He'd seen Alf right enough, but that was this morning and there's still no one around who's seen him since.'

She put the paper down and took off her glasses. 'Sit down and tell me what Mike said.'

He did. He told her the whole story exactly as related to him and when he had finished, still slightly out of breath, he sat back and closed his eyes. In the few moments' stillness that followed he could hear music from upstairs. The girls were at home for a change.

'What the hell do I do now?' he asked plaintively.

'Give Roger Curnow a call?' she suggested.

'No, only as a last resort. The poor man's got to have a day off.'

'Then, what about the watch? Someone on duty might have seen him during the day.'

'Mike said he didn't go back that way. He walked back along the road.'

'Then someone must have seen him, Robert. Pengarth isn't that dead a place, even on a Sunday morning.' She peered at him urgently. 'I think you ought to try the lookout. Who's on duty now?'

'Don't know for certain. I think it might be the Captain.' He hauled himself up from the chair and went to consult the watch bill that hung in the hall. 'Yes, Petroc's got the last watch today.'

'Then, please Robert, I know it's raining, but do just go up there and ask him.'

'I don't need to get wet, old girl, they do have a telephone you know.'

She pulled a face. 'Of course they do. So give him a call. If he knows nothing then we'll have to think again.'

'No peace today,' he sighed as he went out again to make the call. 'When Alf does turn up I think I'll murder him for good measure.'

He dialled the lookout number.

'*Pengarth NCI,*' came the crisp metallic voice of the station manager.

'Petroc, this is Robert Sinclair.' He glanced up at the hall clock. 'Nearing the end of your watch I expect.'

'*The pis aller, old man. Flag down at five o'clock sharp.*'

'I was wondering if you've seen Alf today. No one else has since early this morning.'

'*He's not been on watch today . . .*' Robert could hear papers rustling at the other end and rolled his eyes. '*. . . and I haven't set eyes on him around the village. Not in church. No, Robert, can't say I have. What's he been up to now?*'

'As far as I'm aware he's not been up to anything. I just need to find him rather urgently.' It was never easy holding a conversation with Captain Williams and the telephone was certainly not the right medium for one. 'So, no sighting on the footpath?'

'*No sighting, old man, not even a dictum de dicto of one.*' Petroc then uttered what Robert recognised as his officious cough and added brusquely, '*Better not hog this line for too long, old chap.*'

Robert ignored him and had one last stab. 'What about on the water?'

'*Alf? On the water? What in, a boat?*'

'Yes, Petroc, in a boat.' Robert said with exaggerated patience. 'Alf is too old for water wings and I think he's given up trying to walk on it.'

'*Alright, old man, no need to get sarky,*' Petroc replied huffily. '*Again negative. All the boats I've seen on my watch have been a couple of miles out . . . unless you count Greg's inflatable.*'

'Greg's inflatable? Are you sure?'

'*Looked like him, but that was before the weather closed in. Look, Robert, I really must clear this line in case there's an important incoming call.*'

'Very well. Thank you, Petroc.' Robert said sharply, slammed the receiver down and then slapped a hand on the banister. 'Supercilious bugger!'

'No joy?' Binty enquired when he went back into the sitting room.

'No. Why do I let that man wind me up?' Robert closed his eyes tightly as he gripped the back of a chair, pondering his next move.

'Perhaps you ought to try Alf's house again?' Binty suggested. 'I could come with you.'

He opened his eyes and looked at her. 'Yes, you're right. But, no need for you to come though. Would you just give his home a call while I put on a jacket and pick up his keys. If there's no reply I'll go back down there and let myself in.'

'Are you sure?' She was already on her way to the telephone. 'I don't mind getting wet.'

'Yes, I'm sure. Got to keep someone at base camp.'

He came back from the boot room at the rear of the house, pulling on a waterproof jacket, clutching Alf's back door key and wondering what had happened to his resolve not to interfere. Binty was holding the telephone to her ear and shaking her head. She waited until the recorded message came on and then left a brief request for Alf to call back as soon as he was able.

'I'm not surprised.' Robert gave her a parting kiss and made for the door. 'I shouldn't be too long.'

'What do you expect to find?'

'No idea.' He turned up his collar as a gust blew in through the open door. 'By the way, what does *pis aller* mean?'

'Pis aller?'

'Look it up.' He winked at her and then stepped out into the strengthening breeze.

The rain had driven people indoors so Robert saw no one on his way back down to the bookshop. When he arrived he went through the courtesy of knocking loudly on the back door, but once again there was no response. He turned the key and went into Alf's kitchen.

The room was a mess. He took off his jacket and shook it out over the mat before draping it on the back of a chair. Dirty plates and saucepans were stacked in the sink, newspapers were spread over the table and a pile of clothes had been dropped on the floor at the bottom of the stairs.

Robert went over to the sink, picked up a dirty glass and sniffed. Whisky: neat by the smell of it. He moved back to the middle of the room and faced the stairs.

'Alf!' he shouted, without really knowing why. The house had the dead quietness about it that only comes with total dereliction.

Robert looked up the stairs, but did not make a move for a while. For some irrational reason he was afraid of what he might find if he went up, but at the same time, having come so far, he also knew the job would be incomplete if he did not cover the entire house.

He went up.

The office-come-sitting room door was ajar and he pushed at it gently without going in. It swung open with high-pitched protest from the hinges and Robert stood surveying the interior from the landing. More mess and disorder met his eyes.

Two of the piles of books that he had seen previously stacked in the corner had been knocked over and were now spread like toppled dominoes across the floor. The desk was littered with papers scattered around an old shoebox. Some of the papers had spilled onto the floor and the wastepaper basket lay on its side.

Robert went in and as he approached the desk he saw that most of the papers were handwritten letters, some in their envelopes and some lying open. He hesitated before picking one of them up and reading a line at random. He put it back and glanced at some of the others. The writing seemed to be from a feminine hand, very neat and well formed, but perhaps not the hand of an adult.

Then one of the letters stood out from the rest. The handwriting was different from the others and definitely adult in style. It also seemed familiar. Overcome by curiosity he picked it up and went to the window.

There was a date – some sixteen years ago – but no address at the top. A pencil scrawl in Alf's writing underneath the date stated, *With Lydia's effects*. The letter began, *My Darling Brendan* . . .

He drew up a chair by the window and began to read.

Without his glasses it was a strain in places to decipher words where the writer's idiosyncratic style varied from the norm, but the purpose of the letter was clear. It ended, *With all my love, Lydia*.

256

Robert placed the letter gently on his lap and looked through the grimy window, overcome by a sense of guilt at having read private words of such intensity. Like a penitent voyeur who has been caught in his prurient act he felt unclean, having covertly involved himself in a stranger's uninhibitedly expressed emotions.

Although Lydia had de facto been dead to Alf for many years Robert felt certain that the contents of this letter must have stirred the poor man's mind into a state of turmoil. If Alf had never seen it before it would have been as if she had written the letter only last week and also while still of sound mind. And, if that were the case, then the astonishing fact was that the writer of this carefully crafted sixteen year-old letter had never had the courage or inclination to deliver it.

With Lydia's effects, he had written.

So, what had prevented her from sending it? Had it been from fear of discovery, or had it been withheld in the faint hope that a hopeless situation might somehow become resolved?

Robert stared at the pages on his lap. Could it be that the discovery of this letter amongst Lydia's possessions had cracked the brittle crust of Alf's self-made veneer? It was no good anyone trying to tell him that it was all a long time ago, or that it had been written by a woman coming to terms with her illness, or even that much of what she said in the letter was sentimental tosh, possibly aimed at a person who existed only in her fragile mind.

What went on all those years ago is today's history, Robert reasoned, *so it was pointless now for Alf to torment himself with unanswerable questions*.

But that was Robert being vicariously logical and he knew it. He was sitting there calmly rationalising while Alf had gone somewhere else, alone with his fractured thoughts. Binty's intuition could have been right after all.

Robert shifted his attention to gaze once more through the dirty panes at the lookout and deliberated yet again over what he could do next. As he watched, the stocky figure of Petroc Williams left the hut, strode over to the flagpole and began to untie the stays. Robert stood up wearily, went over to the desk and laid the open letter on top of the others. There was nothing more to be done there.

He began to descend the stairs, but then hesitated on the landing, torn between leaving the house immediately and finishing what he

257

had started. It was against his nature to pry into people's private quarters, but with an involuntary shrug he turned and went up the two steps that led to Alf's bedroom.

The bed was unmade and there was a pile of clothes by the door. One of the windows was open and a curtain moved at the whim of the damp evening breeze. Robert crossed the floor, closed it and then looked around casually, but there seemed to be no significant clues in the room.

The spare bedroom was in immaculate condition, as if prepared for the guest who never arrived, so next he went to the end of the landing and put his head around the bathroom door. He was about to withdraw when something below the basin caught his attention.

He went over and crouched down for a closer look. It was a clump of hair, discarded carelessly on the floor beside a wastebasket. Inside the basket itself he found a lot more hair and there was also some by the soap dish in the basin.

He picked up the hair by the basket and examined it. It took just a few seconds to realise that it was too wiry for cranial hair. This was facial hair.

Alf had shaved off his beard.

Robert stood up quickly and instinctively looked over his shoulder, before dropping the clump into the basket. A sudden flurry of rain tapped urgently on the bathroom window and Robert looked up with a start. A man perplexed and fearful stared back at him from the mirror.

He turned rapidly and made his way down the stairs. There was nothing more to discover in the house. Alf had made a statement and he had gone.

Robert walked briskly up the hill with his head down while the fine rain pattered against his back. All the way home he was troubled by the state of Alf's house. Apart from its general disarray and the shaved beard something was missing, or out of place, and he could not grasp what it was.

Inside his home again, he removed the wet jacket and without greeting Binty, went directly to the telephone and dialled. She came out into to the hall wearing a quizzical expression just as the call was answered.

'Roger, it's Robert Sinclair,' he began. 'Sorry to have to call you at home when you're off duty . . . oh, you're not . . . I see.'

He glanced up at Binty and gave her a weak smile as he listened to Constable Curnow explaining his duty roster.

'No, I don't have a problem myself, Roger. It's Alf Curtis. He's gone missing . . . yes, I know it sounds strange, but no one's seen him since about ten o'clock this morning. He's not at home and his car's still in the garage.'

Binty watched him as he listened to the constable, nodding and occasionally grunting a comment.

'I see, so there's nothing that you can do for the moment?' Robert pulled an exasperated face at his wife, before adding with a note of resignation. 'All right, Roger, I'll let you know when we have anything positive to go on.'

He put the receiver down.

'He can't do anything?' she asked.

'No.' He scratched the back of his head furiously. 'And I take his point. Alf's a rational adult and he's perfectly entitled to go off on his own without telling anyone if he wants. The police won't do anything until they have reason to believe there really is a missing person, who might also be in some kind of danger.'

'I see. And I take it there were no clues in the house?'

'No, not really. Unless you count as a clue the fact that the place looks like a tip. Certainly no indication as to where he's gone.'

He smiled grimly at her, conscious of not mentioning the beard.

'Oh, dear. I had hoped . . .' she tailed off and looked despairingly into his eyes.

'Yes, so did I, but I don't mind admitting that I'm worn out with all this dashing about.'

'Well, why don't you take off your wet shoes, come into the sitting room and put your feet up?' She took his coat from the banisters and hung it on a peg. 'I just hope Roger is right . . . that Alf will just turn up when it suits him.' She did not sound convinced.

'I expect he will.'

He stood frowning for a while and then walked pensively into the sitting room.

Robert was attempting to concentrate on a financial article when just before seven o'clock his daughters returned very damp from a walk with the dog, full of complaints about the fickle Cornish weather. He suggested that they all go out to the Lugger after supper, drinks on him, but that was met with apathy from the younger generation. There was something good on television.

During the course of their evening meal he broke into a conversation to announce that he would go to the pub on his own if no one else was interested. Binty said that was fine by her, as she had to prepare some things for a WI meeting the following day. The usual family banter skidded along the surface, but Robert's concern for Alf's whereabouts continued to gnaw away impatiently at the backdoor of his conscience.

The shaving off of his beard now worried him more than anything else. That simple symbolic act of severance could have been the gesture of a troubled mind, but the absence of any tangible clue as to its significance continued to tease him throughout the meal.

While he helped Binty clear the table after the meal she kept glancing at him, aware that he was fretting, but she made no attempt to lighten his mood. She knew her husband better than to attempt false levity.

With the domestic chores done there was nothing further to hold him in the house, so Robert gave Binty a cursory kiss, pulled on his damp coat and went out. Being with other people in different surroundings, he reasoned, was better that brooding at home.

The pub was quiet for a Sunday night.

Rain and sudden unseasonably cool weather had kept visitors indoors and even the locals were sparse on the floor. Greg gave Robert a cheerful welcome as he approached the bar.

'Morgue-like in here tonight, Greg.' He perched himself on a stool and looked around.

'It's the bloody weather, isn't it.' Greg pulled a pint and pushed the tankard of Rufus Craggs across the counter. 'Too much of this and it'll ruin my trade.'

'Doesn't do mine much good either.'

'I thought you'd finished that job up the road. You know, Mrs Whatsit . . .'

'Watson. Yes, that's done, but there's always another one waiting.'

'I should think you're in demand round here. Can't be many thatchers these days.'

'Oh, there are more than you think. In fact a lot of the old trades are coming back, you know. People are beginning to appreciate the quality of the old ways of doing things. The problem now is in finding the right material for the job.'

'Is that so?'

'Yes. I'm having to go further and further afield for it.'

'Do you work in straw or reeds?'

'I prefer long straw thatching, but its availability always depends on the harvest.'

'But, it's a beautiful job when it's done right.'

'Thanks for saying so.' Robert swilled his tankard and watched the froth gathering in the centre. 'The trouble is that unskilled thatchers give long straw thatching a bad name.'

'Yeah, I suppose that's true of most crafts.' Greg jerked his thumb over his shoulder at nothing in particular. 'At least the new money made in the cities and coming into places like this means that some folks can afford to employ skilled craftsmen. Mass production put many of the old crafts out of business, because mass production meant that suddenly everyone could afford a table, a chair and a wheel off the counter, as it were.'

'And a tiled roof.'

'And a tiled roof,' Greg grunted. 'But now those with the money want to show they can afford something different. It's all coming round full circle.'

Greg was called away to the other end of the bar and Robert drank quietly on his own for a few minutes, studying a stuffed pike in its case on the wall. The pike seemed to be staring glassily at the few dead flies, which lay on the floor of the case just below its jaw.

He turned back as Greg returned.

'Go fishing this afternoon?'

'No, too busy here and also, I didn't like the look of the weather coming up from the west.'

Robert stared at him. 'But you went out in the inflatable.'

'No, not me. She's not left the quay today . . . or shouldn't have.'

'But . . .' Robert felt his insides give an involuntary lurch, '. . . Petroc says he saw you go out during his watch.'

'Saw me?'

'Well, he said it looked like you . . . rowing out to the sloop.'

'Well, it wasn't me, I can tell you,' Greg exclaimed and then a thought occurred to him. 'Christ! Has someone nicked my boat?'

'No, the boat's still there. I saw her this afternoon . . . but the dinghy . . . where was that supposed to be?'

261

'Should have been dangling from the side of the quay . . . or floating when the tide's up.'

'Can't say I saw it, Greg. But then I didn't go all the way down to the quay.' Robert frowned and then a sudden flash of realisation registered on his face. 'Oh, my God . . .'

'What?'

'Petroc didn't see you at all. He must have seen Alf!'

'Alf? Why would he . . . ?'

'Never mind that now, Greg,' Robert said urgently and leaned closer to the landlord. 'Alf shaved his beard off today. You're both about the same height and build. It was Alf he saw in the inflatable. It must have been.'

'Hold on, hold on.' Greg held up his hands. 'What's going on, Robert? You've lost me completely.'

Robert closed his eyes and breathed deeply. This was getting out of hand. He ran a hand over the top of his head and then looked up to see Greg refilling his tankard.

'Looks like you're going to need this.'

'Thanks.' He took a long draught of the beer and then wiped the corner of his mouth with his knuckle. 'The long and the short of it, Greg, is that Alf has disappeared. I've been trying to find him since early this morning. Tried everywhere and everyone I can think of. But now, after what you've just told me, it's my guess he rowed off in your inflatable.'

'But, why would he want to do that?'

'I wish I knew for certain, Greg. I only wish I knew.'

Greg's face reddened slightly, but he showed little other emotion. Then he pursed his lips, turned abruptly and picked up the telephone that nestled beneath a row of exotic liqueurs. 'Just a second, Robert, I'll run a check.'

He dialled and waited. The call was answered and without preamble Greg fired off his question. After replacing the receiver he stared at the bottles for a few moments before facing Robert again.

'That was Jack down by the quay. You're right. The dinghy's gone.' Greg frowned and his face went a deeper shade of red. 'What makes you think it's Alf then?'

'It's a long story,' Robert replied quietly, 'and I still only know part of it. Let's just say something's shaken him up. All I know is that we've got to find the old bugger before he does something really stupid.'

'Ok, I'll go along with that.' Greg thought for a moment and then stood up to his full height, focusing on the far side of the room where two men and a woman were sitting. He put his head back and called out, 'Ted, come over here a minute, will you?'

'Why, what've I done now?' There was laughter from the others at the man's table.

Ted Moss' chair scraped back on the slate floor and he picked up his companions' glasses before walking bow legged to the bar. He was a short sinewy man with exceptionally large hands for his frame. His sunburned and wind lashed face was etched with lines carved by a thousand gales and a scar above his left eye kept it permanently half closed. Ted was one of a very few in the area who still made their living from the fishing trade.

'Guilty of not drinking up fast enough, is it?' The fisherman winked at Robert.

'Have these on me, Ted,' Robert reached into his pocket.

'Oh, cheers, that's Christian of you.'

'Ted, you sailed in about an hour ago, didn't you?' Greg began, as he pulled a pint.

'That's right. Tide was coming in. Not a bad catch too.'

'Did you happen to see a grey inflatable out at sea . . . or anywhere along the coast?'

Moss pondered a while. 'Not at sea, I didn't. In fact I didn't see an inflatable anywhere.'

Greg pushed two pints across the bar.

'Thank you, my 'andsome.' Moss took his drink and slurped it down. 'But, now that you mention it, one of my lads said he saw something that fits the description of a grey inflatable.'

'Where was that?' Robert passed his money across the counter.

'Not at sea. He was pulling in a line over the port side when we were passing Thunder Hole and I heard him say something about a dinghy on the beach.'

'Thunder Hole . . . that inlet about two miles down the coast?'

'That's right.'

'There's a tiny beach there and a cave in the rock behind. You can only get there by boat,' Greg added.

'And you said the tide was coming in?' Robert frowned and glanced at Greg.

'Oh, it's right up by now. That beach disappears when the tide's right in.'

'Just leaves the cave then?' Greg looked keenly at the weather-beaten face. 'So what does someone do if he's stuck at Thunder Hole with the tide coming in?'

'I'd say he either climbs onto the rocks . . . dangerous that . . . or goes back into the cave if he's mad, or gets in his boat and comes home.' Ted looked from one to the other as if anticipating an explanation.

'He was waiting for the tide to turn,' Robert almost whispered and at that moment he knew what was missing in Alf's house. He turned to Greg. 'This may sound peculiar, but I think he's gone out to sea with the tide.'

'Good God, is he mad?'

'Quite possibly . . . or just stone drunk.' Everything in the house had been left where it had dropped, except the whisky bottle. There had been no whisky bottle. Alf must have taken it with him.

'Who'm you talking about?' Ted flashed his sea-reddened eyes from one to the other.

'Alf Curtis,' Robert replied tersely.

'Alf? Where's he to then?' Ted's mouth hung open.

'That's what we want to find out.' Robert drained his glass and squared up to Greg. 'I'm not messing around any more. It's time to call out the coastguard. It'll be dark in about an hour.'

'Can I help at all, with my boat?' Ted gathered up his three glasses.

'No, Ted, you're all moored up for the night. But thanks for the information about the dinghy.'

Ted Moss nodded and then rolled his way back to the table, bursting with news for his companions. Robert turned back to Greg.

'I'm going back up to the lookout and do some tidal plotting before I call the coastguard.'

'Are you up to working out the tidal streams?' Greg asked doubtfully.

'Not brilliant at it, but I should be able to calculate this one near enough. I know when high tide was, the chart has the tidal diamonds and . . . are we into neap or spring at the moment?'

'There you are . . . you haven't a clue.' He lifted the bar gate and stepped through. 'I'm coming with you.'

'But, the pub . . .'

'No problem there. Kev!' A young man in a red pullover stopped talking to a girl and looked up. 'Look after the bar for an hour, would you? I've got something urgent to deal with.'

'Rightho, Greg.' In spite of protestation from his girlfriend, Kevin got up and wandered over to the bar, knowing that he was about to earn a few quid tax-free.

As they stepped out into Fore Street, both men turned up their collars against an insidious drizzle and began the trudge up to the lookout. Sunset – if there had been any sun – was due at about nine-twenty and then darkness would fall quite quickly after that.

They walked briskly and in silence, while Robert did some mental calculations. If he had been right about Alf and the boat, then he would have rowed out from Thunder Hole about two hours ago. He had to row, because there was no outboard, and therefore, even with the tide helping, progress would be slow. Again, if he were right, Alf would be drunk out of his mind by the time he set off, so direction would almost be irrelevant. But, straight out to sea was his guess.

'Bugger,' Greg exclaimed, 'I didn't bring a torch.'

'There's one in the lookout . . . unless the battery's flat.'

I hope to God I'm wrong, Robert kept thinking. *I don't mind making a fool of myself or even wasting people's time if I'm wrong. What I can't be is right and then have done nothing about it.*

The rain had eased by the time they reached the lookout and Robert was able to find the correct combination on the lock without too much fumbling. They went in and Greg turned on the light, while Robert took the chart out of a drawer.

'I expect this light will be seen by someone in the village before too long.' Greg muttered as he searched for the tidal diamond almanac.

'Well, if they do, I hope to goodness they don't tell Captain Pugwash.' Robert allowed himself a chuckle as he laid the plotter and dividers on the chart. 'Ok, Greg, you're in charge.'

For the next few minutes Greg pored over the chart, correlating relevant tide levels with marked tidal diamonds, the neap rate of the tide, the current time and the possible speed of a rowed inflatable. While he did this, Robert called Binty, explained what they were doing and also suggested that she contact Rowena. It had crossed his mind that she, possibly being the last one to speak to

Alf, might have a clue as to why he had disappeared. He put the phone down and peered over Greg's shoulder.

'Right, that's it in theory.' Greg stabbed the chart with a sturdy forefinger. 'He should be about here with the tidal drift.'

'That's not too far out.' Robert began to take the bearing on Greg's estimate.

'There are imponderables though. What we can't tell is how much he's been able to row and the effect of the wind.' Greg turned to look at the weather station on the wall. 'At present it's hovering around twenty-two knots – that's force six, a strong breeze. The last log entry at four o'clock shows fourteen knots, but we don't know how much it's varied in between.'

'That should be good enough for the coastguard, Greg.' Robert picked up the telephone and dialled 999. 'It's the best we can give them anyway.'

The emergency call was answered promptly and Robert asked for the coastguard. He was put through, gave his name and status and then proceeded to give a calm explanation of the situation, with bearings, times and an estimate of where the inflatable might be. The coastguard told him to stand by the telephone.

When he put the phone down he found that he was perspiring. Although the NCI watchkeepers had all done this kind of report under simulated conditions, there was never a substitute for the real thing. Greg nodded at him and murmured a couple of words of encouragement.

'Light's going,' Robert said, looking up at the sky. 'I wish I'd done this earlier.'

'At least the rain's stopping.' Greg looked at the weather station again. 'And the barometer's not fallen since the last reading in the log.'

'You realise this is all conjecture, Greg?' Robert stared intently at him as if seeking reassurance. 'I could be completely up the wrong creek with this.'

'You're doing the right thing, Robert. Someone's out in my dinghy, even if it's not Alf Curtis.'

Robert nodded slowly and then picked up the binoculars to scan the horizon. The sea swell was still only slight, perhaps being flattened by the fresh breeze as it whipped over the wavelets, but that fact offered him small consolation. In the growing gloom he knew that he had little chance of seeing anything more than half a mile away, but looking out there was better than just waiting and doing nothing.

The telephone rang and Greg grabbed it.

'Pengarth NCI . . . oh, hello, Petroc . . . yes, it's Greg.' He looked at Robert and raised his eyebrows. 'Yes, it's Ok, only Robert and me up here. We've had to call the coastguard. Someone's in trouble out there in a dinghy.'

He listened for a few moments, while Robert made frantic neck cutting gestures.

'I'll have to stop you there, Captain, we need to keep the line free for Falmouth. Yes, it'll all be in the log. Goodnight.' He replaced the receiver and his stomach jumped around as he laughed.

Even in the circumstances Robert could not help smiling. It was good to have the comforting presence of Greg Treberthy on hand.

They did not have to wait long after that. The coastguard called back to verify a few points and then confirmed that they would be launching the All-Weather lifeboat.

In view of the fact that the dinghy had not actually been sighted and that there was an element of conjecture in the report of a missing person, they were placing a great deal of trust in the integrity of the Pengarth watchkeepers. But that was the nature of their service.

Robert mentally crossed his fingers as he turned to Greg. 'They're sending out the All-Weather boat, so we should see her in about half an hour.'

'I'll set up the radio.'

Greg flicked the power switch, turned on the VHF radio and then set it to scan.

Neither of them had seen the All-Weather boat in action before, but they both knew its capabilities. It was a Severn Class lifeboat constructed of fibre reinforced composite and could do twenty-five knots per hour, with a range of about two hundred and fifty nautical miles.

Its powerful V12 turbo-charged engines burned fuel at the rate of nearly five hundred litres an hour: hardly environmentally friendly, but necessary for rescue work in extreme conditions.

The six-man crew use a differential GPS satellite navigator that interfaces with a laser plotter chart system and computerised admiralty charts. Those in turn link with a Bridgemaster radar, allowing targets to be plotted and superimposed onto charts almost instantaneously.

Although the coastguard normally requests launching of the Severn only for major offshore rescue work, the lifeboat also carries a small outboard powered Y-class inflatable for shallow operations. There is very little rescue work that this lifeboat cannot tackle and it gave Robert some comfort to hear that the coastguard had chosen it for this rescue mission, rather than the in-shore boat.

He now visualised the crew speeding out to the vessel at its mooring alongside a pontoon in the Carrick Roads.

Another ten minutes passed, the light grew dimmer and the two men in the lookout went through the motions of checking calculations on the chart once more. Any activity was better than idly speculating as to Alf's fate.

Suddenly, without warning, the door to the lookout flew open and the broad figure of Captain Petroc Williams stood at the entrance, breathing heavily and as pink as a watermelon. One eye locked itself on Robert's startled face and the other went walkabout as the wind lifted his hair playfully from behind the open door.

'Phew! Quite a climb up here in the gloamin'' He came in and slammed the door shut. 'Came to help out. Now, what's the score?'

Robert's immediate reaction was one of irritation. There was barely room for three of them to operate in the lookout and he and Greg were managing perfectly well without Petroc on board, however well intentioned the station manager was in sacrificing his Sunday evening.

'Well, that's very good of you, Petroc. You needn't have come out, you know. But, as you're here now . . .' He turned to Greg, remembering that his companion had a pub to run. 'Do you want to get back to the Lugger, Greg?'

The publican hesitated and then shrugged. 'I'm happy to see this through, but, as Petroc's on board . . .'

'Right, settled then.' Petroc removed his coat and slung it onto a peg. Robert caught a whiff of gin and sneaked a wink at Greg.

'All right, gentlemen, I'll go back to my place behind the bar. But, keep me posted, Robert, won't you.' Greg gave him a brief pat on the arm. 'I'm sure they'll find him. Those boys are mustard.'

'I hope you're right. But, it's got to be soon . . . bloody soon.'

Greg bade them well with the traditional wish for a good watch and went out into the half-light of the damp July night. The sky was clearing and he could see a few stars, but the breeze plucked at his jacket as if to remind him of conditions out there at sea.

Back in the lookout, Robert wondered what chance of survival Alf had out there, soaked to the skin, sozzled and lost? But then, maybe that was precisely what he wanted. He turned and looked back up the darkening path and reflected that to Greg this was probably all gruesomely familiar.

He shuddered involuntarily and then turned back to give Petroc his attention, bringing him up to date with the situation, without exploring too deeply the reason why Alf Curtis might be out at sea in an inflatable dinghy with no engine. And, to his credit, Petroc did not press the point.

They saw the spotlight cutting through the gloom first and then even above the wind they heard the throb of the thousand-plus horsepower engines as the Severn lifeboat rounded the point.

At that moment the VHF radio crackled into life. The coast-guard was calling them and confirming the channel to be used for transmission.

The rescue operation was under way at last.

Chapter Nineteen

ROBERT was woken soon after eight by the old dog.

In its younger days it used to bark every morning when the newspaper was delivered or as the postman pushed letters through the door. Now, in its dotage, it merely gurgled a threatening growl, which it did as the newspaper plopped onto the doormat on the morning after the rescue operation.

Robert turned gently to look at Binty. She lay on her back with her mouth half-open and her unblinking eyes firmly shut. He turned back, slipped silently out from under the duvet and tiptoed across the room, avoiding the floorboard that creaked.

He put on his dressing gown as he went into the small room adjacent to the bedroom and immediately caught sight of a fax that had come through some time during the disturbed night. He picked it up and crossed the floor to pull back the curtains.

Petroc had faxed an RNLI service report of the night's events.

'My God, they're quick off the mark,' Robert murmured and then, in the glare of morning sunlight, began to read the report for 5th July.

LIFEBOAT CALL

Lifeboat: All-Weather.

Service: Person believed to be adrift in a small inflatable dinghy, possibly without lifejacket or protective clothing.

Crew: John Hoskin (Helmsman), Mark Trevan, William Martin, Tom Richards, Martin Tremayne and Luke Fawcett.

Location: Wide area off Pengarth Bay.

Weather: SW 5, Moderate sea, Poor visibility, Overcast with showers.

The Action: At 21:10 Falmouth Coastguard requested that Falmouth All-Weather Lifeboat be launched following a report that a person might be in difficulties in a small inflatable dinghy well offshore between Pengarth Point and Poltock Head. The single male occupant was thought to have set out from the inlet known as Thunder Hole between

19:00 and 20:00, with no outboard motor and possibly unsuitably dressed for the weather conditions.

The All-Weather Lifeboat arrived off Pengarth Bay at 21:43 and began a sweep of the bay to a distance of a mile and a half offshore. Regular VHF radio contact was maintained with the Pengarth NCI station and at 22: 20 RNAS Culdrose was requested to stand by in the event that a helicopter might need to be tasked to assist.

At 22:42 a dinghy was seen aground on Shag Rock off Poltock Head, with the casualty still aboard. The Lifeboat inflatable was launched to effect a rescue and this was achieved by 22:58. The casualty was unconscious and suffering hypothermia and was taken by the Lifeboat dinghy to Pengarth, from where the Mobile conveyed him directly to the Royal Cornwall Hospital.

RNAS Culdrose was advised and the helicopter was stood down. The All-Weather Lifeboat was back alongside the pontoon by 23:45 where it was refuelled and made ready for service by 01:03.

This Service Report, sent out by e-mail to all those who subscribed to the Falmouth Lifeboat Service's Shout mailing, was completely accurate, but, being an official report of an incident at sea, it lacked soul, drama and emotion, all of which had surged through the participants during the events of the previous night. An incident had been reported and a mission successfully accomplished.

Robert had finally left the lookout at eleven o'clock and he was waiting on the quay when the RNLI's rescue inflatable came alongside with the prone body of Alf Curtis. The Mobile coast-guard had backed his Land Rover down as far as he could and Alf, wrapped in foil, was lowered onto a stretcher. Robert had only a fleeting glimpse of his friend before he was lifted into the vehicle and then instantly wished that he had held back. Alf looked more dead than alive.

The Mobile had met an ambulance at the junction with the main road and from that point Alf was under professional medical care.

Binty had been on the quay with Robert and together they had walked silently up Fore Street to their home. Most occupied houses on their way up the hill had a light on and some village folk stood anxiously at their front door waiting for news. Robert and

Binty got into bed shortly before two o'clock, but it was some long while before either of them slept.

From early on the following morning Pengarth was buzzing with talk about the rescue. Some people had been there helping on the quay and others had simply stood by watching. Now everyone wanted to know how Alf was, why he had been out at sea on a night like that and where had he been all those hours before. Many questions needed to be answered, but above all else people marvelled at the skill and dedication of the sea rescue service in pulling him off Shag Rock alive. For alive he was. Just.

Soon after reading the Shout report Robert put a call through to the hospital. Yes, Mr Curtis was comfortable and had responded well to treatment. He had suffered badly from hypothermia and dehydration, but thanks to a strong constitution, had rallied and was now out of immediate danger. However, visitors were being advised to stay away for at least twenty-four hours.

Binty was pouring out strong tea when he went downstairs to the kitchen.

'God, you look terrible, Robert.'

'Good morning to you too.' He sat down heavily. 'I'll feel better after a shave and a shower.'

'I was thinking . . .' she began, 'when Alf comes out of hospital nothing will have changed for him. We can't just let him go back home you know.'

'I agree. Whether he likes it or not, he's got to be looked after . . . and probably for quite some time.' He stared at the steaming mug she put in front of him. 'He might not agree to co-operate, but it'll be an opportunity for us to try to help him with his problems.'

'Yes, whatever they are.' She looked searchingly at him and then asked quietly, 'You know, don't you?'

'No, I don't actually, Bints.' His brow creased as he rubbed the stubble on his chin. 'I can't even guess at the reason for his state of mind, and if I did I would probably still be miles off the mark.'

Binty sat down and began to rotate her mug on the table. 'Then I think, for his sake, we need to find out before he's tempted to do something stupid again.'

'He didn't think what he did was stupid. I should imagine people who are disturbed to that extent never do. To them theirs is the most logical action in the world and it's the rest of us who are out

273

of kilter.' He shrugged at his home-spun philosophy and then added, 'By the way, did you phone Rowena yesterday?'

'Yes, I did, and she wasn't very forthcoming . . . at least not about her meeting with Alf. Apparently she had no idea that he'd disappeared.'

'Did she seem worried?'

'Not overly so. On the phone she just seemed a bit distracted.'

He thought about that for a few moments and then stood up. 'I'm going to have that shower before the girls overrun the bathroom.'

'Have some breakfast first, Robert.' She got up and took a loaf out of the bread bin.

'I will when I'm dressed.' He stretched. 'I feel better already after just a few sips of that tea.'

'I'll do bacon and eggs for all of us.'

Halfway to the door Robert stopped and his face creased into a smile at a recollection from the night's drama. 'You know, one thing surprised me about the rescue . . . well, no . . . actually a lot surprised me last night . . . but one unexpected thing was Petroc. He was bloody brilliant. Quite the professional throughout. He even sent me the Shout report this morning.'

He went upstairs chuckling at the foibles of human nature.

An hour later Robert was knocking on the back door of the Lugger. After a few minutes Greg came clumping down the stairs in his dressing gown. He was still in the middle of a yawn when he flung the door open.

'Sorry, Greg, I expect you've had as little sleep as I have, but I thought you'd like to hear the medical report.'

'That's all right, Robert, come in.' He stepped back, but Robert remained on the step.

'No, I've got someone to visit, so I won't stay. Alf's had a comfortable night, he's out of danger, but no visitors for a day or two. That's about all I know so far.'

'Thank God for that. I'll keep in touch with the hospital and see him as soon as they'll let me.' He looked down at his bare feet for a moment. 'Then what happens?'

'Binty and I've discussed that and we're going to take him in for a while . . . whether he likes it or not. We can't let him back to that mausoleum of a bookshop until he's sorted himself out.'

'Good for you.' Greg retied his dressing gown cord and then reached out to tap the barometer glass. 'I nearly cocked it up last night, didn't I?'

'What do you mean? You did a beautiful bit of plotting.'

'Basic tidal plotting was okay, but I didn't allow for the wind.'

'Good Lord, Greg, that's hardly your fault. No one could have known what effect the wind would have. And anyway, thank heavens for the wind – it blew him back onto the rock.'

'Hmm, I suppose so.' Then he smiled ruefully. 'And the rock put paid to my inflatable.'

'Beyond repair, is it?'

'Like a burst paper bag – but that's not important is it?'

'In the circumstances, I suppose not.'

'Well, thanks for the news.' Greg thrust his hands into the dressing gown pockets. 'I'll let you get on now.'

On his way back up the hill Robert saw Tony Gibbins on the other side of the road and dived into the store. Sadie was serving a customer, but caught his eye as he hid behind the cereal shelves. She laughed and called him out once the reporter had passed by.

'He's already been in this morning, Robert, so you're safe here,' she called across.

'I expect he'll catch me soon enough, but I'm not ready for him just yet.' He went up to the counter with a two-litre carton of milk. 'You've heard it all then?'

'With Alf you've never heard it all, but I know what you mean.' She took his money. 'Why did he do it, Robert?'

'I don't know. He's badly cut up about something, but what it is . . .' He shrugged. 'I was hoping you might have an idea.'

'Not me, my lover. Alf and I don't have that sort of relationship.' Someone came up to the counter with a full basket, so Sadie just smiled enigmatically at him.

Robert had not even reached his front door before he had made up his mind what needed to be done next. In the hall he pocketed the car keys and then paused to check for sounds in the house.

'Binty!' he yelled. 'I'm going out in the car for an hour.'

'Ok, Dad, I'll tell her,' came a shout from the kitchen.

He left again before anyone could waylay him and headed off for the garage. It was a guess based on nothing more than an image that had stayed stubbornly in his mind ever since Mike had told him what he had seen, but sometimes hunches develop into facts. It was possible he might have some success in drawing more from

Rowena than Binty had over the telephone. That was what he was hoping as he drove off up the hill.

He was relieved to see her car in the drive and he parked behind it, as if preventing her escape. Then he saw the bicycle, which meant that Louise Dowrick was also in the house.

'Too bad,' he murmured as he pressed the doorbell.

A few moments later Louise opened the door.

'Hello, Robert.' She gave him a cautious grin. 'If you've come to see Mrs Fischer she's in the kitchen.'

'Thanks, Louise.' He stepped into the hall. 'I hope I'm not interrupting anything important.'

She hesitated, then lowered her voice and said conspiratorially, 'I'm teaching her the proper way to make a pasty.'

'Ah, that is important.' He followed her. 'But I hope you can find something else to do for the next half hour.'

She stopped and looked at him and his expression confirmed that he was not asking a question.

'Don't worry, I have lots to do.'

She stuck her head around the kitchen door, told Rowena who it was and then hurried away.

'This is a pleasant surprise, Robert.' She put down a lump of pastry and went to wash her hands. 'Come in and have a coffee.'

'Morning, Rowena.' *I hope it doesn't become an unpleasant one*, he thought, as she fastidiously rinsed dough from her fingers. 'I wonder if you can spare me a few minutes. Some things I need to sort out.'

She did not say anything, but gestured towards a chair and then removed her apron.

'It's about Alf,' he said, coming straight to the point. 'I believe Binty told you what happened last night.'

'Yes, she phoned.' Rowena turned on the kettle. 'He's all right, isn't he?'

'He was in a very bad way early this morning. Another couple of hours and it might well have been too late, but he's recovering in hospital now.'

'Good, I'm so glad to hear that.' She stopped fiddling around with kitchen detritus and sat down. 'So, what can I help you sort out?'

She fixed her eyes on him in a direct, almost challenging way that made him feel slightly uncomfortable. This was not going to be easy.

'Rowena, please don't take anything I'm going to ask you as an intrusion into your privacy. You see . . .' The kettle began to boil and she stood up. '. . . Alf is one of my oldest friends and I need to know what drove him to do the reckless thing he did. If that means asking awkward questions, then I'm sorry, but . . .'

She had her back to him, stirring water into the coffee and Robert felt himself floundering. Rowena's back represented a barricade that somehow would have to be scaled or broken down if he were to achieve any kind of result.

'Sugar? I can't remember.' It was as if she had not been listening.

'No, thank you.' He decided to wait until she was facing him again.

She placed a cup on the table and sat, holding hers in two delicately poised hands, resuming her inscrutable stare. 'When you say *do the reckless thing he did*, what precisely do you mean? Surely you're not suggesting . . . it might not have been an accident?'

'I mean just that.'

She blinked a few times and he saw her hands shake as she lowered the cup to the table. 'My God, Robert, I thought it was just . . . just the result of a careless misjudgement. I had no idea . . .'

'No, Rowena, it was a deliberate act. Alf knew what he was doing, I assure you.' It was Robert's turn to give her the direct stare. 'Very few people know it, but there's little doubt in my mind that it was his intention not . . . not to return.'

'But why . . . ?'

'That is precisely what I'm trying to find out.'

'Why here? Why me? I barely know Alf . . . I . . . I.' She raised her hands in a gesture of helplessness.

'Are you sure you barely know him?'

She blinked again and drew in a sharp breath as if affronted at his question. 'What an odd thing to say. Before he pulled me off that cliff ledge I'd never seen him before. Why on earth do you think otherwise?'

He sighed and toyed idly with his wedding ring. 'Look, Rowena, I just have to try every angle. So, if you didn't know him, perhaps you knew his wife – her name was Lydia.'

'No!' she said vehemently this time through a forced laugh. 'I did not know his wife, his mother or any of his relatives.'

'And yet . . .' he looked at the untouched coffee and launched into uncharted waters. '. . . there was a moment in your garden on Sunday when it certainly seemed as if . . .'

'In my garden?' Her back straightened. 'What do you mean?'

'It seemed to be over some flowers. Something was said between you two and Alf took it hard. I think that might have been the moment he . . .'

'How do you know what happened in the privacy of my garden?' Her voice was husky, but the blue-grey eyes sparked dangerously. 'Has Alf said . . . anything?'

'No, no, nothing like that. As far as I'm aware he's spoken to no one since then. I certainly hadn't even seen him since the cricket match on Saturday. Let's just say that you were seen by a passer-by and this is a small village where secrets are difficult to keep.' He winced as he said it.

'God, what a place! You can't even go out into your garden without . . . ,' she exclaimed and ran a hand through her hair.

He waited and watched while she appeared to wrestle with the probability that the charade in her garden was now an open secret in Pengarth. She pushed the cup away, some coffee slopped onto the table and then, quite abruptly, she buried her face in her hands. Robert could see some traces of dough lodged between her fingers and suddenly he felt deeply sorry for her. She had probably grown to love the village and her cottage in her short period of residence and now they had both let her down. Her bolthole's cover was blown.

'Rowena,' he said softly, 'can you not tell me what that was about? If you can, then it might help me to sort Alf out . . . when he's fit again.'

Her face was still hidden, but then slowly, as if revealing her identity piece by piece, it slid upwards from behind the protective hands until her eyes levelled with his.

'It was nothing to do with Alf,' she almost whispered. 'He just happened to be there when I was carrying out my . . . my act of remembrance . . . my annual ritual of penance.'

He sat very still, with his hands now resting lightly on the edge of the table.

'You see,' she continued, 'it doesn't matter where I am in the world . . . Paris, Geneva, Luxembourg . . . every year on the fourth of July I say sorry. This year I just happened to be in Pengarth, the very place where I made a fateful decision nearly forty years ago. It was a decision I made on a bench in my aunt's garden when I was a young girl. So, I thought it would be appropriate to lay some flowers there . . . and that's when Alf arrived.'

'What was . . . I mean, how did that decision affect Alf?'

'I told you, it was nothing to do with him, so I really don't know why he was affected . . . if at all. And don't ask me to tell you any more, because I've already said more than I ever wanted to . . . to anyone.'

'I understand. That's fair enough. So, you really can't think of anything that might have . . . ?'

She paused for several seconds as if trying to recollect. 'I was quite . . . emotionally distracted at the time . . . I don't know now what I told him . . . I might have . . . I just can't be sure. I didn't even see him walk away, Robert, so I simply can't comment on his reactions. As far as I was concerned I was on my own.'

He exhaled slowly and looked out of the window. A pair of swallows was cavorting around in an impossible demonstration of manoeuvrability, perhaps celebrating a late arrival from Africa, or a new birth in the ramshackle shed at the back. Robert did not feel like joining in any celebration: he was no nearer to solving the riddle of Alf's sudden disintegration . . . if indeed it had been sudden.

Rowena seemed now to have sunk into a slough of introspection and clearly had no intention of volunteering anything further, so he pushed his chair back and got to his feet. It was time to go.

Then suddenly, on a whim, as one last random thrust, he asked, 'Does the name Brendan mean anything to you?'

Initially there was no reaction.

Then, quite slowly, a look of stunned incredulity spread across her face, as if he had slapped her and she was just coming to terms with the blow.

'Who did you say?' She forced the question out as if struggling for breath.

'Brendan.' He gripped the back of the chair, both astonished and perplexed at her reaction. 'On Alf's desk there was a letter addressed to someone called Brendan. It was with Lydia's papers.'

'So, why ask me about . . . this Brendan?' She was still wide-eyed. 'What's he to do with me?'

'I think something in that letter shocked Alf . . . shocked him enough for it to contribute to his state of mind, that's all. I hoped that name might mean something . . .'

'I told you, I'd never seen him before . . . I don't know any Brendan . . . I . . . please leave, Robert . . . just go.' Her fist was up to her cheek and tears were queuing up to cascade.

He hesitated, wondering how he could leave her in this state: a condition of his own making. Then he heard the vacuum cleaner start up in the room next door. Louise had inadvertently come to his rescue.

'I'm sorry to have upset you, Rowena, I really am.' He hesitated. 'I didn't want it to come to this. Believe me, I'm just trying to find a way to help Alf.'

She looked away, her hand still shielding her face, and he slipped out of the room. On his way out he caught Louise's eye and gave a quick shake of the head before reaching the front door. She looked puzzled, but didn't pause from her work.

Robert left the cottage and got into the car. He sat silently for a while before putting it into gear and was about to reverse, when he saw Louise running towards him across the drive. He wound the window down.

'Robert,' she said breathlessly, 'I don't know what you said to her, but she's in quite a state. I should have warned you before you went in . . .'

'Warned me about what?'

'She's a bit fragile at the moment . . . after the news from Geneva.' She looked over her shoulder and then added quickly, 'Will you be at home tonight?'

'Yes.'

'Then I'll give you a ring and explain what I'm talking about. Got to go now.' She turned and dashed back into the house.'

In fact she did not ring back that day and Robert soon stopped wondering what news from Geneva had caused Rowena's fragility. It was well known that Louise was prone to inflate a story in order to fan the flame of gossip. Instead, Robert immersed himself in other pressing matters and he and Binty also prepared the house for Alf's arrival.

Chapter Twenty

THE small grey inflatable boat spun around in the heavy swell, threatening to overturn as each wave lifted it and then tipped it into the next trough. One oar had gone and there was no way of controlling the puny vessel. Rain and seawater had soaked through every fibre of his inadequate clothing, he was without a life jacket, angry at his failure to end it all and cursing at the wind that kept pushing him back towards the shore.

The tide was meant to take him out beyond all hope of rescue and the whisky should have dulled all remaining instinct for survival. But although helplessly drunk and disorientated he remained innately and illogically scared of being drawn down into the dark hostile sea. He had read somewhere that it would be easy. All he had to do was row until he collapsed from exhaustion and then he would slide mercifully into the sea and be immersed permanently in the grave that covered four fifths of the world's surface. They might find the inflatable, many miles from where he launched, but no one would ever find him. Not a damned soul would know where the mortal remains of bloody Alf Curtis lay and, even better, no one would know why he had decided to end it all.

Eventually they would just come to the conclusion that the poor demented fool had gone off his rocker, stolen a friend's boat and tried to reach France in a near gale. Ha ha ha. Let's have another round of Rufus Craggs.

But he had underestimated the spark that remained of an indomitable will to live and had vented his impotent fury against it.

And then, He up there had had other ideas. His little joke perhaps. Alf Curtis a non-believer: why not toss him around a little in the sea, get him a bit wet, then dump the drunken fool on a bird-infested rock to be rescued. Let the poor bugger dangle on the edge of mortality and then drag him back again to face his sins. Another laugh at his expense!

Alf gave an involuntary cough, as if to bring up the last of the salt water and then dragged himself to a sitting position in bed. It was no dream. He was fully awake, reliving with bitterness all the suffering he had borne and of his extraordinary failure to complete the job he had set out to do.

He had planned it all so thoroughly, allowing for tide, nightfall and everyone's total disinterest as to his whereabouts. But, he had not allowed for the wind, or the efficiency of the rescue services, or for the dedication of his friends. And that more than anything else, since he had been able to think rationally again, had shaken and humbled him. There were people out there who really cared what happened to him, unspeakable reprobate that he was. But would that care dissolve in an instant if they ever discovered why he had done it, or, yes God, how he had sinned? How deep is a friendship? How lasting is care and understanding?

The evening light was fading, but Alf's eyes slowly focused on a photograph propped on a chest by the window. There was the best of them all, smiling, sitting on a Dartmoor rock next to his wife, with a dog at their feet. It must have been taken fifteen years earlier, but Robert had not changed that much. A lot of hair had gone since then, but the facial features were the same and the fellow never seemed to put on weight.

Alf smiled and then flinched as the split skin by his mouth reopened. He put his hand up and felt the place, at the same time touching his cheeks. They had shaved off his beard! Then, he remembered. He had shaved himself at home before setting out. My God, how long ago was that? There was about four days' stubble there now.

The bedroom door opened very slowly and quietly.

'Alf?' Robert stood hesitantly in the doorway and whispered, 'Are you awake?'

'Yes, my old flower,' he croaked and then almost laughed at the first of his failed resolves. He was going to give up that particular greeting.

'Fit to talk now?' Robert came into the room and stood at the end of the bed.

'I'll do my best, Rob, but there's still a fair bit of salt in the tubes.' He struggled to sit further up in the bed.

'Right, we'll leave it to another time then . . . when you feel a bit stronger.' Robert moved back towards the door.

'Maybe that'd be best. Still feeling a bit weak.' He raised a bandaged hand. 'But, if you want to talk, I'll listen.'

282

Robert smiled into the gloom. There was too much to be said for the conversation to become a monologue. But at least the patient was showing the first signs of animation, with even a touch of humour as well.

'No, you rest and we'll see how you are tomorrow. Can I get you anything? Water? Some soup maybe?'

'I've got water here, old man, but a slice of Binty's fresh bread would hit the spot. Then I think I'll nod off again.'

'Right, that couldn't be simpler. I'll be back in a minute.'

Alf lay back, staring at the darkening sky, at the wispy cirrus clouds and the swallows as they did their pre-bedtime darts above the garden. At some point in the next few minutes he knew that those swallows would turn magically into bats: it always seemed to happen as if a switch had been thrown. How did one know when to go and the other to arrive? Did they ever overlap, or collide? No, that was unlikely. Their lives were orderly, not like those of human beings. Swallows and bats existed according to their own unwritten but well-choreographed routine and they never collided or overlapped with each other.

Alf closed his eyes and began to wonder how this particularly disorganised human being was going to take his next step towards rehabilitation – if at all – when Robert returned silently and put a plate next to his bed. He then went across to the window and reached up to the curtains.

'Leave them open, Robert. I'm waiting for the bats.'

'You can have them. They make a bloody awful mess in the attic. Anyway, sleep well now and perhaps we'll talk tomorrow.'

Robert moved away from the curtains and trod softly across the room, pulling the door closed as he left.

The Sinclairs had had dinner and Binty was now out at a village function of some kind, so Robert decided to watch a TV programme on wildlife in Cornwall that he had missed first time around. He was halfway down the stairs when the telephone rang.

He walked briskly to the kitchen and picked up the extension.

'Hello, Robert.' It was Louise. 'Is this a convenient time?'

'Yes, Louise, they're all out and Alf's upstairs.' There goes wildlife in Cornwall, he thought. Perhaps a video . . .

'I said I'd explain what I said about Mrs Fischer's mood the other day. I'm sorry I've not called you earlier.'

'Are you sure you should be telling me at all?'

'*Well, it doesn't seem to be a secret, because she told me right out. She just seemed to want to share it with someone.*' He bent down by the television and began to search for a blank video, with the telephone pressed awkwardly against his neck.

'Share what?' He found one, slotted it into the machine, checked the channel and then pressed the record button.

'*Jacques . . . her husband . . . wants a divorce. He phoned her the evening before you came over and said she'd be hearing from his lawyer.*'

'Good grief! *He* wants a divorce? I'd have thought she was the one with the grounds.'

'*Oh, she's not fighting it, but she has been shocked. She says she's known for years that he's been playing around, but now she's got her independence here, it seems things have changed.*'

'Well, good for her, but I don't really see why you're telling me this, Louise, it's none of our business.'

'*I wouldn't have mentioned it to anyone, Robert, but when I saw how upset she was I thought it was something you'd said, not knowing the situation. She doesn't have many visitors, but if people know to be careful what they say before they arrive . . .*'

Her voice tailed off, as if aware of the clumsiness of her explanation.

'Well no, in my case I think you've misread the situation. We were talking about something completely different. Jacques' name wasn't mentioned. But, Louise . . . in spite of what you've just told me . . . about it not being a secret . . . I think it would be a good idea to keep this matter to yourself. Ok?' *Probably too late for that*, he thought.

She hesitated. '*Ok, Robert, if you think that's best.*'

'Yes, I do. I think she's got more problems than divorce proceedings on her mind at the moment, so we'd better all tread carefully.' He wandered through to the kitchen, where the dog was scratching on the back door. 'By the way, what did she do after I left?'

'*She stayed in the kitchen for a while and then went out for a walk with Bruno. She hardly seemed to notice me.*'

He let the dog in.

'You're doing a great job up there, Louise, keep it up. I'm sure she enjoys having you around, quite apart from the work you're doing.'

'I hope so. Well, I just thought you ought to know . . .' she ended lamely.

'I understand, Louise. And thanks for calling.'

He rang off and stared blindly into the night. It was now too dark to see any bats.

Robert and Alf did not manage to have their talk the next day. Alf's voice had not returned sufficiently for the task and anyway Robert had to survey a prospective job for a quote. It was in a village over towards Newquay and he was away for most of the day.

Binty and Sadie had volunteered to take it in turns to visit the bookshop daily, listen to messages and collect the post. Binty had also kept the shop open for a few hours and had actually managed to sell some books. However, Alf had made them promise not to attempt any tidying in his upstairs room, because tidying meant losing things and he knew where everything was kept, however haphazard it might all appear to an outsider. Only Robert knew his real worry was the letters that were still strewn across his desk.

Roger Curnow also stopped by the shop each day for a security check and George Harris had taken it upon himself to clean all the exterior windows . . . using a ladder.

It was on the Friday after Alf's rescue that he declared himself fit enough to hold court. He had left the comfort of his bed, dressed and then wandered around the Sinclair's small garden, inspecting the flowers, breathing in the fresh sea-tinged air and loosening his joints.

He declined a tentative suggestion that they might go down to the Lugger, not yet prepared to face the outside world and certainly not the claustrophobic world of Pengarth; although he made an exception for B.K. Richards. For half an hour they covered Parish business, sitting on a bench in the early evening sunshine.

BK never once referred to the incident at sea.

Robert came home just as BK was leaving and Binty announced an early supper, because the girls were going to the cinema in Truro.

So, it was nearly half past seven on a still, warm, summer evening that the three of them – Alf had insisted that Binty be there as well – sat on garden chairs under the twisted apple tree in the Sinclair's garden, with a cool bottle of Chablis nearby. The angry buzz of a grass strimmer a few houses away, two gulls parading importantly on the ridge tiles of the roof and rigging slapping against a mast near the quay were the only intrusions as the Sinclairs waited patiently for their guest's revelations to begin.

Alf held his glass up to the sky and savoured the crisp flavour of the chilled wine. He was feeling more at ease with himself than at any time in the past three weeks and he also knew now what had to be done, if not to correct errors of the past, then at least to redress the balance somewhat for the future.

He lowered the glass and smiled contentedly at his hosts.

'My dear friends,' he said warmly, 'isn't this magnificent? A beautiful evening, ozone in the nostrils, a tranquil garden and a perfectly splendid Chablis.'

'I'll drink to that.' Robert raised his glass and Binty followed suit.

'What a shame it can't last.' Alf put the glass down carefully and then one hand went instinctively to where the beard used to be.

'What do you mean, Alf?'

'Well, Binty my dear, the time has come for me to move on. If I've learnt something over the past few days it's that time is running out and there's much to be done out there. I could drag out my days in this safe harbour, sheltering from the world while my bones turn slowly to chalk, or I can try one last time to fly . . . or die gloriously in the attempt.'

Robert laughed and slapped the arm of his chair. 'What the devil are you talking about, Alf? I think the wine's clashing with your medication, old chap.'

'Nothing of the sort, Robert. Never more sober or sane.'

A wasp which was about to touch down on his wine glass took his attention and he flapped it away.

'All right,' Robert said cautiously, 'but I thought you were going to explain why . . .'

'In due course, I am . . . maybe not to your complete satisfaction . . . but I am.' He reached for his glass and then continued. 'You saved my life and you're the dearest friend I have in this place, so I owe you that much at the very least. For God's sake, you and Binty are practically my adopted family here!'

'Oh, that's a lovely thing to say, Alf.' Binty beamed at him.

'It's true . . . well, as far as I'm concerned anyway. Now, where shall I begin?' He grimaced for a moment and puffed out his pale cheeks, looking for a moment like a monstrous hamster. 'How about starting with the fact that I am a fraud . . . that my life is a sham . . . a pretence?'

'Oh, I wouldn't say . . .' Binty began, but Robert reached out and rested his hand on her arm.

'Yes, funny how little people really know about each other sometimes. Take names for example. When I went to university and was shopping around the various activities, some wag in the drama department picked up the fact that my initials are ABC, so he dubbed me Alphabet. This in due course became Alf . . . I suppose it should really be spelt A-L-P-H . . . and that stuck for the rest of my life.'

'I never knew that,' Binty exclaimed. 'I just thought the A stood for Alfred. Isn't that strange?'

'Yes, as I said, what you don't know about someone you think you know well is often quite startling, my flower. And, no, it ain't Alfred. It's worse than that!'

'Well?' Robert prompted. 'I know your middle name of course, but I never knew the origin of Alf.'

Alf screwed up his face again and extruded the word as if its taste was repugnant. 'Algernon . . . and don't you dare tell another living soul!'

The Sinclairs laughed spontaneously and Robert slapped his knee. 'Nothing wrong with Algernon, old boy. It's a good old English name. It's just that you don't look one inch like an Algernon. Well, an Algie perhaps . . .'

Alf regarded them with a resigned expression through lowered eyelids and then stretched out to refill his glass as he waited for order to be restored.

'So, how does adopting a nickname make you a fraud?' Binty asked when her giggles had subsided.

'It's just an example of how I began the layers of pretence that have marked out the progress of my life. I started with an ideal . . . a benchmark for my life ahead, if you like . . . but that turned sour when I was still a young man and then I just never seemed to get into step with the rest of humanity. I suppose even the beard was a form of cover-up.'

'Good God, man, that's being hard on yourself.' Robert said and then looked towards the fence as the noise of strimming stopped abruptly.

'Am I? Have you noticed, Rob, how many of us end up here in this little Cornish village, having escaped from something in the big wide world? I'm just another piece of Pengarth's flotsam, washed up under the lee of Shag Rock and I have no delusions about that.' He shrugged and then tipped his glass back. A few flecks of wine landed on his chin and glinted for a moment in the fading sunlight.

There was a prolonged silence before Robert gave a small cough and reached for his glass. He had noted with amusement Alf's adoption of his own flotsam metaphor. 'Fair point perhaps, but most us have had to compromise our ideals, or trim our sails as we go through life. I know if I hadn't done so I wouldn't be . . .' He shrugged.

'. . . Wouldn't be here today?' Alf gave him a lopsided grin. 'I know, old chap, but you had the support of a good strong-willed woman and a loving family.'

'So, was it to do with Lydia then?' Robert searched his face.

Alf met his gaze, but took some time in replying. By asking that question Robert had inadvertently taken the conversation into another dimension, which in turn gave him an opportunity to close some of the doors that remained ajar. He had in any event intended his revelations to be opaque rather than transparent.

'Yes, it probably was,' Alf said pensively. 'Yes, I imagine that a shrink might come to that conclusion after digging through the cotton wool in my head. Perhaps I never really loved Lydia that deeply and maybe I couldn't actually admit to it until after she died. It's an awful thing to say now, but perhaps she was the nearest thing to a facsimile of someone I was actually looking for . . . and then, as her illness developed, I simply went through the motions of being a caring husband, when all along it was probably just an act of conscience-salving . . . a duty that had to be fulfilled.'

'So, when she died . . . ?' Binty prompted.

'So, when she died, all I felt was a release, but that in turn created a void . . . a caving in, maybe. Damn! This all sounds like unadulterated self-pity . . . or phoney psychoanalysis.' He drained his glass and frowned angrily. 'What do you think?'

'Alf, it's not self-pity. No one could have done more for Lydia, for so long, and with nothing back in return . . . emotionally I mean.'

288

He looked at Binty and shrugged.

'And that letter from Lydia . . . was that something to do with it too?' Robert probed gently.

Alf shot him a glance. 'Which letter?'

'The one open on your desk.'

'You saw it, did you?'

Robert looked at him quizzically and then Alf tapped his forehead. 'Yes, of course you must have. Well, maybe . . . maybe it could have been a trigger. Dammit, Rob, there were things in that letter that broke me up . . . really broke me up. What must have been going on in her head that I didn't . . .'

'Anyone would have felt the same way reading that so soon after his wife's death. There's no shame at all in . . .'

'You didn't look at the other letters did you, Rob?' Alf interrupted sharply and his eyes flashed keenly.

'No, certainly not. None of it was my business, but I recognised Lydia's handwriting. I thought at the time it might give me a pointer . . .'

'And now?' Binty butted in as she brushed a fly away. 'Do you think you can push it all into the past now, Alf?'

He was slow to reply, continuing to study Robert's face, as if searching for a sign. Then, almost reluctantly, he turned to Binty.

'I hope so, my dear. But as I began by saying, I think that can only be done properly by moving on.'

'You mean leaving Pengarth permanently?' Robert asked, frowning. 'Giving up everything you've built up here . . . Chairman of the Council, NCI, the bookshop, your friends . . . ?'

'Robert,' Alf leant over to him, 'how can I possibly stay after what happened? How can I face anyone and expect an ounce of respect after what I did? I'm probably a laughing stock already, the butt of every joke in the Lugger and the scorn of anyone with a grain of gravitas in this village. And as for pity . . . ha . . . that would be even worse. Hell, even flotsam gets washed back out to sea eventually.'

'I think you're wrong there. You should give people credit for being more understanding and discerning. As you said, you just never fully know people . . . their problems . . . their deepest fears. You really should give them a chance.'

'No, I've thought it out rationally and have decided how I intend to deal with it. I might start by going to Australia . . . go and see

289

Catherine. It's about time. I've got a new grandson over there you know.'

'What about Rowena Fischer?'

He stiffened and shot Robert a quizzical look. 'And what about Rowena Fischer, my friend?'

'Alf, I haven't mentioned this to you yet,' Robert began and then found something to examine on the palm of his hand, 'but you were seen in her garden last Sunday and you came away looking pretty shaken. Are you sure she's nothing to do with your . . . boating adventure . . . or your decision to leave?'

One side of Alf's upper lip twitched involuntarily. It was a phenomenon, Robert reflected, that he had never noticed under the beard. 'So, I was followed . . .'

'No, you weren't followed. Someone happened to be out walking . . . as you were . . . and you know this village.'

'Well, in that case there's no point in denying it . . . Yes, I happened to be there, at the cottage, when she turned up.' Alf stared at a lower branch of the tree where a clutch of apples hung over Binty's head and he thought for a while before continuing. 'We talked in the garden . . . she told me something very moving . . . very personal . . . to her . . . and, yes, it made an impression on me.'

He toyed with his empty glass and Robert noted the set of his jaws. It was clear that Alf had no intention of expanding on what Rowena had said to him.

'I said once that she reminded me of Lydia,' Binty said softly and Alf suddenly turned to her with a chuckle, which, Robert thought, contained an element of relief. The subject had conveniently been diverted.

'My God,' Alf exclaimed, 'I'd never thought of that. I think you could be right there.'

'So, that's all there was to it?' Robert persisted.

'Yes, my old flower, that's all,' Alf stated with an air of finality. 'I walked on, with a heavy heart for her, but with a great deal else to think about.'

Robert sat back and looked intently at his friend, who suddenly could no longer maintain eye contact. Binty noted the silent exchange and tried hard to think of something to say, but it was Robert who eventually broke the uneasy spell.

'So, when are you going?'

Alf puffed a small sigh and eased back in his chair.

It was as if his inquisition were over; or at least the worst part of it. After all that had been said, he had not actually admitted to the Sinclairs that he had consciously attempted to take his life, but then he had not denied it either. And the same applied to his reason for attempting it. They would simply have to draw their own conclusions from the sparse revelations he had been prepared to let slip through the filter.

'Well, there's a stack of arrangements to be made, people to inform, house to put in order, that sort of thing,' Alf said in a gush. 'I should think that'll all take . . . hmm . . . the best part of a week.'

'Then you expect to be away from Pengarth by the end of next week?'

'Thereabouts, yes.' Alf drew in a deep breath and looked from one to the other. 'Look, I know this must sound very sudden . . . like escaping . . . letting people down . . . but I've had time to think it out. My life's had a severe jolt and I've taken that as a sign that a complete change is called for. I'm not good at explaining these things, but I hope in due course you'll perhaps begin to understand. You see, the sands of time are reaching the bottom of the glass and . . .' he stopped suddenly and simply shook his head.

'Perhaps we will understand in time, Alf,' Binty put a hand on his arm, 'but I have to say at the moment it does look to me very much as if you're running away.'

Alf patted her hand and smiled warmly at her, but did not comment. He had laid out all the explanation that he was prepared to give. He had given himself a shock and also shaken the good people of Pengarth, but he was not about to bare his soul completely for anyone. Not even to his dearest friends.

He intended in due course to apologise to the authorities for the trouble he had caused by his thoughtless action and he would also promise that there would be no recurrence. To himself alone he had concluded there was now another way forward, one that could either fail completely or that could turn his life around for the better, but that plan was in no way on the agenda for public disclosure or discussion. If it all worked out for the best they would eventually discover the truth, or at least an expurgated version of the truth. If it failed then they would simply not see him again. It all came down to that.

'But, I'll tell you one thing, Alf Curtis,' Binty suddenly added cheerily and he raised an eyebrow. 'You look a damned sight more handsome without the beard.'

That lightened the mood and no more was said about Alf's planned exodus. The three of them enjoyed the rest of the evening free from controversy and they were still talking at the kitchen table when the girls returned from Truro.

Chapter Twenty-One

OVER the few days that followed Alf busied himself literally putting his house in order.

He had left the comfort of the Sinclair's home, feeling physically well again and psychologically prepared for what he had to do next. He even opened the bookshop for a few hours each day, but still avoided the Lugger.

The lack of beard served to assist him and to thwart him in equal measure. He was able to move about the village without being instantly recognised, but at other times he found that recognition was essential.

He called on Gloria Bush-Tyke, who actually took a step back into her hall on seeing him looming large on the doorstep. Firstly he had to convince her that he was indeed Alf Curtis, Chairman of the Council, and then persuade her to let him enter her house. After their encounters over recent weeks his character had become somewhat demonised in her eyes and she was not a lady who changed her opinion lightly.

However, after Alf had applied a few layers of charm she gradually defrosted and eventually admitted him into her front room.

After Alf had dutifully admired her watercolours and stroked the mangy tortoiseshell cat, he got down to business.

An hour later he left a smiling Miss Bush-Tyke, who had accepted an invitation over to tea at the bookshop that very afternoon.

Next he went to see Greg Treberthy, who was rolling a keg across his cobbled yard at the back of the pub. They stood in the warm sunshine as Alf offered profuse apologies yet again for the theft and destruction of his dinghy and insisted on paying for a new one. Greg however, delighted to see Alf on his feet again, would have none of it. The insurance company would pay and that was that.

Alf almost told him of his plan to quit the village permanently, but held back, just in case pub walls have ears. They shook hands warmly and then Alf went off on his next assignment.

Petroc Williams slipped his glass of pink gin behind a window seat cushion as his wife ushered Alf into what the captain called the crow's nest. It was an upstairs sitting room with a bow window offering one of the finest views of Pengarth Bay that the village had to offer.

Petroc's cheeks glowed like an autumn sunset as he stepped forward to greet his unexpected guest and they exchanged pleas-antries. However, the mood soon changed to one of disappoint-ment and regret when the captain heard that he would shortly be losing a valued member of his watch team.

'Not an irrevocable decision I hope, Alf?' Petroc wheedled convincingly and Alf took a blast of gin fumes from a short distance.

'Afraid so, Petroc. Time's come to move on. Maybe not for good though – it all depends on how a number of things turn out in the near future.' He offered his hand. 'I'll miss the team and the old lookout, but . . . there you are. You'll find some new blood.'

Petroc's expression showed that he regarded such a possibility with scepticism, but Alf did not stay to hear the captain justify that opinion.

On the way back to the bookshop he stopped at the store for a pasty and a bag of saffron buns, but hurried on home after the purchase. He was not quite ready for a farewell scene with Sadie and certainly not during shop hours.

He ate his lunch with a bottle of beer and then sat down to compose a difficult letter. It had to be quite short, but every word had to count. Everything, his entire future, might depend on what he had to write and on how the recipient might react to what he had composed. It took him two hours and much wasted paper before he was moderately satisfied with the draft.

Having done that, he went downstairs to prepare tea for his visitor.

Gloria Bush-Tyke arrived just after four and Alf went to greet her at the shop door. He invited her upstairs and bade her sit while he went to fetch the tea. When he returned with a tray she was craning her neck to read some titles high on a bookshelf.

'Tea with hot buttered saffron buns,' he announced and she made a small exclamation of pleasure.

Excellent, he thought, *we're off to a flier*.

It was nearly six o'clock when Gloria, as she had invited him to address her, left the bookshop with her head crammed full of information regarding the running of Pengarth's bookshop. There was no formal agreement, no sublet of the property, and no obligation regarding opening hours. There was just a handshake agreement that Miss Gloria Bush-Tyke, an experienced librarian, would run the shop in his indefinite absence. She would bank the takings after drawing forty percent as her commission and she would also be responsible for keeping in good order all other matters relating to the daily business of the shop.

At first she had baulked at the responsibility, but then the exciting prospect of being immersed amongst all those books overcame her apprehension. Also, Alf reassured her by stating that he expected to be able to tell her before that autumn what his permanent plans were to be.

He watched her with amusement as she trotted back up Fore Street, seeming positively buoyed up by the challenge that lay ahead.

Saying goodbye to Sadie was a tricky one. He had never regarded his relationship with her as any more than an entertaining dalliance. She amused him, she flattered his ego and she accommodated him when he felt the need of some warm human company. But, he had never before now attempted to analyse his feelings for her, nor hers for him, and it had certainly never occurred to him that there would ever be a lasting union between them.

She took the news stoically, calmly and in a wholly unfussy way. There were no tears, no recriminations and no promises on either side: just a warm hug and an assurance that he might be back if all turned out well. She did not even watch him walk away.

After that, there were more mundane matters to be organised. Certain people had to be informed, outstanding correspondence to be answered, bills to be paid and his will to update.

Then, on the evening that he expected to be his last in Pengarth, Alf went up to the Sinclairs for a final farewell. He told Robert about the arrangement with Gloria B-T and apologised for dropping him in the Parish Council soup as acting Chairman. They parted with Alf repeating the enigmatic comment about the possibility of returning if all went well. Binty cried a little and Alf gave her a bear hug, while Robert looked sternly at him and simply said, 'Get it right this time, old chap.'

Later that evening, Alf dialled the Dowrick number and Darren answered.

'Alf, I hear you're leaving us.'

'That's right, my old flower, I'm spreading my wings.' *So, the news is out*, he thought.

'Got enough feathers left for that, have you?' Darren laughed.

'I'll soon enough find that out, you cheeky bugger. Now, I need to speak to your sister. Is she in?'

'Yes, I'll get her for you. But, seriously Alf, what about a farewell drink with us in the Lugger?'

'I'll see if I can fit that in, Darren. Now, if I could speak to Louise . . .'

He heard Darren call her name and a door slammed shut somewhere in the house.

'Hello, Alf,' she said breathlessly. 'How are you now?'

'I'm fine, my flower. But, I'm looking for a favour. Are you going up to Smugglers' Cottage tomorrow?'

'Yes, I'll be there quite early, because Rowena's got to leave for Exeter.'

'Exeter!'

'Yes, she's got an appointment with her solicitor up there at eleven.'

'I see.' He hesitated. This was an unexpected turn of events, but perhaps a felicitous one. 'Never mind, you can still do what I'm going to ask. Would you deliver a letter to Rowena for me?'

'Yes,' she replied cautiously, as if wondering why he could not post it or even deliver it himself. 'Yes, I can do that.'

'I'm asking *you* to do it, Louise, because I'm also leaving tomorrow – you might have heard – and I don't think I'll have the time for a detour to the cottage. If I drop it in to you tonight, would you make sure to put the letter into her hands before she sets off for Exeter tomorrow, please?'

She agreed without further questioning. Alf put the phone down and shut his eyes. The messenger was primed and ready: now to type the message from his draft.

As the flamboyant red orb of the sun dipped behind the hill at the back of Pengarth, leaving a smear of wild bloody streaks to mingle with late evening cloud, Alf stood staring silently out of his bathroom window.

Once again, perhaps for the hundredth time, he wondered if he was completely mad. He knew that if there was no answer to that rhetorical question now, then the time was fast approaching when he would find out for certain. All he could hope for was that the eventual revelation regarding his sanity would not cause more pain and distress to anyone.

The Volvo slipped onto the A30 while the newspapers were still being delivered in Pengarth. Alf had on board only the essentials for everyday living, plus a mixed case of his best claret and Chablis. All of his remaining personal items had been locked in a trunk, which he had then heaved into the attic. Everything else had been left in situ and if Miss B-T wished to reorganise furniture, books or anything else, she was welcome to do so.

He had made a small amendment to his will and asked a surprised neighbour to witness his signature to the codicil. Then he had posted the will to his solicitor in Truro. On his way out of the village he had stopped to drop the house keys through Miss B-T's letterbox.

As he sped along the road heading out of Cornwall he continued to tick items off in his brain until he was satisfied that everything was covered. But he knew, even if he had forgotten something, it was by now far too late to turn back.

A few miles into Devon, Radio Cornwall began to fluctuate and fade. Symbolically another part of his old life seemed to be dying through the airwaves, so he switched programmes and turned up the volume to quell any lingering mawkishness in his soul.

He pulled off the main road near the Somerset border and watched a tractor crop spraying in an adjacent field, while he sipped a steaming cup of coffee. After relieving himself behind an oak tree he set off again. There was plenty of time yet, but anything could happen along the way and to be late for the rendezvous might just scupper the entire crazy plan.

Near Andover he stopped again at a service station and bought a bunch of flowers. Rather too garish, but then she would not mind

– not now. Anyway, he had too much to tell her for the colour of the flowers to be a distraction.

It was nearly midday when he arrived in the village.

He took a few minutes to get his bearings – there were so many new houses and the shop had gone – but he soon found the Church. He parked the car, stretched his limbs and then tucked in his wayward shirt.

Wandering into the churchyard through the lichgate he began to search around. It took a while to find her grave, but when he did, the reason soon became obvious. It was out of chronological order with the others. Her ashes had obviously been interred with her husband's remains and he had died many years before her. Twenty-four years before, to be precise.

Alf looked about him but there was no one else in the small enclosed churchyard. The rough hedge that surrounded it was interwoven with brambles, already laden with the dark red knobbly fruit that promised a fine blackberry crop in a few weeks' time. As he bent down and placed the flowers at the base of the tombstone a robin tree-hopped expectantly above his head.

He plucked some lichen from the granite and then stood back to read the lower half of the headstone's inscription.

Mary Elizabeth Cargill
Dearly loved wife and Mother
1912 – 1991

A neat marble base surrounded the grave, but the ground within its perimeter was unkempt and withered stalks protruded from the flower well. Alf knelt and began to do some gardening with a penknife. It gave him a strangely eerie feeling to be back in Lower Deeping after so long.

'Hello, Lady Mary,' he began in a low murmur and then moistened his lips, 'it's Brendan.'

He blinked rapidly, having almost startled himself at hearing his own voice admitting to a name he had not used for so many years. Even Lydia had only ever called him Alf . . . except surprisingly at the beginning of her undelivered cathartic letter.

His attention strayed from the gravestone for a few moments as snatches of unformed memories flashed through his subconscious. He remained staring into the middle distance for a while, until a van rumbling past the church snapped him out of his reverie. He turned back to face the white stone slab, reflecting for a moment that he could almost smell the musty odour of stale soot from the Manor's ballroom.

'I should have come to visit you years ago,' he said, focusing again on the inscription, 'but we always leave these things too late, don't we. Also, I've had no need to talk to anyone before now . . . at least, that's what I thought. If only we would recognise our frailties at times when others can be of help. But no, our innate arrogance forbids that sensible course of action. Well, I'm here now and I've come to confess.'

He tugged hard at a dock, but its deep root refused to budge.

'Do you remember an occasion when I called in on my way to visit my friend Bob in Lymington? That was in the spring of 1967 . . . just before what they now call the summer of love. Bob's my neighbour in Pengarth now, but he's grown back into Robert somewhere since school. Anyway, I never did get to Lymington, did I? I expect you knew that. It was because of a distraction at the Manor . . . a girl called Fizzy. You remember her? Of course you would. You never forgot your young charges.'

He stopped and a wistful expression spread across his face like a nostalgic mist.

'I've never fallen for anyone so fast, Lady M, before or since. I wonder if you recognised the signs. You knew us all so well . . . as well as any mother would.

'Anyway, Fizzy and I went for a couple of walks on that brief visit and on the second of those, just before I heard of my grandfather's illness, we went up to Canbury Rings.'

He stared for a while at the soil on his hands and then, after a long pause, added in a whisper, 'She lost her virginity that afternoon . . . and so did I. That afternoon was the defining episode of my life. I think somehow it set the standard for all that happened to me afterwards. It sounds crazy to say this, but the magic dust has just never washed off or faded.'

He poked at some small bulbs that were protruding above the disturbed soil.

'But then, after I left that day . . . we never saw each other again.'

Reaching out, he brushed a clod of dried earth from the face of the stone.

'We wrote many letters . . . loving letters . . . but never actually managed to get together. Poignant isn't it? There was always some obstacle . . . just something that managed to keep us apart . . . and then one day . . . in late June of that year . . . 1967 . . . she sent me a letter saying that she was going abroad with her parents and that there was little point in us continuing to write.

'For some time I couldn't accept that and I went on sending letters, but after a while I just gave up. I thought I'd die . . . and perhaps a bit of me did die . . . but the memories never did. You can't erase a memory that is sealed and vacuum packed inside your brain.'

The robin had grown bold and it now hopped warily at the edge of the grave, its head on one side, looking for worm activity in the disturbed soil. Alf paused in his gardening and watched it abstractly for a while before continuing his soliloquy.

'In time I went to university, got a decent degree and then went into the City at the right time and made a pile of money in the boom period of the eighties. I met a girl . . . Lydia . . . and married her. We had a daughter. She's grown up now and lives in Australia and I haven't seen her for a long time . . . and my wife . . . well she went into an institution many years ago.

'Then, soon after Lydia died, I found a letter from her trying desperately to explain what was happening to her . . . as she saw it . . . and that really shook me up. Knocked me for six. It's hard to explain why, but it really did.'

Alf shifted his position to ease the pressure on his leg and the robin flew up to perch on the gravestone.

'When I was no longer able to care for Lydia, I moved to Cornwall and opened a bookshop to keep an interest in something. I also immersed myself in local activities, for all that's worth.

'But, I guess at that point it was really about escaping and hiding from the real world . . . don't you think?'

An elderly woman walked briskly from the lichgate to the church entrance, carrying a basket of flowers. She glanced at him before going into the porch and he could hear a key being turned in the ancient lock.

'Then suddenly my cosy little cotton wool world turned upside down. A few weeks ago I rescued a woman from the cliff near my lookout. It was foolhardy and irresponsible, but I'd probably do it again and next time I expect I'll fall to my death . . . but there you are. Anyway, slowly I began to discover more about this woman . . . whose name is Rowena Fischer.

'I saw a picture of her and her sister . . . it was signed *Lucy* . . . I didn't know at first if it was to or from Lucy and that confused me later on when I got to thinking about it objectively. Then, one day, Rowena told me she'd lost a child and I only recently discovered that she really meant that it had never been born. She'd lost it at about three months, you see.

'All of that might still have signified nothing, but then, quite recently, I heard that she had a memento from the Vietnam War. I saw it. It's identical to the one I'd sent to Fizzy.

'Gradually, as all these things fell into place, so also did the truth . . . the appalling truth.

'When we met by accident in her garden, she told me that back in '67 she'd gone down to Cornwall to stay with her aunt near Pengarth, after she discovered she was pregnant . . . her parents were abroad and anyway they were apparently not the understanding kind she felt she could turn to. Her aunt was, so she secretly arranged for her niece to abort the baby. It might even have been her uncle who carried it out . . . I couldn't bring myself to ask. I'm told the poor bugger died a few years later . . . maybe remorse, I don't know.

'Then, several years after losing the child she married . . . but the real tragedy is that she never had any more children.'

The church clock began to strike the hour and instinctively he looked up at the tower. Not much longer now. He closed his penknife and turned back to the stone.

'Rowena told me about her abortion a couple of weeks ago and from that point I put it all together and realised what a terrible thing I'd done. It might sound crazy, Lady M, but in all that time I never knew Fizzy's real name and Rowena didn't know me when we met again. But Rowena was . . . is . . . Fizzy . . . not Lucy as I first began to think.

'You see, I know the birth date of the woman I rescued . . . Robert saw her passport . . . and that would have made her fifty-two. But, Fizzy should have been fifty-four.'

Alf stopped pulling weeds and looked at his hands again. He did not see the soil. He just saw that they were shaking uncontrollably. The poison was all pouring out with each hideous revelation and with every confession. Raising his head slowly he stared despairingly at Lady Mary's name on the stone.

'She told me she was sixteen, Lady M! That evening at the Manor she said she was sixteen, and that's where it all went wrong. On the night we met in your house she said she was sixteen and I never had any reason to disbelieve her.

'Do you see . . . do you understand what I'd done? Up at Canbury Rings that day I'd effectively drugged and raped that girl and made her pregnant. You can't give consent at fourteen, can you? However much love there is between you, it's still illegal and I can never escape that fact. So she went through an abortion . . . never told me . . . and after that terrible thing she never had children.

'D'you understand what it is I've done? I've ruined that woman's life. It doesn't matter a jot that I was only eighteen at the time . . . what happened was totally my responsibility and I can never escape from that fact.'

He lowered his head and stared through misty eyes at the fractured soil.

'And now, nearly forty years on, the event that had been the most beautiful experience of my life has turned as sour as the contents of this grave. She was only fourteen and I was instrumental in destroying her life. How could *I* go on living after that realisation?'

He gave one more violent heave and the dock came up by its root.

'The fact is that I found the truth too awful . . . my dream had become my nightmare . . . so I tried to end it all . . . but I failed even in that . . . and just ended up causing a lot of people a great deal of trouble, as well as making a total fool of myself.'

He pushed some disturbed bulbs back underground and tamped the loose soil down over them. The robin was back and was now almost within arm's length as it eyed a worm that Alf had unwittingly coaxed to the surface. It did not even fly away when Alf pushed himself off his knees with a grunt and then sat back on his haunches.

'But . . . because of that failure, if for no other good reason . . . I've decided now to get on with life . . . but I'm going away instead . . . perhaps to a place where no one knows me. It may sound like an escape from reality once more, but actually I think it's something different this time. I'm not trying to relive anything . . . I'm just having a go at reconnecting with another life . . . that's all. Trying to make something meaningful of what's left to me . . . and yes, perhaps trying to make amends too. It'll be about penitence now, rather than self-destruction.'

Alf scrunched his lips together pensively and wiped a cheek with the back of his hand. 'I don't really expect anyone to understand something I can hardly explain to myself and it's not something I could ever discuss with a living soul. But I knew you'd understand. You always did.'

He stopped plucking at the grass around the concrete edge of the grave and looked again at his hands. 'And that's why I've told you everything, Lady M. Everything.'

He felt physically stiff and emotionally drained. The clock had moved on another ten minutes and it was almost time for him to go.

'After all I've confessed, this bit will probably sound completely mad, but I wrote a letter to her . . . Fizzy . . . before I left. It wasn't easy, but I laid it all out before her . . . explanations, regrets, the works . . . and asked her to meet me . . . today. I've no idea what to expect. She has every right to tear it up and ignore me . . . leave the cottage in Pengarth and go back to her boorish Froggy husband. But, if there's any hope whatsoever, then it'll be this afternoon or not at all. Then, if she doesn't show up . . . which she probably won't . . . I'll stick to Plan A and just bugger off to Australia or somewhere.'

Alf glanced up at the clock once more. He bent forward, put the fresh flowers in the pot and then placed the dead ones, together with the weeds, into the florist's wrapping paper. He stood up slowly and then looked about him for the inevitable compost heap.

'Well goodbye, Lady M.' He smiled down at the gravestone. 'Any rational person will think it crazy, but it's a weight off my conscience just to have spilled it all out to you. You've been a good listener . . . as always.

'Oh, and by the way, I've added a codicil to my will . . . If it's at all possible I want to be buried here one day . . . as near to you as they can get me. So, I'll see you then.'

Alf turned away sharply and then took a detour via the composting pile, dumped the dead flowers and then brushed his hands together as he made for the lichgate. At that moment the woman came out of the church clutching some twigs.

She called out to him and pointed, 'There's a tap over there if you want to rinse your hands.'

'Ah, thank you. It's good soil, but I'd rather leave it behind.'

The woman tittered and then asked, 'Did I see you tending Mary Cargill's grave?'

'Yes, she's an old friend and a very patient listener.'

She followed him to the tap. 'I knew her well too. Such a lovely person.'

'Indeed she was . . . like a second mother.' He turned the tap on and did not hear her reply. When he had finished, he shook his hands in the warm air and turned, but she was gone.

Five minutes later Alf was driving out of Lower Deeping, heading for the intended rendezvous and as nervous as a schoolboy summoned to the headmaster's study to account for a misdemeanour. In a sense it was like that. He was about to ask a woman to forgive him for destroying much of what she might justifiably have expected from her life.

The summer of love, he reflected, *has cast a long shadow before me, but perhaps at last I'm about to reach its edge.*

Chapter Twenty-Two

ROWENA finished her business in Exeter shortly before midday and her solicitor, a friend from university days, invited her to have lunch with him in the city. She had declined graciously, explaining that she had another appointment and then made her way briskly to the car park. She had consulted the map beforehand and judged that it should take under two hours, if there were no hold-ups.

She stopped at a delicatessen near the car park and hesitated over pork pies, before deciding that veal and ham would be more digestible. She bought that, a slice of Edam cheese and two apples.

The legal matters had been surprisingly painless, even though she was stripping away thirty years of marriage. Jacques had sued her for divorce on the grounds of desertion – a hell of a cheek, she had said to the lawyer – and she had responded with adultery and physical cruelty. The lawyer had summed it up as an irretrievable breakdown of the marriage.

It was not until the last paper had been signed and she was preparing to leave the lawyer's office that she fully appreciated the enormity of what was happening to her and also of the step onto the invisible bridge that she was now about to take.

Alf's letter – she still thought of him as Alf – had come as a total shock. Not until that moment had she associated the bluff bearded bookshop proprietor, her rescuer, with Brendan, the beautiful lover of her early teens. Even allowing for the years in between, the contrast was extreme.

Perhaps the first iota of a clue that had begun the germination of a thought had come with Robert dropping his name at Smugglers' Cottage, but even then it seemed to her to be too fantastic an idea to pursue.

And then Louise had delivered the letter.

That had been the explosive device that had burst open the protective fabric of her cocooned memories. What had happened in the spring of 1967 and the subsequent traumas resulting from that brief liaison had long been encased in a separate chamber of her memory bank. But now the sudden pain of its resurrection threatened to overwhelm her reasoning as it all cascaded back with the force of a tsunami.

This could never happen: should never happen. Brendan had gone. She had written the exotic memory of him out of her life's script. She was no longer Fizzy.

She had drifted through that early morning of revelation in a haze, on a different plane from the present, oblivious of anything Louise said to her, until gradually the waters settled in the disturbed pool of her mind.

Curtis is a common name, but why, she repeatedly asked herself, *had it not sparked any thought of Brendan?* She still had some of his early letters, so why had she not recognised Alf's writing? She must have seen it somewhere in recent weeks. But beyond a doubt the eyes were Brendan's. Why had she not noticed that before? How can one look and yet not see; hear but not comprehend? Was it that the memory's encasement had simply been too thorough for any of this to break through?

Then, on the road to Exeter, a new sensation gradually crept over her.

There was an extraordinary and irrational sense of excitement swelling up from within. The gates were slowly opening and beyond them she was catching a glimpse of a possible new beginning: hazy at first, but slowly the mist was rising.

Quite beyond her comprehension, she was feeling the excited thrill of a teenage girl about to go on a second date.

On self-analysis, she found that after all the intervening years she now bore him no ill will. In fact she had never borne him any malice. He was no more to blame for what had happened than she was. She had loved Brendan and he had loved her and that was all there was to it. She remembered now quite distinctly and to her total chagrin that in order to impress him on their first meeting she had foolishly told Brendan she was sixteen. That is what silly fourteen year-old girls sometimes do. So, in not challenging that fateful lie, he had unwittingly made it as much her fault as his. As for what followed, that was simply the result of a force so powerful that neither of them had been able to resist. They had been very young and to be young is to be on another planet.

Now in the autumn of their lives fate had thrown them together again and perhaps the gap of all the years in between was about to close, like the knitting of a flesh wound, or the joining of two continents.

Yes, she was excited.

But even then, nearing the rendezvous, Rowena almost panicked.

She pulled onto the roadside and walked up and down until she felt calmer. Then after returning to the car she sat for a while, forcing herself to breath more steadily, to think more clearly, before driving on.

Just a mile from her destination, she missed the turning and had to check the map again. She reversed, closed her eyes for a moment and then drove slowly up the lane.

The Volvo was parked just where the Beetle had in 1967. What had he called that car? Limey: that was it. Butterflies and other insects were crawling around inside her stomach as she pulled up alongside his car and switched off the engine. She reached across for the lunch bag and got out.

Rowena squinted into the distance towards the circle of ancient trees that stood timelessly on the hill a mile way.

Canbury Rings.

He said he would be there between one and two o'clock and Alf, as she knew by now, had a reputation for punctuality.

They were a long way from Pengarth and it had occurred to her that he could not have known when he wrote the letter that she would be in Exeter today, so he was obviously taking an enormous gamble on her being there.

Was this his arrogant self-belief or simply a wildly hopeful gesture? She *might* have driven all the way from Cornwall out of sheer curiosity, but he could never have known that. Could he? She smiled as she gazed up at the Rings.

Was my trip to Exeter mere coincidence, she wondered, *or yet another twist of fate?*

She crossed the lane, went cautiously over the style and began the long trudge that would take her past a stream, through a copse and across two more fields before reaching the top of the hill.

The recollection of the area was all coming back vividly, but, unlike their previous visit, the sun was now high and slightly behind her, with only a few cumulus clouds blotting the vivid blue of the sky. A few swallows flashed through the summer air in pursuit of insects and a buzzard mewed on its lazy flight high above the copse.

The hollow was only a few yards ahead and knowing that it would obscure her view of the Rings once down there, she paused to see if by chance he was anywhere in sight.

She shaded her eyes, but at first could only see tree trunks beneath thick deciduous foliage. There was no sign of anyone, or even of the old shepherd's bothy: probably now vandalised like so much else these days. Ah, that shepherd's bothy, with its tin roof, spiders and . . .

She was about to walk on when suddenly she saw movement.

Nearly half a mile distant a figure stepped away from the ring of trees, with an arm outstretched. It was impossible to tell for certain, but it looked to her as if there was a bottle dangling from the end of that arm.

You bring the food and I'll bring the wine, he had written at the end of his letter: the letter he had signed, *Brendan*.

Her heart jumped as she raised her right arm to shoulder height and waved the lunch bag. He must have seen, because he now lifted his other arm and held the pose, resembling a well-fed scarecrow.

A smile spread slowly across her face as the scarecrow lowered its arms and then began to walk purposefully down the hill in her direction.

Like a schoolgirl she gave an involuntary giggle and shrugged in a manner that suggested that the whole situation was beyond her comprehension. Then, for a moment forgetting her leg, she almost skipped forward towards the hollow.

. . . *although my eyes were open, they might just as well be closed. And so it was . . . later . . .*

'Will you dance with me this time, Brendan?' she laughed into the still summer air. 'Will you dance in the sunshine with Fizzy?'

Other Books by Nigel Milliner writing as Nigel Horne

All About Face

Only God and the Swagmen

Other Books with a Cornish link
published by Parlores Publications

The Official Encyclopaedia of the Cornish Pasty

Veryan : How Times Have Changed

Portloe : An Illustrated History

Coping with Disabilities

Nigel Milliner

Nigel Milliner is married with three adult children. He and his wife have lived in the Roseland area of Cornwall since 1999, having emigrated from Wiltshire. *Edge of a Long Shadow* is his third published novel.